"Jessica Clare and Jen Frederick
are a force to be reckoned with!"*

Praise for

LAST BREATH

"Clare and Frederick have penned a sexy, thrilling romantic suspense with a strong heroine and a to-die-for hero. Romance readers won't want to miss their latest."
—*Smexy Books*

"Dark, gritty, but filled with hope . . . *Last Breath* is an action-packed, emotionally driven story that will have you reading the pages quicker than you can turn them. The second book in the Hitman [series] has dialed up the action to an almost breakneck speed."
—**A Love Affair with Books*

"Both Daniel and Regan were interesting and wonderful characters, and I loved getting to see them work through their issues and find a way to fall for each other. I'm happy to report that Clare and Frederick knocked this one out of the park for me."
—*The Book Pushers*

"*Last Breath* far exceeded my expectations. It appears as if there is nothing these ladies can't write about, and I anxiously await to see what they will do with the third book in the Hitman series."
—*The Muses' Circle*

continued . . .

"I'm seriously at a loss for words to describe to you how good this book is. It has everything you could ask for. There's tons of action and suspense. But somehow there are tons of sweet and sexy moments in this and it just all works together so well. If I ever have to be rescued by a man—I hope it's someone as dreamy as Daniel. . . . I cannot stress enough how much I think you should read this series and particularly this book. It's one of a kind and you won't regret it."

—*All Romance Reviews*

LAST
KISS

Jessica Clare

Jen Frederick

BERKLEY BOOKS, NEW YORK

THE BERKLEY PUBLISHING GROUP
Published by the Penguin Group
Penguin Group (USA) LLC
375 Hudson Street, New York, New York 10014

USA • Canada • UK • Ireland • Australia • New Zealand • India • South Africa • China

penguin.com

A Penguin Random House Company

This book is an original publication of The Berkley Publishing Group.

Library of Congress Cataloging-in-Publication Data

Clare, Jessica.
Last kiss / Jessica Clare, Jen Frederick.
p.   cm.—(A hitman novel ; 3)
ISBN 978-0-425-28152-9 (paperback)
I. Frederick, Jen.   II. Title.
PS3603.L353L38 2015
813'.6—dc23
2014048285

PUBLISHING HISTORY
Berkley trade paperback edition / May 2015

PRINTED IN THE UNITED STATES OF AMERICA

10 9 8 7 6 5 4 3 2 1

Cover photo by Claudio Marinesco.
Cover design by Meljean Brook.
Text design by Kelly Lipovich.

To Cindy

Thank you for taking a chance on us.

We hope you never regret it.

ACKNOWLEDGMENTS

To our editor, Cindy Hwang, who believed in this crazy series enough to send us into bookstores and libraries around the country.

To Meljean, who has to endure our constant inquiries and requests for changes and general author craziness and who allows us to be her friend when in fact she's the superior author.

To Caroline, for thinking up the perfect name for *Last Hit: Reloaded*. We forgot to thank you before. Please accept this belated, but profuse, expression of gratitude.

To our assistants and publicists, Nicole, Morgan, and Jessie. Would anyone hear of the books without you? We don't think so.

To our blogger friends: Michelle, I don't know why you still open emails from Jen. She bugs you constantly. Lisa, do you ever get tired of those IMs? And to Mel, Lea, and Eagle at SMS Book Obsessions: You crack us up every day. Never stop.

To all of the other bloggers and readers too numerous to name, thank you so much for every word that you've written about this series. You've made it happen and your love and will power us forward.

CHAPTER ONE

One Month Ago

VASILY

"You think to lead the Petrovich *Bratva?*" Georgi Petrovich cries from far down the table. He is so far removed from the main branch of the Petrovich family tree he barely warrants a place here. "You aren't even blood Petrovich!"

"Am I not?" I ask. There's no need to raise my voice. Any emotion indicates weakness. I am not a weak man. "What makes a Petrovich?" I stand then and begin to walk around the table. "Is it blood? Then half of you should be executed on the table for failing to have the requisite DNA. Who shall go first?"

I point to Thomas Gregovorich, a loyal member of the *Bratva* for at least two generations. His father served in the KGB during the Cold War.

He gives a small nod in deference acknowledging that the *Bratva* was a true brotherhood made up of allegiances rather than blood.

"Or you, Kilment, when we took you and your brother in when you were left orphaned on the street, did you believe you became a true Petrovich when you made your first kill? Conducted your first job? When we speak of the *Bratva*, we speak as one voice. What is done to one, it is done to all. Or does that maxim no longer hold true, Georgi?"

There are low murmurs of approval and Georgi sits back, folds his arms, and looks petulantly at the table. We are meeting today to discuss the future of the *Bratva* after the death of Sergei Petrovich. A death I helped orchestrate, and many suspect it, which makes it difficult for me to enact my next step—to kill Elena Petrovich. Two Petrovichs dead so close together smells of a coup. We are an unstable lot, and lopping off the head of this snake would result in chaos. In order to achieve my ends, the *Bratva* must be stabilized.

However, in this den of iniquity, it is not love that holds the loyalty of each man. It is fear. The Petrovichs have held power over us all by setting us one against the other. To rise above, I have eliminated all weaknesses.

What sets me apart is all that I am willing to do. Each of these men at the table has had limits. I have none.

The men that sit at this table are divided. Some view me with awe and respect, and others with disgust. The latter are the ones I respect, because a man who would kill his own sister, a man such as I, deserves to be in a dungeon, locked away from all of humanity.

Instead I stand here as the potential leader of this room of villains and thieves. And it is a position I seek, not because I lust after power, but because if I control the *Bratva*, then nothing is out of my reach. I have one goal now.

"Will you kill your mother to save the *Bratva*, Thomas? And you, Pietr, when your sister whispers to her lover Pavlil Ionov, do you worry that she's telling secrets? Or Stefan, your son, I saw him the other day holding hands with . . ." I stop behind Stefan's chair and rest both hands on the back. I can almost feel him inhale the fear. ". . . a smart young thing. They looked to be enjoying themselves."

Pietr coughs. "So you are willing to kill us all to maintain hold of the *Bratva*? That is not a good reason to follow you."

"No, but you all know that I will sacrifice everything and everyone to protect the brotherhood."

They are all silent because unlike the others, my sister, Katya, is gone. Disposed of by my own hand at the order of Elena Petrovich.

I end my stroll around the room behind my chair. "I am the one who led us away from munitions and dirt to telecom interests. In less than a decade, the *Bratva*'s primary businesses will be legitimate, which means that you no longer have to hide behind your armored vehicles. You no longer have to rely on bodyguards that could be bought off. You need not fear the KGB or the *militsiya*. You can invest in your *futbol* teams and mansions in Londongrad without fear of reprisal."

Leadership means effective utilization of the carrot and the stick. I lead with the stick. Always. The Petrovichs believe in only the stick. For them the carrot does not exist or is viewed with suspicion.

The *boyeviks*—the young muscle our old warlord Alexsandr groomed from urchins on the street to protect the brotherhood— grow tired of the constant threat to their homes and family. They sleep with one eye open, their hand over their heart, wondering if the brother next to them will be killing their mother or raping their sister in retribution for some *Bratva* infraction.

The older generation such as Thomas and Kilment and those

who sit on the Petrovich *Bratva* council are loath to hand over the power of this organization to me, a mere foot soldier sold by his father to repay debts. With Sergei dead and the vicious Elena the only real Petrovich remaining, I am left with a choice. Attempt to wrest control of the brotherhood from the old guard or walk away.

And I would walk away. I have some money stored but I've been a Petrovich for a long time and there are many enemies that would crow over my death. No, in order to survive, the Petrovich *Bratva* must remain strong.

If I have learned anything, it is that people with nothing are victims. It is those with power and money and might who have the ability to protect others.

Thomas rubs a hand across his jaw. "There is one thing you could do."

"That is a legend, Thomas," Kilment groans.

"I will do it." Legends persist because people believe, and if belief means I can bring down Elena Petrovich and secure a peaceful future, then I will pursue this foolishness until the painting is mine. Their desire to recapture the past is absurd and yet another reason the old guard should be replaced. "You wish me to procure the Caravaggio."

Cries of wonder and confusion fill the room.

"So you know," Kilment says flatly.

I pretend no ignorance, for it is a story that Alexsandr shared with me long ago. "I know that a famous triptych painted by Caravaggio once hung in the palaces of the Medicis in Florence, perhaps the Careggi Villa. It was commissioned as an altarpiece but considered to be too profane, as many of his pieces were judged. It was gifted by the Medicis to Feodor the First, who then lost it, and Russia entered the Time of Troubles. When the Boyars rose to power in the seventeen hundreds, it is rumored the painting was recovered by Peter the Great. Citizen Petrovich's grandfather was gifted this set of three paintings and it hung in the great hall of the Petrovichs until it was lost, sold, stolen during Sergei's time. Many say that he who holds it, holds the world."

Thomas nods at this recitation, but Kilment looks unconvinced.

"It is known as the *Madonna and the Volk*," I conclude. The Petrovichs loved the painting because the woman who sat for Caravaggio was purportedly a true Mary Magdalene—a whore. And the *Volk*? It is a man-wolf who is eating Mary, and despite the gruesomeness of the depiction, there is an expression of ecstasy on her face. *Volk*, too, was seen as a play on the old Russian criminal rank of *vory*. Thieves, wolves at the door. We were the predators. Everyone else is prey. I saw it only once, when I was given to Elena Petrovich like some birthday treat. It seemed fitting that Sergei sold it to fund some sordid perversion of his own. "But why is it that it is of any importance? It is a mere painting."

Thomas stares at me. "It is a symbol of our wealth and power, and we have lost it. And no Caravaggio, one of the greatest painters of all time, can be dubbed a mere painting. It belonged to Peter the Great. It is priceless, one of a kind. Why would we not want it? That it is in the hands of someone else is shameful, a blot against the Petrovich name. Now more than ever, we must show our enemies we are strong."

"So you want it, but why is this your loyalty test? Have I not proven myself again and again? Have I not shed the blood of my own family for the brotherhood?" I spread my scarred hands out as if they hold the proof of my allegiance.

"The Caravaggio has been lost to us for years. Many of us

have tried to find it but have failed," Thomas admits. "If you find it, you will show yourself to be a man of resource and cunning, a man who is unafraid. You will restore the pride to the brotherhood and prove your worth as a leader."

I hold back a lip curl of disgust at this. Leadership is not running around the world seeking one painting. Leadership is moving our assets out of dangerous and risky ventures and into more stable enterprises. Leadership is generating loyalty by providing a way for the members to feed their families and protect their loved ones.

This is a snipe hunt, an impossible task designed to make me fail and appear weak amongst those who would support me. Or worse, in my absence they will eliminate those they deem a threat. To kill me here would generate a revolt.

No, this is not about a painting. This is punishment, revenge, retribution. But I am one step ahead of them. I guessed that this is the task they would set before me. They think I will be gone long, chasing my tail for months. I will be happy to prove how wrong they are.

Thomas sits back and looks around the table. He has been a member of the *Bratva* for a long time. They respect his voice. "Bring us the Madonna, and the *Bratva* will be yours."

I smile and raise my palms in a gesture that says *fait accompli*. "Then it is done."

I am not so sanguine two hours later as I sit across the table from Ivan the Terrible. Ivan Dostonev is the leader of the Dostonev *Bratva*, an organization whose base is in St. Petersburg. The Dostonevs posture that they are descendants of confidantes of the tsars. Perhaps they are, but we are all criminals. We bathe in the blood of our enemies and eat our own young.

"I hear the Petrovich *Bratva* is troubled, my friend," he says with studied casualness. Ivan has held power not because he is particularly clever but because he is a man of his word—a rarity in these parts. People trust him—and fear him. He trades in favors and you do not know when your favor will be called in, only that when the time comes you must heed his call or reap terrible consequences.

I owe this man a favor, and I knew from the moment I saw his name on the screen of my phone that my reckoning had arrived.

"When there is a change in leadership, some are disconcerted. That will change," I reply.

"My people tell me that the council has set a challenge for you. Meet it and the Petrovich brotherhood is yours."

I meet his boast that he has infiltrated our organization with my own. "And my people tell me that your son has no interest in following in your footsteps. What will happen to the Dostonevs then?"

"Bah! Vladimir is young. He wants to drink and fuck. Let him have his fun." He swallows his vodka and gestures for me to drink. I do, tipping the glass and allowing the clear liquid to coat my tongue and glide down my throat. "Enough of the niceties. Fifteen years ago, you asked a favor of me. I granted it. Now it is time for you to repay your debt."

"Of course." There is relief in finally discharging my debt. For so long I've wondered, not what I would be asked to do, but when. The uncertainty will soon be behind me. "What is it?"

"I want you to bring me the Caravaggio."

His request astonishes me.

"Why does everyone love this painting?" I'm truly bewildered.

He holds out his arms; heavy jewels adorn nearly every finger. Put him on a throne and one would easily mistake him for a prince of old. "I've always wanted it. It hung in the palace of Peter the Great. It was commissioned by the great Cosimo de' Medici."

"And you thumb your nose at the Petrovichs."

He grins. "That too."

"No." I refuse tersely. "Ask something else."

"I want nothing else." He waves his hand. "You know they are setting you up. This painting means nothing to them. They want you out of Moscow so that they can weed out those amongst your young soldiers who look up to you. The old guard will not give up power so easily."

I stare impassively. The old guard is senile. Their plays are so obvious they are read by outsiders. "I did not know you had interest in the Petrovich holdings. You've always said Moscow is full of peasants."

He flicks his fingers in disgust. "I do not want your precious *Bratva*. I have no interest in your businesses. And frankly, Vasya, neither should you. Let the Petrovich *Bratva* burn. Find me the painting and you can bring her home. Fifteen years is a very long time to have not laid eyes on your precious sister. What would you do to have your family restored to you?"

I fight not to bare my teeth at him, to not jump over the table and strangle him until pain replaces his smug smile.

"I know they expect me to fail and be distracted for months, but when I return with the Caravaggio, they will not be able to deny me. They have prepared their own shallow graves."

"So you have found it?" He quirks his eyebrow.

I shrug but do not answer.

"Well, well. I am impressed, Vasya. It is a shame I did not find you all those years ago. You would have made a marvelous part of the Dostonevs. Still, I want the painting. You will have to find a way to bring me the painting and still gain power within the *Bratva*. For you see Vasya, if you do not bring the painting to me, I will summon your sister home and she will become exactly what you do not wish—a target for all your enemies. I helped save your sister once. It is easy enough to help kill her, too. Choose your course wisely."

"They are setting you on a fool's errand," Igorek announces as I enter my office. He is standing next to the single window that overlooks a dirty alley and the brick wall of the building next door. Igorek is a young warrior with a brother and a mother to protect. He worries, for good reason, that he and his loved ones would be imperiled if I am gone for a long period of time. He is not the only one who has invaded my sanctum. Aleksei, an enforcer whom I trained with as a boy, is also present.

"Only if I cannot return with the Madonna. When I present the painting to them, they will be forced to back me. I will remove Elena to some dacha in northern Russia, and we will jettison any who would hew to the old ways."

"Merely remove her?" Igorek raises an eyebrow.

"What else would I do with her?" I meet his inquiry coolly, for speaking out loud of the murder of Elena Petrovich would not be met in all quarters with approval. She needs to die, but I cannot kill her until the *Bratva* is firmly under my control.

"*Mne pofig.*" He shrugs. *I don't care.*

Of course he cares or he would not suggest it. I, too, care, but it is not the time or place. "Once the *Bratva* is mine, then we will talk about protecting our own."

"Fine, so you look for a painting that has been lost for decades?" Igorek is skeptical.

Aleksei, whom I've known longer, is much less circumspect. "The Madonna? Holy Mother of Mary, are you crazy? Did killing Sergei cause you to lose your motherfucking mind?" Aleksei kicks at a chair and stomps around the room, looking for more things to break. I pull down a Meissen vase that is part of a set we'd recently discovered being transported inside a large set of ornamental—but very cheap—concrete dogs imported from China. Peddling antiques is more lucrative than I had anticipated. We started just a few years ago, as part of my goal to supplant income from the sale of krokodil and humans.

Sergei had been lured to the easy money, but trafficking in drugs and people is not only dangerous but also short lived. The problem with Sergei was that he lacked vision. Now he's dead, his body dumped in a hog lot so that the only thing he's possibly seeing now is the inside of a pig's belly. An ignominious end to the crime boss of one of the largest brotherhoods in Russia, but a fitting one.

"It's out there." I sit at my desk and check my emails. I've been searching for the Caravaggio for months now and while I have not found it, I believe I have discovered a person who can.

"You should shoot yourself now and save yourself the misery." Aleksei exhales grumpily and seats himself in one of the two low-backed leather chairs in front of the desk. I suppose it is my desk now. Once Sergei sat here and before him Roman Petrovich.

I hate the Petrovichs, all of them, both dead and alive. They had promised me safety but delivered only fear and torture. But my revenge will be to rule over this entire *Bratva* until the Petrovich name will be only known in connection with me, Vasily.

"What is your plan?" Igorek asks.

"There are rumors on the deep web of a collector who has not only the Madonna but the Golden Candelabra as well as a few other holy relics."

"Wonderful," Aleksei scoffs. "You know not of but rumors. Even if these rumors are true, one would have to assume that these artifacts are owned by a capitalist and are held in a safe that is virtually impenetrable. Just shoot Elena Petrovich and be done with it."

"If I kill her, who else will I have to kill? Thomas? Kilment? All of them? How about you, Aleksei? Or Igorek? And do I just kill the male members or every issue to the fifth cousin?" Aleksei pales at his name, at the mention of his family. "While it is better to be feared than loved, each act of ill will toward one's own people must be done only when there is no other action. If bringing this painting back means new leadership without bloodshed, it is worth the risk."

He is unconvinced by my speech, but he has a new wife and a child coming. Either of those could be used as bargaining chips against him.

"Igorek, you talk to the others, prepare them for my absence and be on watch." He nods. "How long will you be gone?"

"Not long." My inbox dings and I read the email swiftly. Finally. I give the two a ghost of a smile. "There is one person who can find the source of the postings on the dark web. One person who can lead us to the Madonna. And one person, I suspect, no modern security system can withstand. The Emperor." I lean back in my chair and point to the computer. "The Emperor appeared out of nowhere eighteen months ago and built an untraceable trading network for drugs, guns, flesh. And each of these transactions were paid in digital currency that flowed back to the Emperor in the form of tribute. He has made a fortune. A man who can create that? There is no bit or byte that can hold secrets from him."

"And you think you've found him?" Igorek asks.

"I know I have. He is in Brazil. He is in the employ of the Hudson gang or perhaps another local. But Brazil is the base according to the information we have been able to glean. I have paid for information that should be delivered to an associate of mine. With that, we should be able to locate and extract the Emperor."

"And how will you get the Emperor to work for you?" Aleksei is still dubious.

"By giving him whatever it is that he wants."

CHAPTER **TWO**

Now

NAOMI

Everything is so much easier when everyone follows the scientific method. Science doesn't have emotions. Science doesn't base findings on anything but science. If you have something you need resolved, you formulate your question, do your research, hypothesize, test, and analyze your data. It's all very logical and regimented, and it works.

Unfortunately, most "normal" people don't like the scientific method. They prefer to live through emotion. And by that, I mean they yell.

A lot.

For example, I'm sitting in the passenger seat in a van, and the driver is yelling at me. He's shouting something at me in a language I don't understand. Some Eastern European language. If I had a clear mind, I might try to mentally look for root words to determine the language, but everything is confusion. Five minutes ago, my brother Daniel was in the back of the van, bleeding, but now he's gone. His girlfriend, too. It's just me and this stranger who yells and drives very poorly.

This is all very confusing.

He bellows something at me again. I don't know what he wants, so I scream right back. I'm not sure if we're all supposed to be screaming, or if I've missed a cue somewhere.

The man glares at me, shakes his head, and turns back to driving. "*Bozhe moi,*" I hear him mutter. He looks angry, but at least he's not screaming any longer. I'm still not sure why we were screaming in the first place.

An hour ago, I was the Emperor. Captive of Hudson, hacker extraordinaire and cybercriminal misappropriating funds in exchange for the safety of my family. Now, I'm just Naomi Hays again.

My wounded brother appeared with the screamer and a new girlfriend. Together, they busted me out of Hudson's compound. It was all very A-Team and kind of fun until someone shot a gun and a window shattered near my head. The sound sent me spiraling.

As an Aspie, when I spiral, I get lost in myself. I lose track of what's going on and turn inward in my mind, where it's nice and quiet and safe. I'm out of my spiral now, and in the meantime, my brother has disappeared in all this noise and confusion. All that's left of him is his blood. It's everywhere, too—on my hands, in my hair, covering my arms. Blood's so unclean.

Right now, germs and DNA are all over me. I hate germs.

I also hate new places, new people, travel, and loud noises. Considering that I'm in a speeding van covered in someone else's blood and a stranger is yelling at me, it's safe to say I'm out of my comfort zone.

So I shut down again. I curl into a ball and rock myself, humming my favorite song—"Itsy Bitsy Spider"—to myself. I need to focus. I can't function in chaos. I think of the notes of the song and imagine viewing them on a computer synthesizer. I picture them dancing across the screen in waves. I imagine them, each note a flash of color in the melody.

Eventually I'm so wrapped up in the song that I don't notice anything anymore. My world exists of nothing but a nursery rhyme, and I repeat it over and over again to myself in an endless loop. When the song ends, I start it back up again, my lips moving and mouthing the words. Soon, it becomes a game to see if I can start and stop the song with no breaths in between.

I'm back in my happy place, lost in my mind, utterly content. The only thing that would make me happier is a computer keyboard at my fingertips.

A hand waves in front of my face. "Girl," a voice says. "Emperor." Fingers snap at my ear.

This interrupts my soothing melody, and I blink rapidly, coming back to the world again. I'm not the Emperor right now. The Emperor is a powerful hacker, surrounded by computers, mistress of her domain. Right now, I'm just Naomi Hays. And Naomi is pretty powerless.

I'm tempted to fake a seizure. It's my "go to" when a situation gets too difficult. Hudson and his men never figured out that I was faking. They'd always shoot me full of drugs and leave me alone again for hours, and then they'd be careful not to "antagonize" me again because Hudson didn't like it when they set me off. My fake seizures kept me safe, and the urge to do one now rises.

The man snaps his fingers in front of my face again.

"You interrupted me," I tell him, since he seems to want a response from me. "That's rude."

The look he gives me is incredulous, and I suppose I've misinterpreted his reaction. Maybe he was snapping his fingers in time to my music? I hum a few more bars experimentally, but he only snarls something at me in that strange language.

He doesn't seem very happy. Maybe he needs a happy place song, too. He's pissy and insolent, but he's not hurting me, so I hold off on faking a seizure.

For now.

"Get out of van," he tells me, this time in English. It's heavily accented English, but it's clear he's not from Brazil. He's too pale all over, and people from Brazil are lovely warm tones in skin and hair and eyes. He opens the door of the van and gestures at the street.

I'm not wearing shoes, and I look at the street, imagining my feet touching it. The broken pavement looks filthy. I don't approve. The van is dirty, too, but I already have its germs. Walking onto the street would mean an entirely new set of bacteria, and I don't like the thought. "No."

The pale man puts a smile on his face that's supposed to be friendly, I guess, but it looks about as fake as one of my own awkward smiles. "Come," he tells me. "We abandon van before police arrive. Come."

The second *come* is a command. "Are we going home or back to the compound?"

"Home."

Oh, good. I'm tired of this place with its noise and its blood.

The man waves something at me to direct me out of the van again—a gun. Huh. I wonder if he was the one shooting earlier. Who was shooting wasn't important to me, so I didn't pay attention.

I can't tell you why I'm in a van with this stranger. I can't begin to guess what he wants. I don't know where he's from, where we are, or what day of the week it is, but I can tell you pi to the 3,262nd decimal place. I can recite lines of complex computer code from heart. I can pull apart a car's engine and then put it back together again without a manual.

That's just how my mind works.

I'm special, people say. That's one of those "kind but not kind" words people use when they don't want to say what they mean. I don't know why they don't just say it aloud. It doesn't bother me. I'm autistic. Asperger's, actually, though I suppose we don't call it that anymore. But I've been Aspie for years now, and still am, in my own mind. It means I function differently than most people. I'm inside my own head more than most, and I don't know how to deal with people. I've been called everything from Rain Man to retard. I'm not, though.

I'm like one of the computers back in my garage apartment at home—wired differently for optimum efficiency. I like to think of myself as a custom build. Different from the basic model, perhaps a little clunky at first glance, but the interior's so full of bells and whistles that you overlook the quirks. Mostly.

The man snapping his fingers at me is clearly unaware that I'm an optimized computer. He gestures at me with the gun again, then sighs and rubs his neck. He glances down the street, then puts his gun away and holds out his hand. It's a friendly gesture, but the look on his face is anything but, and I don't know how to interpret this.

Friendly gesture or not, though, I don't like touching. "I don't want your hand," I tell him. "It's dirty."

His scowl darkens. I've probably offended him. My fingers move along the brim of my favorite baseball cap, a nervous tic of mine.

His gaze moves to my cap. He reaches forward and snatches it off my head, then tosses it into the nearby street.

I make an outraged noise. How dare he? That's my baseball cap. I glare at him and then climb out of the van to retrieve it, braving the grimy streets. Now it'll have to be washed, just like my feet.

"Finally, she moves," the man mutters, and shuts the van doors behind me. "Come. We get new car. They will be looking for this one. Come."

I don't know why anyone would be looking for that van—it's all shot up and there's blood on the inside. But he seems to know what he's talking about. I shrug and follow his lead.

We're in a dirty street in Brazil, in one of the favelas. It's filthy-dirty. Perhaps these people don't realize how much bacteria can breed in just one puddle. I did a science experiment once because my mother hadn't believed me when I said things were unclean. She believes me now. One sight of the mold that I'd grown in the pantry to show her, and she'd become a believer.

"Come," he says to me again. "We take that car." He gestures at a nearby junker.

It looks like it's filled with germs. I wrinkle my nose, but there aren't many cars in this area that seem like better choices. And I don't want to stay in this squalid area for longer than necessary, so I follow along. He says he's going to take me home, so he has to be better than the guys that kidnapped me.

"Can I drive?" I ask. I'm not a great driver—I tend to stay distracted and in my own mind a bit too much to pay attention to things like street signs. But I do love to drive—I love the speed of it, the feeling of freedom.

"*Nyet*, I drive. I know area." He tries the door of the car, but it's locked.

"Is that your car?"

"Do you always ask so many questions?"

I do, actually. But this seems to be a chastisement, so I quiet and don't offer to drive again. Strangers are always so prickly and difficult to read.

He looks around again, grabs a nearby rock, and then smashes it through the window. Glass rains down and he sweeps it aside with a sleeve, then unlocks the car door and opens it. More glass is brushed onto the concrete, and then he hunches under the steering column. Long moments pass, and he cusses.

I adjust my cap again and glance around. This man is stealing someone's car. No one's coming out to stop us, though, and I wonder if he's a frightening man. Am I supposed to be frightened? I have a hard time reading emotions, and so I don't get scared of the same people that most do. But I remember Daniel's girlfriend looked alarmed when this man glared at her. I study him as he crouches at the floorboard and jerks a panel off of the car.

He's a large man. Enormous, really. He's taller than anyone I know, and his arms are as big around as a tree trunk. His blond hair is cut short, and his clothes are crisp. That's good. I like neat clothing. Messy people have messy minds. He carries a gun, too, I remember. Maybe that's what makes him scary. I mostly find guns interesting. All those moving parts working in harmony.

After a moment, he swears again and jerks at the wiring. "Are you trying to steal this car?" I ask, since he looks like he needs help.

"Shut up."

"You're not very pleasant." Even I know that this man's an ass.

"Unless you want bullet in brain, shut up."

I don't want a bullet in my brain, actually, so I quiet. But I continue to watch him fumble with the wiring and fail miserably at hot-wiring the car. It's obvious this man's not an Aspie like me. If he were, he'd be able to actually figure out which wires start the ignition.

After a long moment, he swears and emerges from the front seat, a dark scowl on his face. He glances down the street. "Come. We walk."

"We're not taking this car?"

"*Nyet.*"

"But you just broke the window—"

"Walk," he snarls.

I consider this for a moment, then climb into the car's front seat. "Do you have a knife?"

He stares at me. "Come, we go."

This man's favorite word is apparently *come.* Maybe he needs to learn more English. I will suggest a language website for him to visit later, after we've figured out the car situation. "Did you want to take this car? I can hot-wire it for you, but I need a knife."

He stares at me for so long that I wonder if he didn't hear me. Then, he shifts and takes a pocketknife out of his slacks and flips the blade open, pointing it at my face.

It's an inch from my eyeball. Not an ideal place to hold a knife, but all I can see is that it's perfect for what I need. I smile and pluck the blade from him. "Thank you." I take it and jam it into the ignition, then pound on the end until I'm sure it's shoved in hard. Then, I give it a twist. I gun the gas pedal, admiring the way it purrs. Oh, I like this car. It's not pretty on the inside, but the engine is clearly refurbished. "There we go." I beam at it and pet the steering column. I love cars. Then I look at the stranger to see if he's as impressed with my handiwork. "On some older models, you can break the locking pins in the ignition. I've used a screwdriver in the past, but your knife works just as well."

He arches an eyebrow at me—it looks like a blond caterpillar. Then he gestures at the passenger seat. Right, I don't get to drive. I brush a few crumbs of glass off the seat and then slide over. He gets in on the driver's side and pulls away from the curb.

Not a word of thank you. *Hmph.* Disgruntled, I buckle in and try not to touch anything that I don't have to.

Germs, you know.

"You're not a very good thief," I point out to him.

"I am not thief," he says in a rather unpleasant tone. "I am boss."

CHAPTER **THREE**

VASILY

When I pull up to Tivoli Mofarrej in São Paulo, the doorman is affronted. It is a testament to the high ethos of service that he opens the door for Naomi to exit the car. I slip him one hundred euros.

"Shall I valet this?" he asks.

I nod as if I did not just bring a vehicle that is barely drivable to the most expensive hotel in Brazil. I've long since learned that if you act as if you belong, everyone will treat you accordingly. Naomi is planted in the middle of the portico, looking upward at the glass tiles. Placing my hand on her back, I urge her forward.

She jerks away as if I have burned her. "I don't like to be touched."

"It is destiny," I quip. "I do not enjoy being touched either, but standing out in the portico is not enjoyable, so let us enter."

Slowly she moves forward, mouthing something that sounds like numbers. She sounds as if she is . . . counting. Counting the glass tiles? The tiles on the floor? I know not and neither do I care. I want to get to our suite, shower off the glass, blood, and scum, and find our target. I pray it is not here, because Brazil is too hot for my blood. I prefer the harsh, bitter winters to the humid air that at times is as thick as a swamp.

The lobby of the Tivoli Mofarrej is blinding in its whiteness from the sheets of polished limestone tile to the white desks and white limestone wall partitions.

Naomi stops short. "I like this."

"What?" I ask impatiently.

"The white. It's soothing."

Images of the black leather sofas populating the suite we're staying in materialize in my mind. "You'll like black, too," I tell her and push her forward.

"I told you I don't like to be touched. Do you have a hearing deficit?" She frowns. "Because at first I was concerned that perhaps it is your English, but you seem to speak it quite well. Maybe it is your hearing then? You are young to have hearing problems. Is it hereditary? The most common birth defect is diminished hearing. Genetics are responsible for at least sixty percent of hearing deficits in infants so it's most likely your hearing loss is due to your parents. Were one or more of your parents hearing challenged?"

I look at her blankly.

"Deaf. That's what I mean by hearing challenged. *Challenged* is the word you're supposed to use instead of other things. Like instead of mute, voice challenged. Or instead of handicapped, it's

physically challenged. I learned that in college. I'm socially challenged, but maybe it doesn't translate into Russian. You're Russian, right?"

"Yes. What does it matter?"

"It doesn't. There was a Russian student in my art history
course. Your accent was similar. I remember him telling me he
was from a certain region—southern maybe? I didn't much like
the course. My advisor forced me to take it, saying that I needed
some liberal arts to make my education well rounded, but learning about painting and politics did not assist me in creating better code. I like to write code. Code makes sense. Art does not."

"No, I suppose it does not. It is meant to make you feel." She
looks disgusted as if feelings are a cursed thing. Naomi Hays is
an odd girl, even odder than her fast-talking brother. "You are
not much like your brother," I remark.

This makes her scowl deepen. "Because he is funny. Everyone
likes funny people."

After a deluge of words, she shuts up at this. I make note to
avoid comparisons with her brother in the future.

"I do not find Daniel Hays humorous," I answer. "Rather he is
irritating but competent. I suspect that is a trait you both share."

"Competent." She considers that word for a moment, possibly
running through all the dictionary definitions and permutations
before responding. "I'll accept that. Why are we standing in the
lobby?"

I open my mouth to tell her that I have been waiting for her.
Instead, I give her a brief smile and, remembering her earlier complaints, I do not touch her but instead gesture for the elevator. "Shall
we go up to our room?"

"Do I have my own room? I like quiet. I don't want to be disturbed. Will we be going home after this?"

"You shall have your own room. There are three bedrooms in the presidential suite. One overlooks Trianon Park."

When we step into the elevator, I note that she stands in the precise middle and hold her arms close to her sides. She counts again, not the floor numbers that tick by as we speed to the twenty-second floor, but something else.

"What do you count, Naomi?" I ask, curious.

She does not respond or look at me. I realize then that she rarely looks at my face. In the lobby she looked around her and at my chest but hardly ever at my face. At first I thought that she was busy taking in her surroundings, but now I think it is something else. Her fingers brush over the rim of her cap repeatedly. It's so tattered that the white board of the bill is peeking through the loose threads.

Many women like my face. Too many. I've scars but it does little to deter the opposite sex. Yet, she is not interested. I peruse her body as her attention is distracted. She's voluptuous—large breasted, nipped-in waist, and wide hips. If I were a man who enjoyed sex, I would want her.

When the bell rings signaling our arrival on the floor, she does not immediately step off. Instead she watches as the doors open and then as they begin to close again. Swiftly I extend an arm and press the Door Open button and I wait. My body is close to hers, close but not touching. There's a hand's width of space between us. If I leaned forward, we would be flush from groin to ass and chest to back. And still we wait.

Her breathing evens out to match mine. From my much taller

vantage point, I watch her large tits rise and fall with each measured intake and exhale. My hands are oversized but I suspect if I palmed her breasts, they would overflow my palms. My heart rate quickens slightly as an image of her tied to my bed while I fuck her generous tits plays out in glorious Technicolor.

"Your breathing is erratic," she says.

"Yours as well," I note. Her chest is moving rapidly, the rhythm giving a sprightly bounce to her fleshy mounds. I visualize what they might look like at the moment her bra is loosened, how they'd spill out, bouncing nicely. Insane. I shake myself, for I am not one to be transported by lust. I do not like to be touched. I do not like women. Lust is not in my vocabulary.

"Why is yours getting faster?" Her tone holds genuine curiosity. Could it be this easy? Could I seduce her into complying with my demands? I have fucked women I've hated, and I do not hate Naomi. Apparently my body likes her quite well. I glance down at my waist to see if there is visible evidence of arousal. I so rarely feel physical desire that the tightening of my trousers is foreign and almost strange.

"If I share with you, will you return the favor?" I murmur.

"Certainly," she responds immediately.

"I'm visualizing you on my bed, nude. Your hands are tied above your head. Your back is arched. My hands are pushing your breasts together to form a snug channel for my cock. As I shuttle between your breasts, my cockhead hits your chin. Your tongue darts out to lick it occasionally." I take an infinitesimal step forward, still not touching her but so close that the slightest movement would have her pressed against my growing erection. Despite my aversion to touching, there is something about her that calls to me. Her lushness, perhaps? Or merely my own inexplicable physical response to her nearness. I dip my head down close to her ear. "What is your excuse?"

She presses a hand to her chest, touching the top of one of those beautiful tits. "I don't know." She sounds genuinely bewildered—as am I. She won't look at me, but she leans closer, as if compelled. Encouraging.

Before I can question her more, the security buzzer sounds on the elevator. The sharp, intrusive sound causes Naomi to yelp and clap her hands over her ears. Dropping to the floor, she begins to rock much like she did in the van when shots were being fired at our backs.

The buzzing of the elevator along with Naomi's cries fill the room with cacophonous sound and brings Aleksei at a run. Any arousal I felt vanishes. Naomi is my most important weapon in the fight for my sister, my *Bratva*. If she is not well, my trip is for naught. I must be careful with her.

"What in Christ's name is wrong?" he bellows.

"Nothing," I yell back. Disregarding Naomi's desire to remain untouched, I pick her up and carry her into the living room and deposit her on a black sofa. She remains stiff in her crouched position, hands clapped over her ears. The elevator is still buzzing.

"Go, Aleksei," I order. "Get rid of the elevator. And the noise."

Crouching down by Naomi, I ask, "What can I get for you?" Had I shocked her with my words? I curse my low-class upbringing. Naomi, with her tender skin and delicate appearance, is too gentle for my street roughness. No matter that I look like I belong, I do not. I am not born to the *Bratva* or to some higher family. I am simply a killer with an elevated status, looking for an obscene painting that will cement my position as king of evildoers. It is disgust for me that she is displaying.

I cast around for the right words to say to her. "I should not have talked in that fashion to you," I say, dropping my head so she need not look at my face. The sound of the elevator ceases, and the footsteps of Aleksei stop directly behind me.

"What are you doing?" He sounds scandalized, likely affronted that I am beneath this woman. For I am Vasily Petrovich, the ostensible leader of the most powerful criminal brotherhood in northern Europe. We Petrovichs bow to no one and most assuredly not in front of a slip of a woman.

"She is the Emperor," I say simply.

A short silence ensues and then, "I see."

His footsteps carry him away to the far side. I hear the clink of glass and then he returns. "Here, vodka," he offers.

Naomi has stopped rocking, but it is as if she is unaware that we are here. I rise from my crouching position and sit beside her on the sofa. I take the vodka and gesture for Aleksei to bring another. "Bring the bottle," I call when he reaches the bar. Naomi flinches at my loud voice.

I take note of that, too. She does not like to be touched. She does not like loud noises. She likes white. Perhaps I should call the butler assigned to our suite and see if the black furnishings can be traded out for white. I'll see how long we need to stay here before I do. I take a long sip of my vodka. "Good stuff." I tip my glass toward Aleksei in a mock salute.

He cocks his head toward Naomi with a wordless question.

"We are in no hurry," I respond. "Nothing needs to be done today."

Following my lead, Aleksei drinks his vodka and I pour him another. Stretching one arm across the back of the sofa, I turn my body slightly to form a barrier for Naomi. She may not like to be touched, but I want her to be clear that she is safe here.

"What happened?"

"Daniel Hays and I with the help of Senhor Mendoza mounted an offensive against Hudson during his birthday party. Hays discovered his woman and Naomi here in the basement. Naomi is Mr. Hays's sister."

"Ahhh." His eyebrows shoot up. "Mr. Hays allowed you to take his sister."

I laugh, but cognizant that Naomi is sitting next to me, I give a partial truth. "Mr. Hays and his woman went with Mendoza. We came here."

He nods, understanding. "Then all is well."

"Yes, all is well," I confirm.

"I can call for the jet."

Looking at Naomi, who has now dropped her hands from her ears and is currently sitting cross-legged with her hands in her lap but still not fully present, I shake my head. "Not yet. We will wait. But do call the concierge and have some clothes delivered. Perhaps from the Miu Miu store on the corner. Shoes, undergarments. All of it."

With that, Aleksei drains his vodka and then rises. "I will leave you, then. Call if you need more assistance."

I watch him as he leaves. I've brought him along because . . . I do not trust him. Better to keep your enemies closer. When he disappears into one of the bedrooms, I turn my attention back to Naomi.

Setting the glass on the coffee table, I pour another finger. A hand reaches out to stop me from lifting it to my lips.

"Can I try?" Naomi asks.

"Certainly." I hand her my glass and she turns it all the way around until she finds the place on the rim of the glass where I placed my own mouth. Shockingly, her tongue darts out and runs along the edge. I feel the reverberation of her actions in my groin. The cheap wool of my borrowed pants is once again constricting, and the need to reach down and squeeze my cock to ease the sudden ache seizes me. Her lips open then and cover the exact location where mine touched. I muffle a groan. She turns the glass to the opposite side and takes another sip.

"I think it's sweeter when I drink where you drink. Will you try again so I can test it?"

What can I do but agree. "Lift it to my lips, then," I order.

She does and I drink, ensuring a wide placement of my tongue and lips on the glass. The test is run again as she drinks first from my side of the glass and then the opposite.

"Your heart is beating erratically again."

"So it is," I say. My blood is pounding in my ears and in my cock, but I don't make the mistake of telling her this. I do not want to scare her away. Truly, I don't know what I want. I've never sat so close to a woman as fine as Naomi; even with her odd quirks she is lovely to behold and interesting to listen to. I cannot help but move closer.

"Mine too." She places her hand over her chest again. "You were saying things in the elevator and they made my heart pound faster and I felt warm. Very warm."

I shutter my eyes to hide my shock. She was aroused by my words, not disgusted. Carefully I test her. "Would you want me to talk to you like that again?"

I watch her think about it. It is as if I can actually see the gears moving inside her brilliant mind as she considers my request.

"Yes. For science, you understand," she adds quickly.

"For science." I nod. "Would you like to begin now? Or another time?"

"Can we do it now?"

"Of course. But let us choose your bedroom first." I do not want Aleksei to walk out into the living room as I am fucking Naomi, because I do not know how it will end. Will I be able to pleasure her? Will this bring me closer to my goals?

She frowns. "Why will we need a bedroom?"

"What do you think will happen after I tell you about what I want to do to your body and what I want you to do to mine?"

"But you said you don't like to be touched. I don't like it either. Why would we need a bedroom?" she repeats.

I stare at her and this time it is I who needs time to process her statement. She is absolutely right. I do not like to be touched. When I have sex, which is infrequently, I do not kiss a woman. I do not lick her body. I stick my cock in her hole and rut like an animal to my release, usually from behind. Naomi is an aberration. I wonder what her scientific mind would make of that.

"Even if we do not touch, I think the things we would say are better kept between the two of us unless you would like to be observed."

"I don't know if I'd like that. I don't think so but I've never tried it." She shrugs. "I'm not interested anymore. Why am I here?"

Her quicksilver change of subject takes me by surprise, and I struggle to adjust. "Because I am in need of your services."

"My computer skills?"

"Yes. I need you to find someone for me. Have you heard of the *Madonna and the Volk*?"

"I've heard of many things referencing the Madonna, otherwise known as Mary, mother of Jesus. Are you religious?"

"No. I do not like the idea that a power higher than me directs my life. But others believe. The *Madonna and the Volk* is a triptych. In some circles it is much revered but considered blasphemous. It is of the Madonna birthing a *volk*, a wolf, rather than the Christ child. In the second panel, the two are making love, and in the last the *volk* is eating the Madonna."

"That's kind of gross. It's a religious painting?" She frowns.

"Yes, by Caravaggio. It is said to either be punishment for Mary having marital relations with Joseph or the act of a jealous, oedipal son."

She scrunches up her nose, which is surprisingly enticing. "Shouldn't he be eating Joseph, then?"

I smile wryly. "I believe the eating of Mary by the *volk* is metaphorical, a sexual interpretation."

"Oh." She chews on that for a moment. "But you haven't said why I'm here. What do you want me to do?"

"The Madonna was once owned by my organization but was sold many years ago. Recently it has surfaced and was resold to another individual. I want you to locate the owner and ideally, the painting itself."

"Why?"

"Will you not simply accept payment for this project?"

She shakes her head. "I like to know why."

Naomi had been in captivity for two years serving someone else's whims. I understand the need for her to know why. I ruminate for a moment. I can lie to her. Tell her that I am interested in retrieving it for a church or higher cause, but I think that she'd deal better in the truth, in absolutes.

"I want the Madonna because it will help me consolidate power.

If I have enough power, I can protect the people I care about as you tried to protect your family."

"Are you a soldier like my brother?" she asks.

"I was but now I have a chance to lead."

"Are you a competent leader?"

My lips curve up. Competent rather than the moral word *good*. It is like an interview of sorts but instead of being demeaned, I feel compelled to convince her of my worthiness. "I am. I know how to move people to act, which is why I seek the Madonna. It will convince the doubters that I am the correct person to lead the . . . organization. I am clearheaded and make decisions without emotion. I do what is in the best interest of the . . . organization, even if those actions are unfavorable to others."

I leave out that I may have to give the painting to another man in order to save my sister. It is a fact that must remain secret, for a whisper of Katya's existence would jeopardize her life.

For the first time since I've met Naomi, she glances at my face, but before our eyes can meet, her gaze slides away until she's fixated on my cheek or perhaps my ear.

"That does sound like you are competent." Her soft words sound like a compliment. "Will I have to work for you long then?"

"Only as long as it takes. While you search for this person, I will provide everything. Food, equipment, entertainment. Once it is over, I will fly you back to your family and handsomely reward you monetarily."

She waves her hand. "I don't need money. I have plenty. Do you have a workstation?"

"What do you need? Aleksei will obtain whatever it is that you desire."

"Oh no, I like to buy my own things, but I can get started if you have a laptop. It needs to have a good processor. At least quad-core extreme. No netbook. Those things are shitty. I don't know how many scripts I'll have to run." She's walking around looking at things and has already forgotten me. She's forgotten my interest in her body. My story about the *Madonna and the Volk*. My leadership test. When she stops in the middle of the room, she asks the question I've been waiting for.

"Where did you hear the transaction took place for the Madonna?"

"Why do you think I sought the Emperor, Naomi? It was on your creation. The Emperor's Palace."

CHAPTER FOUR

NAOMI

I study Vasily as he speaks words that should not be spoken aloud. My face is calm, but my mind is whirling, calculating things. He knows about the Emperor's Palace. He knows I run the website, and therefore have connections to crime and information that no normal person should have. This makes me dangerous, and it makes him even more dangerous that he knows about it.

Vasily knows a lot more about me than he lets on, which means I will have to be careful. He mentions the Emperor's Palace in such a casual voice that I almost miss it. It is the same way, minutes ago, that he described thrusting his cock between my breasts and fucking my chest.

I . . . don't know how I feel about this. I'm not good at feeling things. Give me a task and something to do with my hands, and I'll get to work. Diagnose my feelings? I will be lost.

I'm visualizing you on my bed, nude.

I lose focus, because then I picture it, too. I picture him devouring me with that intense gaze, the utter focus of his attention, and my lips part. But then I think about all the fluids and horrible unclean things that come with sex and shake the thought away. I must focus on understanding what Vasily wants—what he's saying he wants and what he's not saying, too.

I should not be surprised that he knows of the Emperor's Palace. I set it up to be untraceable by most, and for nothing to lead back to me. Masked IP addresses, borrowed server space, nothing points back to me. Somehow, though, things got messy. I blame Hudson. He never let me take the time to properly cover my footsteps. It was always "create a script to take money out of this account" and "hack into this Swiss bank tonight." Proper dark web transactions take time and stealth, and I was allowed neither.

I've become sloppy. This displeases me.

I refuse to let this stranger know, however. I study him, thinking hard. This is a big man. The set of his mouth is firm, unyielding. He is not smiling. He does not look as if he likes me.

And yet minutes ago he talked of my breasts as if they excited him. And his breathing escalated, like mine is doing right now. At first, I assume I am panicking. Hyperventilation is always one of the symptoms, and when I get overwhelmed, I can panic easily.

But there is not the accompanying spiral of anxiety. There is no tingling in my extremities as if my blood flow is constricted. My stomach does not hurt from stress. This isn't anxiety, then. It's something else entirely.

Excitement?

"You do not speak," he says, and his voice is calm, soothing.

"Tell me what you need. I wish for you to find this transaction on Emperor's Palace and tell who has purchased Caravaggio."

He's dropping his articles of speech; it's a habit of speech of those that speak some Slavic languages. There are no articles of speech. There are also no articles of speech in Hindi, Japanese, Indonesian, and Latin. I read that on a Snapple cap once and researched languages for a week afterward, fascinated by the vagaries of language. Partitives in French are especially fascinating, because—

"Naomi," he says again, drawing me out of my thoughts about languages.

"Hmm?" I've forgotten what we are discussing. "Do you know French?"

"*Un peu.*"

I brighten. "Fascinating. I've always wanted to learn French. I find the feminine and masculine gendering for nouns to be quite interesting. After all, what determines whether or not a lake is actually masculine—"

"Naomi," he says, interrupting me again. "The deep web. The Emperor's Palace. I want you to check the records."

"Oh. Right." I blink rapidly, trying to get my brain off the language rails it's been racing down. "I need my preferred setup—"

"*Nyet.* Start now."

Hmph. "Fine. Do you have a computer I can use?"

He inclines his head in a nod and gestures at a nearby doorway. "Aleksei has brought one for you. It is in the diplomatic suite."

"Excellent." I bounce to my feet and notice his gaze follows my breasts. That makes me feel odd again. I'm fascinated that this man is clearly interested in my body. He finds something about me sexually arousing, when all most people see is a freak. I don't think of myself as a freak, naturally, but I've been called one often enough to know that more people find me disturbing than not.

I think this man is attracted to me. Is this how most women feel? I'm giddy with the thought of it, and I tug at the neckline of my shirt to expose my cleavage like I have seen other women do.

His gaze goes there, and then narrows.

A change in his expression. Interesting. I wonder how most women flirt with men; I'm woefully absentminded when it comes to social cues. I should research this. In the meantime, I wonder if I should touch myself between my legs, like I sometimes do to relax, and see his reaction? My mother told me when I was a girl that it was improper for me to cup my privates when in public, but I'm not in public now, and I get the idea that this man would enjoy seeing it.

"Do you distract me, Naomi?" Those narrowed eyes focus on my face.

I look away, disconcerted. That isn't the look of appreciation he was giving me earlier. I've done something wrong to change his look to one of distrust. Frustrated, I run my fingers along the bill of my cap, soothing myself. My cap is safe to touch. "Computers," I say, refocusing. "I need a computer."

"In that room," he points out.

I move to it and sit down. There's a desk and some chairs and an ugly painting full of colors on the wall, but all I care about is the computer. I flip open the laptop. Immediately, my lip curls. Windows 8. Really? "Kiddie shit."

He barks his companion's name. A moment later, a man comes striding in, his brows furrowed. He says something in Russian, a question, because his inflection goes up at the end of the sentence. Vasily barks out something angrily. The man nods and grabs keys, then heads out the door. Vasily turns back to me. "We will get you better computer."

"Oh, I can work with this for now," I say, taking the mouse in hand and giving it a little shake. It's like settling in with a pair of my favorite pajamas, having a mouse at hand. "But I'm going to put a new GUI on your computer before I go any further."

"GUI?"

"Graphical user interface. This one is not conducive to running scripts. Plus, you have a lot of bloatware. I need to strip things down to run more efficiently."

"Just access deep web," he says, sounding a bit impatient. "I wish to follow buyer of painting. The longer we take to find him, the colder trail gets."

I hear Vasily's words but I'm ignoring them. Working with an unfamiliar GUI is like trying to work with my fingers coated in ice. I'm already at the DOS prompt, uninstalling his hard drive. We're going to erase everything and start over. It's a project. I love projects. "Please keep your backups in a safe location," I tell Vasily absently as the computer goes to work reformatting. "Also, I have voided your factory warranty."

He makes a soft noise that might be amusement.

Hours pass, and I busy myself with installing programs on the laptop I've appropriated. I pick the strongest Wi-Fi signal and tap into it. They'll never notice I'm in their Internets, stealing their bandwidth. Then I add a few of my other favorite scripting programs and tools that will allow me to move through the web without being traced. I work for hours, fine-tuning and tweaking things to how I like them. At some point, someone hands me a bottle of water and an avocado and cheese sandwich on wheat bread. I look at it for any other colors—I don't like eating things that are not white, green, or brown—and when it passes muster, I remove the orange cheese slice on the sandwich and eat the rest without pausing in working. Vasily moves about the room, silent. At one point his phone rings and I glare at him for interrupting me with his noise. He leaves the room.

Then I'm in the deep web and I'm the Emperor. Trillions of bits of data flow at my fingertips, much of it illegal. I've never been interested in merely pirating movies and songs. Not when I can take on—and control—darker information. Morality has no play in such things for me. If I don't know someone personally, I'm not affected by thoughts of them, so I turned my talents to more dangerous information. It's a game for me, to see how far I can push myself. I control more information than anyone else on the web, and it's a heady feeling. I don't do much with the information other than hoard it, but there's a fierce pleasure in the possession of so much knowledge. I access my server records and do a search for Caravaggio, and easily find the information Vasily is seeking.

Then, I delete the records from the archive.

I know after years of being a captive that I am only useful until my job is done. This man knows that I am the Emperor and doesn't seem to mind it, but I do not trust him any more than I trust Hudson, who threatened to kill my family. I know these men are dangerous.

No one is getting my information until I let them. Not even if he stares at my breasts and makes me wonder what it'd be like if he touched me.

So I sit back and begin running an SQL query that looks very intricate but is, in truth, garbage. I finish my sandwich, drink my water, and wait for Vasily to return to the room.

He comes back a short time later and approaches my chair. One big hand presses on the back of it. "Do you find my information?"

"I'm executing a query," I tell him. I'm a good liar because I'm not emotional. I can lie to anyone with a straight face. "I'm cross-referencing these three tables looking for particular sales references. Each table has over two million rows and—"

Vasily pins me with his gaze. "How long?"

"Three days," I lie. In three days, I will have a better idea of what this man wants.

He swears something in Russian. "We must stay here three days?"

"Yes," I lie. "I can't unplug from the network or I have to start my query all over again. You wanted the Emperor. This is how I work."

"We must continue on. We cannot stay here."

I wipe my fingers with a Wet-Nap and poise them over the keyboard. "Shall I abort my query—"

"*Nyet*," he says, and reaches for my hands. His fingertips brush over my skin and I instinctively flinch away. My skin prickles a little, but I remember drinking his vodka. I deliberately placed my mouth where his had been, feeling euphoric. I think of him spreading his germs on my skin with the touch of his fingers against mine. For some reason, I'm not revolted like I normally am. Is it because we've already shared germs?

I think of the stories he told me earlier. He wants to push his cock between my breasts and have me lick it. I picture the scenario, but in every mental image, there are bodily fluids involved. And I'm not sure if I like that.

I had sex once, and it was highly unpleasant. Most think I am a virgin, but I'm not. Like everything, I used the scientific theory.

I formed a hypothesis—can I enjoy sex? I had caught Daniel with one of his girlfriends in the barn at my parents' ranch, and they both looked as if they were enjoying themselves immensely. Therefore, I'd wanted to try it. I'd selected a college classmate I thought was pleasing to the eye and asked him after a study break if he wished to copulate. He had, and we'd found a hotel room. I'd been so distressed by the blankets and the germs that were sure to be crawling on them that I had a hard time concentrating. My memories of sex were him grasping my breasts a few times, then shoving his dick inside me. It had hurt, and there were copious secretions on his end, which had alarmed me more than anything else. I'd screamed at him for leaking on me and ran for the shower.

And that was the end of that.

After that horrifying experience, I'd done more research on sexual activity and now knew that the penis ejaculating semen was normal. However, I did not find any of it pleasant. No touching, because the human skin secreted oils. No kissing, because mouths were filthy things full of germs. And no penises. No penises at all.

But I did like it when Vasily told me what he wanted to do to me. I will allow him to look at me, but not touch. I'm not fond of touching.

"We will stay here," he says. "For now."

I blink at him. I've been thinking about sex and I don't remember our conversation. "Stay where?"

"Here. In this hotel. Tivoli Mofarrej. We will have to be careful. People will be looking for you."

Ooh. I brighten. "Can we have disguises? If we mask our exterior appearances, it will be difficult for people to find us. In one study of police sketches, more than eighty percent were found to be inaccurate—"

"There is no need for disguise," he says, interrupting me. "You will not be leaving hotel."

But I'm already enthusiastic about the thought of a disguise. "I would need a black turtleneck and leather pants. And a haircut! Maybe I will shave my head."

"No head shave. I like your hair." And he reaches out and tugs one lock between his fingers, rubbing it.

I can't feel anything—it's just hair—but I'm disconcerted and pleased. I like direct compliments. So often, people try to hide what they mean and I miss their meaning. He likes my *hair*. "What if I just dye it instead?"

"Dye is acceptable," he says thoughtfully, still rubbing my hair. "What color do you wish?"

"My favorite color is green."

"The idea is to be inconspicuous."

Oh. I think for a moment longer. I'm a natural blonde but I have dark brows, so I won't look too odd with darker hair. "Brown? Naturally brown hair accounts for sixty percent of North American hair colors."

He rubs my hair for a moment longer. "*Da*. Brown. For now."

"And the disguise clothing? Do you need my clothing sizes? I'm a 38-inch bust, 24-inch waist, 36-inch hips. My inseam is 28 inches and I wear a size 8 shoe."

Vasily says nothing, simply regards me and continues to rub my hair between his fingers.

I wonder if I've missed a subtle cue somehow. I can never tell what emotional people are thinking, and I begin to get nervous. "You know I am autistic, correct?"

He shrugs, as if this means nothing to him.

I try to parse that reaction. Normally people recoil, or get a sympathetic look on their faces as if I've suddenly declared myself brainless. But a shrug? A *so what*? I . . . well, I don't recall ever getting that reaction before. He's still touching my hair, though. "Because I am autistic, I will miss subtle clues. You will need to explain things directly to me."

Again, he shrugs.

Flustered, I return to reciting my measurements. "If you need my bra size, I'm a 38C. I'm told that's not an average size, but you should be able to find it in most stores. Medium panty, but it depends on the brand. I've never had my neck measured but I don't think it's necessary. If you have a measuring tape here, we can correct that, though."

"It is not necessary."

"All right." I give one last look at my script. There's nothing else for me to do at the moment. I feel awkward, but I don't want to look at Vasily. If he's giving me cues of what he is expecting of me, I'm missing them. "What do we do now?"

He looks at his watch. "It is late."

"Late" is a cue I know. That's indirect wording for bedtime. I have a routine before I go to bed. I always shower and wash my hair to get the day's grime off of my skin, because I can't sleep if there's a chance that there are germs on me. I also insist on having the blankets and sheets changed every day. It's a quirk my family has always accommodated, and Hudson's people did, as well. I will have to tell this man that I have additional demands. Not as the Emperor, but as Naomi. Naomi is far more delicate than the Emperor.

"Then I should shower," I tell Vasily. "I need shampoo, conditioner, a new bar of soap, and new towels. And flip-flops because there are bound to be germs in the tub."

"I am sure that if the room does not have what we need, it can be acquired." His voice is smooth and easy, and I imagine it as a softly rippling wave of sound. Comforting. Lovely with its bass tones. I like this man's voice. I steal a glance up at him.

"Have you ever been kissed, Naomi?" he asks me, startling me.

"I have, but I didn't like it."

"No? Why is that?"

"Germs," I tell him. "Mouths are dirty things. The average mouth has several hundred kinds of bacteria in it at all times. I don't like the thought of mixing bacteria with someone else's."

"But if their mouth were clean? Teeth brushed? Mouth freshened with mouthwash?"

I . . . I don't know. I've never thought about this. I'm startled into silence.

He's still standing over my shoulder, rubbing my lock of hair slowly. He hasn't moved. I think of him watching my breasts earlier, and his words about stroking his cock between my breasts. I think of the euphoric almost-anxiety-but-not I felt when he looked at me. It's not something I feel often and it's hard to put my finger on. I lick my lips, thinking of my shower. And I wonder what it will feel like if Vasily watches me while I bathe.

I enjoy touching myself and getting clean. I love a scalding-hot shower. And a new, subversive hypothesis forms in my mind. Query: if Vasily gazing at my clothed breasts makes me feel breathless, will him gazing at my naked breasts induce a different physical reaction?

Scientific theory always provides an interesting path to take, and I'm intrigued by where this could lead. I look up at Vasily again. When his gaze meets mine, I break contact and let my eyes focus elsewhere. "I need to shower. Do you want to watch?"

CHAPTER FIVE

VASILY

My hand drops from her hair and I turn her down. "Not tonight, Naomi. I think, perhaps, you should sleep now."

"So you don't want to see me naked?" Frown marks crease her forehead. Her fake confusion generates a wild urge inside me to soothe her, to draw her down next to me on the sofa and rub away the furrows in her brow. The feelings and sensations she is eliciting are startling and unfamiliar.

Impatient with her and myself, I speak to her more harshly than intended. "*Nyet*. Thank you for the invitation but I must decline."

I can see the words tumble inside her head as she debates how to respond, which only irritates me more. I do not need a conniving female on my hands thinking to seduce me. No matter that the thought crossed my mind earlier. My response to her was real and genuine. I am disturbed that she responds with calculation only.

For hours, Naomi had forgotten everything outside of the keys of her laptop and the scrolling screen of black with green text. She tapped away at her screen and muttered how it was too small. When I suggested something larger, she ignored me. I brought her a sandwich but she pushed it away, muttering something about the red looking like blood. She would not eat it. Aleksei and I discuss that perhaps she is a vegetarian and Aleksei goes to speak to the chef. A cheese and avocado sandwich is returned. She eats the avocado and bread but nothing else.

I make note of everything.

Her actions toward me are now calculated. The tug on her shirt to reveal her breasts, the placement of her mouth over the glass where mine touched—all of it seems to be a ploy to garner a reaction. The shower invitation is yet another part of a game she is playing.

But I am still tempted.

"You are—what would you say? Trying too hard," I respond. Even to my ears, I sound petulant and accusatory. A child, not a man. Rising from the sofa, I try for a more modulated tone. "I think we are both too tired for bedroom antics tonight, Naomi." With that, I turn and walk toward the third bedroom. The diplomatic suite had been mine, but Naomi seems to prefer it and the view. Why not simply accede to her requests in this matter?

"It's the bathroom." Her statement stops me short.

"It is what?"

"I'm not asking you to watch me in the bedroom. That's a different room. I invited you to watch me shower. There's water. A toilet. Also nice-smelling things. Steam. It's a different environment. Environments can result in differing outcomes. I'm not interested in the bedroom currently but I may be later. What is it about the bedroom you prefer? You mentioned the bedroom earlier. Is that more conducive to watching things?"

Her words have caught me off guard and worse, I begin to imagine things such as Naomi's ample breasts being caressed by her own hands as she massages oils and lotions and soaps into her skin. It takes little effort to visualize the water streaming over her curves, dripping downward to cling to the blond curls between her legs.

I'm halfway across the room before I realize that she's caught me again. Naomi is clever, and not just with computers. I have forgotten myself. "You have a silver tongue. I will remember that." With a click of my heels and a formal bow, I bid her good night.

I am not prepared for the Emperor to be a female. The fake passports and identities I've brought are all for men. In my room, I take them out and rifle through the identities. The shortest one is a male, five-eight, and that is still taller than Naomi, so disguising her as a male would not work.

This is not a problem I cannot overcome. Rio is a tourist city. There are people—and thus passports—available everywhere.

I place a pair of thin rubber gloves in my pocket and a knife in my boot.

"Where are you going?" Aleksei asks me as I enter the foyer.

I respond coldly, for it is unusual that he is watching me so carefully. "Out."

He knows better than to ask for an explanation but the look in his eyes raises the hair on my neck. It is intense and calculating. I would deal with him now, but I need someone to watch Naomi while I am gone.

"I'll be back shortly," I tell him, part in warning.

He nods in reply.

The hotel we are in is too luxurious for the tour buses, my current target. I walk down the beach and then around to the front of each resort, looking for a bus returning to the airport. At the third hotel, I find the perfect mark. The tour guide is busy corralling guests inside. There is a passenger with a dog who is yapping loudly. The bus driver is leaning against the front, sharing a smoke with a hotel valet.

And one of the passengers is approximately Naomi's height. Conveniently, her purse is left abandoned on top of her suitcase as she chases down a small child. I hunch over, lowering my head, and no one notices as I begin rolling the cases toward the open luggage compartment at the bottom of the bus. Or if they notice, they think I am nothing more than part of the tour package.

When I get to the mother's suitcase, I simply walk off and climb into a waiting cab. Inside the purse I find a passport for an American woman, Karen Brown. Like her name, she has dark brown hair and is the same height as Naomi. It is perfect.

The clothes inside the suitcase will work as well. Satisfied, I give the driver the address of the hotel.

When I return to the hotel, I immediately have the new luggage and passport sent to the jet that is on standby. Upstairs in the suite, Naomi is in virtually the same position she was when I left. Aleksei is in his room, pacing. I retreat to the bedroom and once there, I find myself full of restless energy.

I cannot hear Naomi or the click for the soundproofing is too good in the suite. It is why we chose this particular hotel and set of rooms. Only one way to enter, and no one can hear our activities. Yet now I wish for thinner walls and less space. I wonder if her skin is still wet from the shower. I wonder if, when she cleaned between her legs, she lingered, imagining my touch there.

My body grows tight and ready. I tell myself it is adrenaline from the theft earlier, but I can only lie so many times to myself. Quickly I throw on running shoes and shorts.

"What is the matter with you?" Aleksei asks, joining me in the exercise room, where I have sought my physical release.

"I am hiding," I admit. Sweat drips down my forehead. Without interrupting my long strides on the treadmill, I swipe the liquid away with the bottom of my shirt before it can sting my eyes.

"From the girl?" He smirks.

She is no mere girl. She is a temptress with her luscious breasts and curvy form. I, who am never tempted by women or men for that matter, cannot stop thinking of her. An hour of exercise and I'm still feeling an ache in my balls—*from the girl*.

"She is dangerous," I tell him. "Stay away from her." I do not want Aleksei snared in her web. He is not as strong willed as I. With a mere crook of her finger, she would have him on his knees, begging to be her slave. I do not warn him away because I want her for myself, I warn him for his own safety.

"She is a small thing," he scoffs. "Her skill is with technological things. I can disarm her blindfolded and on my knees."

"Let us not underestimate her," I say. "Remember that Sergei was brought down by a girl."

Aleksei sobers immediately. What Aleksei does not know is that Sergei was tied to a chair when he was shot. He believes that former *Bratva* member Nikolai Andrushko helped to exact revenge for the killing of his mentor, the killing of my mentor, Alexsandr Krinkov. And that Nikolai is now dead by my hand. Only Nikolai's death is just another part of my deceit, for he is alive, living in North America under an assumed identity with his love.

Aleksei considers my words of caution and then asks, "What will you do if she cannot find the Madonna?"

"She will."

"But if she does not?" he presses.

Aleksei was once a friend, perhaps my only friend. We have seen a lot together and I wish I could trust him, confide in him, but his loyalties are torn. We all do what we must to survive. I do not hold any of his actions against him, but I will show no weakness and no doubt.

"Then we return and in time, the members of the *Bratva* will come to appreciate the life of ease that the new direction of our business interests have brought."

"Complacency is dangerous."

"For them, Aleksei. We will be ever watchful." I strike the stop button on the treadmill forcefully. "Get some sleep. I will observe our quarry for the first watch."

Aleksei nods and like the good soldier he is, hurries off to rest so that he can spell me in eight hours.

Over by the vodka, I arrange the napkins and straws before moving to the bathroom.

I take a quick, cold shower. I do not shut my eyes but rather turn my face into the stinging spray of freezing water. Each time my lids drift closed, I think of Naomi in her own shower, under the water, touching herself and how, if I had more self-control, I could have watched her. But I feared at that moment that she would eat me, the *Volk*. Turning away, I sought control in my solitude.

She is dangerous, I told Aleksei, but it is really I who needs the warning. I find her too intriguing, and therefore she is a danger to me and my mission. Because I am not solely focused on the painting or even my sister, Katya. Instead, I find myself wondering how many colors of wheat and gold there are in her hair. I wonder what pure waters have emptied themselves into her eyes to make them so blue.

My hands ache to cup her breasts and my mouth . . . fuck, my mouth is watering at the idea of sucking her tit into it and working the tip until it's hard and erect.

The fine wool of my trousers is too tight and my cockhead is chafing against my underwear. I have never responded to a woman like this. I did not lie when I told Naomi I did not want to be touched. Ordinarily I am repulsed by human affection, but I find myself turning to her again and again in my thoughts where we are *doing* things, rubbing against each other, kissing each other, *fucking* each other.

I scrub a hand down my face and try to will away those thoughts but they are there, lurking behind my other worries and goals.

Outside in the living area, I find there is no one. The lights are low but her computer is humming. On the screen, I see line after line of meaningless letters and numbers jumbled together. *Un peu*, I answered when she asked if I spoke French. I speak many languages, but computer code is not one of them. I should learn. This gap in my knowledge endangers me.

Pulling out my phone, I order two books, one on basic computer language and one on *The Art of Exploitation*. Many good reviews. On the sofa, I settled down to read about buffer overflows and the areas of weakness in software programming.

"What are you doing?" I hear hours later.

"Reading," I respond without looking up. I fear my response to her. Already I can feel my heart rate accelerating from just the sound of her voice. This reaction I have to her is strange, terrifying and yet . . . enticing.

She is like the sirens of old whose voices were so beautiful, sailors followed them on the ocean only to die of heartbreak and longing. I wonder if the songs followed them into the dark, deep waters and if they did, whether the sailors celebrated their watery deaths. A part of me wishes to rise up and walk to Naomi, take her by the hand into the bathroom or the bedroom, and find out what it is like to be touched by her. If her voice quickens me, rouses my base instinct, what would it be like to have my hands on her warm flesh or her quick, clever fingers tripping over my body?

It is those questions, those wants, that keep me pinned to the sofa, my eyes on the words explaining things like heap, stacks, packets.

"Programming is a language just like any other, yes?" I say instead.

"Yes. That's exactly right. Are you reading a book on software programming?" The sofa cushion beside me dips as she settles her weight next to mine. I resist the urge to slide my arm around the back of the sofa and turn my body toward hers.

"*The Art of Exploitation*," I answer.

"Why did you pick that book?"

"Should I have chosen another?"

I feel her shrug. "It's outdated and rudimentary but I can see how it would be useful as a beginner's tool. Why did you pick it? You haven't answered that."

"It seemed like it was the right one."

"There's no art to hacking. *Art* implies that there is an emotional return from coding. There is not. Computer programming is simply the application of a series of prompts and commands."

Her statement belies her tone, but as I examine her face, she shows only earnestness. This topic of rational arguments designed to produce a specific result interests her like none other. Does she not realize that she has a sensory response to her work? She derives satisfaction and, yes, even pleasure. It is written on every feature of her face, evident in the glow in her eyes, the light smile around her lips and the ease in her shoulders.

I move closer to her because she is irresistible. A landlocked siren calling me to my doom in this palatial suite high above the ground and far away from the water.

"You are moved by it," I say, my words no more than a throaty whisper. Her eyes do not look into mine, but drop down to stare at my lips. She never looks me in the eye, but it does not make her gaze any less intense. Her perusal is as corporeal as a touch and I respond accordingly, leaning toward her, closing the distance between us.

"How?" she asks.

"You derive gratification from a well-written line. It is akin to a songwriter penning the perfect harmony or an artist achieving the right color. Your code is your poetry, your art, and you like it."

Her eyes widen as she absorbs my words.

"*Like* is a relative word."

"Too tame?" I arch an eyebrow.

"Too sentimental." Her eyes are still caressing my lips.

"Then I'd say you love it."

We are but a mouth width away because she has not moved as I slowly advanced. But at the word *love*, her gaze falls to her hands and she mumbles, "I don't love anything."

CHAPTER **SIX**

NAOMI

I am fascinated by this man.

It's because I cannot predict what he will do, I think. Most men I've met are fairly easy to intuit, even for someone like me. If I offer something sexual, I expect it to be gladly accepted. This man watches me, but he will not accept.

This is not the result I expected from my hypothesis, and I am intrigued. What is it that causes him to hold back? Is it me? Am I the unappealing one? Or is there something else? I ponder this. Perhaps I will need a new hypothesis. Perhaps my old one is too vague.

After I shoo him away, he settles back down with his phone. He sits quietly and reads the screen, absorbing the information. His eyes flick back and forth, with interest. Too much interest.

I feel my eyes narrow with suspicion.

He thinks I'm doing this wrong.

He doesn't trust me. He's going to figure out how to do it himself and then go around me. *He's checking up on me.*

This infuriates me. Aspies don't take criticism well, and I take it worse than most. Who is this man that thinks he can read one fucking book and become an expert? I inhale sharply, and then begin to breathe faster as the rage builds. "Are you trying to learn how to hack?" I ask, unable to stop myself.

He looks up from one of his books. His heavy brow creases and he studies me. "I simply wish to understand."

Ah. This sounds like a non-answer to me. I hate non-answers, because I'm supposed to interpret hidden "meanings" or "nuance," and those are simply beyond my comprehension. It's like he's deliberately trying to talk around me.

And this pisses me off even more. I look over at my laptop, running my bogus SQL query. I slam it shut and look over at Vasily with a sneer. "You're the expert, you do it."

All my happy feelings about him earlier have vanished. To think that I drank after this man. I scrub my mouth angrily and I leave the room, heading into the bedroom. If he comes after me, I'm going to fake a seizure. Those always shut down a conversation fast.

But he doesn't come after me. Which is fine. If he's so fucking smart, he can run all the queries he wants.

I've done a hard delete of the information he wanted. It's still retrievable, but a little jiggling of the file, a few find/replaces of important strings, and even he won't be able to find it.

Fuck him. If he wanted a hacker, he should have let me hack. Questioning my skill is the surest way to earn my ire.

Even as I stalk away, the hurt thought rises in my mind: does Vasily think I'm stupid, too? Just like everyone else?

Why does this bother me so much?

I doze in bed for hours, expecting someone to charge into my room and demand that I hack for them. No one comes, and this leaves me in a state of confusion. Didn't Vasily tell my brother he wanted me for my expertise? Was it so he could learn from me, or did he want my skills? I don't know, and I hate feeling uncertain. More than that, I hate this strange, opulent room. It makes me uncomfortable. With nothing to work on, I'm reminded that I'm hungry. I pull out the room service menu, but it's written in Portuguese. I study it, trying to match root words with the bits of Spanish that I know. The only languages I'm really proficient in are computer ones.

A man arrives in my room. It is the other Russian. Not the wolf, but the weasel. His eyes are too close together and his teeth protrude a little in the front, reminding me of an animal. I hold the menu out to him. "I want a salad."

He looks at the door, as if expecting an answer, then back at me. "I am not your servant. You are our guest."

"No cheese. No tomatoes. Croutons are acceptable but only if they're rye. Please make sure the dressing is either balsamic vinaigrette or green goddess. Extra avocado. Steak is acceptable as long as it is burned brown. No blood." I'm hungry just thinking about food. All that green.

His eyes narrow at me. "Is breakfast time."

He seems to be waiting for more from me, so I suggest, "And a root beer."

The weasel throws his hands up in the air and mutters something to himself, snatches the menu out of my hand, and then storms off to the far side of the room.

I watch him, because he seems extra twitchy today. He's been twitchy in the past, but today, he's not making eye contact and seems to constantly touch his pocket. Aspie, perhaps? I wait for him to call in my salad.

Instead, he pulls out a cell phone and begins to talk in a low voice, his gaze darting over at me. He speaks in Russian, but I catch one word in broken, heavily accented English. "Retarded."

And then he looks at me.

Hurt spirals through me. He's talking about me. I've been called names hundreds of times before, but this one stings more than normal. This is Vasily's friend, and if he thinks I'm retarded, does Vasily think that as well?

Is that why he doesn't trust me? Is that why Vasily doesn't want to see me naked anymore? Because now he thinks I am "special" and not in a sexy way?

For some reason, this makes me sad. Even though I didn't act on it, I wanted things to be different between us. I liked it when Vasily looked at me with appreciation. When he looked at my breasts. It was like I was a normal girl, however brief. And I liked being normal in his eyes.

I pull the blankets tightly around my body and put my favorite baseball cap back on my head and feel a little better. The brim hides my eyes, which I prefer. The naked face is so open, and I'm told my gaze is weird because I don't like to look people in the eye when I talk.

The weasel nods into his phone, says something, and then

hangs up. I watch him as he goes to the door, checks it, and then looks back at me. "Come with me."

"Where are we going?" I don't get off the bed. I'm not happy here, but I've learned that *come with me* doesn't always mean I'm heading to a better place.

The weasel comes to my side and grabs me by the arm. He pulls out a knife and holds it to my throat. "You will come with me, and you will be silent."

I blink down at the knife. At first, I think, Russians sure do like knives in faces. Vasily shoved one near my eye earlier so I could hot-wire the car. Except this time, I have not asked for a knife.

I look up at the weasel's face. I can't read emotions, but I can see he's sweating despite the cool air-conditioning of the room. Sweat is a physiological response to fear or anxiety.

This man is afraid. Curious. He's holding a knife to my throat and he's afraid of what will happen. This can only mean that he's not supposed to do this.

Suddenly, my own fear strikes. I suck in a breath. His hand could slip and he could slice my throat open. I would die in minutes, because the human body has approximately only ten pints of blood, and if he hits an artery, I can bleed out long before any paramedic could arrive.

The knife pushes a little harder into my throat. "You understand? Good. Let us go to the lobby downstairs. Quietly now. We do not wish to wake the sleeping *Volk*."

"What is a *Volk*?"

"Quietly," he repeats, and the knife digs in a bit more.

I bite my lip so I don't breathe louder than I should, and nod to show I understand. I'm trembling with fear now. It's hard to frighten me, but when I am afraid, it's near overwhelming. I'm having a hard time thinking—my thoughts are frantic, scurrying things, and my hands are shaking.

The man nods as I stand and discard my blanket, my movements slow and quiet. He gestures toward the bathroom door— opposite of the one that will lead to the living area where I last saw Vasily, and we head in that direction. This man is taller than me and he's able to keep the knife at my throat with ease as we shuffle through the opulent bathroom and through the maze of corridors and adjoining rooms that make up the suite. I watch my feet so I don't trip over something and give this man reason to cut my throat. So much DNA would be everywhere. I picture the crime scene and the splatters I would make on the wall, and then force back hideous thoughts.

Itsy bitsy spider . . . I recite the lyrics to myself to calm down.

We make it to the hall, but the weasel avoids the elevator, heading instead for the fire exit stairs. We go through the door together after he carefully eases it open and nudges me forward. He drags me down the stairwell, barely allowing my feet to touch the stairs. When we reach the bottom, he finds a room and thrusts me into it. Once inside, he blocks the door with his weight and pulls his phone out to check it, the knife no longer at my throat.

I don't run. I simply wait. I'm not stupid and I want to live. It's clear this man is doing something that he thinks will get him in trouble. He's sweating so much that droplets are running down his forehead and I wrinkle my nose, instinctively trying to get away so none of his sweat touches my skin.

He sees me flinch away and automatically locks an arm around my throat again. "*Nyet*," he says, speaking slowly. "No. Bad girl."

I want to roll my eyes. I'm not a dog. Nor am I retarded like he thinks I am. My fear is dropping away to irritation as he begins to text something into his phone with one hand. I slide my gaze over and look at his screen, but it's in Russian—Cyrillic. Shoot.

"We wait for confirmation, and then we go." He breathes on my neck, and his breath smells a bit like alcohol.

"Is Vasily sick?" I ask since he's not here. I wish he were. I like him better than the weasel.

"Vasily will not be coming," the weasel says, and my words make his hands tremble a bit more. Aha. Maybe it is Vasily he is afraid of.

"Did the *Volk* get him? Is that like food poisoning?" I ask, repeating the strange word from earlier. It's one of the sneaky things I do. When someone uses a word I don't understand, I throw it back at them. Usually they will then take time to correct the "retard," and I get my answer. It's annoying but effective.

He mutters something under his breath. "It is not food poisoning. Vasily is *volk*. Wolf."

Oh. Right. *Volk* is the word Vasily used when describing the painting. Madonna and *volk*. I think of his fierce features, the cold eyes, the piercing stare. It fits. Wolves are hunters, and I am certainly feeling like prey at the moment. I begin to wonder if Vasily even knows I'm in this hall. I thought he and the weasel were working together, but maybe they are rivals? I don't know.

All I know is that I don't want to go with this man. I'm frightened of what will happen if I do. I think of Hudson, who kept me in a small, dark room for eighteen months, three days, and sixteen hours, simply because he wanted the Emperor to funnel money out of accounts for him. What will this man do with the Emperor? All Vasily wanted was to learn how to hack better than me.

I wish he were here. I feel charged with nervous energy when around Vasily, but I don't dislike him. Quite the opposite, really. I have a feeling that if I don't leave this room soon, I'm not going to like what happens.

Time to pull out the nuclear method.

I jerk in the weasel's arms. It causes the knife to scratch my throat, but I ignore it. Instead, I snap my head backward and straighten my limbs, making my body as stiff as I can. Then, I roll my eyes back in my head and begin to shake as I pretend to have a seizure.

CHAPTER **SEVEN**

VASILY

I lay silently where Aleksei believes I am unconscious from his drugging. Outside of the room, they are talking but their voices are too low for me to decipher the individual words.

Somehow I knew Aleksei would betray me. I knew it yet it still saddened me because it was a loss, and my life has been full of losses.

The door opens and then closes. I wait three more heartbeats and rise.

A quick look at the main living room and the foyer reveals no one. The suite is empty, eerily silent. I open the door quietly and see the elevator is unmoving. The stairs then.

Aleksei is sadly overconfident in his tactics and does not notice he is being followed. At the door of his new room, I pause to listen while Aleksei explains to Naomi why he is spiriting her away and to whom, but waiting is swept aside when I hear him begin to panic. I push open the door that I've surreptitiously unlocked while Aleksei is trying to reason with Naomi.

Inside the room he is bent over a convulsing Naomi.

"Idiot!" I push him aside. He falls away easily. "She's seizing."

I did not realize she was sick, although perhaps I should have noted the episode in the van when we were escaping from Hudson's compound in Brazil. The noise and the guns sent her into a panic and she rocked on the floor with her ears covered, shouting something repeatedly. But I thought nothing of it at the time, because many people do not respond well to bullets ricocheting around and mad men trying to kill them. Rocking in the corner is a normal response. Our disinterest is the oddity.

"Naomi. Naomi." If I hadn't been watching her closely, I would have missed a slight muscle twitch, an interruption in the rhythm of her convulsions that did not seem organic. I lift her in my arms, ignoring Aleksei's protests.

"Don't move her; she'll bite her tongue off," he cries.

"Then she won't be able to talk back, eh?" I say and again, her face moves strangely in almost a scowl. Aleksei hovers behind me like a frantic mother. But what do I know of seizures? It doesn't serve me if she cannot talk. Laying her on the sofa, I pull my belt off and stick it between her teeth. There is a fair amount of resistance as I insert the leather, and I succeed, but not before she bites my fingers hard. Now I'm certain she is glaring. Her eyes snap open and she looks at me with great clarity until her gaze slides away as it is wont to do, past my cheek and over my shoulder. But in that moment, I see her—bright, sound of mind, and mysterious. Her eyes are a shocking blue, fathoms deep like the Sea of Okhotsk. And with that one look, the siren has captured me. My heart races, fast like a bird. There is a shift inside me. A door has cracked open, or perhaps it is my soul that she has speared.

I shudder visibly, unsure whether I want to free myself or dive deeper into her grasp.

"Do you need a doctor?" It is a bit of a stupid question because if she truly is seizing, how could she answer? A quick, impersonal pat along her legs and waist reveal no needle full of medication. If the seizures were a regular thing, she would carry a kit of medication and needles, but none is to be found. One of the Petrovich boys is allergic to bee stings and carries his antidote with him at all times. She has nothing like this.

It occurs to me that I could call her brother, Daniel, and simply ask but I do not want to contact him until we are out of the country, until he is not a threat to us. I've just gained the Emperor. I will not lose her. Not to the traitor Aleksei, not to a rival *Bratva*, and not to her family. She is mine until I see fit to release her.

"What did you do to her, Aleksei?" I ask, coming to a comfortable conclusion. There is a risk, albeit a small one, that she is truly ill. But I think not.

"N-n-nothing," he stutters. "But what are you doing here?"

I am saddened to see such a warrior subdued and sniveling. I am heartsore over what our brotherhood has turned into. I blame this on Sergei and Elena, who have treated us like dogs and set us against each other. "Aleksei." I turn, but keep a hand on the stomach of Naomi—her center. Under my palm, I can feel her steady breaths. She'll not be able to move without my knowing. "You tried drugging me, but I have this." I hold up a straw.

"The straw? It is an effeminate touch." He sniffs.

"It also detects poisons. I have used it for years. A dip into the liquid and the straw becomes striped. A subtle change only visible to someone who is looking for it. I admit I did not believe the traitor in the *Bratva* would be you. We have been comrades, brothers, for so long. Why wait until now to betray me?"

He is silent for once. He glances longingly at the door, calculating whether he can escape before I take action.

I pull out my gun fitted with its suppressor and point it at him. "Come over here. I do not want to shoot you by the door," I order wearily.

Pfffft goes the gun when I press the trigger. He howls like a dog and falls to the ground, clutching his thigh. "Close the door and come sit down," I say with strained patience. "Or next time the bullet will be between your legs and not in the fleshy part of your thigh."

My sorrow over his betrayal is pushed aside. Later, after I have disposed of him, I will mourn the loss of another valuable member of the *Bratva*, but for now I must focus on eliminating a danger.

Limping and bleeding all over the floor, Aleksei manages to close the door and hobble over to the chair. There are tears in his eyes as he glares at me.

"Why did you shoot me?" He whines like a child. I had forgotten he is so delicate and dislikes even an ounce of pain.

"Because you were looking at the door when you should have been crossing the room to sit down." Naomi's stomach clenches at my words and after a pause, her breathing starts up again. I give her a little pat and rise to shove a chair under the door.

I don't know who will be after us, but we need no interruptions at this moment.

"Do you care to tell me who you sold me out to?" I hold my gun loosely at my side. There is no need to point it at Aleksei now. He now knows I will shoot him if I have the slightest belief he is going to do something to annoy me.

"The Golubevs," he says sullenly.

I'm offended. "Those brainless bastards? I cannot believe you dealt with them. Am I such a kitten that you think the Golubevs could bring me down?" I sit again by Naomi, for I feel better with her even breathing behind me.

"They offer me much money."

"Enough to leave Russia? Because there would be no place in Russia or all of Europe that I would not be able to find you."

"Yes, enough. Besides you would be . . ." He trails off.

"Dead?"

He nods.

Closing my eyes, I give thanks that his stupidity is revealed before it can do me more harm. "You are so dumb, friend. I am taking the *Bratva* in a new and better direction, and you could have been part of that. Instead, you sell out to imbeciles, and for what? To have your blood and brains decorate an empty hotel room in Brazil? You could have lived like a king."

Aleksei erupts at my words, shooting to his feet and then falling back down when the pain strikes him. Moaning, he yells at me. "We were making plenty of money under Sergei. Your plan to stop selling krokodil or females who are no better than sheep, because of some grander vision, is insanity. Sergei may have been a bad leader, but you are worse. Your belief that we are a brotherhood, your investments—" He spits out the last word as if it is a curse. "We are criminals! Retrieving the Emperor so he—or she—can run credit card scams, skim off bank funds, or ruin people is a superb idea, but using her to find a stupid painting? Bah." He spits. "You are no better than the Golubevs."

Naomi has sat up now. She cannot hide her intense interest. I turn to her. "It is an immense insult. The Golubevs are petty thieves who survive only on protection money. Their power is in their might, but one stone from a sling can take down a giant."

She nods solemnly. "I've read that story. First book of Samuel in the Bible. David takes down the Philistine giant. Goliath's height was determined to be between six feet nine inches or nine feet nine inches. Either way, quite tall. You know the statue of David by Michelangelo is uncircumcised."

Like me. I'm beginning to follow her wandering mind. "I've seen it at the Accademia. It is quite impressive."

"I'd like to see it," she says.

"Then you shall."

"Now would be a good time. Well, after Rome," she says, and then her eyelids flutter down so that I cannot even see a glimpse of the ocean. But I catch her meaning. She knows something and she's telling me that we should go to Italy. Energized, I smile. Dangerous, seductive, but perhaps willing to help.

"This is not tea time," Aleksei interrupts with a growl.

"One minute, Naomi." I lift my index finger. "I have to take care of this, and then we shall talk about our travel plans."

She gives me a curt nod of her head, one motion up and down. With deep regret, I turn to Aleksei. "As criminals we were *volk*. Dangerous predators, yes, but we were hunted, too. By the law, by other criminals. It is no way to live. To be truly free Aleksei, we must control the *volk*, not be the *volk*."

"You and your fairy tales. It is from being cosseted by Elena Petrovich," he sneers.

"What Elena Petrovich wanted, Elena Petrovich received. She wanted her children to be educated and we were," I answer.

"You are not her child. You were her toy," he retorts. "You are some whelp from a village that Alexsandr stole so that you could become part of his *ubitsya* army."

"I did not realize you were so jealous of me. I am sorry you are not as pretty as I and that Elena did not take a close interest in you," I mock. But Aleksei and I both know he was the fortunate one to have escaped Elena's attention. I did not ask to be chosen by Elena. I did not ask or want to be noticed. At first, it confused me, then it disgusted me, and finally I realized I could use it to my advantage. Her hungry eyes and her touch will always send me to a dark place, but I also know that despite that she is the devil herself, I cannot cast her aside or have her killed. Not yet.

If returning with this painting will solidify my hold on the Petrovich *Bratva*, then this errand is worthwhile. Once I am in control, I will no longer be a pawn of any man or any woman, and my family will be free.

Aleksei looks away, ashamed. Sullenly, he replies, "The *Bratva* depends on girls and drugs. You are trying to push us into things that we do not understand."

"When you were a child, did you understand adult things? Did you understand that you brushed your teeth to prevent decay? That you must eat good food to balance the candy and sweets? That to please a woman, you must do more than plow her field? That when you split open the guts of another man, you can see his spirit rise to the heavens? As a child you know nothing. You grow and learn. We are children in the business world, but we will conquer it because we know certain things can bring success. What we don't know, we will learn by acquiring the right people." I gesture to Naomi. "We need someone who can infiltrate any technological barrier in the world, and now we have the Emperor."

"She is no emperor. She is but a weak, puny girl. Look at her. She can no more break into Neuer Arbat in Moscow than she could into the Vatican or Vauxhall Cross. She could not even break into a grocery store."

"Hey, I can, too. There is no system that I can't breach. I could break into your stupid Kremlin," Naomi protests indignantly. "I can probably tell you in five minutes everything you own, everything you've done in your life. In fact, I could probably tell you where you shit two nights ago."

I bark out a laugh. "There you go, Aleksei. Why do you doubt her?"

"She doesn't eat real food. She stares at her monitor and mouths things repeatedly like a maniac."

"Don't call me that," she yells at him, getting up onto her feet, her tiny hands forming tiny fists. I want to scoop her in my arms for being adorable but this is not the time.

"She doesn't even look you in the eye, not even now." He points at her face, which turns deep red at his accusation. My laughter dies and I place a soothing hand on her arm.

"But, Aleksei, you look me in the eye and lie to me. It's as if you kissed me on the mouth with the same lips that you used to suck the cock of another man, so her lack of eye contact means nothing."

His eyes widen and he opens his mouth to beg for his life, but we have no time to listen to pleas that will change nothing. Before another word is released from his mouth, I shoot him. He falls to the side and then tumbles to the ground.

Naomi flinches at the gunshot but says nothing. Grabbing my belt from the cushions where she had abandoned it, I slide the leather through the loops with one hand while holding the gun in the other. It is difficult to fasten a belt one-handed and after watching me try again, she comes over and bats my hands away. In two swift moves, she has fixed my belt, but the proximity of her hands near my waist and her soft, sweetly scented body next to mine make my pants fit about one size too tight. I step back before I can alert her to this fact.

"Do you need anything upstairs?" I ask.

"The computer."

"We can buy you a new one." I lean against the door to see if I can hear footsteps or even the elevator.

"I have code running on it," she protests. But I have had enough of her lies and subterfuges. She may have captured me, but I am not helpless.

Catching her chin, I look at her and say softly, "I will not hurt you so long as you do as I ask. Be loyal and you will live. Cross me and you, too, will have a hole between your eyes."

CHAPTER EIGHT

NAOMI

"I do not want a hole between my eyes," I tell him. "You do realize that would kill me? A human cannot survive a hole between the eyes, though there have been some medical cases in which a screwdriver or a nail was embedded behind an eye socket and the subject actually was fine until—"

"It was a threat."

Oh. I blink. This is the first time that Vasily has actually threatened me. I frown to myself and study him, trying to figure him out. He's been polite to me before, and caring. I'm taken aback by this change. Maybe shooting the other man has put him in a bad mood.

He grabs my hand and drags me forward before I can protest that he's touching me. "Come. We go."

Not this again. "Where are we going?"

"We are leaving this place. It is festering with Golubevs." He drags me along behind him down the hall, and we make our way back to the fire exit. He takes off his shoes and instructs that I do the same, and we creep down the stairs quietly.

I think of the laptop we left upstairs. It's bothering me. I should have insisted we take it with us, if nothing else, to wipe the drive and erase my footprint. I'll have to hack into it from afar and clean the slate. I don't like leaving my workstation unattended. It's one of my (many) compulsions and it's really getting to me, to the point that I can't think of anything else.

I'm so distracted by thoughts of the laptop that I'm hardly paying attention when Vasily shoves his shoes into my hands. "Wait here."

I tilt my head and watch him stalk to the door of the stairwell. He's moving like a hunting cat I saw at the zoo once, all predatory muscle and imminent danger. Then, the door flies open and he steps through it, grabbing something. I see a flurry of dark fabric and thrashing limbs, and then I hear a snapping noise.

A man in a suit slumps to the ground at Vasily's feet, neck at an odd angle.

Vasily looks in my direction and gestures quickly, impulsively, for me to follow him.

I do, neatly stepping over the body. "Where are we going?"

"Airport," he says, adjusting his jacket. "To Rome."

I brighten. "To see uncircumcised penises?"

"Among other things." He looks around, and then gives me another gesture. I am to follow him into an alley.

I do so, clutching our shoes. We have not put them on yet, but he doesn't seem like he wants to stop. I really should protest about the germs we could be picking up, but now does not seem to be the time.

We round a corner and run into another man in a suit. I gasp, but before I can react, Vasily grabs the man's head and smashes it into a nearby wall. Just *boom*. The man crumples and Vasily continues stalking down the alley, a predator at work.

Fascinating. I admit I'm impressed.

Two more alleys, and we come to a busy cross street. Vasily grabs the door of a cab and jerks it open. He leans in and snarls something, and two people spill out the other side of the cab, running into the street. Then, he looks back at me and points at the cab.

I get in, and Vasily slides in next to me. "*Aeroporto*," he says and pulls out a fistful of money. "*Rápido*."

The man nods and takes the money.

Vasily relaxes as the cab speeds down the street. He glances behind us once, and then grunts. "They do not follow. Dumb fool Golubevs. They will sit in the lobby and wait for hours, thinking they are so clever."

I hand him his shoes.

"You are quiet. Do not be afraid of me." His voice is soft, soothing, as if trying to calm me.

"I'm not afraid."

He arches an eyebrow as if questioning my words. He almost looks affronted that I'm not scared. Vasily leans in and speaks in a low voice. "No more lies."

"I'm not lying. I'm not afraid." A bit surprised at how fast things are moving, but not afraid. No one wants me dead. What is there to be afraid of?

"You saw me kill two men. This does not frighten you? Most women would be sobbing and weeping in a corner."

I shrug. "I don't know those men. Should I be upset?"

"Are you not upset that human life was taken?"

"They were bad guys."

"*Nyet, moy besstrashnyy devushka*, we are the bad guys."

"Then they were worse guys."

He laughs, the sound humorless despite the smile curving his hard mouth. "You have a simplistic view of things."

"I don't feel emotions the way 'normal' people do." I shrug my shoulders and bend a knee, propping my foot on the seat of the taxi so I can put my shoe back on. "I don't know those men. They mean nothing to me alive or dead."

"I am not sure if this makes you a sociopath or the perfect woman."

I've heard the sociopath comment before, but not the perfect woman part. It throws me for a loop. I blink at him and my fingers reach for my baseball cap, to run along its comforting bill.

It's gone.

I realize a moment too late that it's back at the hotel, next to my laptop.

I burst into tears.

"And now the tears come," Vasily mutters, and he sounds disappointed.

"My hat," I moan, weeping. "I left my hat at the hotel."

He pauses. "You are crying over a hat?"

"It's my hat," I wail, my voice getting louder. Clearly he does not understand its importance. "I need it! I can't function without it! Turn around!"

"We are not going back," he says in a firm voice. "You will have to forget it."

"My hat!"

"Forget it."

"My *hat*." The cab driver is staring at me in the rearview mirror. I don't care. I need that hat. It's been with me since I was a child. It's seen me through so much shit. It's comforting in a world of strangeness, and I need that comfort to ground myself. I'm throwing a tantrum like a child, but I don't care. I need my hat. *I need it.* I decide it's time to pull out the big guns again. I start a full-body tremble. He won't stop? I'll make him stop—

The big Russian grabs my jaw and pulls my face against his. For a man that doesn't like to be touched, he sure is touching me a lot. "Do not even think about it," he whispers against my skin. "I know this for a lie."

I swallow hard and go still. The loss of my hat is sending me into a panic, but I know a threat when I hear one.

"Good," he says softly when I calm. His gaze flicks to my mouth, and for an odd moment, I think he wants to kiss me. But that's . . . weird. "No seizures," he tells me. "We do not have time for such things."

Vasily is the first person other than Daniel that has seen through my seizure game. Even my parents have fallen victim to it. But this man? This predator? I can't bluff him. That disturbs me almost as much as the loss of my hat. I chew on my lip, anxiety welling up as I think of my hat, lost and alone in the hotel room. My fingers twitch and I find that I'm twining them in Vasily's clothing, looking for some sort of anchor. I feel utterly lost. "I need my hat," I say softly, and my voice sounds broken. I feel broken. How can I function without my hat? "Please."

"I will get you a new one." He's still staring at my mouth. His fingers are still on my face, and he's still staring at my mouth. I wish I understood what he was thinking.

"It's not the same if you replace my hat," I tell him slowly, and his gaze follows my words as my lips move. "I need that one.

It's my talisman. It helps me sleep. It helps me think. How will I be able to function without it?"

"You will manage," he says. "You are strong."

I don't feel strong at the moment. I feel very naked and vulnerable without my hat. I feel like crying even more, but I know Vasily won't like my tears. I sniff them back and try to calm down. I flex my fingers and release his clothing. "I'm sorry. I'm touching you and I know you don't like that."

He grunts. I don't know if that's agreement or relief, but he lets go of me.

We're silent on the way to the airport. I don't know what Vasily is thinking about, but I'm thinking about my hat and my laptop. I feel as if I've been stripped of all comforting items, and I don't like it. I don't care that men were chasing us; all I can think about is returning to the hotel to get my hat back. Maybe the computer. Maybe.

I wasn't lying when I told Vasily that I have a hard time functioning without my talismans. I like for everything to be in order. Things have to be in their place and just so in order for my brain to function optimally, and my hat is part of my work process. I sit down, put on my hat, put on headphones—but I don't listen to anything. I like silence, and the headphones just muffle things even more. The mouse must be at exactly a ninety-degree angle from the right-hand side of the keyboard, and the keyboard must have a number pad. I need a chair big enough to sit cross-legged in and I must work uninterrupted.

And I must have all these things in order to work. The fact that I won't fills me with dread.

Even Hudson, who held me for two years and was an awful man, let me have my hat. What next? Is someone going to try and make me eat something red? Yellow? Deprive me of hand sanitizer?

The cab stops and Vasily gestures for me to get out. "Let's go."

I look at him. "I refuse to eat tomatoes or squash, just so you know."

He stares at me for a long time. His lips twitch. "Get out of car."

I get out and head for the staircase leading up to the jet. It's a small one, and I wonder how many people will be on it.

When I get on board, though, I realize there is just me and Vasily. If there is a pilot, he's not coming out to greet us. I stand in the center of the aisle, examining the oversized leather seats.

Vasily moves behind me. "Take seat. We are leaving soon."

"I need to wipe it down first," I tell him. Without my hat, my anxieties are surging to the forefront, and I feel the insane urge to sanitize everything in the plane. "Do you have antibacterial wipes?"

He mutters something in Russian and disappears into the cockpit. I hear him talking to someone, again in Russian. He returns a moment later with a package. I open it, pull out wipes, and begin to clean off a chair for myself. My fingers twitch and want to run across the brim of my hat, but of course it's not there, which just sets me further on edge. Finally, though, I sit down and buckle in.

Vasily hands me a small blue booklet. "Take this."

"What is it?"

"Passport."

I open it up and examine it. There's my face, but that's not my name or my hair. The name on the passport is Karen Brown. The woman in the picture has dark hair, not my pale blond. I look up at Vasily, excited at this change. "Are we going in disguise?"

"*Da.*" He sits down across from me, not bothering to wipe

down his seat. I suppose he doesn't care as much about germs as I do. "Once we get into the air, you can go in the bathroom and fix your hair. I am told there is dye there for you." He says this without emotion, but he looks weary. Tired.

I wonder if he's sad. One of the bad guys he killed today was his friend.

I watch him, but I'm not sure how to handle his emotions. The only thing I'm good at is distraction. "Smith is the most common surname in the United States. The most common female name is Mary."

"Yes, but Mary Smith would look very obvious, would it not?" He stands up and goes to the bar at the front of the plane and pours himself a drink. An alcoholic one. It's clear, like water. I like clear. It's so clean. He sips it, then throws the entire thing back and pours himself another.

"I'm thirsty," I tell him.

He gestures at the bar, indicating that I should pour myself a drink. I unbuckle my seat belt and get up, crossing to him. Instead of getting my own glass, though, I take his from his fingers and turn it. I drink from the exact spot that his mouth pressed to when he drank. There are reasons why I do this, I tell myself. One reason is that it's a bit of rebellion, a way for me to control the things that control me. I am forcing myself to win this silent war. So even though my skin prickles with awareness and my brain screams about his saliva, I try to tune it out, because I have a higher purpose.

In the past, when I drank from the same spot Vasily did, his gaze went to my mouth. My breasts, then my mouth again. It's a distraction for my captor, because distractions are the only weapons I have at the moment, and the need for weapons has to override any sort of phobia.

And I glance up at Vasily to see what he thinks of my distraction.

His focus is on my mouth, and when he takes the glass back, he drains it. "Did you know that vodka destroys all bacteria in the mouth?"

"Does it?" He pours more vodka in the now-empty glass and hands it back to me.

Vasily moves closer to me, so close that I can practically feel his breath. His lips are rather attractive this close up, sculpted and fine. "If I kissed you now, I would have no germs to transfer to you."

"That's very . . . interesting," I say, dazed. "Do you want to kiss me?"

"*Da*, I do."

"We should try it, then," I tell him. "For science."

His fingers go to my chin and he angles my face up, until my body is pressed against his and our lips are mere inches apart. "The boys that kissed you before, Naomi, did they use tongue?"

"Tongue?" I struggle to think. It's hard to concentrate when he's staring at my mouth so intently, when he's so close to me. Touching me. I should be revolted.

I should.

I'm not, though. I'm prickling with awareness and ready to be kissed, I think. "Are you going to use tongue on me?" I ask breathlessly. My nipples are pricking, which is an interesting side effect of this.

"Not yet," he tells me softly. "Perhaps when you ask for it."

When I ask for it? I frown at the thought of this and I open my mouth to protest, when his lips cover mine.

And . . . oh.

I think of germs, immediately. My brain has been trained to automatically go into warning mode at the press of skin against mine. But then I remember the vodka. He tastes of vodka, too. I smell it on his breath and on mine. We're clean . . . and I can relax.

His mouth is curiously firm against mine, his lips pressing against my own. They're soft, light kisses. Gentle. Teasing. It's nothing like I'd expect from an assassin. And I'm fascinated by the dichotomy. I relax against him, leaning into each kiss, following his lips when they press mine apart. His tongue flicks against the open seam of my mouth and I gasp at the flare it sends through my body.

"I . . . I thought you said no tongue," I whisper when he pulls away. His eyes are heavy-lidded, and his thumb skims over my lower lip.

"That was not tongue," he tells me in a husky voice, thick with accent. "That was promise."

And I shiver all over again.

CHAPTER NINE

VASILY

I am trying hard not to stare at her lips, the plush ones that pressed against me, but my gaze is caught, like a spider in a web. The way she moves her lips, the circles she makes when forming letters, the soft flick of her tongue as it flashes in and out of view as she speaks.

I want that softness, that wet, fast tongue on my body, running up my neck and down across my chest, and then lower. *Lower.*

My own throat suddenly feels parched, the alcohol drying up every cell in my body. There's something strange and different about her. My earlier threat has no effect at all nor was she affected by my killing of Aleksei in front of her. What is more disturbing is that I'm attracted to her. Me, Vasily Petrovich, who has emotional attachment to no women but the women in my family!

When I have sex with a woman, it is nothing more than relieving a basic bodily function. No different than pissing or eating. In the past, I've struggled to find women who were comfortable with this arrangement. Women like to be touched, kissed, caressed, and they seek to run their fingers over your body, disturbing your hair, wrapping your cock in their soft, limp hands.

And under each caress is a hidden motivation. They want money or for you to save their brother or father or even lover. No one touches me without desire to achieve a boon.

Is she different? The eyes that don't meet mine are full of secrets, and diving down into their clear blue pools will likely be my death. There has been no one who has wrought an orgasm from me fiercer than my own hand. Yet there is something compelling about Naomi and her inquisitive mind and the eyes that seem to take in everything.

And I want her—badly. I want to rip open her clothes and press my body against hers. I want that soft body to feel every plane of my hard one. I want to shove inside her and feel the tight clutch of her pussy around my aching cock. So much that I want and that I cannot have.

Swallowing back my desire, I try to redirect the conversation away from the unhealthy lust I feel for her. "Where in Rome will we need to go to find our contact?"

Her fingers tighten slightly on the glass as she takes a healthy swallow of the vodka before answering, but it is no answer at all. "I need a new cap."

Her distress is palpable. "We will get one in Rome," I promise.

"I want my cap, not a new one."

"Why not a brand-new cap? Your other was worn and old. Perhaps it is not the cap you seek, but a desire to return to Rio." The desire for her old tattered headgear is likely a ruse.

"Because a new cap won't be the same." The space between her brows wrinkles with her frown, and I clench my fingers to keep from comforting her.

Why she wishes to return to Brazil gives rise to a new set of questions. In my short time with Naomi, I've learned that pointed and direct questions result in the best response. "Other than your cap, do you have reason to return to Rio?" I watch her body for signs that she is obfuscating, but she appears only earnest now.

"Yes, I'd like to wipe the computer. I can do it remotely but it's easier when I'm sitting in front of the actual box."

"Your computer . . . and hat . . . are most likely in the hands of the Golubevs."

She scowls. "Then we should go after them. Will they return to Russia?"

"Do you not know their itinerary?"

"Why would I? I'm not a Golubev! I want my hat." The glower on her face deepens, and her whole countenance darkens as if she is wearing a thundercloud as a mask. And the tense and unhappy expression increases my yearning inside to reach over and soothe her brow. To rub my finger along the lines of her forehead and down the petal-soft skin of her cheek until I can trace the hard, jutting bones of her jaw and the soft, plush skin of her lips.

Abruptly, I change the subject. "Why did you not leave Hudson? For eighteen months you have worked for him, running an extraordinarily profitable illegal enterprise. With your skill, you should have been able to send coded messages to someone."

"Yeah, right. To another computer geek? How's she supposed to mount an offensive to fly down to a foreign country and extricate me from a compound guarded by freaks with machine guns? And if I tried and failed? Hudson showed me pictures of what he'd do to my family. Logically it made sense to accede to his demands. Besides, I was shortchanging the pay of his guards. I thought eventually one of them would kill him in anger. Did I do wrong?" The glance she shot me is quick but illuminating. She feels some kind of remorse for her actions, perhaps in part because she didn't do more to free herself.

"Was it peaceful there, Naomi?" I ask gently.

She stares inside her glass for a long time, the occasional swirl of clear liquid the only sign she's still conscious. "Very," she finally says.

"I can give you that . . . and more."

"How?"

"You would like Russia, Naomi. In the winter at the *dacha*, the snow falls and a blanket of white covers everything." I piece together all of the things I know she likes from what little time we've spent together. "It is very orderly, although small. Only seven or eight rooms. I could add on to it if you like. There's a wood-burning fireplace that heats every room and only one way in or out. No surprises."

"Why would you offer this?" she asks, her voice small, but pleasure and curiosity coloring every word.

"It is yours for as long as you want it if you do but one thing for me."

"The Madonna?" she asks.

"Yes, that's right," I reply, because that is the only answer that makes sense now. The feelings of need and wanting possession are too strange for me to comprehend. I push them back but it will be only a matter of time before they overwhelm me . . . and her.

"And if I find it for you, you will take me to this place in Russia?"

"After the Madonna is taken to my home, then you will have

free run of my *dacha*. It is yours to do with as you will. Funds will be at your disposal to renovate and add on what you need."

She could build a mansion out there to rival the tsars of the old country if she would agree to stay. The desire to ensconce her in my private world is so strong that it is a taste on my tongue— both bitter and sweet.

She appears to consider the offer.

"Do I get to go when I tell you where the Madonna is or after you retrieve it?" she cagily asks.

"After it is returned to the Petrovich vaults, then you may go." Her cleverness and quick mindedness impress me. She would make a formidable enemy but a powerful ally. I want her, more than I should, and I will do whatever I can to make it so she aligns herself with me. Right now the carrot is a more viable option than the stick. Threats have little power over her. I cannot tell if it is because she has no fear because she does not care, or if it is because she cannot feel fear.

"All right. I want a baseball cap, too."

"Of course." I hide my satisfaction by pulling out my phone and pretending to review all the messages I have missed in the last few hours. "Why don't you go and color your hair, Miss Karen," I prod her. "You should be ready when we land in Madrid for refueling and then get some sleep. Tomorrow will be a long day." I hope.

"Will you do it?" she asks.

Placing my phone on the table, I peer at her. What trick is she playing now? "I thought you did not like to be touched."

"I don't but I also don't like the color brown unless it's food related, because brown things are normally cooked long enough to destroy any bacteria. I might be sick if I see it on my hands, though." She shudders, holding her hands out as if they are already contaminated.

"I am your humble servant," I say, rising and giving her a short bow. She pushes to her feet. Her oddities are notable. I wonder if she was born idiosyncratic or made this way by some trauma. But we all have our flaws, and mine are so great it would be hypocritical to be critical because she requires things to be done in a certain way or has an attachment to an old, worn cap. There is a medical diagnosis for some and perhaps she is one of those. I am no doctor. What I do know is that parts of me that I believed were buried are throbbing with life.

The jet's bathroom is small despite its luxurious appointments, and it is not made for two people. We are pressed close and when the door falls shut, it is stifling. There is no room for us to maneuver, and my larger frame is dwarfing her. Even if she feels no conscious fear, her hindbrain is encouraging her to shrink away, make herself a smaller target. And my instincts are getting excited by this. My blood is pumping at her subservient stance, and the enclosed space is magnifying every sense. The warm smell of her body wraps around me. She shifts and her hip brushes my thigh, which causes every muscle to tense in anticipation. This will not do.

"One moment, Naomi," I say. Using the bag, I prop open the door to the bathroom, giving us slightly more air. In my absence, Naomi has opened the box and is reading the instructions.

There is a paintbrush, a plastic bowl, and gloves.

"We need a towel," Naomi announces. In a compartment outside the bathroom, I find towels and washrags.

"Put this around your neck," I order. Outside the bathroom I peruse the instructions and then toss them aside. Color and wash.

Easy enough. I pour the ingredients together and the color in the bowl becomes a dark, almost black mix. I hear gagging from inside.

"That's so gross. It's going to feel like mud. I'm not putting it on."

"Then you'll sit in an enclosed space for a very long time as customs officials in Madrid question you repeatedly about your activities. You would like that more, perhaps?" I raise an eyebrow in inquiry.

With pursed lips she shakes her head.

"Then sit on commode and we will begin."

She places a towel on the seat and settles gingerly on the terry cloth. With a deep breath, I enter the room . . . and immediately realize how I've worsened the situation. With Naomi seated, her mouth—her sweet breath—is positioned directly at groin level. My animal response cannot be contained. My cock swells and with each breath grows harder and larger.

"You're supposed to use the gloves." She points to the counter. For a minute I think she's referring to protection. That she wants me to unzip my pants and unwind my cramped organ so that it can be soothed by her tongue and engulfed in her wet mouth. It takes a moment before I register the small opaque rubber coverings are for my hands. Or rather for someone's hands.

"Those are much too small to fit," I say, and then wince at the unintended sexual innuendo. She does not respond to it.

"I suppose they are made for women. There are special products made for men, I believe, which is completely unnecessary. Studies have shown that male and female grooming products are made with essentially the same set of ingredients with scent being the main differential. Men experience baldness at a higher rate because of enzymes in the male body that convert testosterone into dihydrotestosterone. Women have less testosterone so they don't produce as much dihydrotestosterone."

She glances up at me with an expectant look.

"Very interesting." I give her a wry smile. Her comments have allowed me to gain some small measure of control over my unruly body. At least I am not in danger of stabbing her eye out with an unwanted erection. "Shall I?" I point to the bowl and with a nod, I proceed.

She continues to talk about male-pattern baldness, the words becoming a hum of background noise, blending in with the jet.

CHAPTER **TEN**

NAOMI

I whimper when the first of the chemicals touches my head. The overwhelming smell of it, plus the dark color, makes me uneasy. I am reminded of tar, of mud, of all the dirty things I don't like, and it's hard for me to sit still and let him work.

"Shhh," he soothes, and his fingers begin to rub at my scalp. He's still not wearing the gloves, and this feels a little shocking to me. A little dangerous. He's doing it wrong, and he doesn't care what happens. He's going to get all filthy, and he doesn't mind at all?

I wish I were like that. Sometimes, I feel trapped by all the rules my brain has set for me. I'm trying to rebel, to take control, but just pressing my mouth to the same spot on his glass has exhausted my willpower. If I press my lips together, I imagine I still taste him, and I'm not sure I like this. I don't dislike it, but I'm not sure I like it, either. It feels a bit like ownership. I am now owned by Vasily, who wears no gloves and touches filthy hair dye so I don't have to.

His boldness encourages me. This is a man who has said he does not like to be touched, but he's touching me, and he's not even grossed out by it.

I'm starting to understand how he feels. I don't like germs, but . . . I'm fascinated by the thought of being contaminated by Vasily's germs. It's an odd thought to have, but I can't help but press my fingers in the same spots that he has put his. On my temples. Against my hip. Now, his fingers are in my hair, mixing in filth, so I won't touch that, but the temptation is there.

Earlier, I put my mouth on the spot where he drank. I suppose I'm testing myself with these small rebellions. I'm seeing if my mind can handle it. The kiss surprised me. It didn't make me sick. I wasn't even revolted. And now that I've tasted Vasily, I've shared his germs. His mouth is safe, in theory, because it's something I've now been exposed to. Maybe if I'm covered in Vasily's germs, I won't get sick when he touches me, because we'll have communal germs. We'll have been thoroughly exposed to each other's bacteria.

Maybe he needs to kiss me all over.

I rather like that idea—building up an immunity to one person's microorganisms by constant contact.

I wonder if this is what he thinks when he runs his fingers through my hair. He's very quiet, but I feel his hands on my scalp. They rub and rub, and I close my eyes, trying to remain still and remember that he's pushing chemical filth onto my head.

But for some reason, it's bothering me less the more his fingers touch my scalp. The hair dye scent is filling my nostrils now, the chemicals making my eyes water with their proximity, but the rest of my body feels curiously languid. At peace. It's odd.

It's . . . nice.

"Let me know if you're going to vomit," I tell Vasily. I'm seated next to the small sink in the lavatory, and I don't want any splash back.

"Vomit?"

"Yes. Vomit. Expel one's stomach contents forcefully. Purge. Expel. Regurgitate. Puke. Hurl. Throw up—"

"I know what you speak of. Why would I vomit?" He sounds confused.

Now I'm the one that's confused. I frown as he squirts the last of the chemicals in my hair. Both of his hands go to my scalp and he begins to rub again, working the last of the horrible tarlike chemicals in. My eyes almost roll back with the pleasure of his touch—*strange, strange, strange, this isn't like you, Naomi*—but I force myself back to the present. "You have told me repeatedly that you do not like to be touched, yet you are touching me without gloves. As I said, let me know if you're going to vomit. I don't want to be hit by it."

"*Da*." The word is clipped, dissonant. "I will not vomit."

"Then you lied? After all those warnings to me about not lying to you, you're lying to me?"

"Lied?"

"About not being touched," I say as his fingers scrub at my scalp. "Clearly it does not bother you as you stated."

"You state you do not like germs but you drink after me."

He noticed that, did he? "There is scientific reasoning behind putting my lips where yours have been."

"Is there?" He sounds amused, and I resist the urge to smile back at him.

"Lots of science," I agree.

There is a long pause. Then, Vasily announces to me, "I don't like to be touched. You are correct about that."

More lies. Either that, or he's not as familiar with his boundaries as he thinks. I reach out and poke a finger at his arm.

"What did I just say to you?" he snarls, irritated. His fingers stop massaging my hair.

"I wanted to see your reaction to stimulus. No touching at all?"

"None," he grits, and his voice is so black with sudden anger it's practically burning a hole in my head.

Now it feels as if we're both ignoring the fact that he has his hands in my hair. "Have you tested this theory?"

"What?"

"How can you make a blanket statement such as 'I do not like all touches' if you haven't tried all touches yet? I don't like to be touched either, but I like to quantify it," I try to explain to him slowly. Perhaps the inhaled chemicals are getting to his brain, because he is looking at me as if I'm the crazy one. He's the one making broad, ridiculous statements. "Skin contact is unappealing in most situations due to germs and natural skin secretions. Fabric between skin is acceptable, but strangers are never acceptable. You have to start with a control point. What is your control point?"

He stares down me, eyes narrowed like he wants to twist my head off. His hands leave my hair and he pushes me aside, cleaning his hands under the faucet. "We are done with this ignorant conversation."

But I'm not done. I lean over and poke his thigh. He stops what he's doing and turns to stare at me incredulously. His very demeanor says *what did you just do?* All the while, brown chemicals and foam trickle into the sink, clean water rushing over his hands.

He looks pissy but not sick. I gesture toward him as if to say *see?* "You did not snap at me that time. If this was a scientific experiment in regards to touching, I would have to conclude that you dislike touches above the waist, but below the waist is perfectly acceptable."

"I will snap your finger off if you poke me again."

I give him an exasperated look. Does he not know how to run a scientific experiment? "That reaction doesn't count. You're responding to the stimulus of my conclusion, not the actual touch. My theory stands."

The growl in his throat is one of annoyance.

"Shall I touch you below the belt so we can test additional stimuli?" I'm still seated on the toilet, and his hips are mere inches from my face. I examine his belt buckle, the cut of his trousers, and the way his penis fills them out. Judging from the jut of his crotch, he has a very large one. I try to extrapolate the full length of it from the visual I have, but I'm starting to become flustered myself.

"Do it," he says, and his voice is hoarse. It's so quiet I almost don't hear it over the rush of the water in the sink.

Vasily wants to test my theory. He . . . he wants me to touch him near his penis?

I'm encouraged—and oddly aroused by this. I'd like to study my own reaction to the Vasily-stimuli. Am I wet between my legs? Is my clitoris throbbing and sensitive? But I'm more interested in Vasily's reactions at the moment. My hands go to his thighs and I slowly place them there, palms flat against the fabric.

He doesn't move. He's utterly still, perhaps waiting for me to do more.

It's fascinating to touch this big man. This is a safe touch, the fabric under my hands a soft weave that allows me to feel the heat of

Vasily's skin through the material, and the hard muscles of his legs. I run my hands up and down his thighs slowly, but I really want to put them on his penis and see how he reacts to that stimulus. It looks really large at the moment. I find it intensely interesting.

"Are you well?" I ask him, not looking up. I can feel his gaze boring into the top of my messy, chemical-covered head, and I'm not sure I want eye contact right now. Of all things, eye contact is the most difficult for me. It feels too intimate, even more intimate than cupping this stranger's groin would be. "Do you feel the need to vomit yet?"

"*Nyet*," he says harshly. But his breathing has increased in its rapidity. A moment later, he shuts the water off and it's quiet in the tiny bathroom.

He's still waiting for me to do more. A little thrill rolls through my body, and I feel my own pulse responding to the stimulus.

"Can I keep touching?" I ask, and my fingers curl against his legs a little, scratching at his skin through the fabric like I would a skittish cat. It's the same soothing motion he used to massage my scalp minutes ago, and I wonder if it feels as good to him as it did to me. "Or are you overstimulated?"

"Keep. Going." His voice is a thickly accented hiss.

My gaze turns back to his penis and it seems larger in his pants, the entire area tented now. He's aroused all right. I feel smug that my theory has been proven; Vasily does like touches below the waist. But my smugness falls away a moment later when I feel an answering pulse of arousal between my own thighs. I don't need to keep touching him to prove my point . . .

But I do anyhow.

I slide my hands upward, to the tops of his thighs. My thumbs graze along his inseam, and then I boldly press upward, until my fingers and thumbs are framing that area of such intense interest. When I push against the fabric, his erection juts out against it, more bold and prominent than I've ever seen. I'm tantalized by the sight of it, and instead of my careful, flat-pressed hands I've been using up to this point, I want to explore him.

I lift one hand and gently touch my fingertips to the farthest tip of his fabric-covered erection. It feels hard, urgent, as if it desperately wants to escape the confining trousers. I skim my fingertips along his length, gauging it with his hand and wondering at the feel of him. I rather like this, this safe touching and knowing that I'm driving him crazy. It's nothing like my last sexual experience, which was all sweaty skin and fluids. "I wonder if people have sex fully clothed?" I muse. I might be interested in that.

Vasily bites out some Russian word above my head. It sounds like an epithet, and not a happy one.

Immediately, I feel like I've made a mistake. Vasily is staring down at me, and the look on his face is so intense and so personal that I can't handle it. I feel as if I'm being stripped naked and penetrated by his gaze. I blink rapidly and then look away. My hands fall to my lap.

The moment is broken. I don't know that I want it back. I just want Vasily to stop looking at me while I feel so vulnerable. I don't know what to do when he looks at me like that.

The entire world seems to hang in that moment. Then, Vasily reaches over my gross, chemical-covered head and jerks a few paper towels into his hands. "I will return when it is time to rinse," he says thickly, and storms out of the tiny bathroom.

CHAPTER ELEVEN

VASILY

She is a temptress.

I pace in the tiny cabin because I cannot sit, not even for a moment. The blood in my body is running hot, driving me toward the lavatory, but my head tells me only danger lies in that direction. I wish I could plunge my head into a bath of icy water. Or better yet, my hard, aching cock.

I press the heel of my hand against my groin but the discomfort is not alleviated. My own body mocks me, for it will not be appeased by my hand. Instead the pain will linger, like a wound that never heals properly.

I try to distract myself. I pop open my laptop and reserve rooms at three different hotels. I'm not certain where our contact is or what will be our best options. I cannot concentrate well for all my blood is in my groin. My cock pulses painfully with every heartbeat.

"Vasily?" she calls, her voice uncertain.

"Yes, what is it?" I check my watch. Few minutes have passed, and she cannot be ready for me to rinse out the dye. Surely I have more time to gather my composure.

"Are you angry with me? Did my touching bother you?"

"*Nyet*, you are . . ." I search for the right word in my vocabulary to describe her. Dangerous? Yes, but not maliciously so, I do not think. The touch of her hands on my thighs, the tentative and curious caress over my cock all speak of a woman who has only little experience.

She seeks something from me but does not know how to ask, but I know that she is not the woman I should take for a quick fuck in the washroom. I draw a deep breath and then another. And then still another until the pressure below eases. I am not a man who is so enslaved by my desires. I can and will resist the temptation.

"No, Naomi. Your touch was . . . fine," I finish at last. If I tell her the truth, that her touch made me lose my mind, it is too strong of a weapon to allow her to possess. But no matter how many times I tell my body that it does not desire her, my arousal refuses to abate. She does not respond and the air grows heavy with my regret.

Her presence draws me inexorably back. The plush carpet of the plane cushions my feet and muffles my approach. It is the only excuse I can provide for the scene that greets me. Naomi's head is tilted back against the wall, uncaring that the dark dye is leaving streaks of brown against the cream interior. Her delicate neck is exposed, and the tendons of her throat and bones of her clavicle are thrown into high relief.

Her eyes are tightly shut and her hands . . . oh Mary's Christ, her hands are tucked beneath her trousers. The expression on her face is one of frustration as her arm pumps rapidly toward a release she cannot find.

I collapse on my knees and brace my hands—one against the wall to my right and the other on the sink. The force of my arms should buckle the walls if I do not calm myself. All the warnings I have given myself flee. In the face of this erotic vision, I have fallen helplessly into her web. *Take me*, I silently plead. *I am yours.*

"Naomi," I say hoarsely. "Are you in need?"

Her eyes pop open, and to my dismay, her movements still. For a brief moment her eyes hit mine, full of want.

"You can't touch me," she cries. "It won't work."

"Is this an experiment that you've run?" I ask gently.

She nods solemnly. "I tried it once. It was horrible. There was a condom for his penis but not for our entire bodies. I barely made it through."

I suppress a shudder. My own early experiences with the opposite sex were a mass of confusion, self-loathing, and unwanted lust. I learned to fear sex, then hate it. Later in life, when I was in control, I found satisfaction in unsavory ways. I required pain and near disinterest from my partner.

I do not like that Naomi has this feeling toward sex. For her, it should be wonderful as the books say that it can be—as I've longed for it to be but have accepted that it cannot. She has an attraction toward me and I can help her, if I could bring her pleasure it would be one good thing I've done in my meager life.

"Is it infection you fear? Or do you view it as unclean?"

"I have a slight case of mysophobia," she admits.

"I do not know the meaning of that word."

"It's being afraid of germs. I'm not paralyzed by germs like a true mysophobic. I just don't like touching people and people touching me, and part of it has to do with not wanting other people spreading their germs on me or sucking down their awful cologne or smelling the onions on their breath from the fast-food burger they just ate. And most touches are light. Like a hand passing over the tips of your hair, almost like a bug."

I consider her words. She is not saying that she does not like to be touched but rather she does not like certain touches. I probe again to gain a deeper understanding. "But it is not a religious thing. Your mother—or someone close to you—hasn't taught you that your body is unclean?"

"No. My body is fine. I'm immune to my own germs." She rubs herself slightly, slowly as if testing the sensation, and my eyes are pulled like magnets to her movements. I clench my fingers into tight fists to prevent myself from replacing her hands with mine. "But sometimes . . . it's that I can't always bring myself to orgasm with just my fingers. I need more pressure and rotation. A velocity faster than I can move my fingers."

She pulls her fingers out with a sigh as if giving up. No, this will not be borne.

"You would perhaps like a firmer, faster touch than one you can generate yourself," I suggest.

"Yes and I don't need for it to be penetrative. Just on my clitoris." She taps her button through the top of her pants and I shudder with surprised need.

"Would you allow me to assist you?"

"How?" she asks, part in suspicion yet also intrigued.

It is hard to speak. Every organ in my body from my tongue to my cock is swelling in excitement. From my position, I can smell her arousal. Breathing through my mouth instead of my nose is of no help. It's almost as if I can taste her now. I lean forward.

"I will rinse your hair and then wash my hands for five minutes. It is the amount of time a surgeon spends cleaning. You can time me. After, I will touch you with just my fingers in whatever way you tell me is pleasing. You shall direct me as if I am merely an implement of your gratification." I hold my breath with hope as she considers my proposal.

"Like I touched you? Over your clothes?"

"Over or under. Whatever you desire. But I would guess that the exterior of your clothes has more offensive toxins than your delicate and clean skin." It is an educated guess that this line of reasoning will work.

She licks her lips. "Will we do it in here?"

"No, there are two seats that can be made into a bed. You will be more comfortable and it will be easier for you to control what touches you."

She nods in agreement. "Let's do it, then. I'll rinse my hair. If I close my eyes, I won't see the muddy water. You can make the bed."

"I am your servant, Naomi," I say, lowering my head so she does not see my expression of triumph. Rising to my feet, I hurry to pull out the bed. I inexpertly lay a sheet across the cushions and then toss the other blankets aside. While the water runs, I wonder if I should disrobe. I decide to remove my shoes and socks and belt, but leave the shirt and pants on. I will rely on Naomi to lead me.

When she exits the bathroom, her hair is wrapped in a towel and for once she looks unsure.

"Come," I say, passing her. "Watch me while I wash."

I use nearly the whole bottle of soap, lathering each digit and the valley between each finger up to the elbow. For good measure, I wash my face as well, scrubbing every surface roughly. I can feel her intense gaze of me the whole time.

Sopping wet when I am finished, I turn to her, not bothering to dry myself. "Shall I use a towel or air-dry?"

"Towel is acceptable," she says. While I'm drying off, she adds, "I know you washed your face but you can't wash your tongue. I've read that some men, um, go down, on women. But we just agreed to the touching."

"You are not afraid of my mouth germs," I reply, unbuttoning my sodden shirt. "You already tasted me, remember?" I refer to the glasses of vodka she has drunk. "Perhaps you are becoming inoculated," I whisper as I lead her over to the bed. "Shall we begin?"

Naomi climbs onto the bed, but casts a furtive, worried eye toward the cockpit door. "Will the pilot come out?"

"No, not unless I ask him to."

I wait for her invitation but she fiddles with the collar of her shirt. Anxious and diffident, her vulnerability tugs at some dark place inside of me. I want to protect her from all slights, hide her from insensitive and callow individuals who would categorize her as . . . defective because of her differences. These urges are not wholly unfamiliar to me. I am fierce in my devotion to my sister, my true family, but Naomi touches me in a separate way—one born out of lust and want more than brotherly concern.

"What's our current altitude?" she suddenly asks.

"I do not know but I can ask. Why?"

"I was wondering whether I will be a member of the Mile-High Club after this."

I swallow a chuckle. As solemn faced as possible, I say, "No, I'm sorry, Naomi. You can only be a member of the club if you engage in fucking."

Somehow, for the first time, she understands that this is a joke and she gives me a shy smile in return. "If you say so, Vasily."

My name sounds like music coming off of her tongue. "I shall do whatever it is you like, Naomi. I only ask that you say my name again."

"Vasily," she says immediately. Her face is devoid of emotion again, so I'm unsure whether now she is the one teasing me.

"Later. I will tell you later when I want you to say it." I smile now and why not? Rather than pacing the confining spaces of this luxurious cage or trying to sleep, I will be spending the next few hours between this woman's soft thighs bathing her in orgasms. Plural.

Taking two pillows, I motion to her to raise her ass, and slide them beneath her. She looks curiously at me.

"These are to make it easier for me to touch you in only the places you desire. Now shall I remove your pants or will you?"

She hesitates only for a second and then lies back, arms stretched above her head. Her hips are canted upward in a provocative position. Her sprawl is nothing short of an invitation. I do not wait for words; this is enough. With shaking hands, I unzip her pants, revealing her plain white panties that are as erotic as any concoction of lace and satin. Although I will want to adorn her in those someday. I want to see red silk contrasted against her smooth skin or black lace tangled with her blond curls.

My toes curl in anticipation as more of her delectable flesh is revealed. There is a slight dampness I can see on the cotton, likely from when she touched herself. "I like cotton," she says and again there is an air of defensiveness that she ordinarily doesn't reveal.

"You are a beautiful woman, Naomi."

"You've probably seen sexier underwear."

"No," I answer, unable to wrench my eyes from her core. I pull her pants completely off so that her lower half is bared to my hungry gaze. Already I'm imagining what she looks like beneath the white fabric. Will she be wild and untamed or trimmed into a thin patch? Will her lips be pink or brown? How many strokes will it take until the wetness from her pussy coats the inside of her thighs? "No," I say in a stronger tone, "I have not seen sexier. Now tell me, Naomi. Where shall I touch you first?"

CHAPTER **TWELVE**

NAOMI

I hesitate to answer. I'm a mixture of worried and aroused. Worried that he's somehow missed a spot on his hands, and aroused as I realize that he cleaned his face precisely because he wants to put it between my legs and lick me there.

I've never had that happen before. I've never even entertained the thought. It seems a little too wicked even for my own fantasies, and I'm cringing at the thought of Vasily sticking his nice, clean face there and finding that I'm all wet between my legs. He doesn't like touching, like me. What if he's repulsed by bodily fluids, like I am?

"You look . . . unhappy. Shall I wash again?"

I lick my lips, thinking. "Maybe for a minute more." I'm stalling. As he obediently puts his hands back under the running tap, I wonder at him. He's been watching me far closer than I had assumed. He's already figured out several of my peculiarities—my faked seizures, my purpose for putting my mouth where his was. No one's usually interested in Naomi Hays enough to decipher why I do the things I do, but this man watches me like a hawk, and figures me out.

I'm not sure if I like being figured out. It makes me vulnerable in ways that him finding me masturbating did not.

At last he turns, demonstrates his hands, and then wipes them off on a paper towel.

"I'm acutely disturbed at the moment," I blurt out, sitting up on the bench. "I think I shall return to the bathroom so I can finish myself."

"*Nyet*," he says, and there is a hint of amusement in his voice. "You agreed to let me help you. Think of what I can do for you, Naomi." Now his voice is soothing, delicious, liquid like honey. "Think of how my fingers and my mouth can move and bring you to pleasure. Think of how I can suck on your little clitoris until you can no longer stand it . . . and then I will suck even longer."

I shudder at the visual for its disturbing arousal. The truth is, I want to experience what he's offering, but I'm afraid to. I'm afraid I won't like it, and then I'll feel even more of an outsider, more *weird* than ever before.

And what if I disappoint Vasily? Will he think it's because of the way my brain functions? I don't want him to think of me as "less" in any way, and I'm worried I won't be able to experience the pleasure he wants to give me. All of this makes my anxiety ratchet up until I'm practically trembling as he gestures for me to sit back down on the seats.

"So," he says, sitting across from my pallet. "Tell me what

you wish for me to do." He sets his hands on his knees, palms up, as if preserving them for touching me.

For some reason, his businesslike posture makes me feel a bit better. This is another scientific experiment, I tell myself. Right now we are setting up the hypothesis. "I believe," I murmur, thinking, and wet my dry lips with my tongue. "I believe that I will have difficulty coming even if you assist me."

"I do not believe this," he states, still all business. "Will you allow me to touch you freely?"

I nod. That's really the only way our scientific experiment will work. "I shouldn't influence you."

"Shouldn't you?" One eyebrow raises.

Oh. I realize he's right. If I'm to have a control point for this experiment, I need to keep all other variables constant. That means he needs to touch me in the ways I instruct him, otherwise there is no way to determine if it's Vasily that will give me pleasure—or lack thereof—or his procedures. I nod. "Very well." I sit again and spread my legs wide.

"Will you remove your panties?"

I consider this. In the past, I've touched myself through my panties and through direct skin contact. Direct skin contact works more frequently, so I say, "Panties off."

"Shall I remove them?"

I appreciate that he's allowing me control of the situation. I feel more at ease knowing that we're both following scientific principle. "If you're doing the touching this time, you should remove them," I instruct him. I put my legs together obediently and wait.

His hands, so clean they are slightly cool from the water

temperature, brush against my hips. I shiver involuntarily, and his gaze flicks up to my face. "Would you like a safe word?"

"A safe word?"

"A word you say that will tell me you wish to go no further?"

I frown. "Won't you stop if I say 'no'?"

"Some women say no when they mean yes."

Some women are stupid, then, I think, but don't say this aloud. "All right. A safe word."

"Pick something that would not come up in normal conversation."

I think for a minute. "Dyspepsia."

His brows furrow with confusion. "Dyspepsia? *Chto eto znachit*?"

Despite not knowing Russian, I understand what he is asking. "It's the scientific term for indigestion, however, if I was having a conversation, I would say 'indigestion,' so 'dyspepsia' would not come up in a normal situation. It's a good word to use."

He looks at me, and then throws his head back and roars with laughter.

I'm feeling a bit defensive at his laughing. I don't understand it. "What's so funny?"

"You will never be predictable, will you, Naomi?"

"I'm quite predictable," I tell him, pushing my panties off since he's busy *laughing* at me. "I like to eat the same things and sleep in the same position. I count stairs when I go up them. I eat my food in a clockwise manner and I don't like odd numbers of things. You'll find that I'm quite predictable in many ways."

"Quite," he says, but he's still smiling even as he takes my panties from me before I can shimmy them off my legs.

His fingers graze against my calves and I feel another shiver moving through me. I don't like to be touched, but his casual caresses aren't causing revulsion in me. I feel shuddery and weak, but it's not . . . bad. This calls for further investigation. I nudge one of my feet against his hand.

"Do that again."

"Did you enjoy it?"

"I'm not sure."

His fingers brush over my calves again, caressing them. Again, I feel fluttery and strange. I'm not sure if I want to kick him away. Not yet. I watch his hands as they move over my legs, like I imagine a sculptor would on marble. Caressing. Possessive. Enticing.

He has big hands. I watch them as they glide over my skin, noting the differences in our skin tone. He is more golden; I am pale and chalky because I've spent the last two years in hiding. His fingers are bigger than mine, and callused, his nails cut blunt.

"Is this touch pleasing to you?" he asks me. It's clear I should be giving him feedback.

But I don't know what to tell him. "I find it oddly disturbing," I say at last. "Unsettling."

"But pleasant? Sex is not a relaxing thing. It is driving your body, heart, and mind to the brink so you may enjoy the crash."

It definitely feels as if I'm heading toward something. But I'm silent and he stops, his hands resting on my legs.

I frown at him and wiggle a little. "Don't you want to go higher?"

His eyes seem very blue when he looks up at me, and he's smiling. I think that means he is happy. Or pleased. Or trying to seem so for my sake. "*Da*, I want to go higher. But is it what you want?"

"I need more stimuli for this hypothesis," I tell him, and open my legs again. "I feel we should progress more quickly to a centralized area. It will take me a very long time to come if all you do is touch my legs."

His shoulders shake for a moment and his head ducks. I frown, wondering at his quaking, and then a small, muffled snort escapes him. "Are you laughing at me?" This is extremely distressing. I feel stupid all of a sudden, and I close my legs shut so hard that my knees bang together.

"I do not laugh at you," he burbles, clearly trying to hide the fact that he *is* laughing. "Simply at the idea of me petting your legs for hours and expecting you to orgasm."

I scowl at him and wrap an arm around my legs. "I don't want to do this anymore. Go away."

"*Nyet*," he says, and in one fluid movement, he drags my entire body against his. "You are still nervous. Still afraid. It is obvious as you act like a virgin and scowl at me when you become uneasy. I will not hurt you, Naomi. Nor will I cover you in germs and filth. My hands are clean." He holds one up in the air and then gives it a little shake, as if demonstrating. "They have touched nothing but you." Now the hand comes in and traces along my jaw.

I shiver again, but not out of disgust. It's a good shiver. I feel my breasts prickle in response, and my hand slides between my legs, wanting to return to the pulsing throb that feels so very good.

"Now," he whispers, and his face is so close to mine I can see the minute lines around his eyes, the dark blond lashes, the firm press of his mouth.

"Do you wish for me to touch you?"

I nod, sucking in a breath when his thumb skates across my lower lip. I should be thinking *germs bacteria conjunctivitis herpes skin contact pathogens* but all I can focus on is how skittery and excited his touch makes me. My pulse jumps, and I realize that

I'm as aroused now with him talking to me and touching me with his fingers as I was in the bathroom when I masturbated.

He pulls his hand away again, and I realize his other is gripping my shoulder, his arm wrapped around my back. I'm pulled against his chest, and I feel oddly secure here against him. Then, Vasily moves his fingers in the air again, as if to get my attention. I watch as his free hand now moves to my knee and firmly presses it back, nudging my legs apart.

And I'm helpless to protest. I want this. I want to know what's going to happen when he touches me. I'm throbbing and aching with need, and my breath is coming as small, gasping little pants that are registering even in my distracted mind.

"Are you still unsettled?" he asks in a low voice.

"No," I whisper, my tone matching his. "I'm aching."

He groans softly, and then his hand glides up the inside of my thigh, the backs of his fingers skimming along my leg. Then, Vasily's hand moves and he is cupping my pussy. He feels scorching hot against me, and just the sensation of his skin touching mine is making me anxious.

"You are very wet," he rasps, and I notice curiously that his breathing is as rapid as my own. One of his fingers presses forward, parting the lips of my pussy and pushing in. "Very wet."

"I can't help it. It's a natural reaction to stimuli, but I understand if it disturbs you—"

"I like it." His voice is a guttural growl against my ear, and I shiver. I didn't realize how close he's pressed to me but I can feel his breath on my neck, and his head is canted toward mine, as if he is telling me secrets. "I like that your wetness is for me."

"I don't know if—" I begin to protest, but his finger taps against my clit, and I gasp, completely and utterly distracted by that quick touch. It feels . . . different to have a man do it for me. Very different. Intense. Raw. I grab his hand at the wrist and press my flesh against his fingers, asking for more.

"Tell me what you want, Naomi."

"More." I press his hand again, breathless, and my hips twitch. "Start with an even rhythm and circle the hood of my clit. Over time, speed up and increase the frequency of touches. You can change the pattern as you go but don't let up until I come."

He laughs again, and I stiffen, but then his finger begins to move against my clit, stroking it in tiny circles like I told him. "I like that you tell me exactly what you want, Naomi. There are no games with you."

I'm confused at that. Isn't that what he wants me to do? But then a second finger follows the first, and he's rubbing wide circles around my clit, and adding an extra little stroke every now and then, and it feels like he's taking my flesh between his fingers and just rubbing rubbing rubbing . . . And I love it.

"Just like that," I tell him, closing my eyes and falling against his shoulder. I hold my knees open wider so he won't stop touching me, and my hips begin to move, involuntarily following his fingers as he touches me.

"Do you like this?" His voice is rough, biting, and so close to my face.

I nod without opening my eyes, letting the sensations take over. "It feels much better when you do it," I tell him, and cry out when one of his fingers dips lower and touches me . . . deeper. "What are you doing?"

"I am seeing if you like more touches." His nose nuzzles against my face, and I press against him, seeming to need his caresses as much as I need his touch on my clitoris. "Are you frightened?"

"No, but I like the other touch better," I tell him as his finger circles lower. "That one just makes me ache."

"It makes your cunt ache to be filled," he tells me. "Someday, you will let me fill it for you."

I don't reply; I don't need to, because he circles a finger at the entrance to my core a moment longer, and then shifts his hand. My fingers graze over his, exploring—I feel too good to open my eyes and leave the sea of sensations—and I realize he's now working my clit with his thumb. His finger presses deeper again, and I gasp when he sinks it into me.

I'm riding his hand.

He murmurs something in Russian and I feel his mouth press against my brow.

Then, as if he's a car that's changed gears, he begins to press his thumb against my clit rapidly. His speed is so fast that he practically feels as if he's vibrating . . . and these motions carry down to the thick finger that's buried deep inside me.

I've never experienced this double sensation before, and it's overwhelming.

I bite my lip, and when that won't hold my feelings inside, I burst into noisy gasps and my hands start clawing at him, at his shirt. I don't know what I need, but this feels like too much. It's overwhelming and twice as powerful as anything I've ever done to myself. "Stop, stop," I breathe, even as I press my legs further apart and lift my hips against his hand.

"Vasily, stop. Vasily!"

"Keep saying my name like that, Naomi."

"Vasily, please." I pull at his shirt, practically butting my head against him as I writhe against his hand. "I need . . . something . . . more . . . not as fast. Too much!"

But he keeps twitching that intense thumb against my clit, stroking his finger inside me. He's not stopping. If anything, he's going faster.

And all of a sudden, my body can't handle it anymore. I burst and a hard, choked noise rushes out of my throat, and my body clenches and I'm coming, coming, coming, endlessly coming.

I feel as if I'm being torn apart by pleasure so intense it's making my toes curl even as the breath leaves my lungs. And all the while, I gasp like a dying fish and cling to his shirt.

Hypothesis? Destroyed.

CHAPTER **THIRTEEN**

VASILY

We are barely touching. My thumb is on her clit, my three long fingers buried in her cunt, my lips are against her brow. But for those two or three pressure points, we are separated. Yet I feel her everywhere. Her arousal is seeping into my pores, singing along my bloodstream and buzzing every nerve ending.

Does she know? Does her brilliant, intellectual, fact-oriented mind understand how she's infiltrated my very being? She is no siren, but a goddess who can command me with one imperious glare. I want to slide to the bottom of the bed, kiss her feet and await her command. She is the witch and I am her wolf, her *volk*. *Order me*, I think, *tell me what to do.*

I have never felt such a heady rush as when Naomi said *more*. She is not confident enough in her own body, though, or her own orgasms to understand that pain is just a prelude to greater pleasure.

But if she did . . . and she could relay that to me . . . I groan aloud as my whole body stiffens with what could be between us. She would have no boundaries and no barriers. No shame.

What would it be like to have sex with a woman wherein there was no shame? I can almost hear her saying *Lick me with your tongue. Touch me with your fingers. Press them in harder. Bite me. Fuck me. Love me.*

Love me? I do not know where that thought comes from, but it is dangerous. Love is a tender emotion, and Vasily Petrovich does not know tenderness. He knows reward and punishment. Tenderness has no place in my life.

I pull my fingers out, gritting my teeth against her soft moan and her luxurious skin so slick with her arousal that the movement makes an audible sound. A sex sound. A sound that makes my cock hunger for her. With immense effort, I throw myself backward away from her magnetic pull.

But I cannot stop staring at her glorious sex. Her folds are rosy, swollen with the blood of her recent arousal. She is coated with her come, and my mouth aches to taste her. I lick my lips and imagine the tang of her sex on my tongue. This is a visual that will haunt me. When I close my eyes, I will see her face as she comes, hear her sexual moans, feel the tight clench of her cunt around my fingers.

"That was good, then?" I choke out in a hoarse voice.

"Yes. It was good. I mean although *good* is not an accurate term."

I can feel my face fall as she speaks. "Not good? I felt your body explode in my arms. Your eyes rolled backward and your entire frame shuddered with ecstasy."

"Shuddered with ecstasy . . . that's accurate. I agree with that description. Explode, however would not be correct. That would describe me breaking apart into little pieces . . . although I suppose it could be described euphemistically as such because obviously I am still in one piece. But at the end there, when I told you to stop and you refused and kept thrumming your thumb against me . . . It was your thumb, right?" She barely waits for my nod of agreement. "When you were wiggling your thumb against me, it did feel like I was losing control so I guess, all things considered, I'd accept 'explode in your arms' as an acceptable description."

She blinks up at me expectantly. "Can we do it again or do your fingers need to recover?"

I force my hands to curl into fists so I do not fall between her legs and beg to touch her. I need distance from her so I lie. "Yes, my fingers need to recover."

"I thought so." She pulls her legs up and curls into a small ball. "They were working very fast. I suppose they are sore, although I never thought fingers could get sore but they are made of muscles, bones, and tendons and therefore would suffer from the same symptoms as other parts of the body."

Her words are running together as she sleepily continues on about body parts and fatigue rates. After a quick wash of my hands, I throw a blanket over her and settle into a captain's chair close to the exit door, unnecessarily buckling my belt as if this thin band of fabric and quick-release metal could somehow prevent me from throwing myself at Naomi.

Swiveling so my back is to her, I drag a hand over my face. Where are my objectives? The plan was to obtain the Emperor, find the Madonna, return home and wield absolute power over the Petrovich *Bratva*, and bring my sister home. Dostonev's request for the Madonna could be satisfied after I had the backing of the council. Upon finding Naomi, my entire plan has been derailed.

My ears strain to hear her behind me and it is not until her breath evens and slows into the telltale signs of slumber that I allow myself to relax. Slowly I uncurl my fingers from the armrest. Dully I register the marks in the cream leather. The seat will need repairing. I make a mental note of it.

One by one I go through a checklist of items that need to be addressed upon landing. First a call to *Bratva* headquarters. I will need to see the last time Aleksei checked in and with whom he spoke. Which members of the leadership could be trusted? Briefly I mourned the loss of Aleksei. He was a good soldier, capable of taking an order and executing it without a great deal of oversight.

Perhaps I will draw on Thomas for advice, pretend that he is a confidante. I do not trust him but I can make him believe that I find him valuable. That might be sufficient to elicit enough loyalty to hold the *Bratva* together while I'm on this little errand.

My sister will need to be called as well. Dostonev's men guard her and I have allowed myself only minimal contact with her over the years. Those men do not know whom they guard, only that they are paid handsomely to protect one slight girl. She is a woman, I correct myself. Katya does not like to be referred to as a girl, but a girl is all I remember. She was a slip of a girl when I sent her away, when I pretended to kill her so that Elena Petrovich could not whore her out or use her against me.

When I refused to allow Katya to be gifted to a man when she was twelve, I made it obvious where my vulnerabilities were and that either Katya would be killed as punishment for our rebellion or vilely used. I volunteered to kill her myself, and at age seventeen earned a notorious reputation. Another woman might have suspected a trick but Elena was pleased with my willingness to kill, believing that sex is preferable to death. After all, I had chosen that route myself. Sex over death. But not for Katya. I chose to subject myself to Elena for Katya, not so she would have to suffer the same at others hands.

I burned her and brought her ashes back to Elena's trophy case. I recorded it all so Elena would know it was real. With one action, I cemented myself as a loyalist, willing to do anything for Elena, for the *Bratva*. Others were disgusted by my actions but it engendered real fear, for I was Vasily Petrovich, a man so amoral he could kill his own sister.

But none of it was real. I went to Dostonev and promised anything. He delivered me a magician and through the literal use of smoke and mirrors, we faked Katya's death. She lives in hiding now, waiting until I can free her. The Madonna must be acquired. Debts must be repaid.

Then I can have my sister back.

The long list of my duties comforts me. In my own way, I am as odd as Naomi. Finally, I'm able to release a calming breath and fall asleep. During the long flight I wake frequently, but I will myself back to sleep knowing my body will need it once we are in Rome and the hunt is fully engaged. When the pilot steps out to alert me that we will land in thirty minutes, I rise swiftly with a nod. Naomi still slumbers, I note with fierce satisfaction. I have worn her out.

After the pilot returns to engage the landing sequence, I change into the gray suit hanging in the small closet next to a navy wrap dress. This is likely a stewardess's dress but it will serve Naomi better than the luggage full of garish tourist clothes. There's a flight bag on the floor. Opening it I find clean underwear, slacks, and white blouse. This will serve well for Naomi's luggage. I do not want to carry the stolen luggage through customs. Instead the pilot will dispose of it during a different trip. He—and the rest of the staff—are paid well to perform odd tasks without question. Short wedge heels rest on the floor next to a pair of size 14 hand-stitched leather loafers. The two pairs of shoes nestle together as if they belong to a couple. I can see as clearly as if I turn and stare at her, Naomi's lithe body lying alone on the bed, covered with little more than a sheet. Underneath she is nude. I cannot stop the memory of her sweetly convulsing around my fingers as she gripped my shoulders and chanted my name.

I tighten the knot of my tie harder than necessary to draw my attention toward more important matters. My cock is unimportant. The feel of her soft cunt around my flesh is unimportant. The only thing that is important is the Madonna.

Resolutely I shut out the domestic vision of the two pairs of shoes and pull on my suit coat over the shoulder harness. This—unlike the pants and the shirt, fits loosely, allowing for me to hide a gun under my jacket.

I fly private not because I am too good for commercial flights but because I cannot be armed on commercial airlines, and I go nowhere without a gun under my arm and a knife on my leg. In the briefcase in the back of the closet are another gun, six magazines, and a stack of cash. I pocket several for the bribes I will need when we land.

I consider the bookings I reserved while on the plane. We can stay in the more touristy location of the Via dei Condotti or along Embassy Row on the Via Vittorio Veneto. But the Hassler is on the top of the hill looking down over most of Rome. That is

the safest place. I note one particular room overlooks the Spanish
Steps. Ideal. I can see my enemies coming.

"Naomi," I call, standing two feet beyond the bed. I cannot
come closer into her web. I respect her power and know my own
limits.

She rolls over, her voluptuous breasts swaying from her motion
before coming to a rest. She is temptation incarnate. I step back.
Her eyes flicker awake and for a second, they catch mine. As always
I am stunned by their clear, vibrant color. But just as quickly as she
meets my gaze, her eyes slide away to focus on my cheek and then
my ear.

"It is time to awaken. You will get up and get dressed and provide me with a list of equipment needs. I want to procure those
items so that we may obtain our target and finish our business."

As she struggles to sit up, the sheet falls lower and her pale
stomach and perfect belly button are exposed. The sheets make a
swishing sound as she moves her legs to the side. Ah God, I cannot take another moment. I stride to my chair and buckle myself
in, the restraint laughable, but I will take anything to help me
gather my control. My fingers find the indentations I made earlier
and I grip them again, striving to find strength to resist her.

Hoarsely I tell her, "There is a dress and underthings in the
closet. Wear those. Remember you are Karen Brown. We are a
couple taking our first vacation together. We met when you were
a student in St. Petersburg."

"Why not Moscow?" she says, strolling nearly nude to the
closet. Does she know how she affects me and is doing this on
purpose? If so, I applaud her cleverness even as I curse my own
weakness, but given her general obliviousness about many things,
she likely does not realize that her naked body is beautiful enough

to drive men to commit crimes. I take a deep breath and try to calm my rousing body.

"St. Petersburg is more common for study-abroad programs. Outsiders view it as more cultured."

"But it's not?" She pulls out the toiletries bag and the wrap and proceeds to dress. I close my eyes so I do not attack her.

"Moscow is the heart of Russia. St. Petersburg is the gown we've put on to impress all the other Europeans."

"Where is your home?"

"The Petrovich *Bratva* encompasses a portion of the Western Administrative Okrug, one of the twelve districts of Moscow. It is actually in the southwest of the city center."

"Do you rule all of it?"

"*Nyet*. There are over a million people in the district. Most are legitimate citizens. We do not control them. We . . . protect them," I say because while the *Bratva* is powerful, it is because we've provided order. "There are several members of the council that advise our subprefect and above him is a prefect and above him is the mayor of Moscow. There are layers and layers of bureaucracy and nothing can be accomplished in any time without dozens of reviews. And the reviews must be reviewed. And the committees who advise the subprefects or prefects must also be advised themselves. So people come to us for help and we can provide it quickly. We can dispense justice and give out aid if necessary. The *Bratva* provides and protects for those who are within its circle."

"And if they aren't within the circle?"

"Then they must look to someone else."

"It sounds like a big headache and you enjoy this?"

I smile at the sound of her disbelief. "I do."

The noises of her dressing have ceased, which leads me to believe it is safe to open my eyes. But when they land on Naomi in the simple navy dress that accentuates every curve in her body, I wonder if I should gouge my eyes out now and save myself the trouble my attraction to her will undoubtedly cause later. I miss her blond tresses, but there is no denying she is outstanding as a brunette as well. The darker hair color frames her fair skin and deepens the color of her eyes. I am losing my head over this woman because I want to take her to the bed, spread her legs, and take her again and again until my ears ring with her screams of delight.

Teeth clenched, I force myself to the task at hand. Handing her a set of fake papers, I run over the details so that we may pass through immigration with no concern.

"When we land at Ciampino–G.B. Pastine Airport, there will be a hire car waiting for us. Carry your bag in one hand and your passport in the other. They should stamp it. Walk directly to the hire car. Do not speak if you can help it. Now tell me my name again."

She rolls her eyes, undoubtedly tired of me. "Dmitri Luzhkov. We met in St. Petersburg as I was touring Letny Sad at the Russian Museum. You were taking your mother to see the statues and I was taking pictures of the Neva riverbank."

"Very good."

"I'm a genius. You only needed to tell me once."

"Then you should have no problems following my directives when we land."

CHAPTER **FOURTEEN**

NAOMI

I've memorized all the details that Vasily has given me of our "relationship," but he's forgotten one thing about Aspies—we're easily distracted. That, and we don't like new places. The airport here at Ciampino is crowded, people rushing past with carry-on bags and swarming like ants at a picnic. I'm intimidated by this crowd and the unfamiliarity of the airport itself. It seems so big and foreign, and I don't deal well with either. I like comfortable, familiar things.

Still, I manage, if somewhat distracted. I follow Vasily—no, Dmitri—and his big, broad shoulders as he makes his way through the crowd. We wait in line at customs and he's not speaking, which is just fine with me. I'm too overwhelmed by everything around me to try to hold a sensible conversation. I hum "Itsy Bitsy Spider" under my breath to try to calm myself, but it's loud here, and I can hardly hear myself.

No freaking out, Naomi, I tell myself. *You don't want to make Vasily unhappy.*

It's true, I don't. I'm still basking in warm feelings for him since he gave me that orgasm on the plane. I want another when we get back to the hotel, and if he's irritated, it'll be difficult to convince him. I'm thinking about orgasms as Vasily/Dmitri holds out his passport. The man with the stamper speaks to him. Vasily/Dmitri says something. They share a laugh. His passport is stamped and he moves forward. I step up to the spot he vacated, hold out my passport, and wait. Nearby, a baby screams and my nerves rattle, shot.

The man smiles at me. "Are you in the country for business or pleasure, Ms. Brown?"

I stare at the man's mouth. I can't look at his eyes because they're small and piggish and staring, and he's got one tooth that's turned to where it juts out when he speaks. It's like a tusk, really. This man reminds me of a boar. Which muddles up my thoughts from earlier and turns into, "Did you know that a boar can orgasm for up to thirty minutes?"

The man's tusk-mouth moves into an expression like a frown. "I—I am not sure I understand—"

"The female sow doesn't orgasm for as long as the boar does," I continue, still distracted. "But the male has a penis that is spiraled at the end so he can corkscrew into the cervix in order to properly inseminate the female—"

"Karen," Vasily barks at me. "Now is not the time."

I blink. I didn't even get the chance to tell him about the sheer volume of boar ejaculate. "But—"

"Business or pleasure?" the man holding the passport stamp asks me again.

"Pleasure," I say. I look over at Vasily and even though I'm not good at reading expressions, that chilly look on his face tells me he's pissed. I've done something wrong.

"Where will you be staying?" the customs official asks me.

"In a hotel."

I look over at Vasily and his nostrils flare. I wonder why.

"Please step aside so we can go through your luggage." The man gestures, and another customs official in a matching uniform approaches. He takes my bag from my hand and moves me to a nearby table. He puts on gloves and begins to unzip my bag, then begins to go through my Karen clothing.

The new man gives me a quick look, then digs through the dresses in the bag. "Where are you staying?"

"Why does everyone keep asking me that?" I snap.

"Please stand over here," he instructs me, pointing a few feet away.

I'm pretty sure this wasn't what was supposed to happen. I hum even louder and cover my ears, agitated.

Vasily approaches and gives my shoulder a squeeze, then heads forward and begins to speak to the customs official in Italian. I don't catch any of it except two quickly spoken words— Karen and *autismo*.

From there, the look on the official's face turns from annoyance to pity as he studies me, my ears covered and humming. I look away from him, unable to meet his gaze.

The men talk quietly for a moment, but the official is zipping my bag again and then holds his hand out. "Passport, please."

I hand it to him to be stamped, but I'm furious. I'm so angry that I'm shaking. If there's one thing I hate, it's pity. It's everyone looking at me like I'm the local fool, like I'm somehow incapacitated and so stupid that I'm about to start drooling on myself.

And Vasily was the one offering the information. He's betrayed me, and I feel a stab of hurt. I thought we were friends. I thought he liked me. I was even becoming accustomed to his germs. I'm trying to process things logically as he puts a hand on the middle of my back and leads me forward, but all I can keep coming back to is *autismo. Autismo.*

As if that's what defines me.

The look of pity on the official's face.

I'm seething.

No one stops us as we head out. There is a driver with a sign waiting for us, and Vasily nods at him and hands him my bag. Vasily opens the door to the car, gesturing, and I get in.

He slides in next to me and says in a low voice, "I will have many words to say to you when we get to hotel."

I cross my arms over my chest. I'm not waiting for the hotel. "You don't get to finger me again."

The driver gets into the car just as I spit these words out, and he shoots a look into the rearview mirror.

Vasily touches a panel on the door and the glass partition goes up, separating us from the driver and allowing us a bit of privacy.

"We do not do this now, Karen," he says in a menacing tone.

"Fuck you, Dmitri. Just fuck you."

He cusses in Russian, then says, "Now what did I do? I saved your ass back there."

"By making that man think that I'm mentally handicapped! Did you see the way he looked at me? As if I was about to pull my pants down and pick my nose or something." And here I thought Vasily was different. That he cared how I felt. The betrayal feels somehow deeper than usual. Maybe because I'd hoped that Vasily saw me for who I am—the optimized computer—instead of a bunch of broken parts.

"You were creating a scene," he says through gritted teeth.

"I was not!"

"You were."

"Even if I was, I could have handled it."

"By what, faking another seizure?"

My fists clench against my folded arms and I stare out the window. It's a mistake. There's so much foreign scenery flying past as we drive down the street that I feel even more uncomfortable and out of place. I don't belong here. I don't belong with this man.

Sometimes, I feel like I don't belong anywhere, and a burst of sadness overrides my fury.

"I ensured that we got out of there smoothly," he says. "In the future, you will pay attention and not rattle off about pig orgasms." He shakes his head and a short, barking laugh erupts from him. "I do not know where that came from."

I did. It was because I'd been thinking about sex and my own orgasms. My mind's been on sex ever since Vasily slid his fingers out from between my legs with the kind of sigh that people made after a particularly delicious dinner. I'd been wondering all about what would happen if I touched Vasily the way he touched me. Would he object or would he allow me to share my germs with him? I'd been turned on and excited about the prospect of continuing to explore with him.

For the second time in my life, I was contemplating enjoyable sex, and the thought was a titillating one.

All of that excitement is gone now. He's betrayed me in the worst way possible. Up until now, he's treated me like an equal. Like a desirable woman. My guard was down, and when the betrayal came, it was unexpected and felt like a punch in the gut.

And now I feel less than normal. And I hate it.

"We shall have dinner before we get you a new computer," he says grandly. As if the subject is settled. "What would you like to eat?"

I ignore him. If he's ashamed of who I am, he can go eat on his own. I want nothing to do with him anymore.

"Karen?"

Ignored.

His hand touches my skirt, brushes against my thigh. It's an intimate caress. One with germs and transference, and I should be mad that he's contaminating me, but I'm just hurting, hurting, hurting. "Do you play that you are mad at me now, Karen?" His tone is teasing. Light.

I continue to ignore him even as we get to the hotel. I feel like crying. Here I thought I was making a friend, someone I could touch openly, someone I could trust. Someone that understood me, despite all his own quirks and foibles.

He's betrayed me in the worst way and I sniff back tears. The worst is that I don't think he even grasps just how he's hurt me. How could he? He's *normal*. I'm the weirdo.

The car stops in front of the hotel and I ignore everything as we get out. I'm sure the architecture is beautiful and there are fountains and scenery, but all I know is that there are people swarming, and I itch as if there are ants crawling on my skin. I just want to go inside, into a dark, quiet room and hide. Bring out my laptop, sink into my hacking, and forget about the outside world.

Except . . . I don't have my hat. Heavy sadness erupts through my body. I should have known when he didn't want to go back for my hat that he didn't understand me. I've been fooling myself.

By the time we get up to our room, I'm silently crying.

CHAPTER FIFTEEN

VASILY

I have made her cry. These are real tears, not the ones Elena uses when she wants to manipulate me into doing her bidding, but signs of genuine suffering and hurt. Pain and hurt that I have generated. The desiccated place in my chest turns over slowly and then thumps hard, once and then twice.

There's a flow of blood to external extremities, and a tingling erupts all over as if my body was asleep and is just now enduring a painful awakening. The wariness I experienced before when I told myself Naomi was a siren endangering me is a lie. It is myself I should fear. She isn't changing me, but rather causing me to want to change. For her.

My fists clench at my sides as we ride up the elevator to the seventh floor, for I would like to console her but I know not how. The bellman moves stiffly down the hallway, no doubt wondering if we are newlyweds having sudden regrets. I doubt he encounters many unhappy couples. We will have to move soon because he will remember us—the mousy brown-haired crying woman with the dour Russian.

He shoves the room key into the mechanical slot, and the lights flicker to life. With a worried glance to the silent, weeping Naomi, he begins to show us the different spaces in the suite, throwing open the terrace doors. The sudden influx of noise makes her flinch, and at the jerk of my head, the bellman gratefully scuttles out.

Closing the doors, I draw the curtains so light of the afternoon sun cannot filter in. Perhaps her eyes hurt.

In the minibar I find vodka, cheap whisky, and bottles of red and white wine. White, I think. She likes colorless liquids.

She has hardly moved from the middle of the large entry. There is a dining table ahead of her and beyond that the noisy terrace. To the side I spot an alcove near another set of terrace doors. Taking her by the hand, I drag her reluctant body to the cushions and press her down.

"Here, drink," I offer, but my gruff statement sounds more like an order than an offering.

She continues to ignore me instead, wrapping her arms around her waist and beginning to rock. The tears have turned to panic. Her unfamiliar surroundings, the inelegant way I handled immigration, the noise of the crowd at the airport are all taking a toll on her. Soon she is shaking.

Is she cold? Hurrying to the bedroom, I strip the comforter off and drag it into the alcove. I toss it around her shoulders, but still her shaking does not abate. When soldiers are cold, they huddle together and seek warmth from another. The closeness provides not only heat but also comfort. I slide under the comforter and pull Naomi into my arms.

Through the layers of down, the cotton of my shirt, the wool of my suit coat, the violent trembling of her body continues. This close, I can see her head and neck tensely move back and forth in repeated, hectic motion. The uncontrollable nature of her shaking is so markedly different than the seizure she faked in front of Aleksei that I know I will never be fooled again. But then I do not want to see her out of control like this in the future.

"Naomi, I am sorry. I should not have said what I did. You must know I think you are the most intelligent individual I know of. I have searched the world for you." I tell her about my long search for the Emperor. The money I have spent and the places I've been. Rio was one of my last hopes. I talk on and on until her shuddering recedes. Moving to kneel next to the sofa, I try to apologize. "Your . . ." I grapple for the medical term, unsure if it is autism or Asperger's, but it is some social problem. "Your condition means nothing to me. You are just Naomi. Brilliant and—"

"Flawed?" she chokes out.

I am making this worse with my ineptness, my ignorance. "*Nyet*. Perfect. It is I who am flawed." She snorts in disgust as if my words are meaningless tripe. I try again. "We are all flawed, and it is displayed in different ways. I am sorry I was careless with my words, and I will do better in the future. I was worried," I admit. "I have guns in my case and did not want a scene."

"Guns?" She sits up, smoothing her hair back.

"Yes, guns and a few other things such as additional passports. Generally we are not searched coming in through immigrations. It's a stamp and a nod of the head. I'm not certain what was so different today," I muse.

"You should have told me. I could have faked a seizure or something," she exclaimed.

"Yes, I made a mistake." I make no comment on whether this would have drawn more attention rather than less, because she is calmed now.

"Obviously." She threads her hair behind her ears, not even recognizing my big gesture. I never admit to mistakes. That indicates a weakness and I am not weak. Yet . . . here I am on my knees. I shove to my feet.

"Let us eat and then we shall go and buy you a computer."

"What's on the menu?" She begins opening drawers, emptying the paper and pens and pamphlets onto the desktop surfaces and then putting them in piles, first according to color and then according to materials and then in descending order. Unhappy with all of her sorting, she places them back in the drawer. "Well?" She turns back to me as if the episode had never happened. "Food?"

I blink. If it is nothing to her, then it is nothing to me. At least her tears are gone. "We order what we want. Tell me and it will come."

"Anything?" she asks suspiciously. I nod. Her finger taps against her lower lip as she thinks. I stare at it, wanting to run my tongue along those rosy lips and then delve inside. "I'd like avocados and linguine. No meat."

I place an order for our food—pasta for her, seafood for me.

"Was it my words, Naomi?" I cannot let it go as she has. I want to know how to avoid triggering her in the future.

She does not answer me at first but instead rearranges her pens again and again. Patiently I sit because I understand she needs a moment to compose herself and gather her thoughts.

"It wasn't just the words. I thought we could be . . . friends, but you treated me like I was stupid. Why didn't you just confide in me? I could have helped."

"I am sorry and I was wrong. I ask your forgiveness. As for taking you in my confidence, as you can see by Aleksei's perfidy that I cannot trust anyone, not even those in my own organization. I will do what I can to ensure you have every piece of information or equipment you need to accomplish my task but no, do not ask me to trust you. I cannot."

She frowns but begins to think. Naomi is a rational being. She will come to the same conclusion as I.

"But I have not betrayed you," she argues. "And I don't have any reason to."

I can only gape at her. "You are my captive. You have already lied to me at least once."

"When?" she challenges insolently.

"Your memory is so short, then? When you run your computer program and say that you do not have the results but for Rome. When you fake your seizure. When you—"

She raises a hand to cut me off. "Right, but that was when I thought you might kill me or something. I don't think you'll do that anymore. And I'm not really your captive. I mean, you plan to let me go when you get your little picture, right?"

Thomas would shit himself to hear her call the Caravaggio a little picture, but I like it, for this whole debacle is conducted in pursuit of canvas and oil.

"Once I retrieve the Madonna, I will reward you handsomely, and the plane will take you wherever it is you need to go."

The image of my *dacha*, far outside the city center, surrounded by nothing but pines and snow, emerges. Slowly, as if testing the words, I share, "I have a small cabin north of Moscow near Lake

Ladoga. It is primitive, but quiet. There is no one near for miles. Perhaps you would like it there."

She nods enthusiastically. "A place that is isolated, away from people? Quiet? Sign me up. I'll need satellite. And packaged delivery. I like to order stuff online."

My response is delayed by the image of Naomi on my rural property. There is only a small *dacha* presently, as I told her, but I could build something grander, something better suited to her. "Yes, there is a helipad. Deliveries can be made to St. Petersburg and the helicopter can deliver to you daily." It would be expensive, but if I had the *Bratva* under my control, the cost would be manageable. And the thought of letting her go, away from me, is not one I wish to entertain. Some things—some people—are worth all costs. I am fearing that she might be one of them.

"Perfect. I can work with that." She taps her hands. "See, we could make a perfect team. I'll manage all your money, too. I've got really good at hiding it. The Swiss banks are still good and Caymans as well but these days you can even put a lot of it in the United States. Hedge-fund managers are really greedy and accept wire transfers from anywhere. Also I've gotten quite a few tech startups to take suitcases full of cash in exchange for stocks that they already own or in their new company. When they go public you just trade your new stocks."

She goes on explaining all the ways she can turn my dirty money into oligarch wealth. Her words make me realize how shortsighted I have been. I did not need a little picture, as she calls it, to consolidate power. Only Naomi. With her scale, I could wield influence and power over anyone—both my adversaries and allies alike. It is not just financial problems she could bring to me but information—secrets. But I would have to trust her. Her power could render me prey once again. I would be a pawn—a mere tool—in her arsenal.

"It is a good plan," I acknowledge. "And you could do more than secure the wealth of the brotherhood. You could help me bring everyone in line by ferreting out their secrets. But I would look at you and wonder when you would betray me like Judas. It is not you only that I do not trust. I don't trust anyone. Do not take it personally," I add when I turn to her scowling face.

"Of course it is personal. You have insulted my integrity," she argues. "Even Aspies' feelings get hurt. Actually I get pissed off, not hurt, because being hurt doesn't really make sense but being angry does."

She continues in this vein throughout lunch and then in the cab to the electronics store. "Aspies have feelings. I don't want to be called creepy or unfeeling. Also, I'm not a liar. Okay, I've lied a few times, but that was out of self-protection. You should admire my self-reliance. It's a good character trait. Also weird. Don't call me weird. Don't call me weird, creepy, a retard. Or stupid."

She's still detailing all the ways in which she's been insulted in the past when we are back at the hotel with her computer. Of course, she doesn't acknowledge that. Instead she's pretending it's merely a list of traits or descriptions that would piss her off. It makes me ache for her as she hides her hurt behind rationalizations. And I would like to find all these other people and shoot them. Of course, I would need to start with myself.

CHAPTER **SIXTEEN**

NAOMI

It's three a.m. in Italy. I can't sleep. I showered and went to bed like Vasily advised, since our next day would be a busy one. But this new place is making me fretful, and the loss of my cap is eating at me, so I get up and grab the new computer to poke around while sitting in bed. I install software. I hack into my old laptop and send it a keylogger so I can see if anyone uses it. Then, I dig around on the deep web for a bit, uncovering more bits of information that Vasily might find interesting. If we're going to be a team, I need to do my part.

So first, I work on appropriating some additional funds for him. It's not so difficult. I immediately flush all of Hudson's funds into Vasily's accounts. Even though Vasily has taken care to disguise his personal information, everything is available on the Internet if you know where to look. I simply start by looking up

Russians born at approximately this date, and reference back-ward. I've actually been running queries on Vasily for days now, memorizing information as it pops up. He's changed last names, but his first is the same, which makes things easy.

I really should talk to him about hiding his tracks online. I locate his birthdate and domestic passport number with a few advanced searches, and from there, I've got him. Once I find his personal details, I also find what false names he has his accounts under. It's no problem hacking into both with a simple password-testing program—I really need to talk to Vasily about password encryptions too, it seems. Then I start skimming the blockchain where all the Bitcoin—digital currency—exchanges are recorded. It is difficult to move millions of dollars in Bitcoins, but it is easy to siphon small amounts when an exchange occurs. Do this often enough and the small amounts become big amounts. The scripts I've run skim small amounts every millisecond. By the time some-one figures out what I'm doing, I'm gone.

Then, I look up information on the purchaser of Vasily's Madonna. I remember the name, even though I've wiped his transaction information from the site. He is Emile Royer-Menard, and he is known in the underbelly of Europe as a procurer of unusual things. I find that he's in Italy under an assumed name and throws a lot of hedonistic parties, which are described in lurid detail on a master-slave forum. This is something I've never researched before and I'm fascinated by it, spending hours fol-lowing threads about submissive lifestyles until Vasily appears in the doorway. He's staring at me. Or rather, staring at my body. He adjusts himself and then steps into the room.

"What are you doing, Naomi?"

"Did you know that some people still use chastity belts as

orgasm control? The key is given to the dominant in the relationship so he can—"

"That is fascinating," he says in a patient voice, interrupting me. "But why are you researching dominant/submissive relationships at six in the morning? And where are your clothes?"

I look down. Sure enough, my breasts are out. "I sleep in the nude."

"And yet you are not sleeping and still nude."

"I was thinking. I got the computer so I could work. I guess I forgot a step."

"Dress and we shall go to breakfast," he tells me. His gaze is carefully averted.

"Is it safe?"

"*Da.*" At my hesitation, he says, "The Golubevs likely have no idea we are in Italy. Any rival organizations will either be searching in Rio, or waiting in Moscow. We will eat someplace extremely public, enjoy our toast, and I will bring my gun. Will that suffice?"

I think for a moment. "Can I have a gun?"

"Ah, but you have no place to put it," he says, gesturing at my nakedness.

"I can put pants on."

His mouth curls into a smile. "That was a joke, Naomi."

"Oh." I smile back at him, because it is rather silly to think about hiding a gun when I have no clothes on. I consider this for a moment and amend my statement. "Actually, I could put a gun inside my—"

"Clothes," he says, interrupting my rambling. "Then breakfast."

"Is it because you don't trust me?"

"It is that it is dangerous for you to go around with a gun in a foreign country. You might draw more attention than you are accustomed to. And if someone sees you with gun, they might assume you know how to handle it. Do you know how to handle it?" He peers into my face.

"I don't, but I can learn," I tell him brightly.

"Then after you learn, you get gun."

"This sounds suspiciously like a trust issue."

"I cannot trust you, Naomi," he says. He regards me with intense scrutiny. For some reason, I have the oddest urge to have him come and sit in the bed with me, naked. I wonder what he would look like with no clothes on. That's a strange sort of thought for someone like me, and it makes me distrust myself.

"I would trust you more if you shared some of your secrets with me," I admit, getting out of bed to dress. If I stay in longer, I'll keep picturing him in it with me. "Tell me a secret and I won't bug you about the gun."

He thinks for a minute, watching me as I step close. When I move next to him, he reaches for me. And my normal instinct is to flinch away from the touch on my bare skin but . . . I don't. I tell myself I want to see how I react to his touch.

For science.

One finger traces down my bare arm, and sends shivers through my body, reminding me of when he'd fingered me on the plane. I couldn't wait to experience that again. "My reasons for not being touched are different than yours," he says in a thick voice. "It has nothing to do with germs."

My entire body is paying attention to that finger. "I thought you were supposed to tell me a secret? Even I knew that." My breathing has sped up, and not in panic. Instead, I'm thinking about the time he washed his hands for five minutes and then fingered me on the plane. What if I ask him to do that right now?

Will he get naked on the bed with me and put clean hands on my skin and—

He glares at me. "Dress. Breakfast. Now."

Right. I scramble to dress.

Fifteen minutes later, my hair is brushed, and I'm wearing a pale pink polo dress and white Keds with no socks. It's comfortable enough, and Vasily says it looks "sufficiently touristy." He's wearing a floral Hawaiian shirt made of a soft, silky material and man-sandals. His collar is curled on one side, and I automatically reach up to fix it, which makes him pause. His breathing escalates.

"I won't touch," I promise. I adjust his collar. "Did you know that if you have one tablespoon of peanut butter on your toast, you're probably eating 4.2 insect parts and you have a one in seven chance of having a rat hair?"

"That is just what I wanted to hear before breakfast," he tells me. "Let us go." His hand goes to the small of my back to guide me, and we head down to the restaurant at the front of the beautiful hotel.

We order breakfast. Vasily requests *succo d'arancia*, and I ask the waiter if it's canned, because the FDA allows one maggot per 250 milliliters in American food, and I'm not sure what the criteria is in Europe. He changes his order to *cornetto* and coffee instead. I order an omelet made with egg whites and spinach, and drink water. No lemon wedge, as more than seventy percent of them carry microorganisms on the rind, as I inform Vasily.

He simply stares at me as I go on about food safety. "It is a wonder you eat anything. I am surprised you do not try to subside on vitamins alone."

"Actually, vitamins are not regulated by the FDA at all, and have shown that—"

Vasily holds up a hand. "Allow me to eat before you tell me more."

I shrug and polish my silverware on my cloth napkin for a good two minutes in an attempt to rub any germs away, and then tuck into my omelet.

"So why were you looking up bondage this morning?" he asks after eating a bite of his *cornetto*, which turned out to be a croissant, and sipping his coffee, which actually looks like a Starbucks latte.

I turn my plate in a clockwise motion to continue eating the food on the far side of my plate. "The purchaser of the Madonna was Emile Royer-Menard. He also frequents many sex clubs in the area."

He pauses and scrutinizes me. "I am not familiar with this name."

"That is because I deleted all traces of the transaction before we left Rio, so our tracks would be covered." I eat another hearty forkful of eggs. "You should eat more eggs. They're a very safe food because eggshells have a protective coating that prevents bacteria from entering the egg."

He waves that helpful information aside. "Tell me more about Royer-Menard."

So I tell him what I found out. He's a French expat, he's into fetish-play, and he is wealthy and likes to procure extremely rare items that then disappear without a trace. His bank account grows every year despite extreme purchases, so it's a safe bet that he's reselling items to purchasers that do not wish to be noticed. "It's likely he's procured your Madonna and resold it to another party off the record."

Vasily absorbs this in silence. There is no sound but that of his coffee cup being placed on the table. I eye it, wondering if he would be bothered if I put my mouth where his was. I'm growing very accustomed to his germs, and I like the thought of pressing my lips there and seeing what he tastes like this early in the morning—

He snaps his fingers in front of my face, and I realize I've been wandering in my thoughts. "Hm?" I ask.

"I am very upset at you, Karen. What other information have you been keeping from me?" His mouth is pulled down in a frown and I think I've made him angry.

I consider this for a moment. Have I kept anything else from him? "I masturbated vigorously last night prior to going to bed?"

He licks his lips. "While that is good information, I refer to the Madonna."

I shrug. "You know all of it now. If I find out more, I will share it. We're a team." At least we are, now. His murder of Aleksei to keep me safe has brought us together. We are united. "So I think we should go there tonight."

"Go where?"

"To the sex club. To find Royer-Menard."

He makes a noise in his throat, and I don't know if it's agreement or disbelief. "And what makes you think they will let us in?"

"We'll go in disguise. You can be my submissive."

CHAPTER **SEVENTEEN**

VASILY

The fetish-wear shop is doing nothing to quell my thickening cock, which has been half-ready since I observed her nude, hunched over her computer. My once-overriding distaste for sex has been replaced with a near-constant erection. I get hard from hearing her voice, watching her type, inhaling the lingering jasmine scent she leaves behind after showering. It is as if my body is making up for years of quiescence.

In my mind's eye, she is wearing leather boots, a collar, and looking fierce. Nothing else. Her heavy breasts would bounce with every movement and the heels of her boots would thrust her ass out. Bent over, I could use a long bar to separate her legs, opening her to my gaze and touch. With rope, I could bind her hands at her waist or raise them above her head, stretching her body out in one long, continuous line from the ceiling to the floor, allowing me to explore her body with no interference.

You can be my submissive.

Any other woman would expect me to protest to the idea of submission, but Naomi is not ordinary. To her, the suggestion is absolutely rational, because she prefers order and control.

The salesclerk ignores us. We are wearing garish tourist clothes. Likely she believes we have stumbled in by mistake.

Naomi observes the items and touches nothing, but her gaze keeps returning to a leather bustier. There is a collar and a corset connected in the back by a web of leather straps. I lift one away from the rack and hold it in front of us.

"Submission and dominance is not about the acts but about the mental state of the parties. A true submissive is one that enjoys pleasing others, who strives to fulfill her master's desires, who lives for her master's commands." I speak low so that only she can hear. "She would wear this and follow behind her master, and every inch of her body would quiver from his touch. As the eyes of envious revelers land above her exposed breasts, she would get wet in anticipation of showing them even more for the benefit of her master."

She shifts beside me, the fabric of her shirtdress making almost no sounds, but her desire is unmistakable in the lift of her chest, the quickening of her breath, and the hardening of her thick nipples. "Is that what you like?" she asks.

A discernible clink is heard when I place the hanger forcefully back onto the rack. "*Nyet.* I do not share, and I would not allow other wolves to slaver over what is mine."

"Then how do you know what doms and subs do?"

"Merely because it is not what I prefer in the bedroom does not mean I am blind. To many, this is the way their sexual appetites are appeased."

"How is yours appeased?"

"Naomi, if you do not want me to fuck you in the middle of this store, you will cease asking questions," I snap.

Surprise flares in her eyes. Surprise and perhaps . . . interest? Her gaze drops lower to see the proof of my arousal, and I harden, again, under her stare.

"So we won't go?" Disappointment lies heavy in her question.

"I did not say that. I want the Madonna, and if this is the only way to procure it, then I will go and play your pet, but do not mistake my acquiescence in this as a precursor to our bedroom activities."

"We will have bedroom activities?" She is flushed, a juicy plum ready for taking. My tongue aches to taste her, and my fingers curl with the need to touch her.

"Did you think that our business was finished in the plane?"

"You haven't touched me since and I thought you did not like to be touched but you don't have a problem with touching me. You could touch me again. Maybe you could use your penis. Your fingers were great but I feel like I could accommodate something larger."

"Like this?" I pull a dildo down from a shelf. It's long and curved on the end. Her eyes get huge.

"No, I meant . . ." And she struggles for the first time articulating what it is she wants. It is not shyness, I think, but ignorance. She does not have the experience to know what it is to ask for.

"You have suggested I be your submissive. Do you understand how that would work? Because it is not merely you providing instructions and me acquiescing to your bidding. You must control the environment in every way. You must be able to assess every reaction and be able to respond immediately. As a dominant your first instinct must always be to care for the submissive."

She stares at the dildo and then glances back to the collared bustier. "Would I have to wear that as your submissive?"

"No. There are many outfits. I think in a den of leather and chains, that the perfect outfit is not here."

Before we leave, I buy a mask and earplugs along with a dramatic, floor-length cape. Naomi eyes the purchases suspiciously and looks disappointed as we exit.

"Was there something you wish to purchase?"

"No, but I like things that come out of plastic bags. How long do you think that cape has hung in that store?"

"We can have it washed. *Via dei Condotti, numero 66, per piacere*," I tell the taxicab driver.

When we arrive, she protests and points up the Spanish Steps where our hotel, the Hassler, sits like a matron staring disapprovingly down upon her troublesome children. "Are we going back to the hotel because we're up on the hill?"

"Later," I say, pulling her out of the vehicle. She winces at the sound of the crowd, but as we turn down Via Bocca di Leone, the noise fades away and the furrow of her brow smooths out. At the end of the street, I usher her into Letto di Angeli, the bed of angels. It is nearly silent inside the small salon. I draw Naomi over to a small settee.

"*Buongiorno.*" A svelte saleswoman in a cream pencil skirt and silk blouse comes over to greet us.

"*Inglese, per piacere. Il mio fidanzata non parla l'italiano.*"

"What did you say?" Naomi whispers.

"That you do not speak Italian."

"*Allora*! We all speak English. I am Yvette. What can I do for you?"

"We are getting married, yes?" I cover Naomi's ringless hand with my own. "We are looking for a boudoir set. Tasteful yet revealing."

Yvette exclaims with disapproval. "Tsk. Do you not know these things should be a surprise?"

She tries to wave me away with an imperious hand but I know Naomi will not want to be left alone with these ladies who will pinch at her skin and flutter around her like anxious butterflies.

"*Nyet*. I approve all of these things as a man should. Yes?"

Yvette nods slowly and retreats to the back where she can gather her wares. Halfway through the mini fashion display, Naomi loses interest and pulls out her phone. I select several items and ask for modification of the robe.

"I would like all garments to be washed, dried, and delivered in a plastic, sealed bag. We are at the Hassler. I expect delivery by eight."

Naomi looks relieved.

Back at the hotel, I instruct Naomi to nap. I make several calls to find the right outer garment for Naomi. It is summer and tourist season and few stores are selling what I need, but a call to a private atelier nets me one at last. I arrange for it to be cleaned, wrapped in plastic, and delivered to the hotel. Afterward I send emails to my sister and check up on the *Bratva*, and it is then that I notice an alert that I have opened a new account with Islands National Trust. The amount is eye-opening. I check the *Bratva* accounts but there is no change; it is only mine that has been affected.

When Naomi wakes before dinner, I ask her about the account discrepancies.

"I put some of Hudson's money in a new account in your name. He's dead, you know. He won't use it. Do you think Daniel needs some funds? He doesn't work anymore. He used to be in the army but he must not be there anymore."

"No . . ." I pause, unsure of what I should tell her. "He was looking for you."

"Oh. I didn't realize that. How long?"

"Eighteen months."

Her eyes widen. "That long. That's . . . that's the entire time I was gone." Her lower lip trembles.

"He loves you, Naomi. It is what a brother does for his sister."

"Then I definitely need to send him some funds. But it's good he doesn't have to look for me, right? I should let him know that I'm okay."

I look at the phone and then consider Naomi's request. Daniel is too far away to pose a threat, so I nod.

She picks up the phone but does not immediately dial. Her hands press nervously against the metal housing. "What do I say to him?"

"That you desire to help me."

"I don't think he'll buy that."

"Are you worried he will try to come and take you away?"

She nods. "He's very protective and I know he must feel guilty because he had wanted me to get out and make friends. That's why I went to Cancun. I was kidnapped on spring break."

Daniel and I have so much in common. Instinctively I must have recognized this or I would not have relied on him to assist me in ridding the *Bratva* of Sergei Petrovich. Too bad I could not convince him to take out Elena, but he would not hurt a woman. Elena is no woman, though. She is a monster. And she will have her day of reckoning.

"Tell him that you want to repay those against whom you have transgressed and that is the way you can find peace for yourself."

Her troubled eyes turned to me. "How did you know I feel guilty about my work as the Emperor? I've never told you that."

"Because you are a kind person and because Aspies have feelings, too."

She smiles at the parroting back of my words.

"Go, tell your brother that you are safe and that you love him."

She rises with a tentative smile and leaves to make her call. When she returns, her step is lighter and her smile is more genuine. I watch her silently as she returns to her chair and begins to eat.

As she chews her scallop, I wonder if she notices how carefully I have selected her food. The seafood is grilled on both sides giving it a light brown, caramelized appearance. I have tried to order food that fits her dietary preferences without being noticeable. So browned food with green vegetables. And kiwis. There are few green fruits here. Muskmelon. Kiwi. Green apples. "You don't have as much as I thought you would," she admits.

It takes me a moment to catch the thread of our previous conversation. "I was *volk* before. We are merely expendable soldiers. I was paid only a little. The *Bratva* provides."

"Is that why you just have a cabin in the woods?"

"It is."

"You keep saying *volk*. It means wolf, right, but you're not a wolf."

"When I was a child, the wolves were predators in the forests. I thought I wanted to be a wolf because then I could protect my family and myself. When the Petrovichs bought me, they promised to make me into a fearsome wolf. But the *volk* is merely a pawn. The hand that holds the whip and the chain and the collar is the predator. So the *volk* is a tool, a poorly paid one."

"I think *volk* is cool. Wolves are awesome predators. I bet the right wolf could take down a weakling even if he has a whip and chain. I can't see anyone holding you down."

I shutter my eyes so she cannot see my shame. I wish I had always been strong and fearsome, but in the early days I was not. If I think hard enough I can still feel the sting of the metal-tipped leather against my back. I had to rely on the handouts of others. I had to take what they forced on me. But she is right. Someday I will eat the one that held the whip. And the victim will not be smiling in ecstasy like the Madonna in the painting. Thankfully Naomi requires no response but instead chatters on.

"Do you want the Madonna just so you can build a bigger house in the woods? Because I can give you the funds from Hudson's other accounts. He had plenty. You could have a really large house. Maybe a castle even."

"With a moat?" I ask; my dry laugh is not one of humor.

She nods.

"I seek the Madonna because it has power, Naomi. My people believe in this treasure. It will bring us together without more fighting and more killing. Once we are together, we can move forward and away from the krokodil, the insurrection, and the fear. This I believe."

"You're talking about superstition."

"Perhaps." I give a negligible shrug. "But belief is strong. Stronger than rationality. Fear, love, hope—all irrational emotions, but they sway people more fiercely than any fact-based argument."

A knock on the door sounds. It is the porter with our purchases.

"How come you don't tip? In America we tip everyone. Even the hairdressers. Especially the hairdressers."

"That is why all of Europe loves the American tourists as they tip and trip and photograph their way through all the matchless ruins and monuments." I smile. "It is time."

Naomi rises and I pull out her costume.

"It's very beautiful but I'm not sure it's very sexy. You should have gotten the leather thing at the fetish-wear shop. This isn't fetish wear. It looks very bridal." She scratches her head. "I don't think you know what you are doing."

"This is why I am the dominant and you are the submissive," I answer mildly.

Naomi disappears into the bathroom. Sadly, she will not need my help. The cream bustier with the inset cups with the delicate lace trim hooks up the front. The garter belt and panties should hold no challenge for her, either.

As I pull on my black suit, fastening my cufflinks and my belt, my mind drifts to the bathroom. She should be putting a foot up on the commode, rolling up the silk stockings and fastening the tops into the garter belt. Perhaps she smooths the fabric a few times, enjoying the luxurious threads under her palms before pulling on the other garments. She will brush her hair and then sweep a bit of mascara over her lashes and redden her lips with gloss. At the end, she will shrug on the gown that is now a robe. It ties under her generous bosom and hints at the delights below.

"Are you really sure about this?" she asks, appearing in the doorway looking exactly as the store's name promises. An angel in the bedroom.

"Come." I motion with one hand. She obeys, already walking stocking footed across the floor. I open my hand, and a choker of pearls hangs down. I wind my finger and she turns around and lifts her hair before I need to ask. The pearl necklace has six strands, and its extravagant size elevates her chin. I clip a long gold leash to the necklace and let it hang down the middle of her back. The red cape goes over the top to hide her garments.

"If this does not catch the eye of a man looking to acquire something unusual, nothing will," I say. I turn away before she can open her red lips because if she says anything . . . anything at all, I will throw her onto the cushions and fuck her blind.

CHAPTER **EIGHTEEN**

NAOMI

I'm a bit nervous as the cab drives through the winding streets of Rome. I want to fiddle with the pearls at my neck, but they make a clacking noise and it makes me edgy instead of comforting me. I have a cape covering my lingerie, but I still feel rather naked walking around in such an outfit.

Vasily, meanwhile, is wearing a black suit and looks formidable. Even his tousled blond hair is slicked impeccably back. He looks all business, which makes me even more nervous, until he puts a hand on my thigh. For some reason, that touch calms me and I'm fine with the rest of the car ride. Quiet, but fine.

Eventually, the car stops. I peer out the window, but the building looks unfamiliar. It's solid and dark, with no windows at the front. The door is thick, heavy, square wood with a big iron pull ring instead of a handle. Inside, bass thumps loudly enough that

I feel it in the car. I look at Vasily uncertainly. He knows I don't like loud noises.

As if he can predict my thoughts, he produces the earplugs. "Put these in before we go inside."

I take them from him and to my surprise, he grasps my hand before I can put them in. The look in his eyes is incredibly intense. "Karen," he says softly, and then leans in to speak to me. His breath is hot on my neck, and I get goose bumps as he starts to whisper. "You must be completely obedient to me inside. Do you understand?"

"I do," I tell him in an equally quiet voice.

"You are not to call me anything but 'master' once we are inside those doors. I will take the lead and you will obey. If this is to work, this is how it must be."

I nod.

To my surprise, he pulls out the soft black mask and pushes it into my hand. "You will wear this when we go in."

"Why?" I'm to go in blind?

"Have you ever been around horses?"

I shake my head. No one trusts me around large animals, sadly. I don't pay enough attention. But I like horses. They're beautiful and elegant.

"A thoroughbred may become a danger to others in unnerving situations. They are blindfolded so they cannot see the things that bother them. It calms them. It will calm you."

I like being compared to a thoroughbred. "All right. You won't let anyone touch me?"

"No hand will touch you but mine. No matter what I say. If another finger so much as grazes you, I will remove it from the offender's body. Do you understand?"

I blink rapidly. I suppose I do understand that. "I—"

"No hand but mine," he emphasizes. His free hand touches my chin, forces me to make eye contact with him. "Look at me." When I do, he repeats it again. "No hand but mine."

I nod against his fingers. No hand but his.

The look on his face changes, and I wonder if he's going to kiss me. But instead, he releases my hand. "Do you recall your safe word?"

"Dyspepsia."

"That's it." He chuckles. "Put those on and we shall go."

Everything in me is full of worry about going into a strange place, blindfolded and deafened, wearing only a cloak over lingerie. But then Vasily's big hand gives my knee another caress, and I realize that he's got me. He won't let anything happen to me.

I trust him. No hand but his. No germs but his.

So in the earplugs go, on goes the blindfold, and then Vasily opens the car door. It's not that I hear it being opened as much as the air changes on my skin, and then he takes my hand in his and pulls me forward. I ease slowly out of the car, and when I'm standing, his hand goes to the small of my back and he guides me.

It's like being in a cocoon. My senses are dulled—I can't see anything, can only hear the relentless thud of the bass inside the building, and my other senses strive to pick up the lack. I want to hold Vasily's hand, to feel the callus against my skin, but he is the leader, and I am the follower. I wait for gentle signals to tell me what he wants. A quick, flat touch of his hand on my arm tells me to wait. The gentle prod of his hand again at my back tells me to go forward.

Then, the air changes, grows warmer. The wind stops, and the muffled bass picks up. We must be inside. I lift my head a little, trying to sense things, but my cocoon lets nothing in.

We're inside for maybe a minute—time is difficult to tell this way—when Vasily's hand caresses my jaw. Through the blurred mumble of sound, I can barely pick up the tones of his speaking voice, but I can't make out what he's saying, just that he's talking. I lean into his touch, eager for instruction. I want to help. We're playing pretend tonight and he's got the fun part.

His fingers caress my jaw again, and then his hand slides down my throat and tugs at the knot of my cape. I feel the material give as the knot does, and then the entire thing slides to the floor. Goose bumps prickle my arms and legs as they are bared, and I wonder how many people are looking at me in my pearls and pale lingerie. I tremble at the thought, and then Vasily's hand glides down my arm.

And then I think of Vasily. Does he like the way I look? I preen a little, imagining him admiring my breasts, and thrust them out for him to appreciate. With small touches, he guides me closer to his side, and then he takes my hand and puts it to the gold collar at my throat, and then puts my fingers to the chain. It's attached to something, and I follow it down to find the end of the chain clasped in his big, warm hand. My own fingers wrap around his, a silent question. Can he lead me this way?

I lick my lips nervously, and he gives my hand a squeeze in affirmation. And we go into what must be a party.

I lose track of all time with my sight removed and sound dulled. Vasily is right to do so; I'm not nervous. There could be a thousand people an inch away from me, filthy with microorganisms, and I wouldn't care. He's the center of my world right now. I cling to his hand and walk when he walks, stop when he touches my arm and gestures that I stop. People talk around me, but their voices mix with the thrumming bass and don't register. We might have been at this party for five minutes or five hours; it's all the same to me.

The air here is warm and moist, and I find my skin is damp with sweat even though I've done nothing but walk and be led.

Maybe it's anticipation that is making me sweat. Because I feel, at this moment, as if we are building up to something exciting. I have no doubt that Vasily—the big, strong, capable hand that carries my chain—is carrying guns. Will he shoot people? Is he shooting them even now? I think about this and discard the idea. Surely if I can hear the bass and conversations, I'd hear shots going off. I picture him walking sedately through a party and wringing people's necks instead. The image is an amusing one and I smile to myself.

His fingers reach out and caress my mouth, grazing over it, as if he wants more of my smiles. But I want more of his touches. I don't even mind his germs. So I lick the fingers he brushes against my mouth and imagine his response in the silence.

Vasily gives my hand a squeeze and a tug on the chain, and then we are walking. It's a lot of walking. As we walk, the faint murmur of conversation disappears, and the music fades to a soothing thrum in the distance. Now I can hear more of Vasily's voice, and he's talking to someone else. Someone with a piercing laugh. I hear a woman's yelp and realize there are two someones nearby. The woman's startled noise makes me anxious, and I squeeze Vasily's hand again. Mine is sweating in his, and I'm sure I'm oozing germs onto him. He should be disgusted, but he doesn't pull away, only gives me a comforting little shake as if to say he's got me. I calm at that.

We seem to be going somewhere, though. The music fades even more and we continue to walk. Then, I feel the chain move again, and Vasily stops, his hand touching my arm. I stop, and to my surprise, his fingers brush my earlobes and he taps them.

I pull out the earplugs reluctantly, almost afraid of what I'll hear. But the music is a low throb many rooms away, and the air seems to echo here. It's cooler. And it's quiet.

"Is that better, Karen?" Vasily asks. His voice is different. His thick, liquid accent is gone, replaced by a flat tone. It's surprising to me but I don't show it. He's playing a part.

I lick my lips. "Yes, master." I remember my part, too.

"Good." He caresses my cheek and then gives it a pat.

"Your slave is quite lovely," the man with the high-pitched voice says. He's got a hint of a French accent. "Where did you say you got her again?"

"Brazil," Vasily says in that accent. "Best purchase I've made so far. Nice and obedient."

"How's her scream? She juice up when you hit her?"

That seems an odd question to ask. I ponder what this man means, but Vasily answers. "She's not a fan of pain . . . yet. I still have much training to do. We'll get there. Isn't that right, Karen?"

Whatever he says. Inwardly, I shrug at the odd conversation. "Yes, master."

"Well," says the other. "Come. Have a seat and we'll talk business. Cognac?"

"Thank you. Come, Karen," Not-Vasily says and tugs me forward with the chain. I hear fabric—maybe leather—flex and realize he's sitting in a chair.

"Go sit next to my chair, Bella," the other voice says, and I realize he must be talking to the other girl. "You can sit at my feet." She makes a whimpering sound that doesn't quite sound like agreement, but is silent otherwise.

Everyone is sitting down. This presents a new problem. Do I remain standing? Do I sit? Where would I sit? I picture a dirty wood floor. Or worse, an old carpet that's hiding thousands of dust mites. I whimper, unsure what to do.

I feel the chain move and Vasily stands. "Good Karen," he tells me, and his hand caresses my cheek. "You've remembered your training." I'm confused until he continues. "She can sit nowhere that is not mine. I am teaching her that I am the absolute in my world."

"You're a tough man, Dmitri," the other says, and I hear the sound of pouring liquid.

"Just firm," Not-Vasily says, and I hear the rustle of clothing, and then something brushes against my calves. "My jacket is on the floor, Karen. I permit you to sit there."

He knows I don't like germs—except his. I'm so grateful to Vasily for thinking of everything—for knowing how my mind works without me having to say a word—that I sit down and automatically cling to his leg, wrapping my arms around it.

His hand goes to my head and he strokes my hair, and I can't help but preen a bit. I'm doing well at this, aren't I?

"Isn't that a pretty sight?" the other man says. I hear footsteps approach. "Do you share?"

"Not yet," Not-Vasily says, the sound flat. "She's still in training."

"She for sale?"

"Not yet. You interested when she is?"

My arms tighten on Vasily's leg. I know this is a game but the words are still alarming.

"I am."

"I shall keep you in mind, then, Emile."

Emile. Ah. This is the purveyor. Vasily has somehow managed to get him alone into a room so they can talk business. He's a clever man. My hands stroke his leg and I want to touch him. I want to feel connection with him. I slide my fingers up his pant leg and feel his firm calf.

And I feel aroused by touching his skin. His heat, the feel of his fine leg hairs, the muscle that flexes under my touch, I love all of it. I'm not thinking about germs anymore, just of touching Vasily. And I caress and stroke his calf, lost in thought.

I wonder if I can make him orgasm from me touching his leg alone?

My fingers stroke along his skin in the small area I can touch. All the way up to his knee, then down to his ankle. He's so hot; the human body averages 98.6 degrees, but Vasily feels warmer. I pay attention to his silent signals as he talks to Emile, discussing world matters or American politics or something. Their voices are an uninteresting hum, and I'm more interested in the way Vasily twitches, just a bit, when my fingers skate over the back of his knee. My nipples are prickling and I can feel the flesh between my legs growing slick with arousal.

And I really, really want to do more. My hand goes to my breasts, then down to the waistband of my panties. I'm about to shove my hand in there to work myself over when I hear, "No, Karen," in a firm, Not-Vasily voice.

I stop. "Yes, master." But I'm frustrated and sexually hungry and I'm really into this game. Karen wants to keep touching her master. She wants his skin, his taste, his germs, the small shudders he tries to hide as she touches him.

A filthy, naughty idea strikes me and I bite my lip, then get on my knees and press my breasts against his leg. My hands go to his thigh and I realize vaguely that it's gone quiet in the room. I don't care. Vasily is my entire world at the moment, and I'm thinking about the way he touched me on the plane and made me come.

I want to make him come. The shameless thought is eating away at my brain.

"Karen?" Not-Vasily says in that oddly flat voice, all personality and sexy Vasily leached out of it. "What do you want?"

"I want to pleasure you, master." My breath is hitching with my own excitement. "Let me put my mouth on you."

There's a long pause. His hand strokes my hair ever so gently. "Is that so?"

I nod and rub my breast against him, like a cat wanting to be petted. My nipple scrapes along his pant leg, and I can feel the friction through my bra cup and I love it. A breathless little moan escapes me. "Please."

"I will permit it," he says after a moment.

Eagerly, I slide my hands up his thighs and search for his belt. It's there, and resting oh-so-close to it is the hard erection I'm excited to feel. The scent of Vasily is thick in my nostrils, the smell of soap and the musk of his skin, and my fingers glide along his penis before I undo the belt buckle and push it aside. I can't wait to get my mouth on him. I'm excited he's going to let me.

"She's eager," Emile comments as I tug at Vasily's boxers and release his cock to open air.

My hands wrap around his length and my mouth goes to the crown, hiding it from the gaze of the others. I feel Vasily's thighs tense under me, and that small motion tells me that I have his attention. A moment later, his hand returns to my hair, stroking it. "She is."

"And you don't share?" Emile asks again as my tongue licks at Vasily's cock. The crown of him is dripping with a thick, warm liquid that's slightly salty against my mouth. I should be revolted by this. I don't like other people's bodily fluids. But feeling those little shivers moving through Vasily that he's fighting so hard to hide? Those encourage me and I continue to lick him. The taste is strong but not unpleasant.

"No hand but mine," Not-Vasily says casually, but I hear the steel behind his words. "I did not come here to talk about my slave, though. I came to discuss art."

"Ah. Right." I hear someone slurp a drink. Then, the sound of another buckle. "Come, Bella. Learn from Karen. Take me in your mouth."

"Yes, master."

A pause. Then a grunt. "Good girl. So, Dmitri. Any period in particular catch your eye? Are you a fan of sculpture? Pottery? What sorts of things are you looking to acquire?"

"Paintings."

There is a hint of strain in his voice, just soft enough that I catch it. I nuzzle against his cock. It feels huge and hard in my hands, and throbbing with heat and life. I wonder if I can take all of him into my mouth, and I open my mouth wider and rub him along my tongue, sliding him toward the back of my throat. I moan when his hand presses lightly against the back of my head, encouraging me. Am I supposed to love this? Because I do. I know he's clean here—Vasily showers twice a day and he always smells of soap. Even now, my nose can pick out notes of the lavender-scented soap on his skin, and I suck harder, then swirl my tongue around the head of his cock. I have no guide but his hand on my hair, his thighs pressing against my breasts to tell me if I'm doing things right or not. I've never practiced fellating a man. It's not a skill I thought I needed to brush up on. But as I do this, I realize I want to learn the best way to proceed.

It's clear I need to research for our next time so I can improve things.

His hand tightens on my hair and I feel another little shudder move through him. God, I love that. I'm rubbing my breasts against his legs as I lick and suck at his cock, and I'm hopelessly turned on. I know there are two other people in the room—maybe more—but I don't care. Vasily's the only one in my blinder-covered bubble, and he's the only one I mean to please. Karen doesn't care if anyone else is watching. She only wants to please her master.

I have to admit, I'm enjoying pretending to be Karen.

The men are talking business again as I work my mouth on Vasily. He's able to hold a conversation with Emile and they discuss works of art. Emile has a Cézanne in residence if Vasily is interested. I nuzzle at a thick vein on the underside of Vasily's cock, and my fingers brush against the soft skin of his sac. The hair here is crisp, like on his legs, and for some reason, it makes me want to put my hand in my panties again. I know I'm impossibly wet; I can feel my flesh sliding against itself when I press my thighs together, but I don't want to be told no again.

So I concentrate on making Vasily come. I twirl my tongue around the head of his cock as he speaks, and I feel the deep notes of his voice in his skin. No, he tells Emile. He's not interested in Cézanne. He's looking for something more classical. More Renaissance. Does he have any pieces like that?

Emile asks if Dmitri has a favorite. The head of his cock butts against the back of my throat and I moan, because realizing how deep he is in my mouth is making me wet all over again. I release the suction on his cock and lick him for a bit, and he takes one of my curled hands and guides it, showing me how to stroke him.

I'm a fast learner, and soon I'm pumping him with one hand and sucking on the head of his cock with the other.

Dmitri is a fan of the masters, he tells Emile. Raphael. Da Vinci. Van Eyck. Caravaggio. Big names. He's willing to pay big for these, too.

Emile hasn't had one of those come through in a while, he says in an almost musing voice. A Caravaggio last spring but he sold it to a private collector. Someone in Venice.

Vasily's entire body tenses. I think something is wrong, but then he pushes on my head, hard, and his cock goes to the back of my throat. I eagerly take him and suck, wanting to please him, and something hot spurts against the back of my throat. He's so far in I can't taste anything. Fascinating! My throat works reflexively, and I'm swallowing his semen before I can even think to ask if I should.

He's entirely silent as this happens, but I feel the tremble in his thigh muscles that tells me that he's not unaffected. I'm rather pleased that I've made him come, and I lick him over and over, still pleased with myself. I wonder if I can get him to come again if I keep licking. I'm pretty sure I orgasmed more than once on the plane and maybe Vasily can, too—

"Enough, Karen," he tells me in a low voice. His fingers caress my cheek and then he begins to fasten his pants.

I resist the urge to pout, and slowly pull away from him, resuming my spot at his feet. I feel hollow between my legs, like I need something there. I'm aching and wet and unfulfilled, and for a moment, I feel sad and neglected. I lick my lips and taste him on my mouth, and then I lick them again to keep tasting him.

I'm still licking my mouth and thinking about making him

come again when his voice cuts through my thoughts. "So, Emile, I need the name of the man you sold the Caravaggio to."

"My clients are utterly confidential," he says. "I'm offended that you would ask."

"You may be offended," Vasily says. "And you should know that I am prepared to remove each finger from your hands, one at a time, until I get my answer." He pauses and then adds, "With pliers."

CHAPTER NINETEEN

VASILY

Emile laughs, believing my threat to be a poor attempt at humor, but at my continued impassive stare, his laughter turns to a small cough and then silence.

"Dmitri, this is not how I do business. My type of service relies on discretion, and obviously you know this or you wouldn't be here. What is it that you want? I can procure anything . . . and not just art." He dips his head toward Naomi, who's leaning softly against my leg.

"Tell me," I command. Naomi's hands are gripping my thigh. She needs attention and I'm anxious to conclude my business. Individuals like Emile are parasites. They do nothing but siphon money off unsavory deals. They take no risk and expect only reward. He does not even appreciate his good fortune.

As his pet works him with her mouth, he could not be more

unaffected. Ennui is set in the lines of his face, the ones that have had the temerity to creep in after his latest round of plastic surgery. The only real interest he showed was when Naomi's head moved in my lap even though it was doubtful he could see much.

"Boys, girls. Anything really. I'm starting to develop a nice stable of *bacha bazi*. I could get you a toy you'd both enjoy. I find the small, delicate ones nice although there are those who like the strapping young men. It's amusing, I suppose, to see them wear the female dress and kohl their eyes. It's not my preference." Emile's eyes light up with remembered pleasure.

So careless he is with his words as if he is untouchable. As if kidnapping and pederasty is so commonplace that he can speak of it as if it is no different from ordering espresso at the coffee bars.

"Chai boys? A woman for children, a boy for pleasure." I repeat the grotesque expression that the depraved use so casually. I'm careful, so very careful, that my voice does not display my rage at his mention of the chai boys.

The light in his eyes touches his lips as they curve upward in true delight. No wonder the girl in his lap does not move him. "Yes, exactly." He moves forward, brushing the girl to the side. "The rise of the Afghan lords and the fall of the Taliban have made it easier to commoditize the *bacha bazi* trade, and it is far more lucrative than girls. Everyone has girls these days, but trained pleasure boys are rare. So many of the villages still have their boys, and they are careless with them, realizing too late how valuable they are."

Carefully I inhale. I cannot kill Emile yet. Not until he divulges the identity of the buyer. But I can hurt him. Reaching down, past Naomi's plush, warm body, I pull out my knife.

"I'm sorry, Karen, but I need your mask for a moment." Standing to my full height, I order her into the chair. And then I drag Emile by the back out of his. "I do not like the way you conduct business."

"Wh-what are you doing?" he shrieks, and then cries out in pain as I slam him against the wall. The knife slides over the bone of his shoulder to pierce the layers of expensive fabric and pin him to the wall. His shock renders him immobile, and I use the moment of surprise to shove the mask inside his mouth. The girl begins to weep. I'm going to need to muffle her, as I know the sounds will bother Naomi. Ripping the tablecloth off the table, I use my other knife to tear the cloth into strips.

"I'm sorry, but we cannot have you making noise for us," I tell the girl as I wrap the gag around her mouth. Setting her out in the middle of the room where I can keep an eye on her, I bind her feet to her hands. It's a less restrictive pose than she's likely ever done for Emile. Satisfied, I look at Naomi. "Would you like to go to the restroom?"

She shakes her head. "No, why would I?"

Allora as the Italians would say. Turning back to Emile, I pull out my gun. The silver blade is wet with his blood and creating an ever-widening dark stain on his suit. Soon the blood will seep onto his shirt. For someone soft like Emile, the cut through tendon and bone must seem excruciating. He can't stop moaning around the fabric.

"Enough," I say. Raising the gun, I shoot the fleshy part of his thigh. The gun's suppressor muffles the sound, but we all hear the bullet making contact with his flesh as well as his high-pitched keening that escapes even the gag I've stuffed in his mouth.

"I will continue to shoot you in various places until you tell me what I want. I will shoot your other thigh and your kneecaps.

I will shoot your penis and your balls along with your eyes. This gun has twelve more bullets. How many more would you like in your body before I release you?"

He is crying now. Snot and spit are bubbling around his face in a disgusting fashion. While I am not germophobic or mysophobic as Naomi would say, even I find his appearance offputting. A glance at Naomi reveals that she is revolted by this.

"I might have been able to find the buyer," she said with a frown. "But that other guy's records aren't kept on a computer. He must have them written down. If they were digitized, I'd have found them."

"It is a good reason to go paperless, Emile. You would not have ever met Karen and me, and this unhappy little tête-à-tête would not need to have occurred. Now, you fucking pederast, I want to know who has my Caravaggio." I slap him hard to dislodge the spit-soaked mask, and then push the rest of it out with the barrel of my suppressor. He pisses his pants as the gun barrel enters his mouth.

"This is really disgusting," Naomi says. "Like the most disgusting thing ever. Can you bleach the gun? Also the bottom of your shoes? I think those soles are leather and it will soak up his urine. You should throw those away, Vasily." She claps her hands over her mouth realizing she has called me by my true name.

Emile closes his eyes as if accepting his demise. He will not leave here alive. "You have two options. You die a slow and painful death." I pull out a syringe. "This is curare. It leaves you paralyzed. I will shoot you in the gut and then inject you with the drug. It will take hours for you to bleed out and all the while you will not be able to call out for assistance. It is not unlike what you use on the boys you steal and sell. Instead of curare, you use fear, possibly punishment, to keep them silent and subservient. They have no voice. You have taken it. And they bleed to death internally from the heart and soul wound. So your true death should be in this fashion. Only you do not suffer years of torment as they. Only hours. Even in death you get a better bargain. But if you tell me the name of the buyer, then I will shoot you between the eyes and the suffering will be over. You can then face judgment from the higher powers. What will it be?"

"It is in Venice," he cries. "I know not the identity of the buyer. There was another intermediary. His name is Marco Cassano. He owns a mask shop along the Dorsoduro. Please, there must be something you want that I can give you. You do not know all of the information I hold or all the things I can procure for you. I am skilled. I promise. I will help you find the owner. I will. I know Marco very well. You cannot get to him without an introduction. I can provide that."

"I do not want the help of a rapist of boys. Cover your ears, Naomi." I shoot him then. A bullet right between the eyes. It does not feel satisfactory at all, so I shoot him again in the penis, wishing I had done that first. Riffling through his pockets, I find his wallet and a small leather-bound book. Inside there are transaction records, coded with the use of initials. No doubt Naomi could crack the code from the time it takes us to leave this place until we return to the Hassler. Turning back to the young girl, I unbind her.

"Remove your clothes," I instruct. Turning to Naomi, I say, "Take off the robe, shoes, and pearls. You will need to exchange with her. Put my jacket on; there are slip-ons for you in the pocket."

She does so without protest. Anything that can touch her skin is from my body or new. I'm beginning to know her quirks, and it is easy enough to accommodate them. After all, where will I find another who will not flinch when I torture and then kill another in front of her? I did not joke earlier when I said she was the woman for me. I cannot tear my eyes away as she pulls off the diaphanous robe, leaving her standing there with the boned corset forming a tiny waist and pushing her lush breasts high on her chest. She looks like a very naughty bride.

My blood is burning again, but it is not from anger or rage, but adrenaline and thick, hot desire. Some would label me as sick for being aroused after killing a man, but I know Naomi would not. She would understand that the hormones released in my body would spike and fuel a passionate response.

I may not be able to trust her, but I want her. I may even need her.

"Come," I say thickly, holding out my hand. "We must go."

"Are we still in danger?"

"No, *we* are not, but you are."

Her eyes widen and someone, maybe her or maybe the girl, sucks in her breath. The girl shrugs on Naomi's expensive things. I gesture for her to rise and come to me so I can fasten the pearls. She looks nothing like Naomi, but in the dark light and the smoky environs of the club, only the clothes will be remembered. The clothes and the pearls. "Take what you want of his. There are nearly two thousand euros in his wallet. All is yours but remember, if there is a whisper of this night that seeps out into the wind, I will know it is from you and I will hunt you down and make a night with Emile seem like a paradise. Do you understand me?"

She nods. Holding my hand out for Naomi, I dip my head. "Then go and enjoy your freedom."

Naomi tucks her hand in mine, and we exit out of the room and then wind our way through the club, up the stairs, and onto the street. The scene we leave replays in my mind. Naomi's actions and my welcoming of her touch puzzle me. I cannot decipher my own feelings, but Naomi has no compunction sharing hers if asked.

"Why is it that you touched me in the club?"

"I wanted to," she says simply. "Didn't you like it?"

Like it? Such an American word. Russians would say it was pleasant, but her mouth on my cock was more than merely pleasing, it was . . . exhilarating. I set it aside for now, unwilling to examine the event further, for it evokes strange emotions inside.

"We will walk for a while, and then I will find a cab and we will return to the hotel," I tell her. She keeps her hand tucked in mine as we maneuver down the short cobblestone alleyways, skirting the main roads as we move north toward the Hassler. The air cools my body and eases the fierce ache in my loins.

"What is a chai boy? Your leg stiffened when he mentioned it."

I stiffen now. "It is not uncommon in some central and southern Asian countries, although the practice has spread beyond those regions, to take young boys—very young boys—and train them in the arts of . . . sexual servitude. They are stripped of their masculinity. Some are made to dress in girls' clothing. They are like dolls to be dressed up and used according to the whims of their owners. They are called chai boys or tea boys. Sometimes dancing boys."

"Always boys, though?" she asks.

"Yes. Always boys."

"What was that about the Taliban? What did they have to do with it?"

"Was there no sex trade at the Emperor's Palace?" She seems

surprisingly naïve about these matters—the secretive and unsavory nature seemed ideally suited for the deep web marketplace she developed and ran at the behest of her now-dead captor Hudson.

"No, I wouldn't do it. I'd delete those requests and ban the accounts. I never told Hudson and he didn't notice because all of the other money we were making."

I nod, thinking of her days spent in the basement of Hudson's, trying to protect who she could with simple strikes of her fingers against the keys. She was far more brave than she realizes or can even admit. "The Taliban frowned on the practice of pedophilia. They were many things, but apparently rapists of boys was not one of them."

"That's pretty awful. I've never heard of anything like that."

"There are many awful things in the world, Naomi. But people with money and power can protect their own. That is what I seek. To prevent the many awful things in this world from touching the people I care about."

CHAPTER **TWENTY**

NAOMI

We return to the hotel in silence. Vasily is not talking, and I'm rather sleepy. It was exhausting having to leave the club without my earplugs and blindfold. The entire situation rattled my brain until it was only Vasily's tightly clenched hand on my shoulder that kept me from spiraling.

Actually, I probably spiral a little anyhow. I can with Vasily controlling things. He makes the strange situation safe for me, so I can sink into my mind and relax. At some point in the car, I lose track of things and retreat to my safe "Itsy Bitsy Spider" song. When I blink back to reality, I realize it's four a.m. and I'm in bed. Someone has taken off my shoes and tucked me under the covers. I'm still clothed, so I know I didn't do it myself. I never sleep with clothes on.

It constantly surprises me how kind Vasily is to me. I know

he's an assassin and I'm just his bizarre hacker partner in crime, but he is . . . different. More than a friend. In fact, if we weren't in the situation we were in, I'd call him my best friend. No one else ever takes care to make sure that I'm comfortable like he does. It's small things that tell me he's thinking of me and my quirks even when I'm not in my own head. No one, not even my brother Daniel, is so attuned to my needs.

Around Vasily I don't feel like a freak or a weirdo. He makes my idiosyncrasies seem normal instead of strange. And I'm filled with a weird sort of affection for this man . . . affection and fascination.

I wonder where he is right now.

I'm thirsty, so I get up out of bed. My laptop is open, and I'm unable to resist a computer screen, and so I sit, yawning, and begin to do maintenance. I check my sites, handle incoming correspondence, pick through my accounts to see how my script is working, shut down any hacks that have gone over the allowed time. Small, minute, daily things that settle my brain. I set up a script to send money to Daniel every other day at random times. Only a little here and there, dribbling into his account so he won't get suspicious. My brother is very lax with his bank account; I'm pretty sure he only checks it once a month just to make sure he has money in there. It's a good thing I figured out his password years ago so I can manage things for him. I like control.

I set the computer to do a few search strings on past history regarding Marco Cassano and Dorsoduro. I also set the query to look up random spellings of those names, removing or adding an *S* in case of mistyping. I also search for dollar signs in places of *S* and zeros for *O*, since it's another way black hats try to stay under the radar and mask information. I yawn and smile at the computer in satisfaction as the script begins to chug away, picking through millions of bits of information.

There's a sound, almost like a thump in the living room of the hotel suite. I pause and head out to check on it, since I'm thirsty anyhow and want a drink.

When I open the door to the suite, I see the back of Vasily's head. He is seated in one of the overstuffed leather chairs, and as I approach I see he has a glass of clear liquid in one hand, and his gun resting on his knee. He stares into space, not even watching TV or checking his phone.

I hesitate. I don't want to disturb him if he's meditating. But while I pause, he flicks a hand at me, indicating that I can come forward.

I do, and move to the side of his chair. It's curious that he's awake. "The human body requires seven to nine hours of sleep a night. Sleep deprivation can cause memory problems and depression." I peer at him. He doesn't look happy, but I have a hard time telling that sort of thing anyhow. "Are you depressed, Vasily?"

One side of his mouth turns up in what should be a smile, but looks about as false as my own forced smiles do. Sometimes I wonder if Vasily is an Aspie like me, but just hides it better. He seems to be as uncomfortable with things as I am.

I remain where I am, unsure of his mood. Eventually, he looks over at me and as he does, his gaze goes up and down my body. He takes another long swig of his drink, then says, "Someday, Naomi, we are going to have to talk about appropriate clothing." His Russian accent has returned, and it's thick and warm like a blanket.

I look down at my clothing; I'm still in the corset and panties. "If you didn't want me in them, you should have taken me out of them." Of course, picturing him undressing me brings a flash of memories from the club, mostly the scent and feel of him in my mouth. "I'm thirsty," I announce.

"Grab a drink. Join me."

I rub my arms, looking at the glasses set on the bar in the room. They march in a row, lip down, across a paper placeholder. I'm sure they're supposed to be clean but they've been in the open air for who knows how long, and I think of all the hotel documentaries I have seen in regards to cleanliness, and I'm unsettled. My OCD always gets worse when I'm out of my comfort zone, and I am right now. I fight the urge to take the glasses to the sink and wash them; there is no dish soap, no towels, no drying rack. I lick my lips and think, then move to Vasily and take the glass from his hand. I carefully turn it to where he drank, and put my lips there.

He watches me as I drink. It's more of that awful vodka, but it's the only drink available, and so I take it. When I lick my lips, he says, "Why do you do this?"

I frown. "My lips are dry."

"*Nyet*. It is not what I meant." He takes the glass from my hand, his fingers brushing my own, and turns the glass, then touches his tongue to where my lips had been moments ago. "You put your mouth where I put mine. Always. Why is this?"

"I am not certain of the cleanliness of the glassware, but I am already familiar with your germs. If you had a communicable disease, I would have already caught it, so it stands that you are for the most part, safer to drink from than the rest of the lip of the glass."

He snorts and looks at it musingly. "It is never a compliment with you, is it, Naomi? You always tell the truth."

I frown. Did he want compliments? He'd asked me a question and I'd answered. "I . . . don't understand."

He waves a hand. "Ignore me. I am maudlin when I get in a foul mood. I suppose I was hoping to hear that you put your mouth there because you enjoy my touch."

I tilt my head, considering this. "I do enjoy your touch. But that wasn't really what you asked."

Vasily looks up at me for a long moment, and then his gaze goes to my breasts, still plumped from the grip of the corset. To my surprise, he sets the gun on a nearby table and slides a hand around my waist. Then, he drags me into his lap. My thighs are cradled crosswise against his, and my breasts are practically pressed against his face. The chair is not large enough for the two of us to sit comfortably, but I don't think that was what Vasily had in mind anyhow. The look on his face is strange, and I wish I could read him better.

"Are you comfortable?" I ask, shifting on his lap.

"No," he says in a low voice. "I ache. But I shall control it. I do not wish to frighten you." His big hand grips my bare thigh, pressing my body against him.

Vasily's not making any sense tonight. I study him, his face so close to my breasts, and he seems drawn and unhappy. I'm not good at recognizing most facial expressions, but I know when the corners of someone's mouth turn down, it means they want comforting. I'm very bad at this sort of thing, though. I'm not good with emotions, at all. I bite back the urge to spout facts about muscles and frowns, because I want to do more than just distract Vasily.

I want to help him. I want to help him because I like him, and he is thoughtful and kind despite his fierceness. I try to think of what Daniel would do. I picture my brother, and, after a moment's consideration, I pat Vasily's shoulder awkwardly. "Do you need to talk?"

He looks up at me. "Talk?"

Perhaps I've misinterpreted. I'm so bad at this. But I want to be better at it to help him. Seeing him unhappy makes me distressed. I continue to pat his shoulder, feeling out of place about the whole thing. "It's something Daniel always says to me. I thought it might be appropriate here. Did I guess wrong?"

Vasily is quiet for a long moment. Then, he says, "I suppose we should discuss what happened in the room tonight."

Should we? I consider this, and think about what happened tonight in the room. My focus automatically goes to Vasily's lap and my ministrations there. "If you want to talk about it, sure. I enjoyed myself. Quite a bit, really. It was my first attempt at fellatio and I wasn't sure it was something I'd be interested in, but I found I was rather aroused in the moment and I wanted to see your reactions. It was something Karen would do. And I really enjoyed it. I am sad you did not, though—"

"*Nyet*, Naomi," he says, and his voice is soft. "It is not that I did not enjoy it. I enjoyed it. I was referring to Emile."

I wrinkle my brow. "But I didn't want to put my mouth on Emile. Just you—"

"I mean that I killed him. In front of you." He tilts his head, regarding me. "I threatened him, and I shot him. Several times."

"So you did." I shrug. "I didn't know him and he was standing in our way. I'm not sorry."

"And yet you are still not scared?" His hand slowly caresses my arm, as if he's now allowing himself to touch me.

I think of his ability to flip back and forth like a switch. One moment he was shoving the gun in Emile's crotch and shooting his balls, his expression that of a statue. In the next, he was looking at me and staring at me so hard that I'd thought he wants to kiss me right now. I supposed the dichotomy should have bothered me more, but I'm used to people that are wired differently, being one myself. I know Daniel has killed people. I don't think any less of him for it, or any more of him for it. I don't know those people, so I don't care about them. It sounds harsh, but it's true. "I am not scared of you," I tell him. "Do you want me to be?"

"*Nyet*," he says, and his voice is husky. His hand caresses my shoulder, then his fingers trail across my collarbones. Little shivers move over my skin in response to his touch. "Of all the things I wish for you to feel, Naomi, it is not hate." His fingertips skim the cleavage bared by my corset. "Yet I do not think you comprehend what it means when I say I am wolf. Perhaps I should open your eyes."

"You kill bad guys," I tell him, pressing forward so his fingers can tease my nipples. They're so close to where he's touching. If he just moves them down a bit, he can touch them, and I'm getting wet with anticipation at the thought. "You washed your hands, didn't you?"

He chuckles. "You say such things as if they are foreplay. Yes, my hands are clean, Naomi. Do not change the subject. Do you understand what it means for me to be *volk*?"

"You kill for the *Bratva*," I say, not sure where this is going. I study his face, but I see features—his big, strong nose, his square jaw, his firm mouth pulled into a hard line. I don't see expressions. I desperately wish I did, because I can't interpret what he's thinking right now.

"I am the *Bratva*'s wolf. I let nothing stand in my way. Do you understand this?"

"Say it plainly, Vasily," I say, a bit grumpy. I'm ready for him to reach deeper into my bodice instead of quizzing me. "You know I can't read emotions and now you're just irritating me."

"I mean that no matter what is asked, the *Bratva* comes first. It must always come first. This is what being *volk* means." His fingers move up instead of down into my bodice—I stifle a protesting whimper—and then he caresses my throat with his big hand. "If they ask me to kill, I do it. No matter who or what it is. The *Bratva* comes first. Do you understand this?"

His hand caresses my throat, but the wheels in my brain are spinning and the caress takes a sinister turn. He wants me to think about what he means. No matter who or what it is. There aren't many in this world I care about—being Aspie has turned off that part of my brain—but there are some I love fiercely and would die for.

Like my brother, Daniel. Like my parents.

There is a fierce hurt in my heart, and I pull away from Vasily's hands. "You would kill Daniel?"

"If he stood in my way."

I leap off of his lap as if scorched. "What?"

He tilts his head as if nodding to himself. "So now you see. I am *volk*, and it is not always convenient. You do not care if I kill those who are strangers. You will kiss and cuddle me as long as I am *volk* on chain, yes? What if I must kill those who are not? Who stand in my way?"

I stare at him as if seeing a stranger. I see the gun on the table, the glass of vodka in his hand. His shirt is rumpled, but I don't reach forward to smooth his collar. For the first time, he looks . . . menacing.

I don't know what to do. What to think. This is a man who

demands that people clean my purchases and wrap them so I won't be troubled by germs. This is a man who holds me tenderly and dyes my hair so I won't have to touch the chemicals. This is a man who has memorized things that trigger me and keeps me safe from them.

I thought we were a team. I thought he liked me. Not just as Naomi, but . . . like men like women. I enjoyed fellating him in the club. I wanted to do more to him.

And all this time he has been plotting to kill my brother? My parents if they stood in his way? It hurts to think about. "What about me? What if I stood in your way?"

"Ah, that is an interesting question."

"That's not an answer." This is unnerving. "You're worrying me."

"You should be worried, Naomi," he says, swirling the ice in his glass before raising it to his mouth again. Same spot we have both drank from. "I think tonight at the club has made me realize you are not afraid of me. And perhaps you should be."

Maybe I should after all. I stare at him and then retreat to my room, locking the door behind me. I remove my clothes and crawl into bed to sleep, but I'm not tired. I keep seeing mental images of Vasily with the gun. Shooting Mom. Shooting Dad. Shooting Daniel.

I feel sick to my stomach. How can I want someone so much and know they would hurt those I love? How can he be so tender to me one moment and so brutal the next?

CHAPTER **TWENTY-ONE**

VASILY

I should comfort her. Place a hand on her shoulder and soothe her tears, but it's better that she is afraid. Ignoring the tightness in my chest, I pack our few belongings. I do not care that she fears me. I do not care that she is weeping. I do not care that I can still feel her wet mouth covering my hard cock.

I am Vasily Petrovich. I have no feelings.

And I have no excuse like Naomi. I have no feelings because feelings are an impediment to success. If I felt, then I would drown in self-loathing, disgust, and hatred. I would still be that little boy, trying to protect his sister with a fork against the vile beast who begat us. Or the older boy who gave up his body so that his sister could remain innocent. Or the young man who killed and destroyed so that he would not be victimized again.

If I had feelings, I would fly to Moscow, go to the apartment of

Elena Petrovich, and blow a hole in her perfectly made-up face. But feelings don't change the past and they won't change the future.

I do not care.

Not at all.

The weeping.

The fear.

The hate she now stokes in her belly.

None of it matters.

There is only one thing that I seek, and that is power. With power, my enemies will be crushed, and the heel of my boot will grind down on the neck of any who seek to oppose me and mine. I can offer Naomi physical gratification, protection, and maybe even peace.

But I won't give her comfort, affection, or . . . love. Those are for the weak. And even if I wanted to, I don't know how.

My body may burn for her in a way as strong as my desire to kill Elena smolders inside of me. But a warrior's life is one of abstinence and delayed gratification.

It does not matter that I want to fuck Naomi, that I desire to slake my weak body at the fountain of her bountiful one. But as much as I try to shut Naomi out of my mind, visions of her nude body lit by the computer screen or her in the lingerie and filmy robe appear each time I close my eyes. My cock can still feel her wet mouth sucking on its hard length. She is generous and brave and I am none of those things. Even if I could touch her, I do not deserve to do so.

Resolutely I turn to the feeble nightlife stumbling around the Spanish Steps. From my seventh-floor balcony, I could easily pick the tourists off, one by simpleminded one. Despite the earliness of the hour, the street vendors are still hawking their five-euro roses and cheap toys. One at the top of the steps near the hotel, the vendor is repeatedly throwing his glow-in-the-dark gel ball in the air. I pull out my rifle and scope and take aim.

He throws it up and it spirals in the air for a count of five before it descends. He tosses it again. I count off, breathe, and pull the trigger. The moment the ball and the bullet impact, time slows. The neon liquid inside the gel ball explodes, like paint spatters onto a black canvas. At the base of the lamppost, the vendor's head is tilted back and his jaw is dropped.

And then time resumes. The ball falls. Drunk partiers cry out in fear and stumble down the steps. Other vendors start packing up, but the gel-ball male simply stares up in the sky wondering where his toy has gone. The ether has it now.

The position of the moon in the sky alerts me to the time. The forger will be open for business. In the bedroom, Naomi is still slumbering. The lushness of her body is evident even under the linen sheets, cotton blanks, and comforter.

To look and not touch is tormenting. My body tightens as I imagine ripping the covers off of her and diving between her legs. Our mouths would mate fiercely as I thrust into her slick channel, relieving the growing tension between us.

I would not be gentle—not that first time—but I would see that she came. I know many tricks. How to twist my hips to strike the spongy bit of extra-sensitive flesh. The right position so that my pelvic bone rubs against her clit. The precise point between too hard and too soft when my teeth are scraping against her tits. I haven't had to employ these tricks in some time and never really for pure pleasure.

But I would like to see how Naomi would respond, how she would catalog each effort and measure each response.

It takes more effort than I care to acknowledge to wrench myself away.

Below me the taxi appears.

"It is time to go, Naomi," I call.

She stumbles out of the bedroom, dressed in a gown of pale peach. The silky material clings to her peaks and creates enticing shadows in her valleys. Her hair is tousled and the red lipstick she'd applied for the club is smeared. She looks like she was fucked hard and enjoyed it. My cock thickens in response to the sight. Perhaps I should have shot myself after I finished Emile.

I toss her a long jacket. She can change on the train.

"Let's go," I say. My tone is shorter, more terse than ordinary, but gods in heaven, what is a man to do when presented with that kind of temptation?

She shrugs on the trench coat while I dismantle my rifle and pack it away. I want to avoid looking at her, but I cannot. Her stocking-covered legs beneath the knee-length trench hint at what I know is beneath. She looks doubly provocative. More enticing than the vestal virgins probably appeared to the invading barbarians.

In the lobby as we check out, I strain not to pummel the slack-jawed clerk who stares at her with lust in his eyes.

"We need a taxi," I bark. When he does not take his gaze from her, I bark, "Taxi for Termini Stazione. Now!"

My sharp command has him nodding and doing my bidding, but not without one last glance at Naomi. I should pull out my gun and shoot him.

Naomi still blinks owl eyed at me as if not fully awake. "Where are we going?"

Part of me wants to reveal nothing to her. No, that is not correct. Part of me wants to reveal all to her. To place my head in her soft lap and shudder out all my concerns as she pets me like a domesticated wolf. So I give her only the smallest of details. "Firenze."

"Firenze?"

"Florence," I translate.

She contemplates this for a moment, and then her gears engage. I can almost see it happening out of the corner of my eye, because as much as I don't want to gape, I find I cannot look away.

"That's where the statue of David is. I'd like to see that. Oh and the Uffizi gallery would be nice. There's Botticelli's *Birth of Venus*. Have you seen it? Can we go to the leaning Tower of Pisa? I'd like to study that up close to see how exactly it's still upright."

"Those places are crowded. Many people."

"Oh . . . I guess, maybe it would be okay. I could try the ear-plugs again."

I rub a hand down my face. "I am sorry, Naomi. I am anxious to be on our way and that is why I am short with you. Perhaps another time we will do these things, but not this trip."

"Oh of course. I get it."

Her gracious acceptance of my surliness makes me feel even worse, and I find I cannot speak as we ride the taxi to the train station.

Dawn light is peeking through the clouds, casting a rosy glow over the landscape. Even the squat ugly Termini station looks romantic in this light. Throwing the driver money, I pull Naomi out of the vehicle and then grab our bags. I'd chosen the earliest train so as to avoid most of the crowds. The seats I have reserved are in the silent section of the business-class *carrozze*.

I stow our two bags in the seats across from the bolted table and gesture for Naomi to sit. She climbs in without a word and stares out the window. Her lips are moving but I can't make out her words. Throwing my body down into the seat beside her, I slide the compartment door shut. It's like a glass-enclosed tomb now. Silent and oppressive.

Why do I push her away when she has been nothing but accepting of me, my bloody violent ways, and my own idiosyncrasies? She has had opportunity to betray me. Her previous lies *were* out of self-protection.

There's a shift inside me. I no longer want this distance between us, but since I am the one that placed it there, I must remove it.

"Do you want to change?" I ask.

She does not respond.

"Naomi?"

Again she ignores me. She's added a slight rocking motion to her repetitious, soundless words. The train fills slowly, almost agonizingly slow. Tapping my fingers on the table, I stare at the back of her head where the hair is tangled. She can't like that. Naomi is a person of order and precision. That she has not tried to straighten her hair is worrying. Reaching into her bag, I pull out a brush.

"This is a high-speed train. It will take only slightly more than an hour and we will be in Firenze." I pull the brush through slowly, carefully ensuring that the brush does not tug on her roots. Years of brushing someone else's hair has taught me things. I tamp down those memories. Slowly I brush one small section and then another, almost separating each strand individually. "Firenze is an interesting city. It's landlocked, having no access to any major ports. Despite this, the Arno River has wreaked devastation upon the land. In the sixties, the river flooded and knocked down Ghiberti's baptistery doors and ruined countless other precious artifacts. There are markers all over the city noting the flood levels. They are higher than your head, Naomi." Her rocking has stopped and part of the rigidity in her frame has melted, but she still holds herself apart. The tangles are almost gone, but I keep brushing, smoothing her hair into a silk curtain of chestnut and bronze.

"The baptistery doors are outside. In the early morning hours there are few people about. The Cimetière de San Miniato al Monte is open air as well. There would be no crowds there. Inside the Santa Maria del Fiore is an entrance to Santa Reparata. It is the original cathedral, and the Santa Maria is built on top of it. There would be no one down there. It is not Pisa or the *Birth of Venus*, but it is part of the heart of Firenze."

"Will you take me?" she says quietly.

"*Da*," I answer hoarsely. Her supplication is a piercing arrow. I prefer my Naomi to be mouthy and outspoken. "I will, but first, we must go to Guillaume. He is familiar with the scene in Florence and will be able to provide us entrée."

"What type of man is he?"

I smile ruefully, because it is a perfectly worded question. Not who is he, but what kind of man he is "He is a collector of things. Not of the Madonna, though. He would not be interested in a religious triptych. Rather he likes profane and unusual things. A bull's penis used by a holy man in Persia to relieve virgins of their hymens the night of their weddings, for example."

At this, Naomi turns, bright eyed. Her interest is piqued and she cannot resist asking me questions. "How is it not desiccated? Right after death, it would start to atrophy and decay. Is it some sort of mummification? Do you think he would show it to me? What else does he have? I once tried to mummify a frog at school. We were supposed to dissect it but I thought it would be interesting to mummify it first and then dissect it to compare and contrast the aging of the organs, but my teacher wouldn't allow it. He felt that would be an improper use of the frog. But the frog was already dead so it isn't like it would have feelings. It seemed like an entirely appropriate use of the specimen."

"The penis is likely carved out of ivory but I agree. The frog was already dead," I say, amused by the story. Naomi as a student must have been a terror. Smarter than her teachers, no doubt they were ill equipped to handle her questions and thirst for knowledge. "Your parents? What did they say?"

"Oh they moved me out of the school then and put me in a different one, designed for people like me."

"Other Asperger's sufferers?"

"No. You know . . . weirdos."

"You are not weird, Naomi," I respond sharply.

She shrugs. "Whatever. The school was good. We all learned at our own pace, some advancing faster than others. Once you reached a certain level, though, they made you take university classes. One girl told me that those classes were even worse because the professors aren't interested in being challenged and you simply have to regurgitate what they say in lectures during examinations. I stayed in my little Montessori school for as long as possible until they finally realized I wasn't actually doing anything."

"How did you find the university?"

Another shrug. "The same. I was able to do a few independent studies such as the one I did on the Selfish Gene theory and whether it is still applicable given the new understanding of gene regulation—how genes turn themselves on and off. Dawkins coined the Selfish Gene in 1976 building on the late-eighteen-hundreds work by Mendel on gene theory."

At my blank stare, she explains. "Dawkins said that a gene replicates if it is necessary for survival or adaptability and the other genes that are unnecessary die out but new understanding of how genes function are giving rise to new hypotheses. Of course, there's no answer yet, but because there isn't an answer I didn't have to give someone else's. I could make up my own. That was fun."

A knock on the glass door interrupts our discussion. "*Tè o caffè?*"

"*Caffè*. You, Naomi?"

"Orange juice if it's bottled."

"*Succo d'arancia*," I tell the hostess. She pours the glasses and provides us with napkins, a moist towel, and our drinks.

"*Dolce o salato?*" She holds up a bag of cookies and a bag of pretzels.

"Do you wish sweet or savory?" I ask Naomi.

"Savory."

"*Due salato*." I hold up two fingers.

"What is this?" Naomi picks up the slim plastic package with the train's name on the packaging and the words *Salvietta Rinfrescante*.

"It is a cleaning towel. You can wipe your . . . hands."

Naomi already has it open and is wiping her face, neck, and hands. She then proceeds to wipe the table. With horror, she holds it up to me. The Trenitalia train is fast but perhaps not as clean as it could be. Wordlessly I hand her my towel. She rips it open and feverishly begins to wipe.

"I need another one," she pants. Rising, I pull open the door to summon the hostess back, when a black-suited man wearing thin black gloves turns and pulls out a pistol.

"I need another towel," Naomi cries behind me.

"My companion needs another *salvietta rinfrescante*," I say to the pockmarked, tanned face. His lip curls and he raises his gun to my forehead. My two hands fly up on either side of the barrel. In one motion I step toward him, pushing his gun hand up. The action surprises him and he stumbles backward. I thrust the gun into his throat with a punch, flip it to my other hand, and shoot the other black-suited man running down the aisle.

"Naomi, grab our bags," I yell, facing Naomi, one hand stretched down toward the front of the car. My foot is on the throat of the first attacker.

I sense a shift in the air behind me and drop to my knees, rolling over and then up. With one knee up and the other leg bent back, I sight and then shoot. The man stumbles but manages to squeeze off a shot before falling to his knees. I shoot again, this time aiming for his hand, but he topples over and I think I graze his shoulder. A burning sensation on the side of my biceps warns me that one of their bullets has made some contact with my skin. The shot isn't embedded, though. This feels more like it sliced off the outside edge of flesh and muscle. It's of no concern at the moment.

"Naomi," I yell again, running toward the first attacker, "the bags."

She saunters out. "You don't need to yell. I heard you the first time. Raising your voice is only necessary if the listener has hearing impairment or the sound is blocked. In fact, for some people, it's better to merely lower the octave of your voice instead of speaking louder. Studies have shown—"

The attacker pushes upright and leans down to pull at his ankle. I shoot again. One bullet left. Pushing Naomi back into the compartment, I drop a knee on the gut of the downed man. He grunts and I shoot him in the shoulder. At point-blank range, his wound is enormous. Blood spurts out like a geyser. He cries out and I slam the butt of the now-empty gun onto his wound, which causes him to howl like an animal.

"Who sent you?"

CHAPTER **TWENTY-TWO**

NAOMI

People scream around us as Vasily shoves the gun harder into the stranger's wound.

"Who sent you?" Vasily snarls again, and I realize this man is another assassin. He howls as Vasily tortures him, and I want to retreat mentally, to pull away from the noise. But Vasily needs me, so I pop in my earplugs and force myself to take calming breaths. *Itsy Bitsy Spider* . . .

The man grins up at Vasily and grinds his teeth, and Vasily shakes him angrily even as froth bubbles out of the man's mouth. I stare in fascination, wondering what could cause a chemical reaction like that, but then Vasily grabs the bags from my hand and throws them over his shoulder, then takes my hand and drags me forward.

There's an audible sound in the train, muffled by the earplugs, and a screech, and I realize we are braking. The train is slowing, and everything seems to surge forward.

People continue to scream around us as Vasily drags me through the car, toward a door at the far end. He shoves it open, muscles flexing, and then tugs me after him, and we're on a platform outside of the car, a mere foot above rushing track. The ground screams past, even as the brakes continue to squeal.

Vasily mouths something to me and grabs my chin, forcing me to watch him. I'm near deaf from the earplugs but I stare at his mouth as he speaks.

Watch me. Run. Follow.

Then, as the train continues to squeal, he tosses our bags over the side and onto the ground, and moves onto the side of the train, hanging off of a ladder. He looks back at me again, surely seeing my wide eyes, and I catch the word *follow* again before he jumps down to the ground, running alongside the train, legs windmilling until he rolls away.

I just . . . what the *fuck.*

Vasily, that crazy Russian, just jumped off a train and expects me to follow. I can't stay here, but I don't want to jump, either.

Of course, I'm fascinated by the fact that he can do this. I wonder what speed we're at, and if he's hurt himself, but there's no time. I hear more alarms sounding—faint and annoying—through the earplugs. The train is getting slower and slower, and in moments, it's going to stop entirely. I can't stay here. I climb out to the ladder like he did and watch the rushing ground, then jump and run like he did.

The impact on my legs is harder than I thought it would be. I try to run but the ground gets away from me and I end up flailing. I lose my balance and roll down a hill into the green countryside.

The wind is knocked from my lungs and I lay on my back, stunned. I think I've lost an earplug. Or a kneecap. Or both. Everything hurts. If I'm dead, I hope they bury me back home—

A shadow looms over me and I squint one eye open. Vasily. "Naomi?"

I groan. I just jumped from a train. Surely he doesn't expect me to hold a conversation?

He kneels beside me, and his hands run all over my body. "Speak to me. Tell me you are all right."

I wait to see if his hands are going to go to my breasts or between my legs. I'm disappointed when they don't. "The train must have been going a very slow speed, or else we would have broken several bones simply due to the velocity—" I break off as he starts to laugh. "It's not funny."

"I am not laughing because it is funny. I am laughing because I am relieved you are not hurt." He extends a hand to me. "Come. Get up."

"I'm up, I'm up," I grump, and take his hand and get to my feet. Other than bruises and an all-over body ache, I'm fine. "Why are we jumping off trains?"

Once I am standing, his hands move over me again, examining my skin and smoothing down my limbs, as if he doesn't trust that I am truly all right. It's almost . . . sweet. He's obsessed with my well-being, this man. When he is satisfied that I am whole, he speaks. "We jump because several people saw me kill those men, and they will be looking for us. Follow me. We will retrieve our bags and hide until train is gone."

I trot behind him as we head down the tracks. Our bags are nearly a mile away, but we retrieve them and then Vasily hustles me over a hill and into the countryside. We find a copse of scrubby bushes near a road and hide behind it. I can't help but think we look like the criminals we're pretending not to be. Vasily's clothing is torn and grass stained, and I'm sure I look like a mess.

"What is the plan?" I ask Vasily.

He says nothing. His jaw clenches and grinds, not unlike the man on the train a moment before the bubbling froth emerged from his mouth. I watch him curiously to see if the same will happen.

"Do you have a poison capsule in one of your teeth? One of the men back on the train did."

He shakes his head. "I am just thinking."

I pick a piece of grass off of his collar and my fingers smooth his clothing. He looks rumpled, and it doesn't suit his fierceness. "Think harder. We have to have a plan, Vasily."

"I know."

But he doesn't share. I make a frustrated noise in my throat. "You need to tell me what's going on. Were those men Golubevs?"

Vasily shoots me a look I guess I'm supposed to understand. "*Nyet*."

"How do you know?"

"Because the Golubev *Bratva* is filled with fools who bust in and take over buildings. Those men were different assassins. They were professionals."

And I suppose the Golubevs are not. "Emile's men, then?"

"Emile would not have assassins after us. No one could finger us but the woman, and I doubt she will talk."

My brow furrows. "So who else is trying to kill us?"

"That is interesting question, is it not?"

"How many enemies do you have?"

His eyes narrow at me. "All that are not friends are my enemies."

"Okay, how many friends do you have?"

He is silent. Either he is dredging his memory for friendships or he truly does not believe anyone is a friend. I feel a stab of unhappiness on his behalf, which surprises me. I'm not a sympathetic person, but I feel like Vasily belongs to me. His germs, his smiles, his skin, his scent—they are all mine and I am unhappy that he seems alone. I know how that feels.

So I smooth his collar and ignore the hand that swats my fingers away. "I will be your friend, Vasily. For now." Until he threatens someone I care for. I think of his words from last night—he would kill Daniel or my parents if they stood in his way. That is a thought I can't process right now. If I do, my mind will run in endless unhappy circles. So for now, I tuck it away and will turn it over in my head later, when we are not squatting in bushes by the side of a road.

"I do not need friends. I am *volk*."

"That's sad," I tell him. Vasily is no optimized computer like me, so he should have lots of friends, shouldn't he? Daniel does. I feel a stab of sympathy for my friendless wolf. "Aren't we friends?"

"Do you still consider me friend after all I have told you?" He asks the words in a low, intense voice.

I remember our conversation. How he stated he would kill people if he had to. People I loved. But . . . he never said he would hurt me. I think of the way he carefully brushed my hair and spoke to me on the train to calm my spiraling mind. These are not the actions of a man who cares for no one.

I'm torn.

"Consider me one less enemy," I say, unwilling to give entirely.

A faint smile touches his face, and I feel as if I've somehow won a prize. Warmth blooms through me, and I smile back, meeting his eyes.

He glances at the road, the buildings in the distance, anywhere but at me. The faint purr of a distant car approaches, and Vasily nudges me. "Step in front of the car and ask for help. A woman alone is less fearsome than a man. Pretend another one of your seizures if you must. When they stop, I will attack when they open door."

Oh no. A carjacking? I don't like this plan. It's one thing to take a car when someone has left it sitting in the road by itself. It's another to force someone to pull over and mug them. My stupid, screwy mind imagines Daniel driving behind the wheel of the Volvo in the distance and I panic. "We can't just leave a swath of crime throughout the Italian countryside," I protest. I'm inches away from another freak-out.

"Jump out, Naomi," he growls at me. "Hurry."

"No," I say, and wrap my arms around his waist, burrowing my head against his chest. I push the full, limp weight of my body against his in case he tries to ignore me and carjack on his own.

I expect him to shove me angrily aside, and I'm prepared to lock my arms and act like a human sandbag. I feel him stiffen, but as the car drives past, he doesn't move. Moments pass. The engine purr fades into the distance and eventually, Vasily's hand rests on my shoulder. He caresses me, his hand moving through my hair. "Naomi?"

"No more, okay?" I say, and realize I'm close to tears again. "Can't we just buy some bicycles from one of the locals and head to the closest town?"

His voice is soft, so soft my ears strain to hear. "*Da*. We will."

Hours later, we ditch our bikes and limp into a place that Vasily says is called Ferrara. We took our time with the bikes, buying clothes and hats from a tourist stand and then biking through town as if we were sightseeing before heading to a hotel. I have to sit on my skirts and tuck them against my legs to bike, but I manage it.

I'm exhausted, mentally and physically, by the time we get up to our room. One small room, with one tiny full bed. It's nothing like the room we had in Rome, the grand suite overlooking the city. This is small and plain, and the bed is covered with an ugly duvet that looks as if it's full of germs. Using the hem of my dress, I peel the bedding from the mattress and get the towels from the bathroom to lie on instead.

"*Nyet*, do not," Vasily tells me. "We need those."

I pause. "All of them?"

"We both dye our hair again tonight," Vasily tells me. "This time, you are red."

"Like blood?" I whimper. "I hate dyeing my hair, Vasily. The smell and the mess are so bad."

"Is necessary," he tells me. "I will do mine with you. It will not be so bad." He nods in my direction. "Come. Take your clothes off," he tells me, stripping his own clothes. "You do not want dye on your skin. It is a telltale and I do not leave those."

I peel off my dress, still intensely unhappy about the turn this day has taken. "I'm tired of Italy. Can we go to Russia now? I want snow and the *dacha*."

"Not yet," he says. "A bit longer, Naomi." His hands reach out and trace my skin, where bruises are mottling my shoulders. "You are hurt after all?"

"I jumped from a train," I tell him. "I didn't land that well."

He chuckles, his thumbs brushing over my skin in a way that makes my nipples get tight and achy in response. "You were right about the bones. The train was slowing to a stop, or else it would have been a death wish." His fingers hover over a particularly bright bruise, and then his big hands are moving all over my skin. I'm wearing nothing but my bra and panties, but he's still checking me over with a skim of his hands. "You are not hurt more than bruises, are you?"

"I don't think so," I tell him. "Though you might want to look at my pupils to see if I have a concussion. You don't even have to be hit in the head to get a concussion. All you need is a blow that can cause the head to move back and forth rapidly. And traumatic brain injury is the number one killer of people under the age of forty—"

His hands cup my face and he peers into my eyes. My gaze skitters away, but his hands clench on my cheeks. "Look at me." His voice is so firm it scares me a little. I look at him, though I feel weird about it. He gives me the tiniest little shake. "You are not going to die, Naomi."

"Shaking me is probably not conducive to my brain health if I do have head trauma—"

"You're fine," he says, giving me a thoughtful look. His thumb skims my lower lip, and then he releases me. "Now come, we dye our hair before someone else finds us."

It feels like he's rushing me. It's not like him. "Are you stressed? You might be the one with the concussion. It's more common in men than women and one of the signs of concussion is irritability—"

"Naomi, if I am irritable, it is because I am not happy with having a set of new, mysterious assassins. They must be after the Madonna as well. This makes me very angry for a variety of reasons, none of which are aimed at you." He raises a clenched fist and for a moment, I think he's going to punch a wall, but he doesn't. Instead, he flexes his hand and then returns to undressing. I head to the bag and pull out the small bottles of hair dye he has carefully packed away for emergency. Vasily says he is dyeing his hair, too. I think he will be brown. It would look odd if we were both red, though the mental image of that makes me smile.

I turn around just in time to see Vasily peel a wet, sticky portion of his dark shirt off of his body, revealing the wound underneath. There's blood everywhere—blood on his skin, on his clothing, and now leaking onto the towel that he presses to the wound.

Oh God, so much blood. This must be why he's rushing. He needs medical attention. I blink rapidly as blackness swims in front of my eyes. It's not my wound. It's not my blood. It's not. It's nothing.

But Vasily belongs to me, and his wound might as well be mine. I swallow hard, and then I black out.

CHAPTER TWENTY-THREE

VASILY

"You forgot your eyebrows," Naomi says. She's eating crackers and drinking juice in bed. After she passed out from the sight of my puny wound, I bundled her into the bathroom and while she was unconscious I dyed her hair a dull red to match the new papers we will be getting from Guillaume. I knew she would prefer it that way. She came to as I was rubbing the concoction through her strands. Thankfully she closed her eyes and willed herself to not look at the mess. When I was done, I carried her back to the bed and dyed my own hair brown.

I run out and find a pizzeria still open and buy us two pies. Half for her and one and a half for me. Hopefully the cheese is brown enough for her.

In the bathroom I see my error. The hair on my head is rather dark but my face looks pale. I frown. Her face appears behind. She is holding a black tube.

"It's mascara."

I take it out and examine the fuzzy, curved brush covered with a dark brown substance. "Put it on me," I order.

She scrunches her nose. Naomi does not like my orders but she complies. I sit down on the dirty bed that is barely big enough for one let alone two bodies, but both of us are sore from our jump from the train.

We need to rest before we can journey further. It is doubtful I can resist her no matter that the sheets might be dirty or that there is blood on my shoulder and my side. I've resigned myself to my own frailties. I plan to explain this to Naomi before we lie down. She, of all people, should understand neurosis—if not from an intellectual level at least.

Her red hair dangles down around her face. I'm not certain how she colored her eyebrows, but they have a red tint to them as well. She is still beautiful but somehow she is not Naomi. The color is too harsh for her or too red or just not *her*.

"I prefer you as a blonde."

She pulls a lock of her hair and stares at it. "Me too."

She steps between my legs and bends over. The position is awkward for her.

"Why don't you sit on my legs," I suggest.

"But you don't like to be touched," she reminds me.

"This isn't touching. It is merely providing a place for you to be seated while we finalize the details of my disguise."

This explanation must make sense to her, because she nods several times and climbs onto my lap. I cup her back to prevent her from falling off, but my hands drift lower.

"Vasily, I'm too close to you now. Don't hold me so tight."

I've pulled her toward me, I realize. Close enough so that her stomach is nearly flush with mine. Other parts of us are touching as well. I force myself to relax and loosen my grip.

"You're hard," she says as she bends forward with her small brush. Her observation is made coolly and without any indication that it excites her. Having experienced the evening with her at the fetish club, I now know how she sounds and looks when she is aroused. Her eyes glitter and her facts turn provocative. If she wanted me, she would say something like—

"*A man's penis averages around six inches. The vaginal canal might be longer but the G-spot is only one to three inches inside. And most women come from clitoral stimulation not penis-in-vagina sex so six inches is all you need. Six inches is three inches extra, although if someone has like a twelve-inch penis not all of it would be able to fit inside the vagina. And something that big would hurt bad.*"

Perhaps I still need lessons on how to read her. "Do you want to have sex with me, Naomi?"

"Of course. I don't need sex, exactly. But I'd like for you to put your mouth between my legs. And I'd like to feel your penis inside me. I think that would feel good based on prior empirical evidence."

My hands return to grip her tightly. "Naomi, you must be aware that I am not a good man. Are you certain you want to have me touch your body in such an intimate fashion?"

"Because you kill people? It seems like the people you kill need killing. Like those guys on the train? They would have killed us so it makes sense for you to shoot them first. You shouldn't feel bad about that." She tosses her stick to the side and blows on my brows lightly. "Don't touch your eyebrows. The mascara needs to dry. It looks good, though."

"Does nothing unsettle you?"

"Are we back to the killing or something else? And yes, I was upset when you said you would kill my brother or my parents. Was that a joke? I don't get jokes a lot of the time. I mean, I understand them obviously because I'm brilliant, but I don't get why they are funny."

"It was not a joke. You should know that before we have sex. I would kill anyone who stood in the way of what I wanted." I hold her securely, her covered sex against my growing erection, because I don't want her to edge away even though I'm a danger to her, even though I do not like to be touched, even though I know that I'm losing my mind.

"Oh." Her mouth makes a perfect oval at this sound.

An oval that I'd like to plunder with my cock. The pressure is building inside me. I can feel it pushing at every nerve ending, rising to the top of my skin. Behind my pants, my cock hurts. *I've gone without for a very long time*, it reminds me insistently. "You need to be aware of this so that you can make the decision. Tonight we lie down on that bed together, and I will need to have sex with you. If you do not wish for this to happen, tell me now."

She's silent for a moment. "I want to have sex with you, too, but I don't want you to kill my family. I don't really care if you kill anyone else. Wait, kids. I don't want you to kill any kids. Maybe no one under the age of twenty-five. Also, the elderly. I think those people should be able to dictate the terms of their own death to the best of their ability. So like, no one over sixty-five."

I choke back my laughter. "Anyone between the ages of twenty-five to sixty-five would be sanctioned targets."

She nods. "That's the best I can come up with on the spur of the moment. The list might change. Oh, and Regan, Daniel's friend, should be off your list."

I tuck the top of my hand inside her waistband to anchor her on my lap and use my other to trace her fine features. I notice her eyebrows are starting to lighten as the makeup she's applied has begun to rub off. "The parameters you have suggested have already been violated. There are killers who start at the age of ten. All they know is violence. They rise from their beds to kill and they dream of killing at night. And for some, killing is the least of their hated tasks. Sometimes going out and taking a life means avoiding more objectionable things at home."

"What could be more objectionable?"

"Many, many things."

Her brow furrows and then clears. "You don't want to talk of those things? Are they related to why you don't like to be touched?"

"Those things should be buried," I say, not really answering her. "After we have sex, we will sleep. We will then continue on to seek out the Madonna. Once that task is completed, you will go to Lake Ladoga, where my *dacha* is, and wait for me."

"Why?"

"It is dangerous now, Naomi. You saw the men on the train. I do not want you hurt."

She stares at my cheek and with visible effort tries to meet my eyes. There's a blue flash and then they slide away. "You care about me."

Because I am so attuned to her now, I hear it—a longing that she might deny experiencing. Voice low, I admit, "I do but that is dangerous itself. Do you understand? When a man like me cares for someone, that person becomes a target. They can use you to make me do things; they could hurt you just to hurt me."

"How long will I wait?"

How long are you willing to wait? I do not answer her, for I'm too desperate. The need to taste her, to have a physical communion with her is too great. Instead I draw her mouth down to mine. When her small tongue darts out to rub against my lips, I feel only pleasure. I'm emboldened and open my mouth to receive her. She invades me. Her hands come to clench my face and her sex rubs against my hardness.

I did not realize she is as hungry as I until her small mouth devours me, all sharp teeth and wicked tongue. Her pressure pushes me backward and I fall, allowing the bed to catch me. Her fingers pluck at my shirt and I wrest it off.

She whimpers when the contact between our mouths must be broken, but hurriedly removes her top as well. We shove at our buttons and zippers and clothing until it is just her smooth, silky body against my rough, scarred one.

I know I am not worthy of the gift she is to give me—the gift of her body, the gift of pleasure—but I am a bad man and I will take it. But in return, I will bring her to the precipice of ecstasy again and again. There will be no delight she wants that will go unfulfilled.

I could stay here forever with her in my arms in this dilapidated hotel room on this well-used mattress. I have never felt as good in my life before. Not when I killed my father. Not when I sent my sister to Cambridge. Not when I seized control of the *Bratva*. Naomi wanting me, kissing me, making love to me is the pinnacle of *good* in my life, and I do not want to let her go.

Me, a man who loathes touching, who loathes sex, wants nothing more than to lie between this precious woman's legs and sink into her soft flesh. I want her to embrace me and all my vileness until I am cleansed by her acceptance.

"I like your germs." She moves down my chest, tonguing me everywhere. I did not realize my neck was sensitive or that bones were pleasure receptors. She bites my flat nipples and moves down to my stomach, where my cock bobs its head in greeting.

"It's more than six inches," she says, pausing for a moment in her exploration to take in my size. I'm well endowed and have been since a boy. It is why I was picked for certain purposes. Those images threaten to imperil my time with Naomi and resolutely I shove them down into the dark recesses of my mind.

"It is," I admit gravely. "Imagine how much friction I can generate against your G-spot. I can fill you up and stroke every tiny centimeter of your sex. But not until you are wet enough. Touch yourself, Naomi. Are you wet enough for me, or do you need my mouth?"

She reaches between us and slides at least one finger, maybe two, inside her cunt. Her lack of inhibitions is incredibly erotic. One day I will drape her in a floor-length silver fox and nothing else. Her legs will be lashed to the arms of a chair and I will sit fully clothed as she brings herself off. As her orgasm approaches I will kneel between her legs and drink her essence until every cell in my bloodstream is coated with her.

"I'm pretty wet," she says, holding her fingers up for inspection.

I bring her hand to my lips and suck her juice.

Her eyes widen. "That was filthy." She looks scandalized and titillated at the same time.

I hand her a condom. "Put it on and take me inside your body. I am your servant in this."

Her expression is studious and intense as she opens the package and rolls the condom down over my aching flesh. Even that small, innocuous touch makes me flinch. My hands curl into the comforter and I restrain myself from flipping her over and pounding into her like an animal, like a boy with no finesse.

My cock looks obscene under the nearly clear rubber of the condom. The head is nearly purple and hugely engorged, but Naomi does not hesitate. Taking me in one hand and pressing her palm against my chest with the other, she rises on her knees and positions my cock at her wet entrance. She eases the tip in. My eyes are riveted on our connected flesh. Slowly, she descends and it feels . . . as if I am dying. Her wet, hot cunt opens and embraces me. I may never rise from this bed.

"Is this good, Vasily?" she asks, a little breathless, a little unsure.

"Too good," I answer. "I have never felt better in the whole of my life."

She leans forward, bracing herself on my chest. "Is my weight too much? I don't want to touch the sheets, but your body is okay."

Again, I swallow an inappropriate laugh. "*Nyet*. Press harder. I like it rough," I admit. When she doesn't flee, I tell her, "Dig in with your claws. Mark me with your teeth. Make me yours, Naomi. Make me yours."

CHAPTER TWENTY-FOUR

NAOMI

The last time I had sex was nothing like this.

Before, the boy pushed into me and pressed his weight on top of me, until our skin was touching everywhere. He sweated and grunted and got germs all over me. It was a horrible memory, and turned me off of sex for good.

Or so I'd thought. But everything with Vasily is different. I don't mind when his skin touches mine. I don't mind when his mouth touches my mouth and our saliva mixes. I don't even mind when his penis, sheathed in latex so he won't get semen on me, pushes and pushes into me so hard that it hurts a little. He's very big and the position we're in doesn't really allow me time to get used to his girth. One moment he's at my entrance, and the next, he's in me so deep that I'm aching inside and things are stretching.

A small whimper escapes my throat and I wiggle on top of him a little, trying to get comfortable. My position is precarious; the only place I can put my hands is on his chest, otherwise I will be touching the filthy blankets. My knees are pressing onto them as it is; I'll have to shower once we're done. I probably shouldn't be thinking about the bed, but I'm trying to distract myself from the enormous wedge that is Vasily's penis pushing inside of me and making all of my body stretch in response.

"How does it feel, Naomi?" Vasily's voice is thick with his accent, a sure sign he's distracted. His eyes are sealed shut, though, and his hands clutch at my waist to hold me in place.

"Why are your eyes closed?"

"You feel too good. I am trying to keep control. It is . . . difficult for me." He presses his forehead to mine. "I do not wish to hurt you."

Oh. I consider this with another test wiggle. "Your penis is stretching my vagina several inches and causing slight discomfort. You might be so long that you're hitting my cervix, but I'm not entirely sure what that would feel like."

In response to this, he groans as if pained. "Keep talking, Naomi," he rasps. "Tell me more."

I study his face, looking for cues. I'm not sure if he's having fun with sticking his penis inside me. I was wet from the excitement of it, but now that he's in me, I'm not sure that I'm still enjoying things. I feel . . . crammed full.

And his face is tight, his eyes shut, his lips drawn back in a rather feral expression. I'd say he looks upset, but I'm a poor judge of these things. He's in danger of losing control, he says. Am I doing something wrong? I've studied sex a great deal and I don't want to seem like an inexperienced idiot. I debate with myself, and then decide to show Vasily just how much I know.

"The largest penis on record was thirteen and a half inches and over six inches in circumference," I tell him. "I don't think you're quite that big but you're definitely in a top percentile. You feel extremely large inside me." I shift my hips a little, still trying to get comfortable.

"*Da*, like that," Vasily hisses and his hands tug at my hips, lifting them, and then thrusting me back down on his penis. The length of him pushes in and out, causing an intense amount of friction between our bodies.

A noise escapes my throat that sounds embarrassingly like a squeal, and his breath hisses out again, repeating the motion. My palms dig into his chest and I try to move my hips with his hands, since it's obvious that's what he wants.

His big penis pushes into me again, his movements jerky and harsh, and the initial discomfort I felt from his entrance is going away. "My vaginal walls must be stretched to accommodate you now," I tell him. "A vagina can stretch because the walls are pleated like an accordion. I imagine my pleats are rather straightened at the moment—"

He thrusts into me again. This time, I gasp and slam my palms against his chest, startled by the rough movement. He keeps distracting me every time I try to talk, and it's starting to annoy me. I slap a hand on his chest in irritation. "Are you listening to me, Vasily?"

"I hear every word, Naomi. Your sweet lips move like a temptress, and your voice fills my ears as a siren's. Your words are making my cock ache for you," he says, and he opens his eyes and lifts his head to gaze down at our bodies. As he watches, he lifts my hips again and slides me back down on his length. "Does that feel good, Naomi?"

His sweet words are easing my irritation. "I'm not sure. It doesn't hurt anymore."

He shifts on top of me. "If it was good, you would tell me. Am I hitting your G-spot?"

"I don't know. I've never hit my G-spot." But now I'm curious. "How can you tell if it's being triggered?"

"You would know," he tells me and holds me as he sits up, his muscles flexing. He gets to his feet, holding me in place, and I cling to his neck. "Wrap your legs around me, Naomi." I feel vulnerable as he moves, as I feel one step from falling off of him, but he's a man with a purpose. One hand clasps my back and I clench my legs tight around him.

"W-what are you doing?"

He doesn't answer me, just leans over and rips the blankets and sheets off of the bed. I hold on to him like a spider monkey, wondering at the strength he must have to hold me like this. When he's satisfied, he looks at me again, and straightens. "I am going to put you on the bed, Naomi—"

"No," I say. "It's gross! Think of the germs—"

He doesn't listen, just pushes me down onto the mattress and then his weight is on me, his big body covering my own. He's still adjusting things, and grabs a pillow—a filthy, filthy pillow—and shoves it under my hips.

"Vasily, I'm touching the bed," I whimper, and slam a hand against his chest. "I don't like this."

He ignores my protests and begins to thrust into me again, his movements slower and more precise, and he watches my face to see my reaction. When I'm still making distressed whimpers of unhappiness, he leans in—which causes his penis to push even deeper inside me—and whispers, "I read a study where the mattress is the cleanest part of the bed."

"It . . . it is?" His hips swivel against mine.

"*Da*," he growls, and his hand goes to the back of one of my legs, pushing it backward until my knee is almost pressed to the mattress. It tilts my hips even more. His mouth nuzzles mine, a surprisingly tender gesture given his savage movements. "It is always covered, you see. No one ever lays directly on mattress."

This has a curious sense of logic to it, and some of my panic subsides. "I've never heard—" I lose track of what I was saying as his cock pushes into me again and everything feels different. Intense. Like I stuck my finger in a light socket. "What was that?"

"That was G-spot," he says, voice thick. "Do you want to feel it again?"

"I'm not sure."

"That is not a no," he tells me, and rolls his hips as he thrusts again. His penis saws into me at a peculiar angle, and it seems to rub up against something inside me that jolts with nerve endings when he does. I whimper again and my nails dig into him. "It's so . . . much."

He growls low in his throat, like the wolf he claims to be. "Show me," he says, brushing his lips over mine. "Show me how much you are feeling." And he begins to stroke into me again, picking up a rhythm, and every motion seems to rub against my G-spot in a way that is so intense it's almost frightening—if it weren't for the fact that my legs were twitching and my entire body was lighting up in response.

I want to share this intensity with him, but I don't know how.

Mark me with your teeth. Make me yours, Naomi. Make me yours.

The words roll through my mind, and I immediately discard them. He knows I need people to be literal with me, because I don't understand metaphors. But he's watching me so close, his eyes glittering, and he pushes into me hard again.

Something inside me snaps.

I reach out and slap him across the face.

We're both stunned for a minute, and I worry that he's going to get angry. Did I misinterpret him? But he only pushes down and captures my mouth in a savage kiss that ravages my lips and tongue and leaves me breathless. If he didn't like my slap, he's not indicating it. *Mark me with your teeth*, he told me earlier. *Make me yours.*

I am. He's mine.

Vasily wants me to be rough with him. He's definitely not being gentle with me, and it's odd, but I kind of like how brutal he is. He's not hurting me, but he's not tender, either. His thrusts begin to move faster, his hips pistoning against my own on the bed, and the wild sensations continue to build inside me. I don't know how to handle them—this is like the orgasms he gave me before, but deeper, more intense. He needs the intense, too, I think. My hands slap at his chest again, lightly, and then I dig my nails into his skin and rake them down his chest.

He groans, his nostrils flaring. "Yes, Naomi. Keep. Hurting. Me."

His movements are going even faster, and he's now fucking me so hard we might slide off the bed. But I don't care—I'm getting into this. I want to hurt Vasily to show him how intense it feels to have him inside me, rubbing me in that spot that sets everything else on fire. My mind isn't working clearly, or I'd tell him more sex facts.

Instead, I dig my fingernails viciously into his nipple and pinch at his smooth, tanned skin. I want to bite him but he's leaning too far up. All I can do is slap and scratch and hiss at him in frustration as he continues to savagely pound me across the bed, hammering into that spot that's making my entire body tight and tense.

I click my teeth at him, my own face feral with need, and he gets what I seem to want. He leans in and his mouth takes mine again, but when he pulls away, I bite down, hard, on his lower lip.

He groans and stiffens over me, and his brutal rhythm loses its cadence. "Don't stop yet," I yell in his ear. "I need to come!"

"Then come," he snarls at me, and his fingers dig into my thigh as he brutally thrusts harder. It's like he's trying to go from my vagina to my sternum with each motion, but it feels better than anything I've ever felt.

Something elusive and delicious is building inside me and I focus on that, holding on to his neck and biting on his skin everywhere I can—his collarbones, his shoulder, his ear, his jaw, the tendons in his throat. "Not yet," I tell him as I bite, and he continues to pound into me. "Not yet," I tell him with each thrust, my voice growing louder as my pleasure intensifies. "Not yet!" I scream in his ear as I dig my nails into the dip of his shoulder and his movements grow even more ragged, more jerky, more violent with need. I slap at him wildly, fascinated by the growls I get in response, and how it makes him even more erratic.

And then it is there, blooming inside me like a supernova, and I scream, "Right there," in Vasily's ear even as I lock my body around him and dig my nails in, wanting to drag the moment out because it's so good, and so overwhelming. I clench and clench and clench and it just goes on and on like my entire body has given itself over to this impossibly pleasurable feeling, and I begin to cry because it's so intense, I can't even describe it. Over me, Vasily shudders and mutters my name in a thick voice, but I'm not paying attention if he's coming or not, because little stars are dancing in the corners of my vision, and I watch them in dreamy bliss.

That was so good.

Something heavy collapses on top of me, and it's Vasily's sweaty body. He leans in and nuzzles me again, curiously tender after our savage lovemaking.

I squeal as his skin slides against my own, my revulsion for bodily fluids taking over again. "Off," I yell, slapping at his skin again. "Vasily, you're sweating on me!"

He obediently rolls off of me onto the side of the bed, lying there and panting, but his hand continues to clutch my arm, as if he needs to make sure I'm still there next to him.

That's better, at least. I relax and return to my dreamy spiral of pleasure, my thoughts mellow. Postcoital endorphins, I tell myself. These are nice. "So what was that study about mattresses?" I tell Vasily.

"I lied," he says slowly, eyes closed as if in contemplation. "Thought I would distract you."

With a shriek, I get off the bed. He's been grinding me into a mattress filled with bacteria? I can practically feel my body covered in staphylococcus and dust mites. "I hate you!"

"*Nyet*, you like me." He's smiling and he reaches out for me. His skin is livid with welts from where I got carried away, but he looks content. "Come back. We will have sex again as soon as I recover."

"Don't touch me," I tell him. "I have to shower right now. I can't believe you lied to me. You horrible, horrible *volk*," I tell him, and I'm practically bellowing at this point. I want to hit him again, but knowing that he finds pleasure in it makes me stay my hands. "Now I have to scrub myself from head to toe."

I storm to the bathroom. It's time for a cleansing shower at the maximum heat.

CHAPTER TWENTY-FIVE

VASILY

I'm too replete to be angered by Naomi's need for a shower, and for a moment I think about joining her in the bathroom and rubbing the soap down over her thick nipples and between her sex before abandoning the suds altogether and ramming myself into her tight cunt. I draw a finger across my cheek, the one she slapped so suddenly and unexpectedly.

As I rise from the bed, the dirty mirror across the room catches my eye. My chest is a morass of red scratches and nail gouges. I smile at the vision, and then the smile turns into a laugh. "*Okhuyénno.*" I say the outlawed *mat* profanity with wonder as my laugh dies out. Very good. I rub my chest, enjoying the sting. I want her to whip me. To command me to my knees and then draw blood as she strikes me again and again. I grow hard at the thought of the pain and then the pleasure she'd bring me.

Pain is the one thing that made me *feel* in the past. Before
Naomi, sexual intercourse felt no better than pissing or a good
meal, and going without mattered little to me. The few times that
I felt something more than relief during sex was when there was
pain involved, but I never explored it. I don't know that I understood what I needed until Naomi struck me and marked me.
Now I want her to take me again and again. My body aches for
her touch, the scrape of her nails, the bite of her sharp little teeth.

She's an animal. *Nyet.* I correct myself. She is my animal and
I am hers.

With a smug smile, I dress and leave.

Naomi will likely be in there for hours or at least until the hot
water runs out. While she is scrubbing away the germs of the
mattress, I will take care of a few details so that we can be on the
next train to Venice.

Florence is a small citadel of a city. The narrow, cobblestone
streets are peopled mostly by tourists and students, but there's an
obvious unsavory element not so evident in Rome, where they hide
it like the Vatican secrets away its treasures. There, but not seen.

Firenze, as the natives call it, suits me. It is the home of the
Medicis. The epicenter of their power. I pause as I walk by the
Santa Maria Duomo. Inside this church during mass, the Pazzi
family, jealous of the Medicis' power, sought to kill Lorenzo and
his brother Giuliano. Bernardo Bandi and Francesco de' Pazzi
attacked the two brothers in front of the altar, a shocking occur-
rence, but it had been sanctioned by Pope Sixtus, who rightly
feared the Medicis' growing power. Giuliano was killed, stabbed
nineteen times, but Lorenzo escaped. He claimed the hand of
God protected him and surviving the attack close range was a
sign that even the heavens approved of the Medicis. Giuliano's

ultimate revenge was from the grave when his illegitimate son went on to be Pope Clement VII.

The Medicis did not invent the idea of *familia*, but they set forth the blueprints of how to build a dynasty. They were ruthless in their retribution. In just hours after the attack during High Mass, the main conspirators, including Archbishop Salviati and signor Pazzi were hung by their necks outside the windows of Palazzo della Signoria. In the following days, the Medicis cut down nearly every male issue of the Pazzi family, and across Europe, their accounts were plundered by Medici friends.

Yet, the Medici dynasty is gone now. Their buildings having passed out of the family hands for the most part, their legacy one of history rather than current events.

As much as they can be admired, it is important to learn from their fall as well. Being mired in the past can only harm the future. The old guard of the *Bratva* with their nonsense desire for this painting will be their end. *I* will be their end.

I follow the maze of cobblestone roads until I reach Accademia di Belle Arti. Several tiny blocks down, I turn left and find my destination marked by a large green iron door that is as wide as my arm span and twice as tall.

I text my contact and the door clicks, signaling that it is open.

The moonlight spills into the open-air atrium, illuminating the broken pavers in need of repair, but the stairs leading up are almost completely shrouded in darkness. I know from past visits that there is a tiny elevator that Guillaume had installed for his tenants, but I eschew the metal cage for the dark recesses of the stairs. The limestone steps are smooth from the centuries of use. At the top of the fifth flight, I peer out of an arrow slit in the wall. To most, the courtyard, this fourteenth-century building and its crumbling fresco walls would be romantic, but not to Naomi. I suspect she would explain to me how the first floor isn't really a first floor at all, but merely the entry level where light and water were initially collected and then where trade and commerce took place. All the living was done on the upper levels with the kitchen on the topmost floor so that the smells and noise of the workers would not intrude upon the peacefulness demanded by the moneyed inhabitants.

On the fifth floor, the doors are secured by more than a simple lock. A small blinking red light to the right indicates an electronic protection, and there are three keyholes. Choosing the wrong keyhole will likely result in some painful warning. Idly I wonder if Naomi could break into these security systems. As I watch, however, the red light turns green, and the door's locks release allowing it to fall open.

A narrow hallway leads into a large living space, where Guillaume sits in front of a huge bank of monitors. One shows the courtyard, another the exterior door, another the hallway I just walked down. The engines of his machines hum as his fingers fly across the keyboard—the middle one. There are four others. Naomi would squeal in delight at this show of computing power. It is better that I did not bring her. She may not want to leave.

If I lost Naomi to anyone, it would not be to a man with superior looks or money. It would be to someone who challenged her mind more, perhaps someone like Guillaume. He was a French national but got into some trouble after hacking into Interpol to clean the record of a handsome American thief. Others might flee to the beaches of Croatia or perhaps some island in the Maldives depending on the thickness of their pocketbook, but Guillaume came to Florence for no other reason than he said if he was to live in exile from his beloved France, he would do it in a place of civilization, and that there is no other place that would suit him better than Italy.

Like Naomi he will talk only when he is done with his task. Most of the time I do not mind, but I find I am anxious to return to Naomi.

"*Buona sera*, Guillaume. Sorry to interrupt, but I have come to retrieve the items we had discussed."

"*Buona sera. Un momento, per favore.*" He holds up one finger while continuing to type with the other hand. He is so much like Naomi, they could be twins. A thought occurs to me and I blurt out my question before I can stop myself.

"Guillaume are you a—" What does Naomi say? "Aspie?"

"Aspie? *Non capisco.*"

"*Avete la sindrome di Asperger?*"

His eyebrows shoot upward. "How did you know?"

"You remind me of someone." I hesitate, not wanting to reveal Naomi to Guillaume, who trades in information. "The Aspie I know is very difficult to distract from tasks."

"American, eh? They shorten everything. But I am done and yours now." With a flourish, he takes his raised finger and slams it down on the enter key. Those French, always so exuberant. Unlike Naomi, he looks me in the eye at least for a few seconds before sliding away to land on a shopping bag with *Uomo* on the side. He slides the bag toward me.

Rifling through the bag reveals all the items I requested from Guillaume, and a thick cardboard envelope. I pop it open and take out the documents. There are the passports with our new identities as well as the invitation. This time I am from Georgia and Naomi is from England. She stares at me, red haired and lovely. The digital manipulation of the camera-phone still I took earlier is remarkable.

"It's all in there. I wouldn't cheat you."

"Of course not," I say soothingly, remembering Naomi grumble that Aspies had feelings, too. "I am but curious about this invitation."

I pull the thick linen paper out and wave it at him.

"I am curious as well. I don't suppose you would tell me what you want it for. I've never heard that you were interested in that type of thing."

"You would be surprised by what interests me," I murmur, thinking of the marks on my skin.

"Still, this place? The man you seek is reviled by even those whose depravities are unspeakable. You know he collects paintings that depict women and animals together."

"Is that right?" I coolly raise an eyebrow, hoping that I do not betray the quickening of my heart rate over the knowledge that we are close to our prey.

He leans close and his eyes glitter with excitement. "It is said he has Leonardo's *Leda and the Swan* and that last year he acquired a Caravaggio from a Frenchman—"

At my cold look, he shuts up and proceeds to straighten items on his desk—his keyboards, both of them, his mouse, a USB hub, a wireless speaker. Taking pity on him and satisfied that he has provided all the items Naomi and I will need for our visit in Venice, I hand him a pack of cigarettes. He opens the top and nods. "This . . . friend of yours. What makes you say that he is Asperger's?"

"My friend admitted it. There's no shame in the condition," I reply, making no movement toward the bag. Guillaume taps out a cigarette and lights it. The smell of tobacco fills the room immediately.

"You don't think he's too odd with his fits and weird questions and tendency to forget you are even there?"

These sound like complaints Guillaume has been subjected to. Complaints that Naomi has heard. "*Nyet.* We all have our . . . quirks, *da?*" He nods. "My friend is interesting, talented." I think back to the slap across my face and the scratches in my chest. Very talented. "Those things you speak of bother me not at all."

"And in public your friend doesn't embarrass you?"

I recall the incident with the customs official. "I am not embarrassed, although sometimes the behavior of my friend in public can cause problems. But those problems are minor and do not devalue the person in my opinion."

"Then you are different than most, Vasily. Many do not enjoy being associated with us."

"I do not find you weird or odd, Guillaume. No more so than anyone else. My sister, for example, likes things very orderly. And those calcio players have their idiosyncrasies, which everyone finds entertaining rather than off-putting." And me, I think, I like to be hurt during intercourse. "We are all strange in our own way."

"This is true." He takes another deep draw and blows out a long stream of smoke. He's becoming entranced by it. I recognize this focus as I've seen it before in Naomi's eyes as she is distracted by something she finds fascinating. I prefer it to be me, but it can be something as ephemeral as the trail of smoke. "I love the flavor of these but so hard to obtain when I am not allowed into France anymore."

"You but need to ask and more will be sent to you."

He jiggles the pack, listening as the three diamonds inside clink together gently. "I am almost sad that you removed four to make room for these baubles."

I give him a half smile. "I will send you a carton if you but ask."

He doesn't, though. To ask is to owe me a favor. "They say that the Petrovich *Bratva* is in tumult and that its hold in Russia and abroad may be faltering."

I bare my teeth. "Those who say that are full of envy and will soon regret it."

"Do you think you can hold that old family together? You are not a Petrovich," Guillaume says, blowing out another long stream of smoke.

"No. I am better, and those that oppose me will feel my fist and heel on not just their person, but every person in their family."

"But it is called the Petrovich *Bratva* so then you must be a Petrovich, no?"

"Every papal prince changes his name, but the Vatican built on St. Peter's bones remains constant. So, too, is a *Bratva*. The prince who rules formulates his own rules, adorning the walls with his triumphs and writing his victories into the tomes on the shelves of the libraries. But he also preserves the papacy for the next ruler. I am merely ensuring that the *Bratva* is healthy for the next prince."

I leave Guillaume studying his smoke stream. And all around us people are doubting the necessity of the *Bratva*, doubting both its friendly hand and the sting of its sword. But if I . . . *we* . . . could generate the belief within the *Bratva*, that would radiate outward until the entirety of our community would rise up against our enemies if necessary, ensuring that only the *threat* of retribution could keep people safe.

I need peace for those that I love, not just my sister but . . . others. One other. The silly painting is becoming a symbol to me as well. If I can retrieve it, well then, I can rid myself of Elena Petrovich and ensure that Katya and Naomi are able to live a regular life, without fear.

When I arrive back at our little room, Naomi is sitting in a chair that is draped with her clothes and mine.

"Where did you go?" She scowls.

"To get our entrée into Ponte delle Tette. It is an invitation-only fetish club in Venice. Guillaume Beaulieu is a man who can procure many things such as these."

"The Bridge of—"

"Tits," I supply as she struggles for the *tette* translation. "Everything in Venice involves water."

"How come Guillaume can't find your painting?"

"He trades in favors and small gems. He does not take on tasks that would endanger him . . . not anymore, at least."

She makes no attempt to look inside the bag, perhaps afraid of germs, so I open the package for her. The invitations are on heavy vellum and tucked inside a large linen handcrafted envelope stamped with the letters *PdT* in large script. There are two masks, made by Ca' Macana, along with one other thing. Perhaps the most important thing.

"This club is somewhat different. Everyone will wear a mask. Our costumes are thoroughly checked for electronics, particularly cameras or recording devices as well as weapons. Sex clubs in Venice are rare. There is no obvious prostitution nor any red-light district. Only private clubs exist, and this is one of the most discreet. In the club there is every kind of perversion you can imagine. Every kind. Our goal, Naomi, is to find and to place this on our mark." I lay a tag on the table between us. It is a two-inch-by-two-inch square that is made of gold filament.

"Is this an NFC tag?" She grabs it and holds it up to the light.

"It is of the same design, yes, but while a near field communication tag can only be read up to four feet, this can be tracked from a distance. But it is powered by nearby electronics. If our mark goes near any type of Bluetooth or radio signal, it will emit a signal, like a homing device. Because it is made of gold filament, it will register as part of the costuming rather than a banned metal."

"How do we know who our mark is?"

"We look for the right perversion."

"Which is?"

I stare at her. "The *Madonna and the Volk* is the painting he has acquired. Another of his favorites is *Leda and the Swan*."

"Ohhhh," she says with growing understanding. And then, "Ewww."

I smother a laugh. "And this is yours, not part of a costume, but because I promised. And I always deliver my promises."

She stares wide-eyed at the baseball cap in my hands.

CHAPTER **TWENTY-SIX**

NAOMI

I can't stop gazing at the baseball cap in his hands. It's a soft, distressed gray like my old one. There's no fraying on the edges like the one I abandoned, but it's similar, right down to the lack of a logo and the Velcro fitting strap across the back of the head.

He's so thoughtful. Always, always thoughtful.

He holds it out to me, this *volk*, this monster who claims to have no soul. Who says he will destroy my family if they stand in his way. Who says he feels nothing for anyone and does not like to be touched.

But he likes my touch. And he remembered my baseball cap and how miserable I was to lose it.

I reach out and take it from him with shaking fingers.

"I regret we will have to experience another sex club, Naomi. I trust that you will be able to conduct yourself as you did last time? Because you did very well. I have brought earplugs in case you will require them again."

He's talking, but I'm not listening. I finger the Velcro strap. It's so clean, no lint stuck in the tiny plastic hooks. I adore it already. "Has this been laundered?"

"It was factory sealed when I purchased it. I made the vendor remove it from a plastic bag."

Oooh, factory sealed. Germ free. I shiver. Those are magical words for me.

Vasily continues to talk about the club. Something about depravities and masks and historical figures in Venice who have visited the club. I'm not paying attention. I squeeze the bill to give it a little shape, and then adjust the strap to what will fit my head, and then put it on. It's perfect. It's not quite the one I lost, but it's so close and I know he picked this out especially for me.

My heart is doing more of those funny little flips. My *volk*. My monster. I'm not even mad about the mattress anymore.

"I regret we cannot blindfold you this time," he continues in that deep voice, looking at me. "Will you be able to function?"

"I think this cap is made from denim and not the normal acrylics," I tell him, smoothing my fingers along the bill. It's so soft that it's arousing me. And it's not just the cap. It's that feeling I have when I look at Vasily, who's going on and on about some sex club, and who showed me my G-spot earlier.

I know he's a sociopath. I don't care. We all have our issues. But he's my sociopath, and as long as he doesn't hurt me or my family, or make me feel like less, he'll be mine and I'll be his. I'll tell him my conditions and then we can have crazy, slapping sex again.

I liked being wild with him.

"Naomi?" he says.

I look up from my blissful contemplation of my cap and pull it off my head, lovingly placing it on the clothing-covered arm of the chair. I want to wear the cap, but I also want to kiss Vasily's hard mouth at the moment, and it will get in the way. "What is it?"

"You are not listening to me, are you?" His words are words that I have learned are angry ones, but he's smiling at me like I have done something cute. This man is difficult to read. I don't know if he's happy or mad, so I decide that I will distract him.

I get up from the chair and approach him, then straighten his collar a moment before I grab it and mash my mouth against his.

My *volk*.

He groans and his mouth moves against mine, his tongue delving into my mouth, and I meet it with my own. I'm no longer afraid of Vasily's germs—I welcome them. They're mine and I'm his and we're sharing everything, right down to microbes. My anger from earlier has vanished at the sight of the cap. I was seething not an hour ago—from that nasty trick about the mattress to the fact that he'd dyed my hair, again, while I was passed out and left me in a strange city.

But the cap has forgiven all. I'm filled with lust and a peculiar affection for this man. He confuses me, he doesn't always listen to me, but sometimes I think he understands me better than anyone I know.

So I kiss the hell out of him, so fierce that my teeth scrape along his tongue and nip at his lip, and I can feel the shudder that wracks his body in response. I think of the earlier sex, the toe-curling intensity of it, and I want it again. I'm a cat with a new toy, an Aspie with a fixation, and I want more sex.

"Naomi," he murmurs as I release his mouth and bite at the

faint blond beard stubble on his chin. It looks ludicrous with his dark hair but I don't care. The texture of it is fascinating, and the taste of it is Vasily, which means it is mine, too.

"Hush," I tell him. "I'm seducing you. I want more sex."

He chuckles, the sound reverberating low in his chest, and my fingers undo the buttons at his collar and shove clothing aside. I want to see him bare, to press my mouth to more of his hot skin. And I want to bite him. I'm not sure if that's appropriate, but if it's not, he'll tell me.

When my questing fingers reveal his chest, though, I pause. Raised red welts cover his chest, along with small reddish-purple bruises and scratches. I vaguely remember losing control during our last encounter. "Was this me?"

"*Da*," he says, and his voice has dropped to a low, husky note.

I'm momentarily stymied. "Was this . . . inappropriate? Did I go too far? You have to tell me these things." I smooth a hand over his chest, chagrined. "I can't read facial expressions so I don't know—"

His hand closes over mine. Squeezes it. "I liked it," he tells me in a rough voice. "Naomi, in case I have not said it obvious enough, I enjoy being hurt during sex. It makes me very aroused."

Curious, I decide to test this with a little experiment. I dig my nails into one of the scratches and watch his face. Sure enough, his pupils dilate and his breathing becomes quicker the harder I dig. Fascinating. I pull my hand from his and drag my nails roughly across the hard planes of his chest. "Is this a compulsion formed in childhood or is it the result of trauma? Or is this something you were born with?"

"Are you disturbed by my needs?"

That's not an answer, but I let it slide anyhow because I'm

more fascinated by the thought of playing with him. "I want to bite you," I tell him. "Hard. Really hard." My hand smooths over his chest again. "On all these muscles—"

He grabs me with a muffled curse and drags me toward the bathroom.

"Where are we going?"

"I need a shower. And I am going to fuck you while we are in it, since you do not like the bed."

Oooh.

We head into the small bathroom, hand in hand, and it still smells of the cleaning supplies I used. Before I showered, I hunted through the bathroom and found cleaners under the sink, and scrubbed the tile and tub before I stepped into it. I gave them another round of cleaning after my shower, so no trace of the nasty mattress germs remained.

"I smell cleaner," he tells me. "You?"

"Yes, I cleaned everything. Even the tile walls."

"Good," he says thickly. "I am going to push you against one and fuck you."

My pulse flutters to hear that. Oh, wow. That's an erotic thought, and more exciting than anything I've done with a computer in a long, long time. I eye the shower and the now-clean tile, imagining us pushed against it. My nipples harden in response.

"You are quiet."

"I was just impressed that I got wet so fast," I admit to him. "Want me to show you?"

He snarls like the *volk* he is, and then we are kissing again, ripping at each other's clothing. Fabric tears under my fingers, but I don't care. If my violence excites him, I'll give him violence. I want him as aroused as I am.

As our mouths mesh and our tongues twine, I tug at his clothing, snaking it down his arms and freeing his big, brawny, bitable chest. He's ripping at my own clothing, and somewhere in our excitement, he's managed to turn on the water to the shower. Steam begins to fill the room but neither one of us has stepped toward the water. We're too busy divesting the other of clothing.

"Looking at your big body lubricates me instantly," I tell him, pressing my thighs tighter together so I can feel the delicious squeeze of my wet flesh as it slides against itself. "It's interesting that such a physiological reaction can happen so quickly. My body must be very attuned to yours."

"Is that so?" His accent is thick, a sure sign—at least to me— that he's enjoying my words.

"It's true," I say as I step out of my panties. "Feel my secretions." And I take his hand and guide it between my legs. "Very wet, yes?"

His fingers press against my vaginal lips and then dip between them, moving back and forth. Even his hand feels so big that I get even more aroused, and when one finger traces the opening to my vagina, I bear down on it, wrap my hands around his neck, and lean in and bite the hell out of his clavicle.

Vasily snarls and thrusts his finger deep inside me, and I ride it, biting madly at all the skin I can find. I dig my teeth in, wanting to mark him more. I think he likes the marks, so I will leave him with dozens of them to pet and admire.

"You must stop," he tells me.

"No," I say and drag my teeth across his skin viciously.

The breath hisses from between his lips and he fingers me roughly even as he drags our joined bodies back to the sink. I make a protesting noise as his fingers slide from my pussy—so wet that they make a sound as they leave—and cling to him as he tries to roll on a condom while I distract him. I rub my own pussy because it feels good, and then drag my fingers over his hungry mouth as he rolls the condom down his length. "Drink," I command him.

He sucks my fingers clean, and his teeth nip at my skin. When I pull my fingers free of his mouth, I give it a light slap. We're acting like savages, and I've never been so aroused or had so much fun. I love the way Vasily's gaze narrows as I smack him, and his lungs heave like bellows.

And then he grabs me by the waist and drags us both into the shower, and I'm pressed against the wall a split second before he wrenches my thighs apart and slams into me.

I scream with pleasure. The shock of him forcing his way inside is delicious, and I'm so wet that it doesn't hurt. I love his wildness, his frenzy as he hauls my legs higher around him and shoves deeper inside me with the next thrust. I want to claw at his shoulders as he begins to roughly piston his hips against my pinned ones, but the water is making our bodies slick, and there's nothing for me to grab but his hair.

Oh, his hair.

I grab two fistfuls of it and yank even as I lean in to bite at his beautiful, hard mouth, so like the sculpture of a cruel god. His breath hisses out again and he snarls something that I pay no attention to, and he's fucking me so hard and fast that I'm pretty sure he's going to come in the next two seconds. And I want that, so I pull his hair harder. "My *volk*," I yell in his ear. "You're mine, right?"

"Yours," he growls, and gives me one mighty shove, his entire body trembling as he spends inside me. Then his hips shudder against mine and his wild plunges slow down.

He's come and I'm still wanting. So I slap at skin and tug at hair. "More, Vasily, more!"

"Patience," he tells me in a thick voice. I think he's feeling good, but I'm not there yet, and so I yank his hair again, like a child deprived of a pony ride. His hand steals between our sealed bodies and I feel the hard press of it between us as it steals to where our bodies are joined. Then, his thumb rubs against my clit.

My legs jerk. Between the feeling of his still-hard cock inside me and his thumb on my clitoris as he begins to rub, it takes mere moments before I'm screaming my own pleasure, and I come with my teeth sunk into Vasily's shoulder as he continues to work and manipulate my clit. I sigh with relieved pleasure as the aftershocks end and he slowly drops me from the wall to land on my feet in the tub.

"Let us wash together," he says, and peels the condom off.

It's a good idea. We both need to clean up. I step forward into the spray, and his hands begin to run over my wet skin. He unwraps a bar of nearby soap and begins to rub it along my breasts and arms, cleaning me. I stand still and let him.

"You are not uneasy about the sex club?" he asks.

"Hmm?" I'm drowsy with endorphins, and my legs are a little weak in the knees. I feel really good, too. Gosh, I love sex with Vasily, fluids and all. It's clear I've been missing out on something great. I wonder if there are other exciting things we can do in bed. This might just be the tip of the iceberg—

He grips my chin and turns my face toward him so he has my attention. "Naomi. Are you uncomfortable with the sex club we must visit?"

"No? I think I like sex now." My hands move over his chest, reddened with my scratches and bites. One of his nipples is purpling from where I sucked on it too hard. I should feel a twinge of guilt but all I can think is how he must have enjoyed that. "I'm just sorry we haven't had a lot of uses for a hacker at the moment. I mean, you don't need a black hat for going into a sex club, you know? If you wanted me to appropriate funds for you, I could. If you wanted me to take down a network, I could. But suck on your cock in front of others? You don't need me for that."

"I do not need a hacker," he agrees, and my heart momentarily drops. But his hands skim along my wet skin and then cup one of my breasts. "But I need you. You are the only person that can touch me and I do not feel revulsion, Naomi."

I'm pleased by this compliment. "It's because we've been around each other so much that we're likely now immune to each other's pathogens."

He snorts. "If you say so. Or perhaps it is just you, because you are special to me."

I tense a little at the word *special*, but when he clarifies it, I relax. I don't mind being special to Vasily. I take the soap from him and dab my fingertips on it, then stroke them across his now-streaky eyebrows to clean them. "When do we go to this sex club?"

"We go tomorrow."

"Good."

"Why good?"

I smooth my thumbs over his brows. "I want you to find my G-spot again."

CHAPTER TWENTY-SEVEN

VASILY

On my right, Naomi is lovingly stroking the brim of her cap repeatedly. Her fingers must be chafed at this point. I shift in my small seat. My cock is sore today. If she propositioned me, I may have to turn her down. I am not at all certain I could accommodate her request.

In the slow-moving Fiat I appropriated near the university, the images of our bathroom endeavor filter through my mind. First there was her command to locate her G-spot, which was easily done. I have it memorized, and my fingers seek it out without effort. But after rubbing her until she gasped and came around my fingers, I turned her to face her freshly cleaned tile and pounded into her until she was screaming and I was coming harder than I ever had before.

Perhaps we should have stopped there. We slid into the curved porcelain tub, exhausted and weak. With the last ounce of energy, I pulled a towel over us. We must have dozed off, but then I recall waking with my cock in her mouth, her ass bobbing rhythmically by my face. I pulled her over to straddle my face and ate her as she choked around my cock.

Naomi is not a good multitasker.

But when I finally was done licking her juices, she declared that we could not sleep again until my own erection was relieved. I did not argue.

"Did you know that in this position it is much easier for me to maintain firm contact against my clitoris without the aid of your hands or mine?"

"*Nyet*," I grunted in response, lifting her ass up and then enjoying her slam down.

"Our bodies fit really well together. I worried you would be too big. But you aren't too big. I mean, you're big. Definitely bigger than average." Her words went on and on, breathy syllables separated by gasps of air. "Your hair is both soft and scratchy. Why is that?"

"Shall I shave it for you?"

She stopped then. "You would shave? Yes, I think you should. For science."

"For science," I repeated solemnly, and then buried my face into her neck as her cunt muscles began squeezing and releasing me. "What are you doing, Naomi?"

"I'm working my Kegel muscles. Those are—"

"I know what they are," I interrupted.

"Yes, well, I'm seeing if they enhance intercourse. I think it does. It makes me want to orgasm more quickly. I think it's the friction or pressure on various parts of my vagina. Don't you think so?"

"Yes. Squeeze me again," I said through gritted teeth.

"Does it feel good to you?"

"*Da*! Fuck me . . ."

"Vasily . . . Vasily." Naomi tugs on my arm. By the frown on her face, it appears she has been attempting to gather my attention for some time. I shake myself to loosen the sexual memories.

"What do you wish?" She has a new laptop we acquired in Firenze open and is fiddling with the tag we will be placing on our mark for tracking purposes.

"I want to test the range of this tag."

"You have written a program?"

"Yeah, just a simple little code but I can't test how far away this thing will emit a signal when I'm sitting next to it."

"Guillaume said a few hundred feet."

"That's not very precise. How will we track this guy?"

"Venice is small. We will walk around until it goes off."

She frowns at me. "Seriously? That is your plan? That's really bad, Vasily. Pull over," she orders.

I shrug. A break to stretch our legs would be welcome. I drive the Fiat onto the median and engage the emergency break.

"What are you doing?" she asks, confused.

"Pulling over." I open the car door and step out.

"I meant like at a gas station or something."

"This is Italy. There are no roadside gas stations as there are in the United States. It is perfectly acceptable to pull over to piss."

Her mouth forms a circle of horror, and then she digs into her bag, pulling out a bottle of hand purifier. Thrusting it at me, she orders, "Use this after you are done voiding. I don't like urine."

I take the bottle. "You don't seem to mind my come." I throw the bottle up lightly and catch it.

"It's not the same thing." She *harrumphs* and closes the car door.

I walk backward down the median with the tag in my pocket, waiting for her to signal to me. She waves me forward. I turn, jog a few paces, and turn back. We repeat this several times until she finally emerges from the vehicle and gestures for me to return.

"How far is that?" she asks when I near.

"Approximately four hundred feet." I hold the door open, aware of an oncoming Audi traveling at a swift distance. "Get in and move to the driver's side. Your head should be below the window." She hesitates. "Now, Naomi. Go."

I slam the door shut behind her regretfully. It would have served as a nice shield. Pulling out my gun from my shoulder holster, I wait for the car to near. I jump lightly in place to loosen my muscles, allowing my right hand to hang freely along my thigh. A glance to my left reveals Naomi pressed up against the passenger window. I bang my elbow against the glass, causing her to scurry back.

The car is almost upon us. The lights flash once, twice, and then it's gone. I turn and raise the gun almost reflexively before it finally registers the Audi was no threat. Almost regretfully I round the front of the Fiat and climb into the driver's seat.

"What was that? Did you think they were going to shoot at us? Why did they flash their lights?"

"They flashed their lights to tell me that I am an idiot for standing in the middle of the road. You were to remain with your head below the dashboard," I remind her, pulling into traffic and then maneuvering the car into the slow right lane. Not for the first time today I wish for a different car. An Alfa Romeo? We would be in Venice by now.

"I had to see what was going on and I couldn't do that with my head down," she argues.

"If there was a gunman, he could have shot you between your eyes."

"No way. That only happens in the movies. A bullet's trajectory would be moved by impact against the glass, not to mention the vehicle was moving at a high speed."

"Nikolai Andrushko once shot a Chechen warlord in the left eye in a vehicle going 110 kilos per hour while the warlord's vehicle was traveling at an equally swift pace."

"I don't believe it," she says stubbornly. "The thickness of the glass, as well as the velocity of the bullet, not to mention wind speeds, moisture in the air. And besides, if a gunman was that good, hiding behind the leather seat wouldn't be the safest place. Probably the safest place is the engine block. How do you know that this Andrushko character made the shot? It's probably a myth."

"I was driving the Audi that Andrushko was sitting in," I told her.

"Oh . . . well he was a very good shot, then."

"*Da*, one of the best," I agree.

"Where is he now? We should fly him down and then you can drive, I can work on my computer, and Andrushko can protect us."

"He is . . . dead," I say.

"Was he killed by another shooter? Because we should get that guy instead."

What do I say? *Your brother and I faked the killing of Nikolas Andrushko, but he now lives happily ever after with some bosomy farm girl from America?* "I believe he is unavailable currently. You will have to endure my protection services."

"Is that a sexual innuendo? You know I have a hard time catching on to those."

I smile because she might have problems catching them with other people, but she understood mine. "I will protect you all night and into the dawn." The clock indicates that it will take us three more hours to get to Venice. I enjoy hearing her voice and want her to talk. "How was it that you came to be in the hands of Hudson?"

"Oh that?" She scrunches up her nose as if she's smelled something bad. "That was my attempt at being normal. You see, in the United States, kids in college and sometimes even high school kids go to resorts in Mexico or the Caribbean for vacation. They imbibe lots of liquor and have random sex with strangers." My knuckles tighten around the steering wheel at the thought of her with another man but then I remember her . . . idiosyncrasies. She would not have been comfortable there with the strangers and the noise. "Daniel encouraged me to go. I skipped a lot of grades and didn't have many friends my age. He said it would be good for me. But it was so . . . noisy and you couldn't step out of your room without someone running into you. People were very clumsy, too, always spilling their drinks or spitting it out. It was very disgusting so I went for a walk on the beach."

"You were taken then?"

"Yes. I think they were going to—you know—hurt me like they do to women." She meant be raped. "But I convinced them that I could make them a lot of money if they would only give me a computer."

"And you spent eighteen months in Hudson's basement," I conclude for her.

"It wasn't as bad as it seems. It was quiet there. He left me alone mostly. There was one guard who was kind to me. His son was autistic. He brought the son in to meet me and we discussed trains. Trains are like—" she searches for an analogy which is difficult for her.

"Bees to honey?" I supply.

"Yes. That's a great comparison. We love the orderly nature of them. How the tracks can switch back and forth. The timeliness of them. The way we can track their routes. It's fascinating and kind of relaxing." She makes a face. "It's too bad we got shot at on the train before because it would have been awesome to take the train to Venice."

"It is better to be safe than sorry," I say, repeating a famous U.S. idiom.

"What about you? What's the story with you and the painting? Why go to all this trouble? Can't I just buy your way to power?"

"Do you know the story of Pablo Escobar?" She shakes her head no. "Pablo Escobar controlled the manufacture and distribution of cocaine the mid-1980s to the mid-1990s. He was purportedly one of the wealthiest men in the world at the time of his death. What made him so powerful, however, wasn't just the money or the violent way he exercised his authority, but that the people of Colombia revered him. When he died, twenty-five thousand Medellín citizens came out to mourn his passing. He built churches and schools, fed the poor, nursed the sick. And for this, they helped hide his men, his coke, his guns.

"They believed in him like they believed in a deity, and if Pablo Escobar spoke, the people of Medellín carved his words in their bodies. That is real power, Naomi, and it requires more than merely money but a spiritual connection between you and the people around you. The *Bratva* once existed like that for the people around us but it has backslid, concerned more about personal wealth and gain. The current pack of Petrovichs take things, never giving, treating all of those around them like . . . toys." I spit out the last word, feeling revulsion curl around me like a snake, threatening to choke me. "I do not know if I care about the principles of Escobar, the giving, the Robin Hood, mentality. But I know that if I get this Madonna, the *Bratva* will coalesce behind me and I will not be subject to the whims of the Petrovichs again, because I will be the one who holds the power in his right hand and the sword in his left."

Kilometers pass. Village after village flits in and out of our windows, and then she finally speaks. "But what if it doesn't?"

"It will." It must. For this woman beside me to be safe with me, for my sister to live openly and without fear. It must. If I have to burn it all to the ground and rebuild it stone by motherfucking stone.

CHAPTER **TWENTY-EIGHT**

NAOMI

I run my fingers along the keyboard of my new laptop, thinking. Keyboards are filthy things, but this one is practically from the factory, and I wipe it down prior to each use. No germs have touched this but mine.

At the thought of germs, I think of my *volk*. I ache between my legs from our marathon of sex. As Vasily likes to point out, once I have a new toy, I am not easily distracted, and sex with him is my newest fascination. Even right now, I feel the urge to find him and put my mouth on his cock and see his reaction. He tells me it's time to stop because his body aches, but I think this is a specious argument for someone that likes pain during sex. It's more likely that I'm costing us valuable time to prepare.

We're going to the house of perversions tonight, to find Vasily's mark. Our trail across Italy leads to one particular pervert, and once we find him, Vasily can return to his *Bratva* and make a difference in Russia, and I will go to his *dacha* in the woods and . . . what? Relax? Hide from the world and code? Two weeks ago, I would have been fine with that, but two weeks ago, Vasily was not my *volk*. Two weeks ago, I had not found my G-spot. Two weeks ago, everything was different.

I've been abandoned several times in my life. Never by my parents, who love me, and my brother, who is smart and responsible and has never treated me like I'm weird. But beyond that trio . . . I've always been abandoned. Friendships are fleeting, relationships even more so. College was just as lonely as grade school. There is no club, no sorority, no activity I can join and not be an outsider. No matter what I do, I am rejected by those I want to share my life with. I'm used to it by now. It still hurts, but it's an expected hurt.

But the thought of Vasily using me until he gets his painting and then tossing me aside while he reconquers Russia fills me with anxiety and unhappiness. I understand his motives. I felt a twinge of pride in my heart to hear his plans—to rebuild the *Bratva* into greatness and to make a difference in the lives of everyone. It's noble. But I'm pretty sure there's no place at his side for a hacker geek who drifts off on tangents on a whim and who can't be around crowds. If he's to take up the leadership reins, there's no room for Naomi in the picture. Naomi will be at the sad little *dacha* in the woods, isolated and safe and utterly forgotten. No one will touch her G-spot or ask to be bitten during sex.

If there's no room for me at his side, though, I can at least help secure his empire. I flex my fingers before I begin typing again. I start a myriad of searches on the Internet and a second one on my deep web. I'm looking for crime families in Russia, mentions of

Mafia or organized crime, and family names. Once I have the information I need, I'll run a cross-check against clearinghouse deposit records, looking for bank transactions. Once I've narrowed down where Vasily's rivals are storing their money, I can simply peck away, using script after script, until I empty their accounts, one by one.

Money greases a lot of wheels, and if I can cripple Vasily's opponents by removing a tool from them, I will. I'm not like Daniel, who came after me, guns blazing. I'm not good with firearms—the noise sets off one of my spells and I go deep inside myself. But I can be fierce and protective. I can perform my own form of combat on his behalf.

He's my vo*lk*.

"You must not show alarm tonight," Vasily coaches me as we get dressed for the Pervert House. "Do you remember all we have talked of?"

My fingers move up the hooks of my corset, but when I can no longer reach, I pat Vasily's arm. As if we are an old married couple, he spins me around and finishes the hooks for me, without a word passing between us. I think of our preparations for this party. "No blindfold this time. If I get anxious, I am to use my safe word, since that will not cause any alarm amongst the party-goers. Submissives often get nervous in new settings and cling to their masters for reassurance." I parrot the words he told me earlier in a bored voice. "There will be many kinds of scandalous actions there tonight, but I am not to get distracted. I am to look for a man who seeks the attentions of animals. If there are more than one of these kinds of men, we are to look for signs of wealth.

Jewelry, servants, etcetera, etcetera." I even use the same hand motions Vasily did when telling me these things.

He chuckles. "You are getting quite good at mimicking me. And here I thought you were not paying attention." His hands finish the corset and glide down to the satin panties covering my ass, as if unable to help himself.

I don't mind this touch. Anything Vasily sends in my direction, I accept happily. Well . . . unless it's on another dirty mattress. I push that thought aside and turn around, gazing up at Vasily. He's in a dress suit with tails, and we've fixed his eyebrows so they match his hair once more. With the dark brows and hair, he looks saturnine and forbidding. "Is there danger tonight, do you think?"

"I am *Bratva*. There is always some danger, Naomi. It is never far behind."

This is not an answer that makes me happy. "The train was supposed to be safe and men with guns came after you."

He frowns. I know he doesn't like this reminder. "There will be no men with guns tonight, Naomi."

"There weren't supposed to be men with guns on the train, either," I tell him, frustrated. There is a piece of lint on the jet-black lapels of his suit and I idly pick at it, then dust my fingers over the seams, ensuring all the fabric falls beautifully on his big body. "Who sent those men? The assassins in the train car?"

He is silent.

I press on, because I refuse to take silence as an answer. "Golubevs? You said it wasn't them. What other enemies do you have? What about Hudson's men?"

"It was not them," he adds after a moment. "They did not seek you. I think their plans were simply to kill me."

"So who wants you dead?"

He bares his teeth at me. "Everyone."

This is not an answer I like. I continue to fuss with his suit to keep my hands busy. "Do we have weapons planned?"

"The invitation was clear, Naomi. We will be thoroughly searched, and wanded with metal detectors. There will be no room for weapons anywhere. I will rely upon garroting anyone that needs killing."

I touch the necklaces at my neck. Each one has a purpose. One is the tiny gold chain with the tracking device coded to my computer. Another is a thick metal "slave collar" band that wraps tight around my throat. It will protect my throat from similar attacks if anyone should retaliate. Another necklace is made up of multiple thin wires that have a decorative bead but will serve as Vasily's garrotes.

I'm not satisfied, though. "I feel we are not utilizing our costumes to their full ability."

"Oh?" His fingers caress my jaw. "What would you like to add to yours, then, little slave?"

It's something I've been considering all afternoon, ever since I came to the full realization that Vasily would be going into the Pervert House weaponless. I don't like seeing my *volk* without a gun. "I am thinking I should be a naughty slave."

One of those falsely dark eyebrows goes up. "Is that so?"

"Yes," I tell him, with growing enthusiasm for my plan. I want to impress him, to please him with my ingenuity. "Many vibrators and dildos with a vibrating function have a screw base where the batteries go. We can purchase a large one, remove the battery packs, and place a thin, small knife inside. We would have to wrap it with fabric to ensure it did not rattle in the case, but it should work. Then we can return the lid and insert the dildo into my vagina. Once we are inside, we can remove it and extract the knife."

Vasily's face is as unreadable as ever. "Do you propose that you enter this den—"

"The Pervert House," I chime in, since I like my nickname for the place.

"—with a knife in your *pizda*?"

"We should make use of all orifices," I tell him thoughtfully. "Do you think one in the anus as well would be too much?"

"You would do this for me?"

I give him a puzzled look. "Of course I would."

He leans in, cups my face, and gives me a fierce kiss. He mumbles something in Russian that sounds like an endearment, and his thumb brushes across my lips. "Clever Naomi," he says at last.

"It will seem natural," I tell him, since he's not running out the door with credit card in tow just yet. "If I'm your slave and I'm misbehaving, you can punish me. If this is a club of perversions, it won't seem out of place."

"And you are sure you wish to do this?"

I'm not sure, actually. Entering a sex den with a dildo pushed into my vagina seems like a scream for attention, but the alternative is Vasily with no weapon other than a thin wire. "I'm sure," I tell him. "You should go buy me a dildo. A really big one. Big enough to fit two knives. One for me and one for you."

He snorts at this. "Two knives."

"Two," I agree. "If they are thin enough, you should be able to fit two."

"If the blades are discovered, it will be chaos."

"They won't be discovered," I say boldly. "It's the safest place on the planet. You would kill any man that got within an inch of my cunt."

His breath hisses, and I'm not sure if he's laughing or shocked. But in the next moment, his mouth bears down on mine in another fierce, possessive kiss that leaves me shaken. Then, he releases me and heads for the door. "Wait here, Naomi. I will return quickly."

"Quickly" turns into an hour, but he arrives soon enough with a small pink bag, and my heart hammers at the sight. He pulls the toy out with a flourish—hot pink, bulbous, and with a screw-off section like I suggested. For a few tense minutes, I watch as Vasily removes the working parts from inside and pushes two thin, deadly-looking blades into the pouch created. He tucks a handkerchief around them to ensure there's no telltale rattle, and then screws the end back on. He eyes the object, and then looks at me. "Are you wet enough to take this?"

"Not just yet," I tell him, and strip off my panties. Then, I gesture at my now-exposed pussy. "Come give me one last kiss. Then I will be."

CHAPTER TWENTY-NINE

VASILY

I know I should not kiss her on her bare cunt. We will be late and I do not want to walk into that den of iniquity aching for another touch of her body or the taste of her against my tongue. "You must not touch me, Naomi. This is only to help you. I cannot be distracted tonight and you are a very dangerous distraction."

She nods, bright eyed, and holds her hands above her head. I pick up the thin dildo holding the razor-sharp and long, slender blades that are not much wider than a finger. A cut with these would need to be precise, along the carotid artery or Achilles if we mean to maim them. We are crazed. When I kneel down, I can see she is already wet. There is moisture glistening on her upper thighs. I spread her legs farther apart, the smoothness of the dildo pressing its shape into one beautiful upper thigh.

"Do you need my help?" she asks after a moment.

"*Nyet*, just admiring your beauty." I stroke her lips, and pearls of her arousal bead on my fingertips. I lick the juice off and close my eyes, savoring the flavor. Above me she is having difficulty breathing. The air is releasing from her in short pants although I have barely touched her. She is quite responsive, my dear Naomi. "How long do you think I should lick you? How many kisses will you need, do you think, to come for me?" I ask, returning my fingers to her bare cunt, stroking her with a featherlight touch. She quivers and moans but does not answer. "I think you should count."

I lean forward and place the broad flat of my tongue against her swollen sex.

"You are not counting," I say, sitting back.

"One," she replies hurriedly. "That is one. I've never thought about how long it would take you to get me off. I should, though. That seems eminently reasonable. Now lick me again. Two," she orders even though I haven't touched her.

"Are you counting in advance?" I say. "Because that would be an easy way to get confused. Start from the beginning."

"Oh fine. One, damn it. One."

I lick her again, only this time it is short, almost a flick across her clit.

"That's not a full lick," she complains. "I'm only giving you a half for that."

"Count correctly or I won't lick you again," I say sternly.

"Fine. Fine." She restlessly shifts in front of me, her cunt lips playing peekaboo between her thighs. "Two."

I lean forward, press her legs apart, and lick her once forward and then back as far as I can go. Her weak legs cannot hold her, and she nearly collapses on top of me. "Three. Or Four. I don't know. Vasily, just fuck me with your tongue already." She hits me on my back with a tiny ineffectual fist.

I lift one trembling leg over my shoulder and with my palms braced against her ass, I hold her steady for my onslaught. There is no more time for finesse or games. I suck and bite at her sensitive flesh until I can feel her tightening like a coil. In a swift movement, I plunge the dildo in her cunt and she screams.

"My name. Say my name," I order her, pulling the dildo out and pushing it back in. Her body sucks it in, hungry and grasping.

"Vasily. Vasily. Vasily," she chants as she is undone by my mouth and the small toy. I catch her body as it slides down to the floor, unhooking her leg from my shoulder so she doesn't tear a muscle. "I can't stand," she whimpers. "Hold me off the floor, please. There are germs there."

Obediently, I lift her in my arms and then stride to the bathroom. Propping her up on the sink, I wet a washcloth and clean her off. The base of the dildo is still protruding from her. It is very thin and very small but I am unsure how she will walk.

As she leans against the mirror, I splash water on my face and wash my hands. I can still smell her scent, though, as if I've bathed in her.

"Will you be able to walk, Naomi?" I ask her, wiping my hands on a towel.

"Once my blood flow begins to normalize, I should be able to walk without problems. The dildo is small enough that it might chafe lightly but that should not be an impediment. Possibly I will walk with a strange, antalgic gait, but other than that I will appear normal."

"It will look as if I've beaten you, then?" At this club that would indeed be considered normal.

"Or I could have a shortened leg. Many people who have single-leg surgeries to repair broken bones suffer from differing lengths of legs. It often leads to back problems. I wouldn't want to walk around with a dildo all the time," she explains.

"No," I say with amusement. "That would not seem wise."

"It's possible I might orgasm and then because of the temporary ischemic mismatch between the oxygen my lungs need and the amount of blood that is pumping upward to my heart rather than downward, I might stumble."

"Is that true?"

"No, actually I just made that up not about the ischemic mismatch because that's accurate but I'm unsure of whether there is redirected blood flow during orgasms. I will need to research that."

"Certainly, pet, but later."

"Okay."

I lead Naomi through a winding path of narrow alleys, covered paths and bridges until we arrive at Ponte delle Tette. The door is a dark metal, possibly iron, and there is no window. Above me I hear the whirring of a security camera as it tracks our faces. The masks we wear conceal our identity. I flash the medallion that I purchased from Guillaume toward the camera. A *snick* sounds, indicating the door is now unlatched.

Opening the door, I gesture for Naomi to go inside. The door closes behind us. In front, I see a wide glass or perhaps Plexiglas door and beyond that a thin wall separating the entrance beyond into two. The staging area where we will be searched individually. The door slides open and I push Naomi to the right while I step to the left. "I will be on the other side of the wall. I can hear you and will come to your aid if you call out."

She nods tightly and steps forward. A black curtain is swiftly drawn by someone inside, blocking my view of her. If they find the knives in the dildo, will they stab her with them before I can reach her?

Quickly, I enter my own box. A man covered in black leather from head to toe closes the curtain behind me.

"Arms up," he orders. Only his mouth, nose, and eyes are visible. I raise my arms and he frisks me. Satisfied I have no guns or knives on my person, he orders me to step through the metal detector. I have left everything off, even a belt. The metal detector is silent.

Naomi will set hers off. She will explain that she has gold around her neck and a dildo in her pussy. Surely they will not pull that out and inspect it.

"Clear," he says, and I'm pushed through into a dimly lit foyer. I wait, anxious for any sound from Naomi. Seconds stretch out into minutes and just when I'm ready to charge into her room, she stumbles out beside me.

"How are you?" I ask, gripping her shoulders.

She is panting and I wonder if she is close to having an attack. I press down on her shoulders, recalling how the weight of me seemed to stave off a previous attack. It appears to work, as her tense body relaxes under mine.

"I did not like that," she mumbles into my chest. "Don't make me do it again."

"*Nyet*, I will not. I apologize for these indignities."

"They touched me all over. All over," she shudders. "I need to take a shower. Water. I need water. If I had water, it would help. Water."

I press harder.

"What's wrong with her?" A suited man steps out of the shadows. "If she can't handle herself, you both need to go."

"There is nothing wrong with her," I reply with rude haughtiness. "She does not like being manhandled."

He snorts. "Fine, but if she disturbs others then you need to leave."

Inside the club Vivaldi is playing. The wail of the oboe plays a haunting tune. To my right I spot an alcove and duck inside. There are two people fornicating. I cannot tell their genders given the darkness and their shapes nor do I care. I throw five hundred euros on the table. "Out," I order.

They take the money and scramble away. There are plenty of places for them to fuck. Sitting on the edge of the leather-covered banquette, I gather Naomi in my lap. She is still shaking.

"Listen to my voice, Naomi. Take deep breaths. Concentrate on your breathing. In through your nose. Out through your mouth," I instruct. I place my hand on her stomach and press. I breathe deeply myself, letting her feel my chest expand and then contract repeatedly. She begins to mimic me, slowly filling her lungs and then releasing the air. "Again."

She follows and I feel her tremors calm and the tension leach out of her. We sit there for long moments as she gathers herself, one long breath at a time.

She uncoils from me, and I let her legs drop down until her heels hit the floor. "We are not in a hurry," I lie.

"I'm okay," she says, covering my hand still resting on her stomach. "You won't leave me, though? Not again tonight."

"*Nyet*. I will be by your side."

"Always?"

Before I would likely hesitate, weighing my pursuit of power against her request, but now? Now it is only important that she is comforted. "Whenever you have need of me, I will be there." I answer. She does not seem to notice the paucity of my promise. Instead, bravely, she straightens and takes my hand.

"I'm ready."

We exit the alcove and I lead her forward. As promised, there are all kinds of wickedness here. There are ordinary ones played out in households all around such as the binding of the body or the slap of the whip. And then there are the extraordinary ones such that even those who play do not like to admit to. The ones that can't be seen during an ordinary web search or on pornography sites set up by Russian girls for their keepers.

These dark perversions are behind heavily locked doors with discreet signs that only those who are in the know can follow.

"What are we looking for?" Naomi asks, rightfully confused, because to the ordinary eye, we are looking at blank doors, down dark hallways. I lead us up one set of stairs and then another until we are three stories up and I see the sign I've been looking for. The goddess Demeter is carved into a wooden relief above the door.

"Agriculture?" Naomi scrunches her nose in apparent confusion and then it clears. "Ohhh. I get it. Demeter, the goddess of agriculture for the animal lovers. That's kind of gross. I don't think she'd be happy with that."

I pluck the tracking code off her shoulder and then peer down to look at the lock. It's a simple one and strangely enough the thin knives I've hidden in the dildo will work perfectly for those.

Down one floor, I find a bathroom that is unoccupied.

"Naomi, I must remove the implement. Are you ready?" I slide my hands down her corseted sides.

"Yes." She winces. "I could really use a break. I thought it would be sexy but it's actually quite uncomfortable. I think if you were touching me, it might be more pleasurable but as it is I felt like I was waddling. What if it was bigger? I don't think I could even walk then."

I pull her panties down to her knees and then reach between her legs. Even though she said she was uncomfortable, she is still quite wet.

She groans when I pull it out. "Now I feel empty. You should kiss me and make it feel better."

I lock my knees so I don't fall to the floor and fulfill her request. "I will fuck you until you pass out after we are done," I promise and press a hard kiss to her forehead. I unscrew the bottom, and drop the two knives in my hand. "Hold out your hand."

She does so, like a good soldier. Despite her many questions and her nonstop talk, Naomi is one of the best people I've worked with. Generally she does what I ask, and I know I can trust her implicitly. I drop the knives into her hands and then discard the dildo and wash my hands.

The knives are secreted in my pocket next to the tracking device. "You must be very quiet now," I say. She nods.

We exit the bathroom with Naomi's hand tucked into mine. For people who do not like to touch, we seem to be bothered more when we are not connected.

When we arrive at the Demeter door, I make quick work of the lock. I can tell by her swiftly indrawn breath that she wants to comment on this, but she remains silent.

It is not the time nor place, but I cannot help myself from tipping her chin up. Her gaze skitters across my cheek as I bend down to meet her lips. I press against the softness until she yields and opens her mouth with a sigh.

My tongue sweeps in to remind her of my possession—or perhaps to accede to her possession of me, because I'm rapidly becoming obsessed with her. When I should be thinking of other things, she is there in my mind.

Such as now.

We should be entering the room, depositing the tracking device, and leaving. But I'm savoring the taste of her on my tongue and the memory of us joined together, hip to hip, chest to chest.

"Ahh, Naomi, you undo me," I say breathlessly as I draw back.

Her eyes are cloudy with passion and she merely nods. I rub a finger across the lip I've just sucked. It's wet from my mouth and hers. Under my touch, she shivers, and my cock grows diamond hard. Suddenly I'm ready to finish our business so we can return to our hotel and pleasure each other, once again.

Holding the tracking device between my fingers, I gather Naomi to me and then I let the door fall open. The room is small as most rooms in Venice are, and it does not take long for me to encounter another body as we pretend to stumble inside, passion crazed and looking for an empty room

"*Figlio di puttana,*" the occupant cries. *Son of a whore.* "Get out. Get out."

"*Scusi. Scusa.* I am in the wrong room."

"*Porco dio!* I will kill you."

"Is that a—" I cover Naomi's mouth and then hustle her out, shutting the door behind me to the curses and threats.

"Behind you!" she screams. I turn but it is too late.

CHAPTER **THIRTY**

NAOMI

There's a donkey in the room.

I knew coming into this room that Marco Cassano was into animals. Still, thinking it and seeing it in front of me are two different things. The donkey is white and so it stands out amidst the shadows. I'm so shocked at the sight of it—and the man behind it—that I don't realize that there is someone else here.

I hear footsteps and think Vasily is leaving me alone with this pervert, so I turn just in time to see a man behind him in fetish wear.

"Behind you!" I tell Vasily, but I'm a moment too late. The man in the rubber fetish suit throws the coil of a leather whip around Vasily's neck, choking him. To my surprise, my big Russian is neatly trapped against the man. Vasily's hands go to the whip, like something out of a movie, and he strains as the man strangles him.

"*Porco dio!*" the other man is shouting, the donkey fucker. He keeps shouting it over and over again, pointing at us. "*Porco dio!*"

His shouting is making me want to crawl into myself. I freeze for a long moment, strains of "Itsy Bitsy Spider" rolling to the forefront of my mind. I stare at Vasily's purpling face and begin to mouth the words. I don't like screams, so I must drown them out . . .

But even as I start to slide away, I see the urgency in Vasily's face. He's not concentrating on his attacker. His hands are locked on the whip, and they shake back and forth, but Vasily's gaze is completely on me.

Waiting on me.

I blink. Push away strains of the song. Through a hazy blur, I consider things. I can attack the man strangling Vasily . . . or I can do what we came here for. I think of what Vasily would do, and what he would want me to do if I was part of his *Bratva*.

So I finger my gold pendant with the thin tracking sticker stuck to the back of it. I need to get this on that man's skin so we can get the painting. My fingernail pulls up the edge as I run for the man who is screaming in Italian at us. He's pressed up against one of the thickly curtained walls of the room, his genitals gleaming with lubricant. The donkey brays and I skirt it wide, heading for the man. "I'm so glad you're here," I tell him. "I'm scared—protect me!"

He stares at me like I'm crazy and mouths a stream of gibberish Italian at me. "*Allontanati da me!*"

"I'm scared," I repeat, and fling my arms around his neck, clinging to his side and avoiding his filthy genitals.

He pushes at me, shouting obscenities, but I'm clinging to him like a tree vine as I maneuver the tracking sticker off of the pendant. My fingers brush his nape even as he shoves me roughly. Success.

His hand slams into my jaw and I lose hold of him. I stumble to the floor, and his lubricant is all over my legs and stomach. I whimper with horror, knowing what I am covered with. "Vasily," I moan. "He's so gross."

"*Putta!*" the donkey fucker shouts at me. He gibbers something else, pointing at Vasily, then at me. I can guess what those instructions are—kill me, too.

I look over at Vasily and my gaze meets his. He's utterly calm. It's like he's waiting for me. So I nod. It's done.

His nostrils flare, his only outward sign that he's caught my signal. I see something metal flash in his hand, and then he stabs behind him.

The man in the rubber gimp suit bellows with pain. He was not, I think, expecting to be stabbed. Vasily grabs the whip and yanks it away from his throat. His hands move, so very fast, and I watch as he stabs and stabs the man behind him over and over again.

My assassin was never in any danger, not really. It was all a ploy to give me time.

However, I am in mortal danger now of catching a staph infection from this man's lubricant. I shudder and vomit on the floor, unable to control my stomach. The "Itsy Bitsy Spider" returns, and I curl up around myself—my dirty, dirty self—and begin to hum and rock while the room goes to chaos around me and the donkey brays and brays and brays.

Hands press down on my shoulders. "Karen. Karen. Wake up. It is time to go."

Who is Karen? The pressing becomes harder, the voice familiar. Vasily. Then I remember I'm supposed to be Karen. And we're in the pervert room.

It's not the place I want to have an episode. My eyes snap

open and I see him kneeling in front of me. His fingers caress my cheek and it hurts. I wince and pull away.

"It is time to go, Karen," he tells me again, and I nod.

He takes my hand and pulls me against him. I look over, expecting to see the donkey fucker shivering in the corner of the room. But the donkey fucker is laying in a pool of his own blood, his throat cut. His eyes are gazing up at the ceiling, seeing nothing. I turn and the assassin in the gimp suit is also dead. His mask is ripped off and the face there is not one I recognize.

Vasily has killed our target. I'm . . . pretty sure this wasn't part of the plan.

"Um," I question as Vasily takes my hand and leads me out of the room. "Why is our target deceased?"

"Not now," he tells me, touching my cheek and pulling me through the club's maze of hallways. We pass by people, but no one is paying attention to us—everyone is too busy with their own perversions. I shudder as we stumble past a group of people, one dressed up like an animal of some kind.

When we pause in a doorway, I can't hold my questions back. "Who was that man that tried to kill you?"

"Karen, I will answer all questions but it must not be now," he says, voice gentle, and I realize in his other hand, he grips the other knife. Oh. We're not safe just yet, then. I follow his lead as we duck through more rooms. Vasily opens a new door and I cringe, anticipating another donkey, but it's just another side room that is empty. Music plays, violins slicing through the quiet. I wait, tense, as Vasily locks the door we came through, then rams one of his knives into the doorknob, jamming it.

He heads to the opposite side of the room while I stand in the middle of the floor, shivering and not entirely in my own mind. I watch as he presses his ear to the wood of the thick door, then moves to the curtains and wipes his hands clean of blood. He spits on his hands, wipes, and spits some more. It strikes me as horribly filthy, but there's no shower in this room.

And I want a shower so bad. I think of the germs I have on me: the strangers that touched me when I entered, the man's lubricant, the secretions from the donkey he was fornicating with, the floor I sat down on, any blood that might have spattered . . .

I feel faint.

"I'm going to be sick," I tell Vasily in a weak voice.

"Good," he tells me and moves to my side. "Vomit down your front. It will be convincing."

I swallow hard, but in the end I lean over and throw up on the nice Aubusson carpet. Vasily pulls my hair back as I puke, and then he pulls me into his arms, carrying me.

"I'm filthy," I protest. "Don't touch me."

"Shh," he says, and his voice is soft.

I'm in a haze as we go back to the entrance of the club. His slave is sick, Vasily explains, and we must leave early. I must look rather frightful because they give us our coats without question, and off we go back into the streets of Venice. Vasily immediately heads for the water's edge and summons us a water taxi.

We climb in, and I suck in deep breaths of the clean night air. We say nothing until we return to the hotel, and then Vasily locks the door behind us and then barricades it with the nearby dresser. "Into the shower," he tells me, voice firm but hands gentle.

I nod, but I'm still hazy and Vasily has to undress me out of my costume and then leads me to the shower. The water is scalding hot, but I start to feel like myself again once it pours down on me. Then, I grab the soap and begin to scrub every ounce of my body. Clean. Clean. I need to be clean.

Vasily steps into the shower next to me, and then he takes the soap from my hands and begins to rub it over my shoulder blades. "I am sorry," he says to me.

I start to tremble. "It was a rough evening."

"*Da*. It was bloody." His fingers are gentle as they soap my skin in circles. "You were clever to think of the knives. They came in handy."

I scrub the washcloth over my stomach and thighs. "Do you think I still have donkey vaginal secretions on me?" I ask in horror, and begin to dry heave again.

"We will make sure you are clean," he assures me. "Do not worry." And he continues to soap my skin, helping me scour every inch of dermis that might have come into contact with anything tonight. Eventually, the water cools from its blistering temperature and my skin throbs but it feels . . . better. I start to feel more human again, and I switch places with Vasily in the shower, letting him have the spray.

I lean against him, exhausted but still full of questions. "Why was there an assassin tonight?"

His hands drag through my hair, stroking it. Petting me. I never realized how good it felt to have someone pet you like a cat. "Someone knew we were coming," he says.

"Who was that man?" I ask. "You took his mask off. Did you recognize him?"

"*Da*," he says, and his voice is flat, thick. Angry, I realize. "He is one of the Alexsandr's pets. Nikolai knew him well."

"Who is Alexsandr?"

"Alexsandr was a very important man, once. He trained many young boys into assassins, including my old friend Nikolai. Both he and Alexsandr are dead now."

I'm not connecting things. "I don't understand." I press my cheek against Vasily's freshly scrubbed chest, listening to his heartbeat. "The man tonight . . . he was working for the enemy?"

"He works for the Petrovich *Bratva*." Vasily ducks his head under the spray, his way of avoiding my questions.

I sit up and wait until he's done. "So someone sent a Petrovich assassin after you?"

"It would seem so." He reaches over and turns off the shower, so casual.

"Is that why you killed our mark? I thought the plan was to track him. When did that change?"

"I killed him because he was braying worse than the donkey," Vasily says as he steps out of the shower. He picks up a thick, fluffy towel and wraps it around me, tucking me into its warmth. He begins to dry my skin with tender motions, and it's an odd dichotomy—this caring, thoughtful side of a man that ruthlessly killed two people earlier. "And because he is no longer necessary."

I frown. "Why is he no longer necessary?"

"Because Elena Petrovich must have the painting at this point. She has beaten us to it, somehow, and now seeks to eliminate me. We walked into her trap."

My eyes widen. "What do we do now?"

"Now, we go after head of snake." His eyes gleam and I wish, for the millionth time in my life, that I could read emotion.

CHAPTER THIRTY-ONE

VASILY

"It is very small and not white," I say in apology. The flat I've brought Naomi to is barely larger than the train cars we traveled on in Italy. "It is a place that is safe." I debate whether I should share the routes of escape and the cache of weapons but decide against it. I will not be gone long. "I have a meeting and then I will take you to Lake Ladoga. We are only three hundred meters from the Solnechnaya Station should you wish to leave," I add. "There is a park across the street. In Russia, dollars are accepted everywhere. Euros too."

She runs a hand lightly across the gray stone counter that separates the foyer from the kitchen. Beyond the stove and small refrigerator is a table and beyond that a bed. Nothing else besides clothes, cash, and guns are present.

"I like that it's small," she says, moving farther into the single room. She drops onto the bed and smooths the coverlet she has wrinkled. My heart tightens at the vision of her in my small space. The need to succeed is greater now for I want her here, with me, always. We have not talked much of tomorrow, only that the idea of the cool, white *dacha* in the north appeals to her. But how long will she stay there? How long will she want to be with me if her existence is threatened at every juncture? Peace will not be won with a simple painting but instead through violence. I can only pray that it is not her blood nor mine that flows. No, praying is not my only tool. I flex my hand.

I've been the killer of the *Bratva* for two decades. I came to them when I was ten. Alexsandr, the old warlord, trained me to think as well as kill.

Elena taught me to hate.

This woman? She is teaching me to . . . love.

For her, for my sister, I will find peace for us if I have to kill everyone in the south of Moscow to achieve it.

"And I don't mind sitting here because it has only your germs. Your germs are ok but I have access to a lot of money so we can buy a bigger place if you like." She looks at me through a veil of lashes. "If you aren't mad at me for screwing up in the club, that is."

"*Nyet*," I say fiercely. In two strides I have her hands in mine. She does not look at me, of course, but I do not care. She sees me all the same. "You were brave. Very brave. Put it out of your head, Naomi. I am sorry that you had to see those things. I should be whipped for taking you there."

"But you'd like that." She grins to herself, so pleased at the small joke she has made.

Worry gives way to laughter for I cannot hold back my smiles at her amusement "Yes, perhaps that is no punishment. Then I should be tormented in another way."

"Why do you like it? I've figured out you don't like to be touched softly and that the harder I bite or scratch you, the better it is. I guess that makes you a masochist." She answers her own questions as she is wont to do. "Does that make me a sadist because I like it when you get excited?"

"These labels mean nothing, Naomi. I like your firm touch because it is yours. Nothing else." It's not a full truth, but I do not feel like explaining my sordid past to her. She would stare at me in horror and disgust much as she did the donkey fucker if she knew what I have done.

She shrugs. "You haven't talked much since we left Venice. I figured you were pissed off. I can't read people well, remember?"

I squeeze her hands tightly. "I do not wish to cause you more distress. Elena Petrovich has summoned me. I must go and see what it is that she wants. Once that is over, I will take you away and we will begin to reconstruct the *dacha*." I walk to the kitchen and open the sink door. Under the sink I pull off a taped brick of cash. "There are dollars and euros here if you need them."

Naomi barely looks at the cash. She's rubbing a pattern in the bed covering and appears lost in the motion. I gather my gun and an extra magazine. Undoubtedly Elena will have me searched, but I will bring these regardless.

"Is that who called you on the phone when we arrived?"

"*Da*, it was."

"Who is she?" It's whispered and I almost miss her question.

I hesitate as I have brought so much filth to Naomi that I regret exposing her to even more, but she deserves to know. She deserves to know who she has taken into her body, who professes to keep her safe.

"She is the daughter of the old *Bratva pakhan* or boss. She is one of the last true Petrovichs. The rest of us are . . ." I search for the right word. "Fostered into the family and given roles. When I joined, my sister and I were given to Elena until I proved I could be a fierce soldier, so then I became *boyevik*. *Boyeviks* are the footmen of the family. We enforce the will of the Petrovichs. When Sergei comes to power after his father's death, he makes me head soldier—but he does not trust me and rightly so because I plot his death. Once he is dead, I think, then I no longer am the *Bratva* soldier because we are of the old ways. A woman cannot lead the men. I say this not because women are weak but because Russian men—we are closed minded. But the old guard does not turn to me. They say I am not a Petrovich no matter that I have spent two decades in their service. And I cannot kill Elena so closely after Sergei's death or no one will trust me. So when the council places this test before me—obtain this painting—I accept the challenge and cling to the idea that it can bring about a painless revolution. But I am returned. The painting must be in Elena's hands, so I will go to her, see what kind of threat she presents, and return.

"Sounds dangerous. Maybe I should go with you." She continues to rub a pattern in the sheets.

"*Nyet*. Stay and wait for me. I will return to you shortly." I hold my breath. *Wait for me forever, no matter what*, is what I want to plead but I do not. I cannot. She inclines her head and I take that small agreement with me all the way to the exclusive neighborhood that houses Elena.

When Elena Petrovich is in the city, she stays in a grand

penthouse flat on Ostozhenka, the "Golden Mile." When her father was alive, they lived off Tverskaya, where the tsars once inhabited palatial homes, but the old staid flats of velvet and gilt-covered ceiling reliefs were thrown away for a modern residence of gleaming chrome and marble.

"Vasily Kuznetsov Petrovich," I announce myself on the intercom. The doorman nods his head and points his white-gloved hand toward the far elevator. I watch as he keys in the code for the penthouse.

Elena's manservant—a boy no more than fifteen by his budding facial hair—greets me with a short bow when the elevator arrives at the top floor. The marble floor and walls are blindingly white. There is hardly a speck of color in the main living room. On the floor is a plush white rug, and there are low-slung white leather couches that are positioned to showcase the view of the city.

"Vasya! Finally you are here," Elena cries, flying toward me in rush of silk, brown hair, and Chanel perfume. Elena has always worn Chanel. The scent makes me sick. "You must see my latest acquisition. I just received it yesterday."

She takes my hand and leads me down a hallway that opens off the entrance. The door to a walnut-paneled office is open. Inside there is a glittery white and glass—or perhaps in Elena's case crystal—desk, a white leather chaise lounge, and two chairs. To the right of the desk is the triptych, hung with the center panel elevated. "What do you think?" Her sly smile challenges me but I do not rise to her bait.

"I think that to hang it in your study invites unwanted questions." The security in Elena's apartment is something I oversaw. It will be easy enough for me to take it from her.

"Now Vasya, don't pout. The owner called me the other day

and asked why the Petrovich wolf was after him. I played dumb because I did not know why you are chasing all over Italy for some *mat* painting."

The real purpose of the errand reveals itself. The council sent me on this trip hoping I would not only fail but be killed in the process. Have they been working with Elena all along, and when I got too close to achieving what they thought was impossible, the strings were pulled and I was yanked back to Russia? Or are there only a few betrayers?

The only thing that prevents me from leaving is the possibility that Elena will reveal all to me as she gloats.

"Why didn't you tell me you wanted this painting? I would have procured it for you."

"My task was to procure it for the *Bratva*. If it was just a test, then it appears I have succeeded. I found it and it is now returned to the bosom of the family."

Her tight smile betrays her frustration, and she fists her hands as if she would like to punch me. *Oh my dear Elena, not as much as I would like to choke the life out of you.*

"Vasya, I feel like you are drifting away from me. I heard you had a companion with you at several establishments that I didn't think you would like to visit. Perhaps you have changed in the years you have served as a soldier for my family?"

"I am the same as I always was," I reply, but I employ serious concentration to prevent a shudder of fear from showing. I do not want Naomi to be known by this woman.

"You have secrets from me, and I do not like that." She sits on the chaise and toes off her red-soled stilettos. "Must I remind you that we arranged for you to move from warrior to general together? I fear you have forgotten all that I have done for you."

Her words are heavy with disappointment. "After all, how many stupid little street boys are sent to be educated at Cambridge?"

"It was your brother that promoted me after Alexsandr's death."

"But it was me that told him to do that and you know it!" she exclaims and stamps her foot. "Look at all I have done for you! You are the only Petrovich street boy to go to Cambridge. I arranged for that and for your sister. I did that, Vasya, so that you and I together could run this family." Her tone turns cold, sharp like the point of an icicle. "But here you are, running off to Italy on some treasure hunt. You should have come to me the moment the council presented you with this challenge. You do not need a mystical painting to secure the *Bratva* as your own. You need me and me alone. The fact that you went on this hunt without warning or consultation makes me concerned that you have lost your way."

So then only a few betrayers on the council. Someone—Thomas, Kliment—revealed the council's offer to me and Elena, fearful of the possible loss of her status, intervened.

"I serve the *Bratva,* not just one person with the organization. This was the council's edict."

"You should just kill them like you killed my brother."

We stare at each other, because this is the first time she has voiced the suspicion that others must have held.

"I did not kill your brother. That was done by Nikolai Andrushko, and we have disposed of him."

"I'm having trouble trusting you," she pouts. Her one foot rubs up against the calf of her opposite leg. Elena is a beautiful woman. No doubt other men would respond, but I have nothing inside me for her but hate. "I need you to prove your loyalty once more. Like you did when I asked you to kill your sister."

Yes, she needs to die. I will kill her and take Naomi and disappear. There are other places in this world that are quiet and remote.

I hear a rustling and see the silk of her dress pool on the floor, and I'm thrown back to the early days of my time here when my cock responded to a woman's touch without much understanding. When my body responded to vile stimuli and I learned to hate myself.

My stomach clenches and my balls shrivel. Already I feel contaminated—like Naomi with the blood of the donkey fucker smeared over her. It has been so long since I've been commanded to perform for her. I can hardly believe she wants me again. I am too old, scarred, and hairy for her and have been since I was fourteen. That was when she decided that Alexsandr could have me. My thick fingers and hairy balls displeased her. It was one of the best days of my life.

"What do you ask of me?"

Her laughter trills out. "I am giving you a choice, Vasya, because I care about you." She claps her hands and this time I look up. A young naked boy is led into the room by the manservant. The boy is ten, perhaps eleven? It is hard for me to tell. He is prepubescent. There is no hair anywhere but on his head.

My throat tightens and my tongue feels thick. He looks at me with luminous eyes. Fear is there as well as disgust and confusion. His member is stiff and red. The young manservant barely older than the captive does not look at anyone but his hand is fisted at his side.

"Come in my dears, you are blocking the entrance." Elena motions the two boys farther into the room. Two more people enter and this time I can barely hold my bile down. It is a terrified Naomi being led by Ylofa Yavlinksy, a thug brought in off the streets and well known for his delight in raping women. I had planned on executing him and a few others when I seized control of the *Bratva*.

At the sight of Naomi in their grasp, fear rushes over me followed quickly by rage. I am willing to sacrifice but to require it from the pure Naomi who has done nothing but to love me? No, this injustice cannot be born. I want to leap forward and tear Ylofa's neck open like a true wolf and devour him.

I will torture him. I will keep him alive in the basement of a dacha in the woods and visit him monthly to renew his wounds. He will beg for death and I *will not give it to him*.

Naomi has one hand on her baseball cap and her lips are moving. She is seeking inner strength and I pray that she finds it.

Whatever Elena wants, I shall do. I shall do this and then wash myself for three days and beg for forgiveness. I shall do this and return to take the painting, and once I have delivered the painting to Dostonev, Elenaida Petrovich will be on the shelf of grotesqueries.

"Ahh, we are all here. This is so wonderful." Elena claps again. "Vasya, here is your loyalty test. You have three choices. My new initiate, Grigory, can pleasure me. He is ten years old and has only had a few lessons. Perhaps you could give him instruction on how to touch me? After all, I never had as good of a student as you." Naomi flinches at this. She will never let me touch her again. "Or, you can watch as Ylofa rapes your woman. That would be less physically pleasurable for me, but perhaps as entertaining. I do not know. We will have to test it out."

"What is the other option?" I ask. Nothing she requests of me will be too much so long as the others can go.

Elena clucks her tongue. "Always the protector, eh? It is so strange to me that you and Nikolai have such strong protector instincts when all you have been trained to do is kill. Why do you care about this *blyad* and *mudak*? They are disposable. One woman? One boy? They can all be replaced. But you, Vasya, you are important to me. I've trained you, educated you, and positioned you to lead the *Bratva* with me at your right hand—your consigliere—to use an Italian term in keeping with your little vacation." She giggles.

"What is the third option?" I repeat.

Sighing, she opens a drawer and draws out a slender filet knife. "You are made a eunuch. If you are so willing to sacrifice yourself, then you sacrifice your manhood and you once again become my *volk*, for what woman would have you?" She smirks. "Ylofa will not take your cock, of course. That is unnecessary. He will only cut open your sac and remove your balls."

I stare at Naomi, for she is staring at me. The blue of her eyes is so pure—like heaven. "Would you still have me?" I ask. Her brows furrow but I tell her with my eyes that I will have hands to touch her and a mouth to kiss her. I can pleasure her with my fingers, tongue, and toys. I do not need my cock as long as she will accept me once we are finished here.

She widens those blue spheres until they are all I see. There is no *Bratva* or Moscow or Russia or Elena. There is also no rejection as I feared. Her stare is one of acceptance and . . . love? I am unsure exactly what is there but it welcomes me, forgives me, comforts me.

"I will do it," I say to Elena but I refuse to look away from Naomi. "Allow the others to leave and you may take whatever you like from my body."

CHAPTER **THIRTY-TWO**

Earlier . . .

NAOMI

I am not as fond of Russia as I had hoped.

Vasily left me in the apartment alone. For an hour or two, I was entertained. I found cleaning supplies. I scrubbed. I straightened things. I organized the few dishes in the kitchen. I washed linens. Cleaned the tiny fridge. And then I got bored.

There is no Internet in this place, and my newest laptop is utterly useless without it. Vasily must connect through a cell phone service, but there is no Wi-Fi for me to tap into. We are too remote. I fiddle with my computer for a bit anyhow, coding theoretical scripts and imagining the results once launched, but it's useless if you can't test anything, and I quickly tire of this game. I could use my phone as a hot spot, but it would be too slow for me to do anything productive. I pout.

Vasily was still gone, so I call my brother Daniel to say hello.

"About fucking time," he greets me. "I was hoping to hear from you again sooner. I thought you were going to call me back when you were in Italy. How come I'm suddenly a millionaire? Ten times over?"

"I cleaned out a few accounts of Vasily's competition."

"And sent it to me? Do you hate me that much?" His voice raises a little in anger and I hear a feminine voice murmur to him on the other end of the phone.

"I don't hate you at all. I'm surprised you think that."

"Sarcasm, sis. Sarcasm."

"Oh. Well, don't worry, you paid an estate tax penalty on things. It all will look very clean on your banking records."

"Jesus Hermione Christ, Naomi. You can't just hand me illegal money like that. I near about had a fucking heart attack at the sight of it."

"You should get your cholesterol checked," I advise him. "You're far too young to have a heart attack. How is Regan? Does she like the ranch?"

"Regan is beautiful and kind and charming and gracious and she has the best ass in tight jeans I have ever seen." I hear a feminine chuckle on the other end of the phone. "She's also standing right here. Do you want to talk to her?"

"Why?" I ask, puzzled.

"Just to say hello?"

"I have nothing to say to her after hello?"

"Right. She might not get our conversations. I think I'll just stay on the line." His voice is warm even though the words are chiding. It's a conversation we've had before, many times. As an Aspie, I am abrupt with people and not good with small talk or managing conversations, and Daniel has had to "soothe ruffled feathers" in the past, as he likes to say. I'm not sure what I said that set him off, but I go on.

I want to tell Daniel about the places I've been and seen—he would be impressed that his introverted little sister has been to Florence and Venice and ridden on a train. But Vasily has cautioned me about mentioning locations so I look for a different topic. "Did you know that there are men that like to fuck donkeys? I saw one. I wasn't entirely sure that he could reach the donkey's vagina but apparently you can with the appropriate footstool. The donkey must have been trained to stand still for his attentions, but I imagine that is a difficult thing to train for. Do you buy a donkey fully trained for bestiality or do you suppose that someone buys a normal donkey and has to slowly introduce it to—"

"Whoa whoa whoa—" Daniel bellows into the phone. "Where the fuck is that dipshit Vasily taking you that you're seeing someone fuck a goddamn donkey? Put him on the phone right now."

I frown. "Daniel, I am making conversation. It was a bad place, but don't worry. Everyone died."

"*What*?"

"The donkey is safe," I assure him.

"Naomi," Daniel says, and his voice is flat. "Put that sonofabitch on the phone right now."

"Vasily is visiting Elena Petrovich," I tell him. "I am in hiding until he comes back, and then we're going to have sex again. Maybe more than once."

"Oh my Christ, someone please burn my ears off of my head," Daniel moans into the phone. "I am going to kill that bastard for taking advantage of you."

"You'd better not," I tell him with a frown. "I don't want you killing Vasily."

"Sarcasm, sis," Daniel points out again.

I sigh. Always with the sarcasm. I never can pick up on it. Daniel was a sniper in the army, so it is reasonable to think he might come after Vasily. I should probably caution him when he returns.

There is a soft knock at the door.

I tilt my head, thinking, and look at the plain clock on the wall. Vasily should not be back this soon. No one is supposed to know that I am here. This is not good.

"Someone is here," I tell Daniel quietly into the phone. "Something bad has happened with Vasily."

"Where did you say he went again? Regan, get me a pen."

"To visit Elena Petrovich. She has summoned him. She probably knows I am here." I speak quietly, but the person knocks at the door again and tests the doorknob. It will not be long before they attempt to break the door down, and they can't catch me with the phone, or Daniel will be in danger. "Can you come?" I whisper quickly.

"Give me thirteen hours and I'll be there with bells on," Daniel tells me in a worried voice. "Go with them. Do whatever they want, but stall, do you hear me? Stall. I love you, sis."

I hang up and stuff the phone between the cushions of Vasily's chair. "Coming," I call out, and approach the door. I briefly consider Vasily's brick of money under the sink, but anyone that is coming for me will not be bribable, I suspect. Better to just stall, as Daniel has said, and wait for him to arrive.

So I open the door and paste (what I hope) is a happy smile on my face. "Yes?"

The man that stands there is in a black suit that somehow looks cheap and ill-fitting. He is bony-thin, with hollow cheeks, and tall. His hair is greasy from a lack of bathing, and his nose has been broken multiple times. And he returns my smile. "You are to please come with me." His accent is very thick and sounds like Vasily's. "Your friend Vasya is in danger."

For a moment, my heart skips a beat. Vasily is in danger. But then I remember the situation; Vasily did not send this stranger, so his mouth is full of lies. I have to pretend I don't know this, though. "Oh no," I say. "Can you take me to him?"

"But of course," the man says, and grins at me far too widely for it to be natural.

We get into a black sedan with tinted windows, and the man opens the back door for me. I get in, and there is another man in the driver's seat. He barely glances over at me in the rearview mirror, but starts the car. The skinny man sits in the front, gives me another false smile, and then murmurs something to the driver. They both laugh.

"Where is Vasily?" I ask. "Where are we going?"

They laugh again, and continue talking in Russian, ignoring me. At this point, I am almost positive they are laughing at how gullible I am. See, they are probably saying. She is stupid. She comes without asking questions.

But my actions have purpose. These men are going to take me to Elena Petrovich, who has Vasily's Caravaggio . . . and Vasily.

And Daniel will be here in twelve hours and fifty-five minutes.

Now

When I see Vasily next, it's good I don't have to hide my fear. I'm terrified of this big place with its ornate furniture and the fact that there is a naked, wide-eyed boy in the room with us. Elena Petrovich is beautiful—and also naked—but I don't like her face.

I especially don't like her after she offers to have the man holding me—Ylofa—rape me. And then the next is the worst.

"Ylofa will not take your cock, of course. That is unnecessary. He will only cut open your sac and remove your balls." Her voice is irritating.

I'm trying to digest whether or not this is a serious threat— removing balls? Really?—when Vasily gives me an intense, soul-searching stare. If he's trying to communicate something, I miss it.

"I will do it," Vasily says. "Allow the others to leave and you may take whatever you like from my body."

And I've had enough of this shit.

"This is incredibly stupid," I say. "You are the worst castrator ever if you think removing his balls is going to be an effective method of castration."

Elena turns to me and her jaw drops. Her face flushes a mottled red, and I'm filled with glee.

"*Nyet*, Naomi—" Vasily begins.

"I'm serious. This is kiddie shit," I point out. "That is the stupidest punishment I have ever heard. What, do you think every man that has his testicles removed from testicular cancer is suddenly a castrato? That's idiotic and absurd. Anyone with more than two brain cells to rub together would know that a man without his testes can still get an erection and have sex. Removing the testicles will simply remove his ability to produce semen and reduce his testosterone—which, I might add, can be artificially increased with medication and thus take care of the sex-drive problem. So really, all you're doing is creating an incompetent scenario in which you are not solving the problem at all. Why not remove his spleen and pretend that turns him into an eunuch as well?" I snort, amused by my own joke. I even hold up a finger. "Oh look, I have a paper cut. This must make me a eunuch!"

"Someone shut her up," Elena says in that annoying, tight voice. "Or I will cut the bitch's tongue out."

"Why not just castrate me?" I mock. Everyone is looking at me as if I'm insane—Vasily included. The hand holding my arm is bruise-tight, but I ignore it. I have my plan: stall for time. Elena Petrovich won't kill me. She needs me alive to hold Vasily. If she wanted me dead, they would have put a bullet through my brain back at the apartment. I know this, and I use this confidence to continue to needle her. "You do realize you can't believe everything you read on the Internet, right?"

"That bitch is yours, Ylofa," she snarls, her face a dark, ugly red that suggests she is losing control. Her breasts are heaving with anger. "I have changed my mind. I will take Vasily's balls and you can rape the *pizda*."

A low growl sounds through the room, and I realize it's Vasily. His hands clench, and there is a mad look on his face. "You will not fucking touch her," he says in a cold voice. "Do so over my dead corpse."

Elena reaches for her robe and pulls it back on her body, scurrying backward. She shouts something even as the man holding me grabs his gun and pulls it out.

"No!" I cry, but he holds the gun over my shoulder and shoots before I can react.

A dart appears in the raging Vasily's chest mere moments before he can attack Ylofa. He collapses at our feet, and I realize Vasily is tranquilized, not dead. This man is not armed to kill. Elena wants all of us alive.

The room falls silent. Elena puts a hand to her heaving breasts and mutters something in Russian. The naked boy scurries to action, along with the manservant. They each grab one of Vasily's hands and drag him across the room.

"So," Elena says to me after a moment, speaking in English again. "You are determined to ruin my fun tonight. Now we must put Vasya in a cell and wait for him to wake up. I wish for him to be conscious for his castration."

"His useless castration," I point out.

"Cunt," she says in that sneering voice of hers. "Enjoy your time with Ylofa."

The man holding my arm grabs me and hauls me out of the room. I glance over my shoulder one last time to see Vasily's unconscious form being dragged slowly across Elena's rug. *Hold on for eleven and a half hours more*, I tell Vasily silently. *Daniel is coming.*

We go down a few side halls, and then Ylofa slams the door shut behind him and locks it. I can't read expressions normally, but there's no mistaking the evil leer on Ylofa's face as he looks me up and down.

I take a step backward in alarm. "Don't touch me." I back up against a nearby chair. I'm scared, I admit it. I have a plan, and I'm hoping the plan works. If not, this is going to be very, very bad.

He continues to advance. His long, bony arm snakes out and grabs my wrist, and then he hauls me against him. "On knees," he tells me, and pushes a surprisingly strong hand onto my head, forcing me down.

I collapse to my knees, unable to withstand his strength, and he begins to unzip his pants. As he pulls out his member, I begin the next part of my plan.

My eyes roll back in my head and I begin to convulse. My body stiffens, and I begin yet another fake round of seizures.

I can't watch him this way, of course, but I hear his breath suck in even as I collapse and fall backward onto the carpets. He won't try to stick his dick into my mouth now. Not with me arching my spine and drooling all over myself in a rather convincing seize.

"*Chto yebat*!" He sounds startled.

I hear a metal clicking, though, and I can't place the sound until I hear the swift *pshew* of his gun as it fires another dart. Pain shoots through my sternum, and my eyes flick open just in time to see Ylofa glancing around, as if checking for watchers.

As I slide unconscious, I think to myself that perhaps this great plan of mine is not so great after all.

CHAPTER THIRTY-THREE

VASILY

When the drug wears off, I find myself in a plush room. The young manservant is sitting cross-legged, chained to the floor. He is nude but from the nonchalance of his stance, I can tell this is not an uncommon place or position for him. The younger boy is nowhere to be seen.

"Why are you here?"

He shrugs. For a fifteen-year-old boy he has experienced too much already. "I assume she will ask me to pleasure you or perhaps you to pleasure me. You are very old but she appears to have a special affection for you."

I want to tell this youth that I was born old. Poverty does that to you. I reach down to touch my groin but there is no pain.

The boy notices. "You are untouched. I think the crazy lady convinces them to not harm you."

"Do not refer to her as crazy." I give him a grim smile to soften my reprimand. His return roll of the eyes indicates I should not have tried. Too much American television for this boy. Russian boys do not roll their eyes. "Is it a brother or sister that she threatens?"

This makes him look at me in surprise and then with narrow-eyed suspicion. He thinks he is the only one? How can he be so naïve? But I need him for whatever might come next. I must convince him that the time to act is now, rather than waiting.

"My brother. How do you know this?"

I begin to examine my bonds as I talk. "This is the way that she tells herself that she is not evil. You—and I and the others—do as she asks without force. When she hunts she looks for those who have vulnerabilities. At times you wonder if you should just kill yourself or the ones that you love to put an end to it all. Cut the thread on Damocles's sword yourself and if it falls and beheads you, then your suffering is over."

"But if you are gone, the one you have sacrificed for all those years remains unprotected." He's listening to me. His insolent, lazy pose has been replaced with one of alertness. He is standing now, holding his chain off the ground.

"True. So you take the sword up in your hand and wield it."

At this he scoffs. "If it were only that easy, I would have knifed her years ago. She watches me and my brother constantly. All of her puppies have watchers. You do not do as she asks, and vulnerability"—he spits out the word like it is contaminating his mouth—"is brought before you. A warning the first time and the second—"

"The second time, she makes them suffer," I interject. "At least she has not changed. I know her well."

"But you are still dog on a leash," he sneers. "You have no

sword, and your crazy girlfriend has been tranqed. Now you will perform, both of you, like trained bears at the circus."

"That is one outcome," I agree. "But we can make others."

He wants to turn away, but the carrot of possibility is too strong for him to ignore. "I don't believe you can make change."

"Watch me," I say. There is a chain around my wrist. I follow it to the base, which appears to be bolted to a floor joist. Several jerks fail to move the bolted plate. Another delicate chain is wound around the base of my cock and balls, which is attached to my wrist. I cannot lift my dominant hand more than shoulder height or it begins to pull on my balls, but if both my hands were free . . . I look around for something small but heavy I could use. There is a plaster bust on the built-in chest behind me and the chair of the sofa. Either will do but the plaster bust will be easiest. "Where is she being held? My friend," I clarify, snatching the bust and tossing it in the air. It is not as heavy as I would like, but with a few blows it should do the trick.

"Next door. Elena is calling her friends for an impromptu party."

"Who has weapons here?" Elena does not carry weapons nor does she know how to use them. It disturbs her vision of herself as a wealthy noblewoman. We are her weapons.

"Ylofa. Later, the bodyguards of her guests." He is eyeing me warily. "What will you do with that?" He pushes his chin toward the bust.

"Free myself." I tip the chaise lounge on its side, for the base is much harder than any other part. Kneeling before it, I place my balls on top. "Your brother? Is he watched?"

"Yes every hour of every day." His voice is growing faint.

"Are you allowed to contact him? Is there a safe place he can go for a couple hours?"

He gnaws at his lip and stares at me with growing horror. "You do not plan to use that, do you?"

"I am no dog on a leash." I lift the bust in the air.

"Stop!" he cries.

I pause with the bust halfway down to my balls.

"What are you doing?" he says. His chest is heaving as if he is the one who has suffered the crushed testicles.

"I am loosening the leash."

"I do not understand." He steps nearer to me. "How will this help you?"

"After I crush my testes, I will be able remove the chain and move my right hand freely."

"You are crazy like your girlfriend."

"Perhaps." I bare my teeth in a gruesome smile. "It is first compliment you have made."

"Here." He tosses me a thin, shiny object. "I store this in my mouth for the times she likes to lock me up and I no longer wish to be restrained."

I catch it. It is a thin metal pick with a hook on the end. "Thank you."

In a few movements, I have released myself and him. He rubs his ankle.

"What will you do now?"

"Find Ylofa, of course. He will be the only person with weapons. We disable him, rescue Naomi, kill Elena, take the painting, and leave."

"You can do all of this?"

I toss the pick in the air. "Yes. I will take the sword and stick it into Elena so many times, the blood will run out of her like a sieve." I bare my clenched teeth. "Come with me and you will have your turn."

This time it is he who bares his teeth.

"Where is Ylofa?"

"Where else but watching porn on his phone when he is supposed to be guarding Naomi."

I am not able to loosen the larger chains from their bolts on the floor, but the manacle and chain that bound my body together will serve a fine purpose. I whip it around and toss it out a few times to measure its length and spin. Yes, it will do well for me. "Come, then, and stay behind me."

He nods. I unpick the lock from the inside and open the door slightly. The hallway is empty. I creep out and head toward the living room.

"Your friend is the other way," he hisses. I press a finger to my lips to silence him.

I want to know who else is in the apartment other than Elena, Ylofa, Naomi, this manservant, the young boy, and me. The study where we were tranqed is empty, but there are two piles of clothes. I take mine and dress while the boy does the same. I rifle through the cabinets but as I suspect, there are few weapons here. I do find a pair of scissors in a drawer and hand them to the boy.

I see nothing in the living room space but a raised podium and a small leather bench. Around it the furniture has been arranged for optimum viewing, but at this point it is empty.

I tip my head back toward Ylofa and Naomi. Outside the door, I listen but hear nothing. Slowly I pick the lock, not wanting to make any noise to alert Ylofa to our presence. When I disengage the tumblers, I position the boy to the left of the doorway and indicate for him to open the door. This way the wall will protect him and should Ylofa come to the door, I can take his eye out with the manacle.

At my nod, the boy pushes the door open, the latch making a small *snick*. But even that small sound is too loud, for Ylofa jerks up from his chair, pulls out his gun, and shoots at the door. Both the boy and I jump back. Wood splinters as the bullet pierces the wooden door and lodges in the plaster wall. I motion for the boy to get down. He obeys immediately.

"Get to the study," I shout, but point to the room we were just in. He nods and crawls quickly down the hall. Ylofa charges out. I jump up and ram my head into his stomach.

He grunts and shoots again but only manages to hit the floor behind me as the momentum pushes him back into the room. I keep running until his back strikes a wall or a bookcase. A few items tumble down, striking the both of us, but I barely notice. Adrenaline is pumping through me. I punch up with my chain-wrapped fist but manage only a glancing blow. He tries to push me off, bringing his knee up into my chest repeatedly but I hang on. This close, he will never be able to deploy a fatal shot.

But a ricochet bullet could hurt Naomi, who lies still on the lounger. I do not see any evidence of assault on her body, but it enrages me that he's had his hands on her, that he has seen her unclothed magnificence. For that alone he should die.

I wish I could kill him a thousand times for her. My rage at her mistreatment empowers me.

His elbow digs into my shoulder blade, but this time when I strike him, I hit his cheek, and his face snaps into the wall. I get two more blows and bloody his nose before I pull him away from the case and then wrap my arm around his neck.

Dropping the gun, he pulls on my arm and then tucks his chin toward his body in order to bite me. With a flick of my wrist, I uncoil the chain and then, angling his body away from Naomi, I whip the chain around his neck. In one motion, I release him from my arm chokehold, catch the free end of the chain, and with both hands, draw the chain tight.

He claws at his neck. Ylofa is a big man, but he's served Elena far too long. A young foot soldier on the streets may have been able to withstand my tranquilized and diminished strength, but not Ylofa. He gasps for air, but I only pull tighter and start to saw at his neck. If he doesn't pass out, perhaps I will simply sever his neck from his shoulders.

The chain in my hands has turned red from my blood as the links bite into my skin.

"Vasily, he is getting his blood on you," Naomi observes from the lounge. She has pushed herself into a reclining position but looks too weak to stand.

"*Da*, I will need to shower after this." I strain against his resistance. "Get up, get the gun."

She rises slowly. "What time is it?"

I shake my head. "The gun, Naomi."

"I need to know the time." She is agitated but I do not have a watch to answer her. At least she is responding, which tells me she must be okay.

"You are stupid *pizda*," Ylofa gasps out. He has much air in him, this windbag. I bring up a knee and jab him in the back.

"I do not know the time, Naomi. Please, my dear, the gun."

"I need the time," she repeats.

She cannot help herself.

"We have been out two hours," the boy says from the doorway.

"Oh, that's not good," she replies, but finally pushes away from the lounge and walks over to get to the gun. I maneuver Ylofa away from her but when his body finally goes limp, I let him go.

"We are leaving, though. That is good," says the boy.

Naomi hands me the gun. I use it to shoot Ylofa. None of us flinch.

I gather her body against mine and bury my face into her hair. My knees are weak with relief that she is alive.

"Are you hurt?" I hold her slightly away from me and inspect her quickly. She does not appear to be harmed, but I know many injuries cannot be seen from the outside.

"No. You came in time, but Daniel won't be here for another ten hours." She rubs the top of her head like she used to do with her cap.

You came in time.

I hear nothing else. I press a kiss on the crown of her head. Then her forehead and then, because I cannot stand one more minute without reassuring myself she is alive and well, I capture her mouth and sweep my tongue inside.

She responds instantly, molding her body to mine and ravages me back.

We break away, panting from our passion.

"Daniel?" Her words finally sink in, but before she can explain, I smell smoke.

I check the magazine. There are only six bullets left. Ylofa is a fool, wasting seven shots on us. Down the hall, I see smoke coming out of the study. "Find a service elevator," I tell the boy. He runs off.

The smoke is rising into the hall but through the doorway, I see the Caravaggio burning on the floor. "No!" I shout, running forward. I stamp on the flames but there are too many and the painting, old and fragile, is like tinder. The laugh of a mad-woman trills out beside me. Turning on Elena, I grab her upper arms and shake her until her teeth chatter, but she laughs on.

"What have you done?" I demand. Horror is freezing my blood, turning me to stone. I hear the cold words of Dostonev proclaiming that he is wealthy and indolent and wants the painting. This stupid fucking painting. My sister's life depends on this painting being given to him. I wish I could kill Elena a hundred times.

She cackles again. "You want the painting so badly that you would sacrifice your manhood for it? That you would tie yourself to another woman? No," she sneers. "You can have the painting in ashes."

I shove her aside and draw a hand over my mouth. The deal I made with Dostonev for the safety of my sister burns in front of me, and I watch the flames eat up her life until there is only smoke and ashes left.

CHAPTER THIRTY-FOUR

NAOMI

I'm still groggy from the tranquilizer as I follow Vasily into the smoke-filled room. Elena sits on one of her couches, laughing like a crazy woman as Vasily lays the Caravaggio flat and stomps on it with his boot. It's really no use—the painting is five hundred years old and crafted from oil and canvas. If anything remains, it'll be a miracle.

The item we have spent so much time searching for—Vasily's holy grail, our reason for our wild quest across Europe—is now nothing but seared edges of a wooden frame and bits of curling canvas. It's done for.

But as I watch, dazed and sleepy, Vasily tries to pick up one corner and hisses, shaking his fingers. He's going to hurt himself.

What we need is a fire extinguisher. Practicality takes over and I ignore the crazily giggling Elena to go hunting for an extinguisher before my *volk* singes off his fingerprints. I leave the room and step over Ylofa's body, racing down the hall. Two rooms and half a corridor away, I uncover a familiar red canister tucked next to a hutch full of Fabergé eggs, and snatch it from the wall. I race back to the room and unhook the hose from the extinguisher. Now one of the drapes is on fire and is being ignored as Vasily tries to piece together the charred edges of the painting on the floor, and Elena just smiles at him as if she's won the lottery.

Why all this mooning over a single painting when the world is burning down around everyone?

I hose down the burning drapery with the fire extinguisher, getting rid of the worst of the fire. Now there is only smoke in the room, and the three of us.

"You are too late," Elena says in a mocking voice to me. "The Caravaggio is burned into ashes, much like poor Vasya's hopes for the *Bratva*." She begins to laugh again.

She's pissing me off, so I turn the fire extinguisher hose in her direction and give her a good shot to the face. "Shut up, you."

Elena coughs and sputters as I head to Vasily's side, the canister stuck under my arm. I peer at the pieces he's trying to reconstruct, but there's nothing that shows that this was once a triptych created by a master artist. There's nothing to show a wolf, a Madonna, anything. It might have been a finger painting that he mourned for as much that remained of it.

"Vasily, what now?" I ask him.

He ignores me, and his entire body language is that of a man defeated. I think, perhaps, this painting symbolized more than he cared to think about. Either that, or being in the presence of the awful Elena has undermined his confidence to lead. Regardless, this is not the Vasily I am used to, this man picking through the soot. If it is this big of a deal to have a distasteful painting, perhaps we can buy another. Maybe with the donkey fucker.

Donkeys have been on my mind quite a bit lately.

I'm contemplating this when someone shoves me from behind, knocking me to the floor. Elena's screech of anger barely registers. She's knocked me onto the fire extinguisher, and it slams into my ribs, causing them to creak painfully and for the breath to be forced from my lungs. I gasp and choke on the carpet, even as she climbs over me like a malevolent spider monkey.

"Whore," she shrieks. "*Pizda*!"

She must not have liked being hosed in the face with the extinguisher, I think dully as I try to get my breath back.

Hands claw into my hair and she wrenches my head backward, and I moan in pain. "Vasily," I cough. "Help!" I'm not good with physical fighting. My weapons have always been bots, scripts, and code. I flail uselessly on the carpet, trying to get her heavy body off of me. "Vasily!"

"Get off her, Elena," Vasily says and I recognize the danger in his voice. I scrabble to grab her with my hands, but she's pulling my hair and flexing me backward in a way that spines don't bend.

Then, there is a loud crack, and for a moment, I think she has snapped my back. But I fall forward, and she lands on top of me, still.

I cough. My ribs feel like they're on fire. Maybe they've caved in. I moan, and then Elena rolls off of me, and Vasily's big hands are helping me stand upright. He caresses me, his hands moving over me in that tender way I've come to recognize as his touch.

"Are you hurt, *lapochka*?"

I press a hand to my ribs even as I lean against his big, reassuring chest. "I think my lungs caved in."

"*Nyet*," he says in a curiously flat voice. "Else you would not be able to scream my name."

He doesn't sound like himself, so I look up. He's not even staring at me. His gaze is on the woman huddled on the carpet. Elena's eyes are open but her neck is at a weird angle, and she's not moving. That snap I heard was her neck. Vasily has killed her.

I'm not even sorry. She was a bitch. "Good job," I tell him.

"It was so easy," he murmurs tonelessly. "Just one quick snap, and all problems are solved except one. Now the *Bratva* has no leader. We will crumble into dust, like ants without a queen."

I frown. This sounds defeatist, and this is not my Vasily. I pat his arm and wipe a smudge of soot from his sleeve. "Sounds like you're in charge, to me."

"*Nyet*," he says, and his voice is so soft even as he continues to stare at Elena's dead body. "The painting is destroyed. With it, I could have shown them that I am no mere foot soldier. Now, I am simply another upstart with no claim."

"You still have the painting," I point out. "It simply needs some restoration work." I think of the meme on the Internet about the elderly Italian woman who tried to restore a priceless painting of Jesus and utterly destroyed it. Her painting looked more like a melting head than a masterpiece, and I think of the *Madonna and the Volk* given similar treatment and giggle madly.

Vasily touches my cheek, his thumb stroking my skin. "Now is not the time for laughter, *lapochka*."

His touch is gentle, but those are words used for reproach. I'm unable to tell if he's upset at me, so I try a different angle. "Tell me what the painting changes, Vasily?"

"What do you mean?"

I nudge the burned canvas frame with one shoe. Even that small movement makes my ribs protest, but I ignore them. "Tell me what the painting does," I repeat. "How it makes you the leader."

His eyes narrow at me but he is looking more like himself, the dazed look in his gaze disappearing. His fingers continue to stroke my cheek, smoothing his germs on me. I don't mind in the slightest. I have decided I like his germs, and I like him. "The Petrovichs owned the Madonna for years. It was a symbol of our strength."

"She had the painting," I point out. "And now she's lying on the carpet with her neck broken."

His lips thin, a sign that I am learning that Vasily does not like my argument.

"Wouldn't your, um, group respect the man that had the painting and burned it? It's a huge rebellion. Plus, ding-dong, the witch is dead, and you killed her. You can't be the only one who hated her. Heck, I knew her for five minutes and I hated her. And what about emptying the bank accounts of all your enemies and filling your own pockets? Wouldn't people get behind that?"

He continues to stroke my cheek, saying nothing. At long last, he says, "Perhaps . . . you are right. Perhaps."

"Of course I'm right." I'm a little miffed he has to even question it. I'm always right. My mind is a repository of knowledge. But I don't point this out to him because he already knows this. Likely he is just distracted and has forgotten. "And what will you do?" he asks me.

"Wait for Daniel," I tell him. "He will be here in a few hours, and I suppose we should be around to explain to him that we don't need his services after all." Even as I say it, I'm a little sad.

Because really, this is where our paths split. Vasily will take over his *Bratva*, like he has always wanted, and I will . . . well, I will do something with myself. Go home, I suppose. Return to a world of anonymous hacking and fucking with bank accounts that should not be fucked with, just to keep myself from boredom.

Vasily won't like to hear that, but the truth of the matter is, with me at his side? His control will be undermined. People will think he has hooked up with a crazy woman, or an idiot, or worse, a "retard" in their eyes. I won't be able to be at his side openly, because no one will understand me.

Vasily wants me nearby, of course. Tucked away in his dacha in the woods. To think that such a small frame of time ago, it sounded ideal. Peace and quiet and no disturbances, no need to do anything but work on my computer and help Vasily with any sort of hacking he might need.

But . . . I have changed my mind. I'm not sure I want solitary peace and confinement any longer. I think of my hours in Vasily's apartment. It was surprisingly lonely. In a short period of time, I have grown used to my *volk* always being around, needling me with questions, teasing me, having sex with me. Touching me. Caressing me. Finding my G-spot. Fixing me specific lunches that he knows I will eat, because he cares for me. I think of a life hidden away in his *dacha*, only seeing him when he has time to put aside in his schedule and have sex with me.

That is no life, not really. I don't want to be an afterthought.

So I shall go home with Daniel, and Vasily will rule his men with an iron, absolute fist, just as he's always wanted.

CHAPTER **THIRTY-FIVE**

VASILY

"Come, let's go." I gesture to both Naomi and the boy. The commotion has brought the caterers and staff hired to man the party down to the study. I wave the gun at them. "Be gone. There is no business here of yours," I shout to them in Russian.

They scatter like flies.

"Why didn't you kill her before?" the boy asks me.

"I had just killed her brother. Killing Elena so soon after would have destabilized the organization. When the council presented the opportunity to take control if I fulfilled a small task, I seized on it. I would have killed shortly after. My mistake. I underestimated her and we all suffered."

"But you are Vasily Petrovich," the boy protests. "I've heard of you. The *volk* of the Petrovichs. Breathe wrong and he will kill you. It does not matter if it is even his own beloved sister."

The mention of Katya makes my knees buckle. Killing Elena does not rewind time and make the painting magically whole. Today I have become the target of not only the Petrovichs but the Dostonevs as well. My sister is a target. The beautiful, brilliant woman I have come to love standing in front of me is a target.

I will go and sacrifice myself to Dostonev, plead for my sister's life, for Naomi's protection.

"If I go before the council empty-handed, I will be killed. It is better for me to leave. Naomi, I will be able to protect you until your brother arrives. And you, little one, can you scurry off to safety with your brother?"

"But you can still lead." The boy is like a dog with a bone. He will not let go.

"I am no one now."

"Who were you before?" he asks.

"I was no one before. I came from the mud, the dirt, the garbage." Naomi puts her soft hand on my shoulder. "I'll follow you."

"Me as well."

"Me too," pipes up the ten-year-old. The older boy had rescued him while Naomi and I were busy dealing with Elena.

I stare at them. "Without the *Bratva*, I have nothing. Everything I possess is owned by the *Bratva*."

"What do you mean?" Naomi asks.

The boy interjects. "It is true. When the *Bratva* takes you in and gives to you, it is only temporary, for the period of time while you are part of the brotherhood. When you leave, you depart with only what you had when you entered."

I show my empty hands to Naomi.

"I came in when I was ten and had nothing but my sister, so I leave with nothing."

She scratches her head. "But I have money and access to a lot more. Can we buy our way in?"

"*Nyet.*" I shake my head, bemused by her generosity. How does she want to stay with someone like me? Tainted and befouled? "The brotherhood rests on loyalty."

"So what would the head of the *Bratva* do in case of a coup?"

"He would call his soldiers home," I tell her. "Devise tests for their loyalty. See which men will be loyal regardless, which will question the new rule, and which need to be weeded out. Then, he will do the weeding and establish his rule."

"Then that is what you do," Naomi responds, patting my sleeve.

The boy next to her nods. "Many would follow you. The *boyeviks* all speak of you with awe."

He is saying things I want to hear only because he is afraid to be alone. I take Naomi's hand in mine, for I need the comfort of her touch.

"Go to your home, boy. If the Petrovich *Bratva* has no leader, it will become a bloody turf battle. Go home with your brother and protect yourself."

After some indecision, he nods and runs off.

"Let us go somewhere safe as well."

She does not protest.

I take her to another safe house. I will not be able to afford the rent on many of these in the future. If by some chance I make it out alive, I will hire out my gun and become *ubitsya* like Nikolai. A man without allegiance.

"You can shower while I call my sister."

Naomi whirls to me. "Your sister isn't dead?"

Confused, I realize I have never told her my greatest secret. I am so used to pretending I have no sister. I feel a smile spread across my face.

"No. She is not. She lives." The smile dies quickly. "I made a bargain with another devil to keep her safe, pretended to kill her, and have not seen her in years."

"Oh, Vasily," she sighs. "That's a lot of time not to see your sister."

I nod solemnly. "Too long."

"Does everyone believe your sister is dead?"

"*Da*. Everyone. Everyone but you and the devil."

I can tell by the light in her face that she likes this, being the sole possessor of this knowledge.

"What would happen if you were dead? How would she find out?"

"Dostonev, a man who I had planned to deliver the painting to after I obtained backing from the council, would tell her. His men have guarded her since she was twelve."

"What if you weren't dead, but just captured?"

"She should still act as if I am dead, because I would not be captured without a fight."

"Logically, you should walk in and tell them what happened. That Elena had the painting all along and that she burned it to spite the brotherhood. Everyone will be angry with her and support you."

"Is that right?" I cannot stop staring at her. How long until all I have are my memories? I wonder if tonight will be the last time she will allow me to touch her.

"Yes. Do you want to shower with me? You look like you do. Ordinarily I can't read facial cues, but your whole body becomes tense and your cheekbones become more prominent when you want to fuck me. That and your cock is hard." She points down to my waist.

I follow her gesture to stare at the obscene rise in my trousers. "I am always hard for you, Naomi."

"Then come shower. I will wait for you."

I dial the number without thinking.

"Vasya, what is wrong? It is not our scheduled time."

"Hush, Katya," I say, my eyes still on Naomi. She is wandering around my tiny apartment. Like the other safe house, there is only room for a bed and a small table. There is a shower, however. "I was not able to retrieve the painting. Elena knew of my plans somehow and burned the painting before I could present it to the brothers."

"That stupid bitch," Katya curses. "I wish I was there. I'd snap her twiggy neck like a brittle branch."

I cough. "I actually did that."

"You did?" She sounds gleeful, and then in a more subdued tone says, "What happens now? What about Dostonev?"

"I do not know what the council will decide tomorrow. Perhaps . . ." I pause, for emotion is threatening to overtake me. I have not seen Katya in ten years. Not since I killed her. "This might be my last night. You must go into hiding."

She begins to sob. "No, no, Vasya. Run away. Run away tonight. Come to me. I have saved so much of the money you send to me. We can go to America and get jobs. I will wait tables and you . . . you can . . . you can . . ." She trails off because there is no occupation that I am suited for that does not involve killing.

"I love you, Katya. Leave now. Do not wait for me to call again. Assume I am dead and that you will be exposed. Maybe if

I am gone, my enemies will forget you. I love you." I hang up then. My head feels too big, too heavy for my neck. Sorrow weighs me down, and I find I cannot release the phone, as if it is my only link to my sister left.

I do not know how long I sit there, clutching the phone in my hands. Naomi is beside me, smelling fresh and clean. Her skin is scrubbed and looks dewy soft.

"My sister," I croak. "She will be left alone without me. And you." I cannot bring myself to formulate the words.

"I will help watch over your sister. Daniel will watch over us both," Naomi says. I push to my feet, for if tomorrow is my last day, then I want to be inside of Naomi for as long as I have left. "Come on." She tugs at my arm. "Water makes you feel better. It's proven."

"If you say it, then it must be true." I run my hand over her freshly washed hair. "Will you join me?"

She nods even though she has just dried off. It seems we can deny each other nothing.

Inside the shower, the hot water washes over us in slow dribbles but neither of us mind. I watch as rivers and tributaries form on Naomi's pinkening skin. With my tongue, I begin to traverse those waterways. One stream flows over the rise of her breast and breaks over the nipple. I suck on the one nipple and thumb the other. Under my mouth and hand, I feel her heart rate quicken. The nipples stiffen beneath my ministrations.

Moving lower, I dip my tongue into the well of her belly, the area so sensitive that even light contact causes her fingers to tighten around my scalp. Lower still, I find her tart liquid clinging to her inner thighs. I kneel, the tile sharp against my knees. The sharp sensation brings me alive and hardens my shaft.

Tenderly I lift one leg over my shoulder. "Talk to me, Naomi. Tell me what I am doing to you." I need to hear her speak of her pleasure again.

"Ahh, you are going to lick my clit, right? I hope so. That's what I like the most, although I do enjoy your cock inside me. It would be great if you could lick me and fuck me at the same time."

"I can." I'm delighted that she wants toys and saddened that I might not be able to enjoy them with her. The thought of her with another man angers me. I fall upon her sex like a beast then. I will make her come so many times tonight that every man that follows me will be a disappointment. Instantly I am regretful and soften my tongue lashes against her tiny clit.

Her nails dig into my scalp. "Why did you stop? I liked your tongue hard against me and your chin scraping between my thighs."

"Did you?" I say and turn to press a kiss against her leg. "I attacked you because I thought about another man between your legs, and it angered me. But then I do not want you to be lonely and unsatisfied for the rest of your life."

She tugs on my hair, pulling me upright. Holding my face between her palms, Naomi forces her eyes to meet mine. As always, the shock of blue is stunning. She holds me there for one second, maybe two, and her eyes slide away. I know that she is still staring at me, though, her eyes seeing things that others would never, no matter how long they met my gaze.

"I will have no *other* than you," she vows. "So you better fix things tomorrow."

I lift her on top of me, for I cannot wait another minute without the feel of her cunt surrounding me.

"There is no better feeling in this world than your soft, wet walls hugging me tight," I gasp. Bending at my knees, I push her against the tile. "Mark me, Naomi, with your claws. Mark me well so that tomorrow I remember what I am fighting for."

She digs her nails into my shoulder and catches my ear between her teeth. Her cunt sucks at my cock, dragging me in when I withdraw and embracing me when I thrust forward.

Relentlessly I pound into her, uncaring that the water has turned ice cold and that the shower is too small for our gymnastics. I want only to fuck her and fuck her and fuck her until I am nothing but bone.

I wrench the door open and stagger out of the bathroom and onto the bed. Tumbling her backward, I follow her down so that we are not separated, not once, not even for a second.

I pull her legs upright and press them together. "You will feel me deeper this way." I push in slowly this time so I can see how deep I can go without hurting her. She moans her pleasure. "Touch yourself, Nadya."

I've taken to calling her by a diminutive at her request. She says that if I call my sister Katya and that I am called Vasya by those I love then I, too, must call her something special.

So she has become Nadya to me. Naomi, Nadya, it makes no difference what I call her. She is my everything. The beginning of the day and the end of it.

If this is the last time I am ever inside her, I will remember it, and my soul will find hers again and again until someday we are together again.

Her fingers press in the valley of her legs, slow and tentative at first. "It's not as good as when you do it," she admits. I brace one hand next to her head and press forward, the weight of my body pushing her knees toward the bed. With my free hand, I reach around her thighs and place my thumb over her fingers.

"Touch yourself," I repeat. Beneath my hand I feel her move. "Can you feel your wetness? Your arousal?" I breathe deep. "I can smell you. After I am done fucking you, I want you to sit on my face. I will eat you until you come again, until my mouth, my throat, my lips are covered in your juice. But first you must come." I pull out and flip her over onto her belly and before she can take her next breath, I'm entering her. She stretches to accommodate me, my cock thicker, heavier, longer than before.

She exhales with each thrust, moaning her approval and encouragement. Her hips tilt upward. I rock into her until the head of my cock is buried deep inside her channel. I feel as if I can never have enough of her. My head is clouded with need and want. I can see only one thing. Naomi, Nadya, Mine.

I tuck my hand between us and touch her as she so desperately needs. Her pussy is swollen, stretched, and wet against my hand. She grinds her ass against me, her breaths are harsh, racked pants. Around my cock and against my hand I can feel her stiffen as ecstasy catches her up. Delirium sets in and I pound frantically into her until my hot seed shoots into her endlessly.

We collapse on the bed, wet from the shower, wet from our passion. I push aside the blankets until we lie on the dry sheet. For two people who do not like to be touched, we cling to each other and as night settles in, we reach for each other again and again.

"I love you, Nadya," I whisper into her hair. "I have lived a worthy life now that I have had the chance to love you."

CHAPTER **THIRTY-SIX**

NAOMI

He's given up. It's strange to see. Vasily's face is as unreadable as ever to me, but there is a slump in his shoulders that makes my heart ache with frustration. He believes that tomorrow he will meet his end at the hands of the *Bratva* he has fought so hard for.

All because of a stupid painting. If I could print out a reasonable facsimile and pass it off, I would. If all they want is a painting, I will draw them something. The result would be just as ugly as the one that bitch Elena burned. But they seem to want that painting. I don't understand it, but I have never understood art.

But I do understand Vasily. And I understand his despair.

So I kiss him and caress him as the hours tick away. He is desperate with need, my *volk*, and the next time he takes me, his touch is more savage. I reply in kind, scratching and biting and hurting him in the way he adores. By the time he collapses on top of me, spent, his cheek is red from my slaps and his neck is scratched up, and his skin is covered in sweat.

We are both content, even as his weight presses me into the mattress. This time, I don't complain about germs or microbes. I don't point out that he has come inside me twice now with no condom. If he is to die in a few hours, I want all of his germs, all of his fluids, everything he can give me.

But he'd better not die, because I will lose my shit and start killing people myself.

Eventually, he presses a kiss to my mouth. "The hour nears. We must dress and prepare ourselves."

I want to protest, to pull his body back down over mine for one more quick round of lovemaking, but I don't. I'm panicking. I don't want Vasily hurt. I try to calm myself instead, searching for my old fail-safe—the scientific method. But right now, it's failing me.

Ask a question: will the *Bratva* kill Vasily?

Do background research: there's no time for it.

Construct a hypothesis is next. But I can't construct one without letting emotion cloud my judgment. All of my heart screams that they won't hurt him, that they wouldn't dare. But my logical brain has no idea how things will go down. I don't know enough about *Bratvas* and coups. Vasily does, though, and he seems to think his end is near, which terrifies me.

And after the hypothesis is constructed, you "test" things. But the test will come when Vasily approaches the *Bratva* and they either fill him with bullets or let him go in peace.

My breathing quickens with anxiety until my chest hurts. When Vasily finishes dressing, I straighten his tie and smooth his collar. It barely covers the marks I have left on him. "We don't have to go right away," I inform him. "We can wait. Maybe give them a few days to cool off, see how things shake out—"

Vasily grabs my chin and tilts it up until I'm looking him in the eye. Even though it's hard to keep eye contact, I do so, some-how. "*Nyet*," he says softly. "I am *volk*. I do not hide, not from my own people. Whatever judgment they seek for me, I shall accept."

"We could get back into bed," I say desperately. I begin to unbutton his shirt, undoing his work of a few moments ago. "You can find my G-spot again—"

His hand covers mine. "All will happen as it should, Naomi," he tells me.

But you are not fighting, I want to say. I know why he does not—because he is *volk*. He is *Bratva*. He is their creature, and if they have decided to put him down, he understands this. It is me who makes excuses and cannot understand.

So I drop my hand and watch him fix his buttons. "Let us go find Daniel, then."

I don't mention the council. I don't want to even think they exist, and that they are ready to pass judgment on my *volk*.

We are silent on the car ride to the *Bratva* headquarters. I sup-pose there is nothing to say, not really. When we arrive, a familiar man is waiting in front of the double doors to the room where the council will pass judgment on Vasily, a rifle cradled in his arms.

"Daniel," I call out joyfully. "We're here now!"

"Naomi!" He rushes toward me, slinging his rifle across his back. "Oh, thank Christ." When he gets to me, his arms wrap around me in a massive hug, and I sit and endure it awkwardly. He squeezes me for what feels like forever. "I know you don't like hugs, sis, but suck it up for your big brother."

"I am," I tell him, though I'm relieved when he releases me.

Daniel's eyes are curiously shiny as he steps back and studies me. "Nice cap," he says, flicking the brim of my ever-present baseball cap.

"The old one was lost to Golubevs when they tried to kill us," I tell him.

Those shiny eyes narrow and he glares at Vasily. "I thought you said my sister would be safe, you goddamn prick."

"She is safe," Vasily tells him. And it's true, I am.

Daniel's mouth scrunches up in the way that I know means he's not done arguing. "I take it the Golubevs are the reason for the hair color choices?" He looks at Vasily. "You forgot your eyebrows."

I wave a hand dismissively. "Eyebrows are not important at the moment."

"That's right," Daniel says. "Where the hell have you two been?" he asks. "I've been here for hours and worried out of my goddamn mind."

"Sorry," I tell him. "I had to go have good-bye sex with Vasily. He is depressed." Vasily makes a noise in his throat, echoed by Daniel.

"Oversharing," my brother says.

I blink at him. "I'm sorry. Should I have lied?"

"To your brother, yes. When it comes to sex? Always." He looks over at Vasily. "Not going to ask me for forgiveness?"

"Not this morning," Vasily says, his tone rather blank.

"Shame. I feel a bit like whipping your ass after you touched my sister."

"You shouldn't," I point out to Daniel. "It arouses him. If he needs a whipping, I'll do it."

"Oversharing. Jesus Christ. I need mental bleach right about now." Daniel scrubs a hand on his face. "I don't even want to ask about the scratches on your neck."

"I left those," I tell Daniel proudly. "You should see his penis."

"Aaaaargh!" My brother waves a hand in the air. "Can we please, please not have this conversation? Sis, I am ecstatic to see you whole and in one piece." He grasps my hand again and squeezes it even though he knows I don't like touching. I endure it, since Daniel clearly needs this. "I'm even glad to see Vasily's sourpuss face if it means he's kept you safe."

"He has," I tell him. "I don't even mind his germs or his semen." This is a declaration of love from me, and I look over at Vasily, wishing I could read his face. Does he like hearing this? Or does it make him sadder because he thinks going through those doors that Daniel is guarding will be his execution? A secret, awful part of me hopes he will hear my words and change his mind, and he will grab my hand and we will run off to the *dacha* he has mentioned. I will let him fill me with semen as often as he likes and I will love every moment of it.

Just as long as he doesn't die.

"Now you're just saying that shit to freak me out," Daniel says. "I will pay you a million dollars if you never mention the words 'Vasily' and 'semen' to your dear brother ever again."

"I gave you that million," I tell Daniel easily, but my fingers betray my anxiety. I can't stop twitching, and my fingers skim my baseball cap. The hall is utterly quiet other than our conversation, and I wonder what is happening behind the door that Daniel is guarding.

"You can have it back," Daniel says.

"I don't—" I begin to argue, but Vasily cups my chin.

"Keep the money, Nadya. You might need it if I am gone."

No, no, no. I don't want to hear this. I turn to Vasily and begin to straighten his tie. It is askew by an infinitesimal amount, and I don't like that. I adjust the knot, smoothing my fingers down the dark silk.

"What's he talking about?" Daniel asks.

Quickly, Vasily recaps what happened earlier. The burning of the painting. Elena's death.

"You need to see what is inside," Daniel says, his voice growing low. It's clear that our earlier conversation was for anyone who could listen, but this is for Vasily and my ears alone.

"Is it bad?" Vasily asks.

"It's . . . interesting," Daniel replies. "I don't know if it's good or bad, to be honest."

I don't like interesting. Desperately, I smooth my hands over Vasily's collar and tug at his sleeves so they hang correctly. I'm obsessing, my fingers checking his buttons to ensure that he is not rumpled. His hair is starting to show hints of yellow against his skull, and it looks strange against the dark brown dye. I smooth a longer lock off of his forehead and tuck it behind an ear.

"Nadya," he tells me softly. "I look fine."

"Your tie is not straight," I tell him. "I should take it off and retie it so it hangs properly." But I don't. I just smooth and smooth and smooth the fabric. "You don't have to go in," I blurt, dangerously close to tears. "We can turn and run. I can drain money into a ghost account for you. You and I can go find another *dacha* and we can hide out—"

"I cannot," he tells me, voice soft. His fingers caress my cheek again. "I am *volk*, no matter what."

I blink repeatedly, trying to calm myself. Trying not to cry. Vasily doesn't like to see me crying. "I told you once that I didn't love anything. But I do. I love you. I love you and I want you to come with me." I don't want to lose him. Not now, not ever.

He tilts my face toward his and leans in. His lips brush gently against mine in a whisper of a kiss. Then, he releases me and looks at Daniel. "Keep her behind you at all times," he tells him. "If there is bloodshed, I do not wish her to be harmed."

Daniel pulls two small guns out of holsters tucked under his arms. "You got it."

I want to cling to Vasily's leg and beg him not to go as he turns and faces the double doors. Facing his future, however long or short it may be.

Then, he pushes the doors open and steps inside. Ahead of him, I see rows and rows of chairs and men seated in the chairs. Is it a firing squad? I push forward, dragging Daniel with me like a shield. I have to see what is going to happen.

As I push into the room, I take everything in. There are at least thirty men seated in here, all of them young. I do not see a single one that is bearded or gray haired. They are all young, and fit, and they wear the same cold expression that I have seen on Vasily's face so many times. They are *Bratva*. Killers. They are all dressed in dark, bland suits so they can blend in.

And they all have guns on their laps.

As Vasily steps inside, I admire his broad shoulders and his form. He is the biggest out of all of them, proud and unyielding. He is not asking for forgiveness from these men. He dares them to speak against him, despite the fact that they are all armed. My breath catches in my throat, because he is magnificent.

He is *volk*.

He regards them, and speaks short words. *"Petrovich Elena umer. Ya ubil ee."*

They take this in silently.

He continues to speak, no doubt telling them of what has occurred. I can't make out any of it, and I decide I need to learn Russian so I can participate in future conversations, if there are to be any. For now, I imagine the words he tells them, picturing Vasily as the narrator in a story. *Yes, yes, Elena was quite the cunt. She was a raging bitch and she tackled my sweet Naomi, so I had no choice but to dispose of her crazy ass. Now you will all kiss my feet and thank me for this.*

I paraphrase, of course. The reality is likely more somber, because not a single person is smiling.

Vasily says one word, then drops his hands as if to say he is done. Silence reigns.

One person stands up in the front row. It is the older boy of the two that escaped with Vasily. He is carrying a gun, dressed in a fine suit. As he stands and approaches, a surge of panic rises in my throat. Is he going to be the one to kill Vasily for daring to want more for the *Bratva*?

But to my surprise, he turns his gun around and offers the butt of it to Vasily. He speaks, saying something long and dramatic. I catch none of it except *volk*. But the offer of the gun gives me hope. And I watch as one by one, each man stands and turns his gun, butt facing out. It is an offering to Vasily.

And I don't need to know Russian to know that they want him for their leader.

CHAPTER **THIRTY-SEVEN**

VASILY

I walk through the crowd of men, brushing the stocks of the guns. There are thirty or so of my brethren here and they stare at me with faces full of grim expectation.

What has happened here?

Naomi has somehow orchestrated a near-bloodless coup. In my narrow-mindedness, I failed to see the potential in my brothers. I failed them by not trusting.

If it were not for her love and belief in me, I would be dead or on the run. I would not be standing here, new leader of the *Bratva*. It will not be an easy transition. Outsiders will challenge us for territory and power.

But we are young, strong, and still idealistic in our own strange ways.

I've carried out dark deeds with many of them, all for the

purpose of extending or, at the very least, protecting the Petrovich power. But what has the *Bratva* done for us? I reach the end and turn toward the assembled group. Heart so full I can barely form words, I begin to speak.

"When I was a boy, I believed that being *volk* would save me, save my loved ones. But I soon learned that being *volk* for Petrovichs meant having no loved ones. The *Bratva* comes first, yes?"

They nod as one. "And if we did not place the *Bratva* first then a *boyevik*, a soldier, would be sent to bring us back in line. One of our own would suffer. The *boyevik* would not want to inflict the pain but he would do so, because to not obey would imperil what he held dear. A mother, a father, a brother, a lover." A sister. "I wake up one morning alone in my bed and think this is no better than Communist Russia, when our grandfathers feared they would be sent to a work camp where we would die at the hands of Soviets." I raise my palms in surrender. "I think to myself that I no longer desire to be *volk* and I set out on a quest to obtain the famed Caravaggio that had hung on the walls of the *Bratva* palace for a century until it was lost by Sergei. I am here to tell you that the Caravaggio is gone. It is dust." Murmurs move like a wave through the room. "I have nothing to offer you in terms of power or money." Naomi coughs but ceases at my glare. "Nothing but my weapon, my body, and my vow. I will fight for you so that you can live without fear for your loved ones, for your own soul."

I drop my hands to my side and wait.

Igorek walks forward and picks up my hand. He pushes a heavy signet ring on it. I frown at him but he remains silent, only waiting for a reaction. The ring is made of silver and is tarnished in the deeper recesses. A person not skilled at cleaning wiped off the surface black to reveal the wolf's head.

"The white-furred gray wolf lives in the harshest of climates, in the coldest of lands, and still thrives. It is an honorable species who has killed off its competitors and risen above its challengers to live with its pack in the snow and ice and tundra of Siberia. The gray wolf is a survivor." He pulls down my hand and kisses the wolf. "We are your pack, Volk Vasya. You can choose to eat the Petrovichs or abide with them. Tell us and we will carry it out."

The sound of thirty bullets being chambered in unison fills the air with ominous harmony. One by one, the *boyeviks* come forward and kiss the ring. It is awkward and discomfiting, but the ritual is necessary for them and perhaps for me.

"Is it time for the loyalty tests?" Naomi asks in a loud whisper. Igorek ducks his head to hide a smile.

"Nah, Naomi, they don't have time for that. Vasily has to work fast."

"You should call him Vasya, Daniel. That's what all his friends call him. Nicknames are used by people who have affection for one another," Naomi informs her brother, who looks at her as if she is talking gibberish.

"I don't have affection for that asshole," he retorts. "I'm here for you."

Before the two can devolve into a sibling argument, I intervene. Pulling Naomi to my side, I admit, "Daniel is correct. We must act swiftly." I turn to Igorek. He will be my second. "We should call a meeting with elders. If the majority of the elders oppose us, then we will leave and form our own organization."

"With what funds?" asks Stefan, a new *boyevik* just moved up from the lower ranks.

"We have lots of money," Naomi pipes up. I shake my head as Daniel pulls her aside. She should cease speaking. Already too much curious attention is paid to her. I do not wish for the *Bratva* to know of her worth. In this uncertain period, she could be seen as a bargaining chip. I will not allow for this to happen. The more that she shows her value, the greater a target she becomes.

"Let us not worry about money at this time," I suggest, but already I see the *boyeviks* eyeing Naomi with interest. I press my lips together. "Call for the meeting."

Igorek nods. He motions for two others and they follow him out the door.

"How will you know if they are lying when you ask them if they will be willing to follow you?" Naomi asks.

"I will watch them."

"I could make a polygraph," she suggests.

"How?"

"A polygraph measures breathing and heart rate. There are a lot of false positives, and a true sociopath has no problem passing but given that your test subjects would be unawares, it could provide you a data point greater than, ah, watching." She says that last word with no small disdain.

I cannot help but allow a small smile to curve my lips. She is a wonder. "What do you need?"

She describes her tools. I send two of the remaining *boyeviks* for the supplies.

"These phones have a heart rate monitor for your finger. Require everyone to place their finger on it. We'll use these photo diodes from these exercise watches and tape them on the neck. That will measure two pulse points. I'll monitor the results here." She points to her computer, which is set up next to my seat at the head of the table.

"I didn't come all this way to watch my sister be cannon fodder," Daniel interjects. He picks up the laptop and sets it down in the corner of the room and then drags boxes around it, effectively screening Naomi off from the rest of the room.

"I can't see anything back here," she complains and picks up the laptop. Daniel blocks her exit. She looks toward me once and then twice, and then with an extraordinary effort, she meets my gaze. "Please, Vasya. I want to sit next to you."

I can deny her nothing. I wave my hand for Daniel to move. He glares at me and refuses to budge, but when Naomi pushes by he does not stop her. I pinch her chin between my thumb and index finger. "If you sit by me, you must not talk. You must do everything I ask of you. Like at the club."

"Which club? The one where you killed Emile or the one where you killed the donkey fucker?"

Predictably Daniel explodes. "Jesus Hermione Christ, you shit stain, what the fuck were you doing with my sister? This is fucking unacceptable."

"Daniel, you can reprimand me at another time, yes?" I nod toward the *boyeviks*, who are watching with unabashed interest. He grits his teeth but nods.

"The rest of you prepare for the meeting." Most of the *boyeviks* leave although a few do not. Some have come to the *Bratva* with nothing. Alexsandr, our old general killed by Sergei, believed in taking orphans from the street. Treat them kindly and they will follow you with blind loyalty. He was not wrong. I have been a loyalist from the age of ten, willing to do anything the *Bratva* asked of me. But when Elena tried to keep me in line by threatening my sister, discontent lodged in my heart, and with each day that she was imperiled, the seeds of treachery took root and grew.

Outside the window of the warehouse, I see nothing but gray streets and small, battered cars.

Naomi places her small hand on the windowsill next to mine. The contrast between us is monstrous. Her hand is pale and lovely with elegant fingers that do extraordinary things. Mine are scarred and beaten. Already they look like the hands of a man two decades my senior. It is a wonder she allows me to place my hands upon her form. When we are alone, I will ask her if she wants to leave. She should not feel compelled to stay with me. I've taken her from one captivity and placed her in another. That Daniel has not taken my head from my shoulders speaks to his honor and elevated thinking. It would be a privilege to be referred to as Vasya by one such as Daniel.

"When this is over, the *dacha* is yours, Naomi," I croak out hoarsely. These words are hard to give voice to so they are quiet, little darts in the air. I want to grab them and eat them up.

"What do you mean, it is mine?" Her eyes narrow and I look away, out the window again. The bleak landscape mirrors my aching heart.

"It is yours alone. I will not be there but by invitation," I say.

"I don't understand," she says impatiently. "You know you have to be blunt with me. I don't like this. You—"

A commotion at the door interrupts her, and Igorek appears with his two men, the elders trailing behind him. Whatever she wants must wait, for the meeting is convening.

"What is the meaning of this?" huffs Georgi.

Thomas, the most sedate and serious of the elders, nods his head. "Do you bring us the Caravaggio?"

"Please be seated." I wave my hand toward the table. "As you can see, each seat has a sensor. Press your index finger there when you desire to talk. The diode is for your neck." I sit at the head and attach myself to Naomi's wires. Some of the leaders do as I ask. Others do not. I grab the hand of Georgi, who sits next to me. "Georgi, you do not wish to participate?"

He sneers. "I am not your lackey."

It is with little regret that I shoot him in the shoulder. Shocked silence ensues at the table. I repeat my request. "Please ensure that the pressure is hard against your veins, or we will shoot you for not having a pulse."

Thomas speaks again. "Where's the Caravaggio? We told you that we would vote for you as boss if you brought us the painting, a return of the glory of the Petrovichs."

"The Caravaggio is dust and Elena is gone."

Some of the pulses must have jumped, for I can see a spike in the heart rate lines of Naomi's program.

"Then you are done with the *Bratva*," Georgi gasps, his face white with the pain from the gunshot wound.

Ignoring Georgi, I address the remaining men. "You elders have a choice. You can follow me as head of the Petrovich *Bratva*, or I and all of the *boyeviks* will leave, and we will form our own brotherhood. And hungry for territory and power, the Petrovichs will be our first target." I steeple my fingers together and lean back. "So you can fall in line, leave, or present a united front against us. What will it be?"

Georgi, pale as snow, leans forward. "You think the son of a whore will lead us? Never."

"That is one vote against. Who else?"

Toward the end of the table, Pietr clears his throat. "I will follow you, Vasya. I have always liked you."

"Ohh he is lying. Look Vasily," Naomi interrupts. The graph is spiking wildly. I do not entirely understand what I am looking at, so I look at Naomi and read her expression. She is delighted that her machine is working. "Ask him something else, something that would make him lie again."

"Do you fear this woman?"

"No," Pietr scoffs, but he is unable to meet my eyes.

The graph is wild again. She claps. "I love it. He is afraid of me. That is a first. Ask him if the sky is blue. For a control."

"Is the sky blue?"

He does not answer. I lift my gun. "Pietr, is the sky blue?"

His answer is sullen. "Yes."

"Is the grass green?"

"Yes."

"Do you love your vodka."

Hesitation. "No."

"These are all true," Naomi hisses. "Ask him another question like . . . has he raped a woman?"

"Well, Pietr have you?"

He purses his lips together. "No."

The graph goes crazy.

"A lie." She scowls. I pick up my guns and shoot him twice, first between the eyes and second in the heart, for good measure.

Georgi pushes away from the table and runs for the door. Igorek shoots him before he can make it to the end of the table.

"This is a fucking shitshow," Daniel growls behind me. "You need to end it before someone we care about gets hurt." He jerks his head toward Naomi.

"Place your fingers on the phones, please," I ask. The commotion has caused people to move away from the devices but at my command, everyone obeys. They know now to speak the truth or die. It is simple.

"I do not like the way the *Bratva* was run under Sergei and Elena. They rotted it out from the inside. In another generation, this brotherhood would be dead. Do you wish for that?"

There are many shakes of the head.

"True," says Naomi.

"I would like for us to move forward, under a new regime. We give to our people as the *Bratva* had in the past, providing for them generously with education opportunities, housing, and other necessities of life. If you are loyal to the *Bratva*, then you do not want. Loyalty is not paid for in sexual servitude or threats to family members. Anyone who is part of the *Bratva* is here because they wish it, not because we have blackmailed them into it."

"We will be smaller and weaker," Thomas warns.

"Then we will be smaller. But not weaker. Today we are only as strong as our weakest leak. When we weed out the traitors, the disloyal, the malcontents, then we will be left with a true brotherhood, one that serves together because it suits them, because we cannot bear to disappoint our brothers. Not because we fear their reprisals. Fear is what we will foment in our enemies. Never within our brotherhood."

"Then yes, I am with you," Thomas says. Once Thomas agrees, the rest follow except for the last, who hesitates. I note his reluctance and mentally mark him for watching.

"Meeting is dismissed." I rise and wait for everyone to leave, but Igorek stops them.

"Kiss the ring," Igorek demands. Thomas hesitates but then turns and strides toward me. Thomas is an aged warrior, and it is odd to see him bend over to lift my hand to his mouth.

"I pledge my loyalty to the *Volk*." Then he raises my hand in his. "Long live the *Volk*!"

The *boyeviks* echo the cheer loudly while the elders watch. One by one they come and kiss the ring. Naomi stands behind me, one hand on my shoulder as the men pledge their homage.

CHAPTER **THIRTY-EIGHT**

NAOMI

Vasily is in control. Like a king, he takes the homage of his people with due accordance and gravity. Me, I'd be giggling like a loon each time a pair of sour old lips came up to press themselves against the ring.

And then I'd scrub the ring, because of germs.

But my *volk* is standing tall and proud. This is everything he has ever wanted, everything he has dreamed. It will be a tough road from here, carving out their niche once more, but if anyone can do it, it is Vasily, who wears his determination like a second skin.

I'm a little sad I won't be here to see it.

Okay, a lot sad.

But now that the painting is gone and Vasily is in control, there's no more need for me at his side. I'll leave him all the tools

I possibly can, of course. I'll keep his bank account loaded and protected to ensure that my *volk* will always have enough money to run his organization. I don't need to be with him to be helpful, but my body will miss his body.

And I'm going to miss his germs, his wolfish smile, and the way he strokes my skin as if I'm the finest thing he's ever touched. I'm going to miss challenging him and caressing him, and just having someone listen to my crazy conversations and actually having them listen instead of tuning me out.

Vasily is meeting with his *boyeviks* late into the night. There is much to be discussed, including current jobs, current enemies of the Petrovichs, future enemies, and a trail of minutiae that leads from one side of the world to the other. The Petrovichs have a messy empire and it needs tidying, and Vasily is the man to do it. But he's so busy that I retired to another room some time ago, needing to get away from the people and the sounds. Daniel hangs out with me in the ornate study, eyeing the ridiculous furnishings and occasionally picking one up and saying things like "Do you think Regan would want a vase covered in naked babies?"

"Cherubs," I correct him, not looking up from my computer screen. I know the vase he speaks of. It's gaudy and hideous and stands proudly on the mantel of an equally gaudy and hideous lacquered fireplace mantel. "And does Regan collect Sèvres?"

"Sèvres? Is that what this is? Shit, it's ugly." I hear him plop it back down on the mantel. "Whoever ran this place before liked some seriously terrible shit."

"It is rococo style," I tell him. "A very shitty style." It hurts my eyes, all its frills and gaudy swirls and endless color and carvings. It's not a restful style in the slightest. I think of the pale white *dacha* Vasily mentioned with longing, but it's not to be.

I don't want to be there alone, close to him and yet not together. And I know he can't be there with me, not if he expects to rule his empire. It's just not going to work. My heart hurts at this realization, and I continue moving funds around on the computer, electronically scraping off any sort of trail so I can later deposit the money into one of Vasily's many accounts.

I've cleaned out his enemies, which means they will be coming after him. But they would anyhow, especially if the leadership has been shuffled. So it's best he has a shit-ton of cash in order to grease palms.

"How much longer do you think Vasily's going to be out there?" Daniel says, and I hear a yawn in his voice. "Regan's going to want me home soon. She's still not good at being alone for long periods of time." He says it easily but I hear the strain in his voice. He's worried about her, and he's eager to leave.

I suppose I've stalled for as long as I can. With a stab of regret, I close my computer and bite my lip. "I'm ready."

I'm not ready. I'm not. I want to run into the next room and grab Vasily's arm and cling to it as if that will somehow change things. But that will only highlight how incredibly wrong I am for him, and so it's time for me to go. I feel like crying. I want to bury my face in some antibacterial Kleenex and weep for days, but I dare not, because it will distress Daniel. And then I'll be even more distressed, and we'll have an endless circle of unhappy emotion and I'll retreat within myself, unable to process.

Which isn't a bad idea, really, but I want to be present for my last views of Russia. It is a cold and unforgiving country, but it is Vasily's, and I will savor every last glimpse of it.

"You want to say good-bye to Vasily before we head out, then?" Daniel asks me.

I do, but it's not wise. I know I'll end up weeping uncontrollably, and I can't handle intense emotion like that, not right now. So I shake my head and tuck my laptop under my arm. "Let's just go," I tell him.

"Can your dear ol' brother point out that this is a crappy idea? Because I'd really prefer for an enraged Russian to not follow us to the airport with some idea that I'm kidnapping you home. I really like my nuts and would prefer to keep them."

"Vasily won't want your nuts," I tell him. "He likes women."

Behind me, Daniel sighs. "Sarcasm, sis."

Right. "You know I'm not good with that stuff," I tell him, annoyed. "Speak plainly."

"I am saying," Daniel enunciates, coming up from behind me. He grabs my shoulders, taking care to touch my sleeves only and not my skin, and he turns me around. "That you shouldn't run away like a chicken."

And he points me toward the door.

It's on the tip of my tongue to point out to him that chickens are rather speedy runners, when I realize Vasily is standing in the doorway.

Oh.

I blink, and then my gaze slides away from his. It feels like too much to look into those blue eyes right now. I inspect his clothing, instead, the perfect way it lies against his big, muscular form. The clenched fists at his side. The tension in his body.

"Where are you going?" he asks, and his accent is thick, a sure sign he is agitated. Maybe tired. It has been a long day for all of us.

"My lovely sister is running away," Daniel says. "And I'm guessing you'll have something to say about that."

"I'm very irritated with you right now, Daniel," I tell my brother, scrunching my mouth to stop from frowning. I need to look calm. "And Vasily, Daniel and I were leaving to go home. You're in charge, so we're not needed any longer."

The fists at his side clench so hard that I see his knuckles whiten. "You are leaving? Why?"

Daniel's hands lift from my arms. "This is my cue to skedaddle on out for a bit. I'll be in the hall if you need me, sis."

"Now who's the coward," I taunt him, but I don't move. The truth is, I'm still a coward. I did try to run away. I set the laptop down on a nearby twiggy-legged table, and then my fingers flick at my sides, helplessly. I pull off my cap and clench it in my hands, running my fingers along the bill.

Vasily strides forward to stand in front of me, and he moves so close that now I'm staring at one of his buttons on his shirt. I hear the door shut, and Daniel has left the room. Warm fingers— the only fingers I like touching me—brush under my chin, and Vasily lifts my head until I'm forced to meet his gaze.

"Why do you leave, Nadya?" His voice is achingly soft.

It hurts me to hear it. All of this hurts me. I feel as if I'll never recover from the heartache echoing through every ounce of skin and muscle in my body. "I can't stay, Vasily. You know I can't."

"I know no such thing."

"I don't belong at your side."

"Who has told you such?" His fingers tighten, imperceptibly. "Has Daniel said such a thing? Shall I remove his head from his shoulders?"

"No," I tell him, surprised at the vehemence in his tone. My gaze skitters over his harsh face, so beloved to me now. "No one has said this. I am saying this."

"But why? Is it me?"

Now that's just ridiculous. "It's me, Vasily. Of course it's me. It's who I am. I can't be at your side. You have to rule with an iron fist. No one's going to follow you if you keep company with a retard."

His nostrils flare and he tenses against me. "Never call yourself that again. Never."

"I don't really think I'm retarded," I tell him, and my voice is soft. "But others will."

"Do you think I care what others think?"

"Don't you?" His tie has become slightly crooked with his movements. I reach out and straighten it absently. "You needed the respect of the *Bratva*, so you hunted the painting. Now you have them, but my presence might undermine you, and I don't want that." I tug at the knot, then tighten it, and smooth my fingers down the fine, dark silk.

"I do not understand where you get this. Of course you are meant to rule at my side. As the *volk*'s woman."

I search for a hidden meaning in this, but I'm not finding one. He can't possibly be telling the truth, though. So I try again. Perhaps he needs a visual. "Have you ever seen the movie *Forrest Gump*?"

"I do not know where you go with this—"

"In the movie, Forrest is looked down upon by everyone because his brain works differently. People think he's stupid. They mock him. No one understands him. And he falls in love with a beautiful girl." I keep smoothing the tie, because I need to touch something. "And she turns him away because she's embarrassed by him. Because he doesn't think like everyone else. Because he's different."

"Naomi—"

I rush on ahead. "But she's happy to be with him in private, of course. Because no one can look at them and laugh. And I thought at first that I would be okay with that. That I could hide out at your little *dacha* and be your secret. That it would be fun. I'd have the best of both worlds because I'd have you when you have time, and I'd have my silence. But now that we have been together in all these noisy places and spent our days and nights at each other's side, I realize that's not what I want at all." I run my fingers over his tie, over and over, even though it's aligned perfectly. "I don't want to be someone's ugly secret. I don't want you to be ashamed of who I am and hide me away. I don't want your love only when it's convenient. Now do you understand?"

He touches my cheek, and I realize that it's wet. I must be crying. I didn't notice. My entire world is down to that tie, to the soft pattern of dark lines in the silk, to the angle of it lying against the paler shirt. The tie is all I see. It's all I can focus on, because if I let my brain pan out, I'm going to lose control. I just know it.

Because I thought I could handle this without emotion, but I'm very, very wrong.

"Nadya," Vasily says to me. "Look at me."

"I can't," I say, and there's a hitch in my breath. "I really can't."

"I would never be embarrassed by you. Never. You are special to me—"

I flinch. "I hate that word, special."

"Then I will not use it," he declares. "You are unique. Original. One of a kind, like the Caravaggio."

I think of the painting with its wolf doing terrible things to the Madonna. "I am like the donkey fucker?"

"*Nyet*," he says, exasperated. There's a laugh in his throat. "I am saying this all wrong. You are priceless. You are so rare and valuable to me that I would chase you all across Europe in search of you. I would destroy men that stood in my way. I would worship at your feet, if you would let me." His fingers brush over my tear-wet skin. "And your weeping destroys me," he says in a soft voice, and kisses my cheeks. "So come, let your Vasya show you what you mean to him."

He tugs me into his arms and I go willingly, because I love it when he touches me. To my surprise, though, he hauls me up, one arm under my legs, and one arm against my back, and carries me like he would a heroine from a black-and-white movie. We head back into the antechamber that is still full of assassins awaiting their orders from their new leader.

Daniel is off to one side, and he is smiling as if he knows a secret I do not.

Here, Vasily sets me down. He turns, one hand clamped on my shoulder in case I try to run away, and he addresses his men. "This is Naomi Hays," he tells them. "She is my queen. She will rule at my side. She is the brains to my brawn. If I am the wolf, she is my keeper. If I am the gun, she is the hand holding the trigger. Do any of you question this?"

The room is utterly silent.

"Good," Vasily says, and he leans in and kisses me hard in front of all. He kisses me so long and so thoroughly that my knees are weak when he releases me, and I have to lean against him for strength. His arm goes around my shoulders and he pulls me against him. "Now you are not leaving my side," he murmurs into my ear. "Are you?"

"No," I say, dazed. "I suppose not."

EPILOGUE

VASILY

"Did you put the soundproofing in so I couldn't hear the helicopter or so that no one could hear me scream?" Naomi asks as she collapses against the sheets.

The white sheets and the white walls could be blinding to some but it only serves as a focus. There is nothing I want to view other than Naomi.

I prowl up her body, licking my way from her cunt to her breasts. "The helipad was a bother to you," I say noncommittally. I am not certain if she would be pleased or offended that some of the *boyeviks* call her a very loud girl, but in Russian, so she may not understand regardless. "It is for the safety of the workers," I declare piously. "If they heard you they would be distressed by their own performances in the bedroom. The pressure would lead to more failure and then women all over Russia would blame you for their lack of orgasms."

"You lie well, Vasya," she says. I shiver at her use of my diminutive on her tongue.

"You are a *dachniki* living here." I smile. "A summer person even though you are here year-round."

"I like that," she says. She comes to Moscow if I am gone too long, the helipad making it easy for her to travel but she prefers to spend time here at the *dacha* in her retreat of white silence.

Dostonev was disappointed when I could not present him with the painting, but he has not called in my favor yet. With Elena gone and the *Bratva* under my control, I was able to bring Katya back from London. His passive acceptance over the loss of the painting was an acknowledgment that his threats lacked any teeth. I still owe him and I will repay, but not with pieces of my heart and family.

That Katya was alive was met with astonishment and interest. Instead of viewing me as a monster willing to kill his own sister, my deceit helped to humanize me to the young *boyeviks*. I still might have to kill many of them for the lustful glances they shoot her way when they believe I am not looking.

She spends much of her time in London, though, as it has become her home. But we are together again.

And I am lying with my beloved.

Lowering my face between the valley of her lush breasts, I whisper, "It is no lie. Should any of them behold you in this state, they would be struck blind by your beauty. They would be forced into the woods, where they would tear at their skin in despair or sit outside your doorstep and waste away until they were nothing but skeletons until they had but one more view of your perfection."

"Is that how you feel?"

I take her hand and place it on my cock. "I feel as if I could fell a thousand giants when your hand is on me. Does it not feel strong as steel? A blade worthy of your sheath?"

She strokes me roughly just as I like. "I don't think the blade is a good comparison word for your penis. A blade would really hurt me. I'm not into that kind of pain and even if I was, wouldn't that ruin your pleasure because you wouldn't be able to fuck me for a long time? I think a knife wound takes a month or more to fully heal. And depending on the knife, it could damage nerve endings, which would result in declined sensation. How about just your cock in my pussy?"

I smile against her skin, licking the inner curve of her breast. Out of the corner of my eye, I see her nipple tighten and lengthen, readying itself for my mouth. "You may call it whatever you like so long as you keep touching me in this manner," I reply.

"Okay. I enjoy rubbing your penis. The heavy ridges of your veins creates an interesting contrast. When you get very hard, as you are now, the head juts out."

"The head would like for you to squeeze him in your hot little hand."

I take one delicious nipple inside my mouth as she continues her explicit and heat-inducing examination of my shaft. Her back arches to shove the nipple deeper into my mouth. I suck hard, so hard she gasps and is unable to continue speaking.

My hand dips into the well my mouth drank from just moments ago. She's slick, juicy, and ready. I bring my knee forward to press her thighs apart, and she guides my cock to her entrance.

"Naomi, will you instruct me?" I ask, poised to thrust forward. I want to gaze into her blue depths, just for a moment. It takes her great effort to do so, and my heart leaps as those eyes make brief contact and then slide away. "You are so true, so beautiful." I stroke her cheek.

"I want you inside me."

I push inside, just a little. "You need to be more explicit."

She slaps me impatiently on my flank. "All the way. I want you to fill me up with your cock."

I do as she asks and then . . . pause.

"You are playing with me," she says.

"I am," I respond solemnly. "I enjoy hearing your voice. I enjoy hearing you describe the filthy things we do in your very remarkable way. So, Naomi, tell me. What is it that you want me to do?"

"I want you to pump—no thrust. Thrust is a better word. Thrust inside of me."

I start to move, slowly dragging my cock along her swollen tissues. Her mouth falls open and a moan colors the air.

"At what pace should I move?"

"Faster," she says, and thrusts against me. At her command I begin to thrust faster, drilling into her fiercely enough to make her breasts shake in her chest, hard enough to push her palms into the headboard, deep enough to feel her womb at the end of my cock.

I push her knees up higher, press her thighs open wider so that there is no place inside her that is untouched.

"What else?" I say through gritted teeth.

"Touch my clit."

My hand trembles with passion as I place it over her mons. I pinch her little organ between my fingers, and her hips rise off the bed.

"I live to be inside you, Naomi. Everything I do in Moscow,

in London, in Hong Kong, is to be able to come here to our *dacha* and slide my cock inside your sweet cunt and fuck until we are mad, mindless things."

She does not respond with words, only with increasingly louder moans of pleasure. Her face is rapt and her body is tense under mine. Ready to receive, ready to give.

I drive her into the mattress, following her, and drive into her lush body again and again, because we are hurricanes of need. Our mouths feast upon each other and our hands knead, stroke, and strike skin against skin until we are a blur of ecstasy.

In the wreckage of our lovemaking, we lay breathless.

"You are my heart," I murmur against her hair when I'm able to speak and form thought again.

"You know what, Vasya?" Naomi sits upright, captivated by a thought.

"What?" I trail a lazy finger up the knobs of her spine.

"You and I are like the Caravaggio. *We* are the Caravaggio."

"How so?" I'm bemused.

"You are the *volk* and I'm the Madonna. You devoured me in the woods just like in that painting!"

"So as long as we are together, the power of the *Bratva* will be unimpeachable?"

She nods solemnly. Naomi so rarely tells a joke. She is very literal and in this moment, I do not know if it is joke or real. I think and then come to the conclusion I do not care. For she is not entirely wrong. I am the wolf of Russia, and she is the woman who saved me and in doing so saved many others. Without her I am nothing. So . . . we are the Caravaggio painting come to life. The *volk* and the Madonna. It is good.

Turn the page for a bonus Hitman Christmas story,

LAST GIFT

exclusively in print in this edition only!

To our fans!

DAISY

Nick watches the cars heading down the side street next to our apartment building. It's unusually busy, and I can tell it's making him tense. It's evident in the stiff set of his shoulders, and the way he ever so gently bends down the mini-blind so he can peer out on the snowy streets, unnoticed. When his hand brushes at his waist as if looking for his gun, I realize just how on edge he is.

I lick my fingers and put aside the Christmas cookie batter I'm making, and move to his side. "Nikolai," I say softly. "What is it?"

He looks over at me, his beautiful eyes dark with worry. "It is nothing, Daisy."

But I know it's not nothing. Every inch of his body is telling me that it is something. So I move to his side and peer out the window, trying to see what he sees. There are cars in the street, moving slowly, but it's to be expected. In the distance, there are

Christmas lights covering every inch of the nearby buildings, all sparkling and pretty. I see nothing unusual, but I am not an assassin, so perhaps I am missing something. I turn to Nick. "What is it?" I repeat.

He nods at the window. "Many cars. They slow on this street. They watch something."

I blink for a moment, and then laugh. "Of course they watch something. They're slowing down to look at the Christmas lights." I point at the nearby buildings, festooned with green and red and white lighting. There's even an animatronic nativity that I passed by earlier. It's garish, but still impressive. "I imagine it's parents taking their kids out to see the decorations."

His shoulders relax a little. "*Da?* Is tradition?"

I nod firmly and link my arms around his waist. "Tradition. Nothing to be worried about."

His breath exhales slowly, and his hands rub my back. "I still think like hit man."

He does. I imagine it'll take time for that to work out of his system. My Nick needs a distraction. "Do you want to get in the car and go drive past the lights?" Nick gives me such a disgruntled look that I laugh despite myself. "That must be a no." I snuggle against him, loving the slow, possessive feel of his touch as his fingers skate down my back. "What Christmas traditions do you have?"

"I do not celebrate."

This surprises me. I pull back and look up at him, puzzled. "Not at all?"

He shrugs. "You forget my upbringing."

I do. My face immediately softens in memory. My poor Nick, brought up since childhood by the *Bratva*, raised to be a killer.

Any kindness or softness he might have known before me was all an act, something he paid someone to do for him. The *Bratva* trained him to be an assassin; they did not train him to be a normal man.

I was foolish to ask. How could I not know the answer? It's there in the way his hands have tightened around me. He realizes he is missing a vital part of a normal life, and it bothers him. It is another missing puzzle piece, and he wants to be whole for me.

I feel cruel for asking. I will distract him instead. I am good at distracting. "I think we should get some mistletoe for our apartment."

"*Da?*" His voice is musing, almost playful, and it makes me feel achy with need. I love it when Nick is playful. "You wish to hide underneath and surprise me with kisses?"

"Surprise parts of you with kisses," I agree breathlessly, and my fingers go to his belt. He stiffens again, but when I go down on my knees, his fingers caress my jaw with such love that I ache inside. I unbuckle his belt and pull it free, and by the time I tug down his zipper, he's erect underneath his jeans and hard at what I'm suggesting.

I slide his clothes down his thighs and his cock pushes free, firm and beautiful and inches from my face. I am learning what pleases Nick as we live together. We practice a lot, I think with a smile, and I'm getting better at driving him crazy. I don't reach immediately for his cock. Instead, my hands stroke back and forth on the thick muscles of his thighs, and I watch his cock jerk in response to my touch. There is a drop of pre-cum beading on the head, and I want to taste it.

I will, but not yet.

Nick's hands are moving over my face, my jaw, my hair, frantically touching me but not wanting to interrupt what I'm offering. I know he loves this; it's because he loves it so much that it gives me such great pleasure to do it. I love pleasing Nick. I love seeing his face when my mouth is on him. This angle will make it almost impossible to watch his expression, but I will picture it instead.

Slowly, gently, I move my massaging hands up his thighs and curl them around his heavy balls. He groans as my fingers stroke them, and I feel his body twitch again. When another drop appears on the head of his cock, I lean in and lick both of them up, not wanting to lose that precious flavor.

My love makes a sound low in his throat, and it is beautiful to hear. "Daisy," he breathes, and follows it with a nonsensical rapid-fire comment in Russian that I can't make out. I'm taking Russian in one of my classes at school, but he's speaking too fast for me to pick it up.

I close my mouth around the head of his cock, and my hand goes to grasp the base of him. Nick can stand it no longer. His hands tangle in my hair and then he's pushing deeper into my mouth.

I loosen my jaw to welcome him, to take him as deep as I can, and moan deep in my throat when he thrusts into my mouth. He's a little rough, but I love it. I love him losing control; it's not something Nick does easily, and it's not something Nick does around everyone.

But I love it.

Then he's fucking my face, his cock thrusting into my mouth, the head pushing at the back of my throat, and I do my best to take him. He's big, though, and I'm still inexperienced, and so when I pull away, my gag reflex working, he lets me. I cough a little, and then give him a faint smile to let him know I'm okay.

Nick takes his cock in hand, wet and gleaming from my mouth, and begins to rub the head of it against my lips, watching me with intense, fascinated eyes. I part my lips, feeling the hot, soft skin brushing against my own, feeling him glide the pre-cum on my face.

Then, he pumps himself hard and he's coming on my face, splashes of heat spattering on my cheeks, my mouth, my lips. I lick them, because he likes the sight, and I love the taste of Nick. So wonderful.

He groans at the sight of me, face upraised to him, covered in his come. Then, he strips off his T-shirt and begins to mop at my face. "You are too good for one such as me, Daisy, my love."

"I love you, Nikolai."

I'm rewarded by that intense satisfaction in his eyes.

I'm pretty sure I burned the cookies in the oven. I'm pretty sure I don't care, either.

Tomorrow, I decide, I will go to a gun shop and look for the perfect present for Nick. Something dangerous and beautiful, just like him.

NIKOLAI

"You seem preoccupied today," a soft voice on my right says to me. It is some girl whose name I cannot remember or, more honestly, a name I do not care to learn. She's the interrupter. All she does is constantly interrupt me while I draw, while I dream. Today she has broken up my replay of last evening's decadent lovemaking.

I try not to be angry with her. Perhaps she has no Daisy in her life, no one who adores her and she adores back. Another person would feel, I suppose, sympathy because of her lack, so I try not to scowl at her. Daisy would tell me to be polite.

"I am occupied with thoughts of my beloved," I tell the interrupter. There. That is polite. I smile at myself. Daisy would be proud of me. I will tell her of this later when I pick her up from class.

Thoughts of my vehicle turn my smile into a frown. We are driving a rental because we have fierce arguments over the type of vehicle I want to buy for us, for Daisy really. I want to buy a Maybach with armored sides and bulletproof windows. Daisy screamed when she looked up the price for one on the Internet. I think it is just the right price but her face was like a little thundercloud when she shook her phone at me, the one I have bought her.

She tells me she cannot drive yet because she has no license, and unlike lingerie or fur coats, I cannot buy her one. She must take a test. I tell her she drives fine, but she demurs. Public transportation is fine, she says. There are buses that can take us everywhere, not to mention the train that runs from the interior of the city out to the suburbs.

Public transportation would be fine for me, but not for Daisy. There are other people who could touch her and even harm her.

It is perhaps paranoia, as she calls it, but I think it is just good sense, like leaving the house with a small revolver in my boot or Ka-Bar knife in my backpack. I have only a few tools of my former trade in our apartment—some of them are known to Daisy. Others I have failed to tell her about, such as the handgun in the closet and the one in our kitchen and the one I have taped under the front hall table. I will not leave Daisy undefended but I know she would feel uncomfortable with all the firearms. She asks,

"Where are all your guns, Nick?" And I tell her sadly, "There is gun in nightstand and I have this small one."

This is not a lie; more like not bothering her with unnecessary details. I am in charge of protecting my sweet Daisy so that she can give me all her tender love. I smile to myself, happily lost in the dream of her once again. I pick up my pencil and begin anew.

"Your beloved," I hear the interrupter say. "That's so old-fashioned but sweet."

"Yes, sweet." What would Daisy have me do? She would want me to smile at the interrupter. Daisy smiles at everyone. I try to smile at the interrupter. Is her name Patty? Dotty? Kitty? I cannot recall.

"You're very devoted, aren't you?" I finally look at the interrupter. Her dark hair is curled and lies in waves around her shoulders. She has very long eyelashes, like the legs of a spider. I think some would think she is attractive, but she looks nothing like Daisy. "What're you giving her for Christmas?" she asks.

Giving her for Christmas. The words strike a chord in me and I slowly turn toward the interrupter. "Giving for Christmas . . . ?"

"Yeah, I mean, she's your beloved, so you're getting her something, right?"

I nod. Yes, I am, I think. Gifts for Christmas. Beaming at the interrupter, I ask, "What would you like, if you could have anything?"

She blinks at me and places a hand over her chest. "God, what I wouldn't give for a guy like you to be so over the moon about me. Where'd you two meet?" Spider-lashed lady sets her face on one of her hands and moves closer to me. I'm uncomfortable by her nearness and by her strange eyelashes. I may draw these in my next work, giant long-legged wisps of black, like whiskers on the eyes.

"We meet . . ." I trail off and think of what Daisy would like me to say because the truth is that I spy on Daisy while researching a hit, a kill. I know Daisy would not want me to tell the truth. "We meet in coffee house."

"Your accent is just delicious. Do you have any brothers?" Flick, flick, go the eyelashes.

"*Nyet*, no brothers. No siblings." I check the clock. Our time in class is almost up and I have not yet completed my project. Sighing, I begin to pack my things so I am not late to pick up Daisy. Last time I lingered overlong speaking with the professor about the darkness in my sketches and how I needed to incorporate lighter shades. By the time I arrived at Daisy's campus, there was a horde of males surrounding her. At least two or three. Daisy said she was making new friends and so I hid my dismay.

"Well, if you and your girlfriend ever want to hang out, you should call me. Want my number?"

At first I shake my head in the negative, but Daisy would like more friends . . . so perhaps yes? "*Da*, you write it down for me."

"Just give me your phone and I'll put it in."

I frown, unsure of whether I should do this, but then think of Daisy's laughing face when she was talking to the other students. I hand over my phone, the public one—not the one I use to text Daisy. That phone has private images and private texts that no one should ever see but me.

The girl smiles at me and the legs of the spider flutter up and down. Once my phone is back in my hand, I see her name is Callie. "Thank you, Callie." I hold out my hand to shake hers. She looks at it strangely and then shakes her head.

"You're an odd duck. A hot one, but odd. Good thing I like odd." She takes my hand and squeezes it tightly, holding on a little too long. "God, your hands are so big."

My hand looks normal, I think, holding it up in front of me.

She laughs. "You're so literal!"

"Thank you," I say, and try to bring her attention back to the Christmas gifts. "You are a woman, Callie," I say.

She rolls her eyes. "So nice of you to notice."

Of course I notice. I notice everything. "Yes, I notice." Impatiently, I continue. "You like Christmas?"

Her eyes light up. "Who doesn't?"

"What is it you like the best?" I ask. Traditions are important to Daisy. I want to start our own traditions.

"Gifts, of course," she smirks.

A few other art students have wandered over. I ask all of them, "What is best gift you receive?"

They shout out answers.

"Jewelry."

"Xbox."

"Car."

The last is from Callie. I point to her. "You get a car as a gift?"

"I wish," she shakes her head. "But I'd like one. You giving them out?"

I nod slowly. "Yes. Yes, I think I am." I clasp Callie around her shoulder, like she is a good comrade. "Thank you for your friendship."

Turning, I head for the rental car. I am excited. Very excited. I am going to buy Daisy a car for Christmas.

When I arrive at Daisy's college campus, my spirits are high and I care not that Daisy is surrounded by males—two at least.

The third I am not so sure of. There are females there too. I wonder what they discuss. Perhaps gifts. I hope one of them wishes for a car so that Daisy will understand how normal this gift is. As I approach, I study the other individuals surrounding her to see what they might have that Daisy does not. Her coat is keeping her warm. I would like to buy her a fur but Daisy says that she doesn't like the thought of wearing all those dead animals.

"Nick!" Daisy hails me immediately. She draws me into the crowd and I lean down to kiss her, just a small brush of my lips against hers. Then, to be sure everyone understands that Daisy is under my protection, I place my gloved hand around the back of her collared neck.

"All done, *kotehok*?"

She nods eagerly and waves good-bye to her friends. "You seem in a pretty good mood."

"*Da*, I run over motorist on the way here. Very satisfying."

"Nick," she exclaims, batting at my arm.

"Little hit man humor," I joke.

Suddenly she stops and turns me to face her. "You never joke." Her eyes are searching mine but she cannot see the gifts I have in mind for her, only that I love her, so I stare back into the rich blue depths and think of her heavy eyelids the night before as she sucked me deep into her mouth.

"Last night," I whisper to her, "so good, *da*?"

"*Da*," she agrees.

"Tonight it is my turn." I bend down close to her ear so no one can hear the words but her. "Tonight I will kneel between your tender thighs and I will lick you until you are screaming for mercy, but no mercy will be yours. Instead, I will torment you with my fingers and tongue and cock until you are senseless, until you feel nothing but pleasure in every nerve and fiber. There will be no centimeter of you that is not touched by me. When you arise from our bed tomorrow there will be no memory in your head but of me fucking you."

Her knees buckle and I clasp her to me. "You shouldn't say those things to me in public," she gasps, glancing around.

"No one but you and I matter in this world, Daisy," I tell her in all seriousness. "But come, let us get home so the fucking can commence."

This elicits a giggle from her. "You're so filthy and formal at the same time. I love it."

I hold open the car door of the cheap sedan. It will be one of the last days Daisy will ride in this. Climbing into the passenger seat, I hand her my public phone. "I make friend for you today."

"Is that right?" She takes the phone and flicks it open. "Is it this Callie person?"

"*Da*, she offers you her phone number so you can meet her."

She snorts and then closes the phone. Leaning her head against the seat, she says, "I'm thinking she wants to be friends with you, Nick."

"*Nyet*, she invites you to have coffee with her. I will come with so you are not alone," I offer magnanimously, as if it is a big gesture for me to accompany Daisy to a coffeehouse when in truth we both know that I am desolate without her. "But she is a little strange. You should not sit close to her. Her eyelashes look like giant spider legs. It is hard to concentrate on what she is saying when those long black things are creeping close to you," I advise.

Daisy sighs. "Okay, Nick, if we decided to hang out with Callie, I'll be sure to sit back far away from her." There is a tone in her voice, one that suggests she is holding back a laugh. I take a moment to glance at her before focusing on the traffic in front of me. "What is funny then?"

This time she does laugh outright. "She's probably wearing fake eyelashes, Nick! And she was flirting with you. She wants you to call her to take her out for coffee."

"But I am with you, Daisy, for always. Why would I want to have coffee with a girl with spiders on her eyes?"

She reaches over and lays her head against my arm. "I love you, Nick. I love that you are completely clueless, because otherwise I'd probably be tormented by jealousy."

"There will never be anyone but you." A break in traffic allows me a moment to drop a quick kiss on the top of her head. "Also, we will be home soon. I will show you what I mean."

She shivers. "I can't wait."

Me either.

I am riveted by the sway of Daisy's hips as she walks up the stairs in front of me. They seem to be saying something. This is the first refrain of the siren's song. *Follow me. Follow me.*

"I am," I whisper beneath my breath. "Any way, even unto my own death."

"What's that?" she says.

"Your hips," I tell her, for I keep nothing from my Daisy. Well, almost nothing. The car is a gift and so that will be secret until it is delivered. "They call to me. I think your body wants something from me."

"Is that right?" she murmurs. Her innocence has given way to naughtiness and it is a change that I revel in. The words she says are subtext for the want simmering beneath the surface, the desire that has been building since we climbed into the car.

"It is so, *kotehok*." I have reached the step that she is standing on. I'm taller than Daisy, stronger, too, but she does not shrink from me. Instead, she rises on her tiptoes and places her mouth against my chin.

"What do you think my body wants?"

"I promised to show you." I lift her effortlessly into my arms, although my muscles tremble when she begins to dot open-mouthed kisses along my jawline. My knees become weak as her tongue finds the hollow of my throat. I am but putty in her soft hands. Somehow I manage to unlock the door and carry Daisy to our bedroom. It takes a superhuman effort and I think I am only upright because my cock is so hard that I can barely bend over to lay Daisy on the covers.

Her eyelids are heavy again, weighted down by lust. I dispense with my clothes swiftly. I know she likes to watch but I'm too eager to be inside her. I confess my weakness.

"I cannot wait to feel the hot glove of your cunt squeezing me."

Her eyes flare at my words. Holding my heavy erection, I stroke it roughly, squeezing out drops of come and spreading them around the thick member for lubrication.

"Come here, then."

At her invitation, I fall upon her, pulling off her coat and sweater. I pause then to savor her pendulous breasts that are swaying with her effort to remove the rest of her clothes. Palming each breast with a hand, I bury my face in the valley between the pale mounds, my thumbs rubbing gently over each nipple. They are erect almost immediately.

Her sensitivity astounds me and I am tempted to simply suckle on her breasts until she grinds to completion riding my thigh. But the ache in my cock is unrelenting. Later, then, I promise myself, and kiss the tops of each breast before removing the bra that confines them.

Impatiently she makes a frustrated sound that her tights and skirt are caught at my hard thigh. Moving, I help her until we are flesh to flesh. We fall back onto the bed, my mouth on hers and my hand between her legs.

She is wet, always so wet for me. Her thighs tighten around my hand and she begins to ride me even before I've touched her.

My fingers thread through the curls that shield her lower lips and her eager little clit that pushes up and demands attention. I ignore it, though, spreading her labia apart and reveling in the juicy sounds her cunt makes as I ease two fingers inside of her and thrust quickly.

The thready sounds of her need fill the air. "Yes, Nikolai, I need you."

"I can feel it," I growl, moving down her body. "I want to taste it first."

I nip at her clit and feel a corresponding tightening around the two fingers moving relentlessly inside her. Her soft flesh against my tongue makes me close my eyes in pleasure. I need the taste of her to flood my throat and coat my mouth. Using both hands, I spread her wide for me and spear my tongue inside her. She grips my head with both hands, tugging at me and pushing me away at the same time.

"God, Nick, the feeling—" Her words are choked off as I attack her clit with my tongue, lightly nipping it and then sucking it into my mouth to soothe the tiny pains.

I will never get enough of her. Never. I drink at her fountain, working her with my tongue and lips and teeth and fingers until she is thrashing and crying meaninglessly above me. The fervor of her want makes me crazy with lust and I rear up on my knees and thrust inside her, one swift motion that sets her off again, and I can feel the soft walls of her vagina hotly clutching at me. I grit my teeth to keep from coming at that very moment.

I have no restraint now. I am no better than an animal. Dragging her hips up, I pump into her.

"You feel amazing, always so amazing," I gasp between thrusts. Daisy looks up at me, wordless with love, and I bend down to take her mouth in mine. I rub my tongue against hers, the same profane motion I make with my cock inside of her cunt. She moans and I revel in the dual sensations of being surrounded by her wet, hot enclosures.

"Faster, Nick," she pleads with me. "Don't stop."

Her hips are now moving in that same round motion that she made when she walked up the stairs, only faster now and with less perfect rhythm. The glide of her hot cunt against my shaft feels like heaven. The pleasure of our joining is almost too much.

Her fingers dig into my thighs, and as I feel the bite of the nails in my flesh, I recognize how close she is to coming again. My balls tighten as I increase the pace of our mating.

"Now, come for me now," I demand. Her body rises off the bed, bowed by the force of her orgasm. I shout out my release and pound into her until I feel like I am jetting my come throughout her entire body. Nothing in this world is as good as being inside her. I collapse, sweaty and spent, onto her body and her arms and legs close about me, holding me close.

"You are my beloved, Daisy, as I am yours. Do not ever let go."

"I won't, Nick," she whispers into my ear. I do not know who clutches the other closer but I think it is me.

DAISY

I never thought Christmas would be such a delicate situation. But then again, I never thought of myself with someone like Nick.

I stuff my hands inside my coat pockets and watch my breath blow, frozen, into the air. I'm skipping class. I should be prepping for finals, but somehow, I am here on the street, waiting at the bus stop. This is more important than classes. It's imperative that I get Christmas right for my Nick, so that we set the tone for our future together. I want to show him how good life with me can be. How sweet it is to be loved purely for who you are, not who hires you.

It's these thoughts that go through my mind as I take the bus to the rougher part of town and hop off two blocks from a gun store. I walk briskly. It's cold and icy, but it's early and there's hardly anyone on the street. I feel safe, oddly enough; my love is a hit man, and I have met the *Bratva* head on. Street thugs seem almost a foolish worry now.

I head into the gun store and smile at the man behind the counter.

He gives me a skeptical look, as if I've taken a wrong turn. "Can I help you?"

"I'm looking for a Christmas present for my . . . boyfriend." I frown at the word. There's probably a better one for what Nick is to me. He is my everything. But we're not married. We're not even engaged.

"What kind of gun?" the man asks.

I step up to the counter and peer at the weapons there. Immediately, I'm crestfallen at the sight. It's not that there's anything wrong with the handguns, pistols, and assorted weaponry in the cases.

It's that I realize it's an entirely wrong gift for my Nick.

We're trying to move away from guns and death, he and I. If I got him one, what kind of message would I be sending? *Here is what you are, and what you will always be. A killer.*

I bite my lip. This feels wrong. My Nick is so much more than this, than a man who deserves nothing more than weapons.

"Actually," I murmur, "I think I have changed my mind." I give the man a quick smile and turn and leave, heading right back for the bus.

I think about Nick as I wait for the bus, and I think about him on the way back to the part of town where we live. I'll go back to the campus shortly, so he won't suspect I've been away, but I head to our apartment first. I have an idea of what to get Nick after all.

My Nick loves art. My Nick loves me. I think of his lean, tattooed body and how gorgeous he is to me. Perhaps I will get a tattoo—one of his beautiful, haunting sketches—on my body. He will see it on my skin and know I am his forever.

I like this thought. I dash up the stairs to our apartment, unlock the door, and hustle to the desk set up in the corner of the spare bedroom. It is Nick's office, though he does not spend much time in here. We prefer to cuddle on the couch, and my love has gotten quite good at sketching with one hand, the other wrapped around my shoulders and holding me close while I watch movies or read a novel. I used to read nothing but romances, but the reality of Nick has ruined those silly fantasies for me; now, I read cozy mysteries about crime-solving cats.

Nick's sketchbook is carefully set on the desk, amid boxes of charcoals and pencils. I pick it up and begin to flip through the pages, as always fascinated by the inner workings of Nick's mind. The sketches are dark, and some are disturbing, but all of them have a beauty and a grace to them. I pause over one sketch of a woman that must be me, asleep in bed, the covers tangled about my body.

My heart aches with love for this man, and I bite my lip.

It's not right for a tattoo, though, and when I skim a few more pages, I find just the right picture. Clutching the book to my breast, I race back out of the apartment, time not on my side. I must make a photocopy of this and get back to school before Nick realizes I am gone.

Days pass and Nick suspects nothing of what I plan. We have a small tree in the corner of our apartment, but there are no boxes under the tree yet. It's like neither of us wishes to be the first one to put something there and declare the holiday, so we hold off. Instead, Nick helps me decorate the apartment with garlands, and we play Christmas music, and kiss under the mistletoe, so much mistletoe. Nick has practically filled the apartment with it.

On the twenty-fourth of the month, I tell Nick that I am going to do my father's Christmas shopping. It's a tiny white lie; my father is a firm Amazon shopper and ordered all of our Christmas presents weeks ago. He even got them off the porch himself, which is a big step for my father. I'm proud of him. I'm not visiting him today, though. I take the bus downtown and head to the tattoo parlor I have picked out, where I have an early appointment.

The place is empty when I walk in, a counter full of body jewelry and bottles of disinfectant in the front of the store. The walls are covered with colorful tattoo designs. Behind the counter, a sleepy-eyed man is sitting at one of the chairs. He turns at the sight of me. "You Daisy?"

I smile nervously. "That's me." I pull out the drawing I have kept in my purse for the last week. "I need this drawing tattooed over my heart."

I lay the artwork flat on the counter in front of me and smooth it out nervously.

It is a picture of a red heart, surrounded by darkness and delicately cupped between sketchy suggestions of fingers. There's a banner across the center, and where Nikolai had written my name, I have modified the drawing and put his name in the banner across the heart. It is in Cyrillic: Николай.

I love it. It is darkness and hope. It is Nick's heart in my hands, and I will put it over my heart as a double meaning—that the one that beats in my chest belongs solely to him.

The man looks at the drawing. "Nice work. Kinda dark for a pretty little thing like yourself, though. You sure you want that?"

"I do," I tell him. "Right here." And I tap my chest, right where my breastbone is. "Can you do that?"

"I can. Go ahead and take your shirt off." He heads to the back with my paper.

I'm a little shy about taking my top off in front of a stranger, but the man couldn't care less about my naked breasts. He doesn't even look in my direction as I step inside the tattoo parlor and begin to disrobe. Before I am totally topless, he offers me a towel and tells me to use that to cover up my breasts but to leave my chest bare. Thank goodness.

The man is kind as I sit in the chair and he begins to disinfect the spot. He talks of the weather, and Christmas, and his girlfriend's children. I smile and talk with him. They are looking for an apartment downtown; I suggest to him our building, which will be ready in another month, and I will make sure Nick gives this man a discount. He seems nice.

He warns me the tattoo will hurt, but the feel of the needle on my skin is more irritating than anything else. The black lines he draws sting and drag on my skin like a pencil is jabbing me at high speed, but I don't mind; I think of Nick's face when he sees how I have stamped him on my body forever.

"So, can I ask what this writing is?"

I smile dreamily. "It's a name: Nikolai."

"Husband?"

"Boyfriend," I admit, and again, that word tastes wrong on my lips. Nick has never asked me to marry him. I know he won't, either, because I told him that I would ask him when I was ready. I like to be in control of things, and Nick gives me control.

Maybe I'm ready now. I consider this as the man swipes at my stinging skin, then bends over the tattoo some more. "How long do you think this will take?" I ask him. "I have one more place to go today."

Hours later, my chest is throbbing, I carry a bottle of disinfectant in my purse, and my new tattoo is bandaged under my sweater. My skin feels scraped raw, but the picture is vivid and dark and gorgeous and I can't stop staring at it. Even now, I want to rip off the bandages and touch Nick's name branded over my heart. I love it.

But I head to a jewelry store instead. I pick out a man's ring and a matching dainty one for a woman. It feels weird to be the one picking out the rings, but these are simply bands. I will let Nick pick me out an engagement ring to go with the band later, if he likes.

It's simply important that I claim him for myself, for good.

I go to the grocery store and pick up a few things on the way home, then begin to make Christmas dinner. We have a ham already cooked, and I am making mashed potatoes and a pie. We will be going to my father's and bringing food for Christmas dinner, but I can't wait for Nick to come home. I'm brimming with excitement. I can't wait to give him my gifts.

I already have the rings wrapped in a tiny box in my pocket. Under the tree, I have small things, like a set of art pencils and a new leather sketchbook that he will love.

And as I wait for Nick to come home, I touch my chest over and over. I took off the bandage, but the skin underneath is red and blotchy, and I'm a little dismayed that it's not perfect for its unveiling. The man at the tattoo parlor told me it would take time, but I have waited until the last minute to get my tattoo. There is no way I could have kept a tattoo secret from my Nick; he likes to kiss every inch of my skin on a daily basis.

The door opens and I rush into the living room to greet Nick, all smiles. He's unwrapping his scarf and grinning at me, looking pleased with himself.

"You're home," I exclaim, and head forward to wrap my arms around his neck and kiss him.

"You miss your Nick?" he teases, and his cool eyes light up with genuine warmth, just for me.

"Always," I murmur, and drag his face down to mine for a passionate kiss. His tongue sweeps over my mouth possessively, and for a moment, I'm entirely distracted by him. Then, I bat at his jacket and pull away. "I have your presents."

"You do?" For a moment, he looks so boyishly pleased that I'm giddy, and I can't help the excited giggle that escapes me.

"You get them early if you're nice to me," I tease, and saunter back into the kitchen, making sure to sway my hips.

He gives a soft groan, and in the next moment, he grabs me from behind and drags my body against his. "Do you tease me, Daisy?" he murmurs in my ear, and I shiver with delight as he nips at my earlobe.

"I do," I murmur. "Can I show you your gift?"

"Will I like?"

"I think so," I tell him, and turn around in his arms. I am wearing a red cardigan with the neck buttoned up to my throat, and as I smile at him, I slowly undo the buttons. His eyes light up, anticipating a strip show, but I don't correct him.

Instead, I bare the tattoo I have had painted over my heart, and wait for his reaction.

NIKOLAI

I stare at Daisy and the red angry welts on her skin that rise around the dark outline of a heart and the letters of my name etched into her body. My bones have liquefied and I stagger to the wall and press my arm against it so that I do not fall on my face.

"Painting is a blind man's profession. He paints not what he sees, but what he feels, what he tells himself about what he has seen." I quote Picasso at her because I have no thoughts of my own.

Her smile wavers.

I rush to explain, my words tumbling out like a torrential rain—hard and scattered. "I dream of being owned by you. In my fantasies, you wear my mark to tell everyone not that you belong to me but that I belong to you. But it is only in my mind. Never would I dare to give voice to this . . ." I cast about for the right word. "This *want*."

"You once told me that your tattoos tell your story and I want mine to do the same." Her lips tremble with emotion.

I lunge at her, unable to stand here this full of love and not hold her in my arms. We sink to the ground, our arms wrapped around each other. I hold her loosely to my chest so I do not rub against her tender skin. There is a wetness on my face and at first I look up to see if there is a leak in one of the exposed pipes, but I realize it is me. That I am the one leaking moisture.

Daisy brushes away the tears. "I'm hoping these are tears of joy?" Her voice holds a gentle teasing.

I try to speak but the fullness in my throat prevents any words from escaping. The gift I've purchased for Daisy seems callow compared to hers. I swallow and try again. "When I am born, it is to a woman who has no name. She is a prostitute for the *Bratva*. They take me from her and maybe she bears more sons or daughters. The *Bratva* is my family. The gun is the teat from which I draw my sustenance. I grow strong feeding off the suffering of others until one day it sickens me and I turn away, abandoning the strict principles I have been taught as a *Bratva* soldier. But in turning away from the *Bratva*, I leave the only family I know. It is fine, I tell myself, because I need no one. Until you, Daisy. When I see you and your smile, I suddenly realize my whole soul's purpose was to find you and become yours. I am clay in your hands. My life, my heart, it is all yours. That you would claim me as your own is the greatest gift you could have ever given."

Now Daisy is crying and our tears are mixing together. Our embrace is not sexual but spiritual. We are touching each other more deeply in this one moment than in all the moments we have been naked and together. "You're my heart, Nick. I claim you."

I shudder at her words and she repeats them, this time more loudly and with more force. "I claim you."

She pushes me away slightly and digs into her pocket. Unfurling her hand, she presents to me a ring box. She hastily unwraps it and pulls out a pair of rings.

I am dumbfounded as she slides one onto my left hand. "I claim you," she whispers, kissing me softly, her lips dragging along mine. I try to capture them but she is too quick for me. A metal object is pressed into my palm. It is the other ring. Trembling, I lift her left hand and slide the ring onto her finger.

"I am yours, then, and you are mine," I say.

Her smile lights up the room and it is as bright as day inside our apartment. I see her beautiful soul, white and glowing, and next to it is my soul, smaller, but within her circle of light. Satisfaction burns straight through me and transforms into desire. Later, after we have confirmed our union with a physical coupling, I will give her the car keys. I know she won't protest because it is nothing compared to the gift she has given me.

I manage to stagger to my feet, still overwhelmed. Sweeping Daisy into my arms, I walk purposefully toward the bedroom. Gifts, I realize, are not measured by their monetary value. I could spend and spend and spend on Daisy and never match the spirit of what she has handed me. Human life is short, a mere blue dot in the universe that appears and then disappears in the blink of an eye.

But the love of two people? It is the very essence of being.

Coming soon from bestselling authors
JESSICA CLARE and JEN FREDERICK

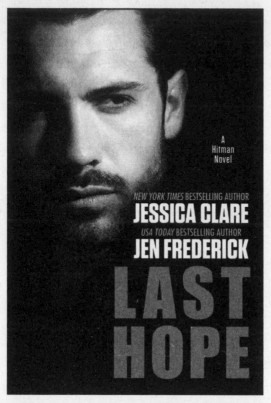

A Hitman Novel

NEW YORK TIMES BESTSELLING AUTHOR
JESSICA CLARE
USA TODAY BESTSELLING AUTHOR
JEN FREDERICK
LAST HOPE

In the explosive new Hitman novel a jungle mercenary
and his female target find love on the run...

AVAILABLE SEPTEMBER 2015

Praise for the Hitman novels:

"Sexy, thrilling romantic suspense." —Smexy Books

"Phenomenal."
—*New York Times* bestselling author Sara Fawkes

jillmyles.com
jenfrederick.com
penguin.com

Penguin
Random
House

T467-0215